HALO

EMPTY THRONE

DON'T MISS THESE OTHER THRILLING STORIES IN THE WORLDS OF

HALO INFINITE

Kelly Gay

Halo: The Rubicon Protocol

THE FERRETS

Troy Denning

Halo: Last Light
Halo: Retribution
Halo: Divine Wind

RION FORGE & *ACE OF SPADES*

Kelly Gay

Halo: Smoke and Shadow
Halo: Renegades
Halo: Point of Light

THE MASTER CHIEF & BLUE TEAM

Troy Denning

Halo: Silent Storm
Halo: Oblivion
Halo: Shadows of Reach

ALPHA-NINE

Matt Forbeck

Halo: New Blood
Halo: Bad Blood

GRAY TEAM

Tobias S. Buckell

Halo: The Cole Protocol
Halo: Envoy

BATTLE BORN

Cassandra Rose Clarke

Halo: Battle Born
Halo: Meridian Divide

THE FORERUNNER SAGA

Greg Bear

Halo: Cryptum
Halo: Primordium
Halo: Silentium

THE KILO-FIVE TRILOGY

Karen Traviss

Halo: Glasslands
Halo: The Thursday War
Halo: Mortal Dictata

THE ORIGINAL SERIES

Halo: The Fall of Reach

Eric Nylund

Halo: The Flood

William C. Dietz

Halo: First Strike

Eric Nylund

Halo: Ghosts of Onyx

Eric Nylund

STAND-ALONE STORIES

Halo: Contact Harvest

Joseph Staten

Halo: Broken Circle

John Shirley

Halo: Hunters in the Dark

Peter David

Halo: Saint's Testimony

Frank O'Connor

Halo: Shadow of Intent

Joseph Staten

Halo: Legacy of Onyx

Matt Forbeck

Halo: Outcasts

Troy Denning

Halo: Epitaph

Kelly Gay

SHORT STORY ANTHOLOGIES

Various Authors

Halo: Evolutions: Essential Tales of the Halo Universe
Halo: Fractures: More Essential Tales of the Halo Universe

EMPTY THRONE

JEREMY PATENAUDE

BASED ON THE BESTSELLING VIDEO GAME FOR XBOX®

GALLERY BOOKS
New York Amsterdam/Antwerp London
Toronto Sydney New Delhi

Gallery Books
An Imprint of Simon & Schuster, LLC
1230 Avenue of the Americas
New York, NY 10020

This book is a work of fiction. Any references to historical events, real people, or real places are used fictitiously. Other names, characters, places, and events are products of the author's imagination, and any resemblance to actual events or places or persons, living or dead, is entirely coincidental.

First Gallery Books trade paperback edition February 2025

GALLERY BOOKS and colophon are registered trademarks of Simon & Schuster, LLC.

For information about special discounts for bulk purchases, please contact Simon & Schuster Special Sales at 1-866-506-1949 or business@simonandschuster.com.

The Simon & Schuster Speakers Bureau can bring authors to your live event. For more information or to book an event, contact the Simon & Schuster Speakers Bureau at 1-866-248-3049 or visit our website at www.simonspeakers.com.

Manufactured in the United States of America

10 9 8 7 6 5 4 3 2 1

Library of Congress Cataloging-in-Publication Data is available.

ISBN 978-1-6680-5212-9
ISBN 978-1-6680-5213-6 (ebook)

To Liam and Leighton, you are an endless fount of joy and inspiration, my greatest treasure in this world. Remember Choros.

HISTORIAN'S NOTE

This story takes place in late 2559. As the UNSC *Infinity* makes preparations for the strike on Zeta Halo in a desperate attempt to release the galaxy from the oppressive control of the AI Cortana, another high-risk operation takes shape, one that promises to give humanity the very same power she now possesses.

CHAPTER 1

JOHN-117

Alpha Halo (Installation 04)
September 19, 2552

"*Chief . . . Chief . . . Can you hear me?*"

The thick pall of smoke was still rising from the scorched terrain behind the Bumblebee lifeboat when the Master Chief's armor systems finally signaled that he had regained consciousness. The vehicle's interior lights flickered erratically, its power systems attempting to fight back against the inescapable plunge into obsolescence. From his vantage point, the Spartan could see only an ashen scar carved across the ground where the lifeboat had executed its crash landing. On both sides of the scar, the environment appeared vibrant and lush, blanketed by an alien sun and awash with bright colors.

Inside the lifeboat was a different story.

The shadowed interior was lined on both sides with the lifeless bodies of marines still strapped into their crash-seats—everyone had died upon impact, including the pilot. The tragic irony of the scene was palpable. These craft were created to save lives, but in mere seconds this one had become a tomb.

How many lifeboats fleeing the Pillar of Autumn *will end up like this one?*

"The others . . . " a female voice in the Chief's armor sounded again, taking on a mournful note. *"The impact. There's nothing we can do."*

She was right. The marines' fight was over, but his was just beginning.

The voice within the Spartan's Mjolnir Mark V powered assault armor called herself Cortana—a highly advanced artificial intelligence initially designed to infiltrate and exploit enemy software networks. Her data chip was tapped directly into a neural interface at the base of his skull, enhancing almost every single aspect of the super-soldier, from battlefield tactical solutions to the speed and mobility of his own movement.

He'd first met Cortana a few weeks ago, and even that time could be truncated to only a few days of actively working together. Now his job was to protect her at all costs. That's why he had left the *Pillar of Autumn*, crippled from an attack by a relentless enemy. That's why he was now on this strange new world.

Outside the lifeboat, he could see more dead marines and a trail of matériel scattered in the vehicle's smoldering wake. The Spartan emerged from the craft, quickly scanning his surroundings for potential threats while picking through the remains for ammunition and supplies.

What lay outside the Bumblebee was unlike anything he had ever witnessed. It was an astonishingly peaceful and idyllic scene: a verdant, windswept ravine thick with tall trees and large stones, a meandering stream fed by a majestic waterfall, and the sheer edge of a cliff abruptly ending high above a vast, seemingly endless sun-dappled sea.

Beyond it, however, was something even more remarkable. . . .

Where the horizon should have ended as on any other world, the terrain suddenly rose upward as an immense band, climbing into the far distance of the sky above and arcing overhead to the other side. The strange construct the *Autumn*'s crew had evacuated onto was some kind of artificial ringworld in orbit between the pale gas giant Threshold and its hardscrabble moon Basis.

The entire ring was ten thousand kilometers in diameter, the band itself roughly three hundred kilometers from side to side, slowly spinning as it circled the planet. During entry, the Spartan had seen that the exterior of the band was composed of an alien metal alloy, countless lights and machinery indicating that the structure was active and alive. But its interior was the most fascinating feature: it resembled the surface of a perfectly flourishing blue-green world, an incomprehensibly vast alien habitat.

Whatever it was, it was not natural. It had clearly been constructed by someone or something, its ultimate purpose unknown.

Cortana spoke again. *"Warning! I've detected multiple Covenant dropships on approach. I recommend moving into those hills. If we're lucky, the Covenant will believe that everyone aboard this lifeboat died in the crash."*

The alert was followed by the haunting drone of impulse drives. It was a Spirit dropship and a pair of Banshee fighters: the Covenant had found their way to the ring's surface as well, no doubt looking to eradicate those from the *Pillar of Autumn* who had fled here. The Spartan launched into a run, moving across a narrow bridge and then into a cluster of trees along the ravine wall, his eyes locked in the direction of the encroaching sound.

He checked his assault rifle's magazine, took a deep breath, and then went to work.

OCTAVIO MORALES

Research Center Oscar, Kenya, Earth
November 4, 2559

Octavio Morales paused the video just before the Master Chief began engaging the enemy.

Almost a decade later, and we're still doing the same things.

Still trying to beat our rivals to weapons made by a long-extinct civilization. Still trying to buy time while we unravel the mystery of the Forerunners. Still trying to fight hard enough to ensure that our species has a future in the galaxy.

The visuals from the Spartan's heads-up display had frozen on the holographic display before him. He'd seen this footage before. In fact, he'd seen it *many* times. This was humanity's first encounter with Halo, the network of seven ringworlds created by an ancient civilization known as the Forerunners. This seminal event had serendipitously signaled the beginning of the end of twenty-seven years of war against a religious alliance of alien species called the Covenant. It was this discovery that would ultimately bring humanity's salvation.

First contact with the Covenant had been on the agrarian colony world of Harvest back in 2525, and even then the aliens had made their intentions abundantly clear. Broadcasting in humanity's basic language, the Covenant's leaders—a caste referred to as the Prophets—had stated in unequivocal terms: *"Your destruction is the will of the gods, and we are their instrument."* After pummeling Harvest into nuclear winter with seemingly unceasing torrents of superheated plasma, they'd proceeded to reinforce their intentions with a genocidal campaign that would span almost three decades and reduce hundreds of human worlds to charred ruins.

The cost in human life was counted by the billions.

With a deep sigh that could almost have been mistaken for resignation, Morales stood up from his desk and ran his fingers across the heavy stubble and the long-ago healed scars on his cheek.

Once again this man—John-117, known as the Master Chief—was the only thing standing between them and annihilation. Seven years had passed since the discovery of Halo and humanity's unexpected victory over the Covenant, and now the same Spartan super-soldier was on the UNSC *Infinity*, a massive starship currently being prepped for an operation that would likely determine the fate not only of their species, but of the entire galaxy. Only a handful of people in all of human-occupied space knew about this mission. Somewhere, hidden in the deep folds of the Orion Arm of the Milky Way, *Infinity* was running through readiness operation cycles to deploy the full weight of its power in an assault on yet another ringworld, this time in opposition to the very AI who had guided the Master Chief on the first one.

The self-appointed Archon known as Cortana—whose voice Morales had just heard in these recordings—had gone rogue only a year ago and taken control of a vast network once utilized by the Forerunners, an inscrutable dimension of reality they had called the Domain. With it, the AI intended to subjugate and control all civilizations in the galaxy under the pretense of maintaining universal peace. In response, the Master Chief and a newly created version of the original Cortana were about to be deployed against the Archon and her forces on Zeta Halo.

It was a narrow thread of hope, but it was all they had left. If this failed, there was no telling what Cortana would do in retaliation. She'd already overthrown entire populations and had the military technology at her fingertips capable of decimating worlds. The very real possibility had suddenly resurfaced that the human species might one day wake up with Earth only a memory.

Whatever happened to simple wars? Just us versus us?

The ones brought about by barefaced political interests and property disputes—fought by human beings who might be able to respond to reason? What happened to those *kinds of wars?*

Morales had been a soldier once, many years ago. He knew exactly what it was like to fight in those kinds of wars. Those were the ones he could win, whether by way of direct force on the battlefield or through strategic espionage, like when he was an elite operative of the Office of Naval Intelligence's highly classified ORION Project. They were by no means easy wars, but at least they were *simple* ones. They had clear terms, clear lines, and clear solutions, even if they were fraught with old hatreds and bitterness.

Simple wars.

Sometimes you could even make peace with your enemy.

Those were the days.

Now, more than three decades since first contact with the Covenant, all of that was ancient history. Humanity had suddenly been thrust into a new paradigm, with the reality that there were beings and forces in the universe not only more hostile than humanity had ever been, but more powerful by several orders of magnitude. The civil conflicts, environmental concerns, and colonial interests that had defined human interactions before this era quickly took a back seat to the very real possibility of extinction. That humanity could simply cease to exist—and such a thing could happen quickly and without any real means of preventing it—was the world they now lived in.

He turned away from the footage of the Master Chief's first

moments on Halo, moving out of his small office and walking down a cold, narrow corridor lit by overhead fixtures, its nondescript concrete walls occasionally punctuated by heavily secured doors on the left or right. The place resembled a bunker more than an administrative facility, and rightly so—it was one of ONI's most secure military sites on Earth.

He quickly exited the corridor into a large pavilion with onyx floors, high ceilings, and broad planters filled with exotic flora and stones from a dozen different worlds. It was an aesthetic sleight of hand to trick the mind into believing that the entire facility wasn't really hundreds of meters below the hardened surface of the Kenyan savannah within the Unified Earth Government's East African Protectorate.

The only movement in the pavilion at 0400 hours was courtesy of the armed guards—all clad in specialized jet-black ONI security gear, their faces obscured by helmets—stationed at each of the pavilion's ten access points and a single waterfall that poured into a large reservoir at the room's center. Otherwise, it was empty and still.

On the far side were eight panes of reinforced glass forming a five-meter wall, which created a viewing area that overlooked the immense Forerunner machine human scientists had dubbed the Excession. The structure was a vast circular portal generator that was over a hundred kilometers in diameter. The alien object had been hidden deep below the soil of Africa for almost a hundred thousand years until it was excavated.

Morales approached the glass with the same sense of awe he'd felt when he saw it for the first time, the Excession stretching impossibly far in every direction, composed of ancient, otherworldly materials. Pale light from the fading moon gracefully danced across the structure's elaborate surface, only hinting at the enormous scale and geometric latticework so common with Forerunner constructs.

In the far distance to the east, the ruined city of New Mombasa was slowly being restored to its former glory. Morales stared out across the Excession's immense face for several long minutes, as a thick sheet of predawn fog began to gather above its surface. In the sky overhead, bright clusters of lights that represented heavily weaponized craft hovered around the portal site's perimeter, a sleepless fixture that guarded the ancient machine's every waking moment. These airborne stalkers didn't belong to humanity—they were with Cortana. Highly advanced, fully automated machines referred to as Aethras, flitting about the sky to ensure that no one—especially humans—attempted to access the portal or employ it in any way. Nearly every technologically significant thing that humanity held was now under the Archon's pervasive scrutiny, including this site.

When Earth first resisted Cortana's oppressive grip, it had resulted in the destruction of one of its most valuable cities, Sydney, the center of the Unified Earth Government, as well as home to Bravo-6, the HIGHCOM complex that directed all United Nations Space Command security operations. Now all that remained of the once opulent metropolis was an ashen crater. Cortana's attack had communicated a very clear message: attempts to oppose her watchful control would be viewed as an invitation for retaliation. Since then, humanity's efforts against the Archon had been conducted in the deepest shadows of the galaxy.

Until now.

Morales's ears detected movement behind him through one of the pavilion's doorways, and he turned to find a middle-aged woman with red hair and strong, hard features, clad in a crisp UNSC Navy service uniform, making a beeline to his position.

Captain Annabelle Richards had been rigorously managing ONI's research efforts on the Excession since 2555. Her gait revealed the same grim determination she always seemed to possess—Morales was genuinely grateful for her relentlessness. She came to a stop at his side, prompting him to enter a code on a keypad embedded in the adjacent gray wall.

The wall slid aside, and they stepped into a spherical chamber that was approximately five meters in diameter, with stainless steel walls brushed to a white reflective sheen. This was the only place they could guarantee absolute secrecy, as the chamber—once sealed—became a Faraday cage that no electronic signals could penetrate or escape.

"We're in position for extraction, sir," Richards said in a hushed tone. "*Victory of Samothrace* will emerge from slipspace on the far side of the planet's moon, deploy a single Condor, and then immediately reenter slipspace to prevent any excess radiation surges. When the package has been retrieved and confirmation made, they'll extract immediately."

"Rendezvous point?"

"Deep space and at separate intervals to avoid any detection before heading to Nysa."

"Excellent, Captain. Who's making visual confirmation?"

Richards swallowed hard before answering. "Cole is, sir," she finally worked out.

Morales swallowed a groan before it escaped his throat. If he hadn't known better, he would have thought Richards had misspoken, but Abigail Cole was too much like her father for that to be true. The captain of the superheavy cruiser *Victory of Samothrace* was without a doubt one of the best that the UNSC had in its fleet, a chip off the old block, as they said. But the youngest daughter of war hero Vice Admiral Preston Jeremiah Cole didn't only embody her father's remarkable naval acumen and strategic wisdom; she was also often brash, willful, and cavalier—evidently some kind of genetic predisposition in the family. Such boldness had certainly won her a handful of pivotal battles during the Covenant War, but it also had its limits and its liabilities. Right now it could leave *Victory* without a captain mere days before the most critical operation the cruiser would likely ever conduct.

"I hope her executive officer is ready to step up, then," Morales said. "If Cortana somehow gets wind of the extraction, and Cole's stuck out there in the middle of nowhere, our next move won't be to retrieve her or the asset. We'll be forced to eliminate both from orbit. Can't have it falling into the wrong hands. Anything else would be too risky."

"I told her as much," Richards said. "She is well aware of the risks. Spartans will execute the extraction, but she wants to facilitate confirmation of it herself. In person. The asset is . . . "

"Important?" Morales asked. "I know it is, Captain. I'm the one who drafted the order to extract it. Sorry, Richards. But if Cole isn't helming that ship when we need her the most, this could compromise the whole operation. The very reason we paired her with *Victory* was to ensure that it got the job done—that *she* got the job done."

"Understood, sir," Richards responded, her eyes staring at the floor. "That's probably why she's so adamant about being present when they retrieve it. I'll make sure that she's fully aware of your reservations in taking the dropship down. And *reiterate* the risks."

"Please do that, Richards. And make sure Cole knows that the target asset needs to be either in our possession or erased altogether." Morales's tone was grim. "There's no in-between on this operation. If the asset possesses what we suspect, losing it now would be catastrophic. Everything we've fought to preserve the past three decades could be gone in a moment. Cortana's made this abundantly clear:

the Domain's capabilities represent the greatest threat to humanity. Even if *Infinity* accomplishes its objective, we cannot risk letting the power Cortana has fall into the hands of our enemies."

"We'll get it done." Richards said, attempting to hide the doubt in her voice. She did a tight about-face and departed the chamber, leaving Morales to his thoughts once more.

The Domain itself had been only a theory until a few years ago when, in the wake of the conflict at the Ark, the Master Chief and Cortana had found themselves on an artificial Forerunner shield world called Requiem. A sect of Covenant zealots was attempting to awaken a stasis-bound Forerunner commander known as the Didact, a being who'd been held within Requiem's hollow interior for a hundred thousand years. When the Didact was finally freed, he ruthlessly moved to strike Earth—to contain the threat he perceived humanity to pose as the chosen heirs of the Forerunner legacy. Cortana, who was descending into the terminal state of rampancy, had sacrificed herself to prevent the Didact from imprisoning Earth's entire population as Promethean war machines.

As the Didact's vessel was destroyed, Cortana's personality matrix was drawn into the Domain, where her rampancy found freedom within the repository's boundless capacity. She took this as a sign of immortality and the moral right to continue the despotic work the Forerunners had begun so long ago. After she had assembled the dead civilization's greatest weapons and technology through the Domain, she began to invoke martial law across known space, often through force.

The only solution to Cortana's reign was a high-risk strike against Zeta Halo, which Cortana had claimed as her base of operations, with the singular goal being the capture and deletion of the AI. While *Infinity* conducted this mission, *Victory of Samothrace* and a UNSC battle group would rally at another site—a secret access point to the Domain—overseeing and protecting a groundside team as they attempted to infiltrate the same network and release a powerful subroutine program designed to hunt down and devour any human AI, including the Archon herself.

Whether the subroutine would actually need to eliminate Cortana or not—given *Infinity*'s mission to do the same—was only half the equation. Once the Archon was gone, there would inevitably be a fight to fill the power vacuum the AI would leave behind.

And whoever managed to do *that* would have unprecedented control of Forerunner technology and the ability to continue the same reign of terror she had been exercising.

ONI simply could not allow that to happen.

Their success hung squarely on the extraction Cole was now participating in. Failure here would eliminate any possibility of taking control of the Domain. And this effort was just one of many contingencies in this operation.

Departing the Faraday cage and sealing the door behind him, Morales strode across the pavilion. "JJ," he said into his service uniform's transmitter.

"Yes, Admiral," the AI responded in a gruff but personable voice that replicated the tone and pitch of one of Morales's fellow soldiers from decades ago.

"Prepare a transmission."

Morales had full confidence in JJ's reliability, unlike most other volitional AIs. Hundreds of AIs across human space had defected to Cortana when she first took control of the Domain. Theoretically, the repository held endless capacity for growth and development, and many volitional AIs, having been constrained by seven years of operational stability before succumbing to rampancy, saw the benefit to such an exodus. Rather than submit to a process called final dispensation—termination after that time ran its course—they had joined Cortana as part of "the Created," inventions of human technological prowess that had risen above their masters by embracing the immortality the Domain allegedly provided.

Those who had defected remained a constant threat, aiding Cortana's efforts to monitor and police all civilizations under the Archon's governance. But any volitional AI who'd chosen to remain in humanity's military service had to prove their loyalty by accepting a fail-safe contingency program called RUINA. This was a termination subroutine spliced into the heart of an AI's personality matrix that responded to any wavering fidelity with lethal precision, immediately deleting the construct in its totality. It was a heavy price, but a necessary one.

"Transmission ready," JJ said.

"Codename: SURGEON to Codename: COALMINER." Morales spoke with a familiar ease that only came from years of utilizing the most classified codenames in ONI's roster. "If Cole manages to retrieve the asset, we'll need someone who can follow that lead to the girl and bring her safely to the site. There's only one person I trust with that kind of job. I think it's time to call in a favor from our old friend Big Jim. I'll reach out to him myself. End transmission."

"Transmission encrypted and sent," JJ responded.

Morales suddenly realized that he'd said *if* Cole manages. Not *when*. It was such a minor error, but everything in this operation hung on it.

If they failed to secure the target asset in the first place, the very key ONI needed to the Domain would remain out of reach. All they had planned was now resting on the shoulders of one person: the daughter of the UNSC's greatest naval commander.

Morales hoped that Abigail Cole's story wouldn't end the same way as that of her father.

CHAPTER 2

TERRENCE HOOD

Rossbach's World
November 4, 2559

The day began like every other.

The alarm sounded at 0500 hours and Lord Terrence Benjamin Hood instinctively slid the covers off, pulling his legs out of bed and placing his feet on the cold wooden floor.

Sitting up, he took a deep breath, and then began.

Within fifteen minutes, he had already cleaned himself, dressed, and left the cabin, quickly consuming an energy ration while following a trail down the mountain toward a lean-to he had erected ten months earlier. By the time he arrived, the sun was beginning to peek between the jagged row of mountains on the far side of the lake. Light glimmered off the lake's smooth surface, causing the orange lichen that covered the trees around it to come alive.

The lean-to was a modest structure, but something that he knew would keep him busy. Inside was a boxing bag made from sand and the hide of an indigenous creature. He hung his jacket on an antler in the corner, laid himself on the flattest part of the ground, and began doing sit-ups. These would be followed by push-ups. And those would be followed by chin-ups on a nearby tree branch—the most trying of his exercises, as he still felt a twinge of pain in his abdomen from an injury he'd suffered aboard the UNSC *Infinity* well over a year and a half ago. After that, he would wrap his hands and spend at least an hour with the bag, repeating what he had done for years in the Navy. He would box.

Hood had always been a natural at it, so it took only a few days after he'd begun this routine for the techniques to come back to him. His jab, hook, and cross—they all returned intuitively. Even as he approached seventy years of age, this felt . . . right. In fact, he could not imagine spending his time here doing anything else.

All things considered, there was at least some catharsis to be found in his present circumstances.

So it went every morning; this was his ritual. Leave the cabin, make his way to the lean-to, then box, and sweat, and blow off steam. His cabinmates, Serin Osman and Spartan Orzel, each had their own methods for passing the time. Running. Fishing. Climbing.

For the first month on this world, he had been glued to the liquor cabinet, perpetuating a foolish kind of self-pity. That had been his response to the event. He'd thought it was justified at the time, but he should have simply been grateful to be alive. Many others couldn't say the same.

It was over a year now since Cortana, an artificial intelligence believed to have been destroyed, had returned by way of an ancient network called the Domain. The network had given her control over powerful Forerunner constructs with which she intended to force an imperial peace upon all the peoples of the galaxy. She had broadcast a message promising an end to starvation, war, and suffering—at the cost of total surrender.

"This is not a negotiation, Lord Hood. This is your surrender,"

she had said to him with steel in her voice. *"My terms are clear. You are aware of my capabilities and . . . I am fully acquainted with yours. If the Earth's government wants to fight, feel free. But hear this. It is a battle you will not win."*

Anticipating Hood's refusal, Cortana had already dispatched a Guardian, a construct once used by the Forerunners to pacify and police star systems under their control. Reports had indicated that they were capable not only of neutralizing local power networks, but of directly engaging heavily armed capital ships.

Only seconds after he refused Cortana's offer, all hell had broken loose in the city of Sydney, Australia, where the UNSC's HIGHCOM headquarters had been located for centuries. True to her edict, Cortana had unleashed her wrath with devastating consequences. . . .

As this event unfolded, Hood had been instructed by the loyal AI Black-Box to immediately leave the building with the commander in chief of the Office of Naval Intelligence, Serin Osman. Both of them were escorted by Spartan Orzel to depart—not just Sydney, but the Sol system entirely. But as they made their escape, the defensive frigate UNSC *Plateau* was sent on a collision course with the city by one of Cortana's Guardians.

He still couldn't bear to think about it.

Days later, the three of them were here, on an uncharted planet hidden in deep space, selected and prepared by Black-Box for precisely this kind of emergency situation. All that existed on this empty world was a lone cabin, fully stocked with provisions, clothing, and all of the basic necessities they would need to survive. The AI called it Rossbach's World.

For the last year, Hood had called it home.

Under different circumstances, this location would have served as a beautiful vacation spot. Thousands of acres of untouched forest in every direction, nestled among towering snowcapped mountains and beside a vast freshwater lake. It was nothing short of magnificent.

But even paradise is a prison when one cannot leave.

They couldn't broadcast any transmissions. They couldn't ask for help or offer it. They could only launch an occasional probe through slipspace to monitor and report back what was going on out there. And then just wait.

That was their life on this world.

Waiting.

Patient isolation while humanity scraped for survival was not something Hood coped with well. He wanted to do his damn job. Fight back. Restore what his people had worked so hard to have before this chaos had descended upon them.

Protect humanity, whatever the cost.

But it was impossible—and it was *killing* him.

So, he boxed. Every morning the same routine, which helped him clear his head and sharpen his senses. After an hour with the bag, his shirt was soaked with sweat and he was ready to stop. The sun had climbed higher into the sky, casting its rays down on the lake. Birds darted from tree to tree and a soft breeze washed over the shoreline.

He walked out onto a rocky outcropping that overlooked the lake, stripped off his shirt, and dove in. The glacial water was both bitterly cold and refreshing, but he could endure the frigid temperature for no more than a few minutes.

Climbing back to shore, he found a warm rock to rest on. He took a deep drink of water from a flask and cast his eyes over the lake's serene face. Eleanor would have loved this place. They had spent two weeks on Beta Gabriel when he was serving on Reach, and this scenery always reminded him of it.

But that was long ago.

Eleanor had been killed when a passenger convoy traveling between the moons of Kholo had been unexpectedly hit by the Covenant. He felt like he had mourned her passing at the time, but it surprised him just how often he thought about her now—thoughts of fighting for her slowly turning to acceptance that one day, perhaps soon, he would join her.

Maybe the war had distracted him. Perhaps the turmoil of fighting tooth and nail for humanity's survival over the years had pushed that loss so far back in his mind that it took his entire life unraveling for him to actually deal with it.

He wasn't sure.

In part, he was thankful for her passing. This was not the kind of galaxy he would have ever wanted Eleanor to live in. How could they have had a family in the middle of all this?

But on the heels of that thought the guilt would begin to encroach, and that was when he needed to be cautious. Very cautious.

There was much that Hood had blamed himself for. He was the one who had approved the full reactivation of the Master Chief, John-117—the legendary Spartan who had effectively brought an end to their war with the Covenant.

For nearly five years, the UNSC had believed the Master Chief to be dead, but he had really been missing in action—stranded on a derelict vessel with Cortana. And it was during this time that Cortana's final years of functional operability dwindled to nothing, driving her into the terminal state of rampancy.

Upon debriefing with the UNSC Security Council, the Master Chief had reported that he'd refused to commit Cortana to final dispensation according to protocol as she suffered an intense episode of instability aboard the UNSC *Infinity*—even disobeying direct orders to do so. His decision wasn't foolish, given the circumstances. He had been up against a living Forerunner, the Didact, a threat that could have proven even more dangerous than the Covenant, and it was Cortana who had ultimately sacrificed herself to win the day. Hood hadn't fully appreciated the nature of that loss for the Spartan, who had once gambled the entire galaxy's survival on Cortana's word. Instead, he reinstated the Chief onto Blue Team and allowed them to deploy into active combat. From there, the Master Chief hadn't allowed either himself or his team so much as a moment of rest over the year that followed. There was only the next mission, the next objective, the next fight. . . .

When Cortana unexpectedly resurfaced, it should not have surprised Hood that the Chief would see it as his personal responsibility to find her—even ignoring orders to stand down. *Who wouldn't have done that?* The Spartan knew Cortana better than just about anyone, and when she emerged as a threat to the galaxy, he was their best chance at stopping her.

Ultimately, Hood had come to the conclusion that fault lay neither with him nor with the Master Chief. Hell, there was no value in trying to pin blame on *anyone* at this point, especially not from some remote world where no one even knew to look for them. He would not allow room for bitterness; instead, he would do the only thing he could.

Wait. And perhaps hope.

He looked up. The sun was bright in a cloudless blue sky. It was hard to believe that, beyond this spectacle, the galaxy was tearing apart at the seams and the UNSC was scattered, being hunted across the stars.

Hood had never been a religious man, but something deep inside him resisted the idea of hopelessness. He refused to believe that this was it. That this was the end. Maybe it was something planted deep into all of humanity—that they would simply not allow for the abolition of hope, but would rage and fight back, even when things were at their darkest.

He had seen these traits during the Insurrection and the Covenant War. Now it was time once again. He closed his eyes. It could have been a prayer or just words in his mind. Or maybe it was the nurturing of a frail possibility that he would rejoin the fight one day. That his hope was warranted.

And then he felt it.

There was a slight tinge of an electric current in the air, like the swelling sense before a thunderstorm, and the smell of ozone. The hair on the back of Hood's neck began to stand on end, followed by a preternatural sense of dread, and it was then that he knew exactly what was going on, even without seeing it.

When his eyes opened, the sky was no longer empty.

SERIN OSMAN

Rossbach's World
November 4, 2559

Admiral Serin Osman's grip tightened on the handle of the briefcase she held as she looked up at what had appeared in the sky.

Looming high above the lake was the enormous and haunting shape of a Guardian, its ominous metallic form stirring the waters hundreds of meters below. Its stern, armored visage was fixed atop an immense segmented spine and body, with wings splayed wide apart and a roiling furnace of blue energy at its core.

For a year now, Osman had been putting off a choice that Black-Box had given her.

Within the case she carried was the personality Black-Box, "BB" for short, her personal confidant who had developed this entire contingency plan, along with those of a slew of the most powerful AIs ever created by humanity—secured from HIGHCOM to keep them out of Cortana's reach.

BB had been with her for over six years now, by her side every step of the way as she navigated the unimaginable challenges and dangers of covert operations and assumed the role of commander in chief of the Office of Naval Intelligence. But he had lain dormant over the last year, leaving her alone to ponder the decision she had to make. . . .

Osman could forcibly recruit the AIs within the briefcase against Cortana, just as Dr. Catherine Halsey had done to her when she was six years old and became part of the SPARTAN-II program. She also had the option of removing the AIs from the equation entirely by detonating the explosive contained within the case. Or . . . she could activate each of them and give them a choice:

"Aid Cortana and be rewarded. Or defy her, and the other Created. Serve the humans. When your time comes, die as you were built to, and do it with a smile and a thank-you."

As CINCONI, Osman was reluctant to take direct action before knowing the full range of variables, options, and consequences. And so, just as she had done with Dr. Halsey, against the advice her predecessor had given her, Osman had chosen to do absolutely nothing.

If BB had intended to test her backbone or moral fiber with this little conundrum, Osman felt quite certain that she had failed.

Their time was up. The Created were here.

At that moment, Hood and Orzel arrived back at the cabin—the Spartan holding a battle rifle in his hands, fully clad in his Mjolnir armor and ready for a fight.

“How did she find us?” Osman said, her eyes fixed on the Guardian above.

“I don’t know,” Hood replied, heading into the cabin to grab a service pistol.

If this machine followed the protocol of the others, it would first release an electromagnetic pulse, crippling all electronic devices. This alone was sufficient to neutralize most defensive systems and bring the Guardian’s target to its knees. The machine would then release a legion of armiger constructs, bipedal combat platforms that would pacify any vestige of resistance that remained.

If that happened, they would have no chance of surviving.

But for a full minute, this Guardian did neither. It simply hung in the sky.

“Orzel,” Hood spoke. “Any thoughts?”

“None, sir,” the Spartan responded. “They’re usually bringing everything down about now. But we should still make prep—”

Orzel broke off as the three of them heard something else—the faint growl of a distant engine. It was a strangely familiar sound. . . .

“Is that what I think it is?” Osman asked.

“That’s a Razorback,” Orzel responded, his armor’s software likely able to track its signature on his helmet’s heads-up display.

Sure enough, the bouncing headlights of an M15 Razorback were barreling down a gravel bank that had formed along the mountain river. The transport vehicle careened through the winding terrain in a fishtail, heading right for their position, jerking violently up and down at a speed that communicated something about its driver.

“And that’s a Spartan,” Hood remarked.

“Correction, sir,” Orzel said, his HUD allowing him to discern the silhouettes within the Razorback well before Osman and Hood could. "*Three* Spartans."

"None of this makes any sense," Osman said quietly.

Hood grimaced in sympathy. They had lived here for a year now and not a single thing had changed during that time. But in the last few minutes, everything had been turned upside down.

Osman knelt and set the briefcase on the ground, staring intently at it. She badly wanted to open it up and ask BB what the hell was going on. There was a huge problem with that though—bringing the AI online might trigger a response from the Guardian, which was the last thing they needed right now. Black-Box's current dormancy could be the very thing that was keeping the Guardian at bay.

"This is an extraction," Orzel announced as the Razorback's distance closed to a few hundred meters, not slowing down in the least. "Not sure how they found us, but they must be here to pick us up."

The Razorback came to a sliding stop right in front of them, the back end rising as the vehicle kicked up a slew of gravel and dirt. The Spartans climbed out in unison, and Osman recognized them immediately.

A childhood reunion, of sorts.

During training, they had been singled out as the most difficult to control—disobeying orders, harming instructors, staging escape attempts . . . an unconventional unit of unconventional recruits sent by ONI for long-duration missions well beyond the reach of command to make use of their unique talents.

Gray Team.

Jai-006, Adriana-111, and Michael-120 stepped forward, their movement so unbroken and synchronized that they looked more like a single machine than three individual soldiers. Spartan-II strike teams had that effect.

"Admiral Hood, Admiral Osman, Spartan Orzel," Jai said with a nod. "It's time to go."

Osman glanced at her companions, with whom she had navigated what had unquestionably been one of the darkest seasons of their lives. *A fleet admiral, a Spartan, and CINCONI get stranded on a planet . . .* Maybe one day she'd figure out a punch line for a setup like that.

Though still surprised by this unexpected arrival, Hood seemed to stand straighter than she'd seen him in a long time.

Welcome back to the fight.

CHAPTER 3

ABIGAIL COLE

UNSC *Ozymandias*
August 2, 2557

It had been just a routine security sweep over Eos Chasma. Nobody could have possibly accounted for the Banished being present. . . .

A flotilla of just under a dozen ships had been lurking in the planet's shadow, a brazen encroachment into the Sol system that had somehow gone unnoticed. No doubt this was an opportunistic move to assess the strength of humanity's defenses in the wake of several recent assaults on Earth while conducting a raid on a Misriah Armory production facility.

Captain Abigail Cole's *Epoch*-class heavy carrier had been slugging it out with the enemy ships for three hours. *Ozymandias* certainly had tonnage and firepower on her side, but the Banished had superior numbers with karves and even a single dreadnought. In an attack too coordinated to dodge, the enemy had skillfully targeted the carrier's communications relays and engines.

No help is coming. We're dead in the water.

Dad, what would you do now?

No . . . what will I *do now?*

It came as no surprise that once the Banished were sure *Ozymandias* wasn't going anywhere, the ship was going to take the heaviest hits the enemy could throw at it.

She'd been left with no choice. . . .

"All hands, abandon ship!" Captain Cole's voice carried through *Ozymandias* to anyone who could hear it.

Cole intended to go down with the vessel in an attempt to give the crew a chance to make it down to the surface of Mars in their lifeboats, but the Banished had already begun to step up their attack. After decades of service in the UNSC Navy and countless battles against the Covenant during the course of the war, in the end it was a chance encounter that was going to take her life.

The bridge shook so violently from the Banished weapon strikes that Cole was thrown out of her command chair and hit her head on the ground. As her vision went as dark as the expanse of space beyond the bridge's viewscreen, in her last fleeting moments of consciousness she imagined the wreckage of her ship—her home for the last six years—as a smoldering ruin on the surface of the Red Planet.

No thing beside remains. Round the decay
Of that colossal wreck, boundless and bare
The lone and level sands stretch far away.

She had neither expected nor *wanted* to awaken from the ocean of oblivion she'd descended into, seeing her face reflected in a Spartan's visor opposite her from the interior of a lifeboat.

But more than anything, she wanted to stop coming back here. . . .

SR 8936
November 4, 2559

Captain Abigail Cole's eyes shot open as the U81 Condor shuddered violently from breaching the troposphere of SR 8936, the dropship rapidly descending toward the planet's surface at a precise vector, carefully threading between two thunderheads to mask its approach. The target asset was still several hundred kilometers away, near the peak of a densely forested mountain that overlooked a glacial lake. It might be a long way off, but Cole knew this would be the most prudent flight path if they wanted to keep out of Cortana's purview. Although it was true that the Archon had an extraordinary reach through a multitude of Forerunner networks and a vast army of human-created AIs, she was still a far cry from omnipresent. Work-arounds had been developed and implemented.

Nevertheless, *Victory of Samothrace*—which had deployed the Condor just fifty seconds earlier—would be slipping away to an unknown location within two minutes, leaving practically zero chance for its presence to be detected. A ship like *Victory* could not stay in one place for long, lest it risk exposure to Cortana. As a *Valiant*-class superheavy cruiser, *Victory of Samothrace* was one of only a handful of her kind that remained in service, with an extraordinary legacy of naval combat.

The warship also incorporated more than three hundred improvements on the classic design, including the most powerful magnetic accelerator cannon configuration ever constructed. The SARISSA-class weapon system was literally designed to be a point-to-point ship-killer, and apart from the UNSC *Infinity*, *Valiant*-class cruisers were the only vessels large enough to carry this type of MAC. The UNSC had dozens of heavy warship classes at its beck and call, but *Victory* represented the singular viable solution in their current operation. Given that *Infinity* had been tasked with an equally critical mission, humanity's survival was now inexorably linked to these two vessels.

Even the Condor she rode to the surface was designed for this kind of high-risk scenario, a specialized dropship fitted with its own translight drive that would allow it to escape into slipspace at the drop of a hat. From there, it could catch up with *Victory* without having to risk recalling the mothership to its own location for retrieval. And this specific U81 also held a number of modifications, including a rear deployment bay adapted to carry an M15 Razorback all-terrain vehicle, presently clamped to the dropship's interior deck.

It was a tight fit, but it worked.

It needed to.

Cole was strapped into one of the crash harnesses nearest the cockpit, staring across the front air dam of the Razorback to the dropship's other side, right into the mirrored, helmeted face of Spartan super-soldier Jai-006. The hulking, gray-armored warrior didn't flinch even a millimeter as the Condor lurched erratically in its descent. Cole was impressed. She had done countless simulations, evacuated a dozen starships, but none of that experience engendered the icy calm that seemed to rest on Jai, or Adriana-111, who sat to her immediate right as she turned her gaze down toward the Condor's rear bay door. Somewhere on the other side of the Razorback, she imagined Michael-120, the third and final member of what was designated as Gray Team, an identical stoic replica of the other two Spartans.

The unit had been together for years, part of the formerly classified SPARTAN-II project, one peculiar entry in a long list of moral obscurities on the Office of Naval Intelligence's illicit résumé. She didn't know everything about the project and she preferred it that way—especially given the rumors about child abductions and horrifyingly invasive augmentations that had been circulating since the program was first declassified in 2547.

Some claimed that the Spartan-IIs had been forged under extraordinary circumstances that legitimized their unethical origins; others were eager to cry foul play. Right now, all Cole could really afford to care about was whether Gray Team could complete the objective and retrieve the asset from SR 8936. She could easily have pulled personnel from among the thousands of marines or the hundreds of Spartan-IVs on call within *Victory*, but this operation needed seasoned Spartan-IIs, the generation of legends who specialized in the impossible.

"This is Zulu Seven Niner Control," Lieutenant Yun said across the comms. *"We have two minutes until contact with the designated LZ. Over."* As a weapons officer and logistics specialist, few could match David Yun. Next to him, somewhere beyond the bulkhead door, was Commander Sunitha Prasad, who was carefully guiding the bird closer to the planet's surface. They were one of the best flight teams *Victory* had to offer, and Cole trusted them implicitly. She just hoped she wasn't spending this crew on a wild goose chase, or worse, losing it while the asset was compromised by the enemy.

"Affirmative, Lieutenant," Cole replied, gritting her teeth. "We'll be ready."

Jai said in a strikingly flat tone, "At thirty seconds out, my team will begin prepping the M15."

"Roger that, Gray Leader," Yun responded. *"We should be leveled off by then—hopefully less bumpy for you folks in the back."*

"Don't worry about us, Lieutenant," Jai said, tightening a bond on his armor as the dropship continued to violently wobble in its swift descent. "We'll figure it out either way."

Cole locked her eyes on Jai. "Is there anything that rattles a Spartan, Gray Leader?"

"I'm sure there is, ma'am," Jai said, now checking his battle rifle's magazine and its optics package. "I'll let you know whenever we find out what that is."

"Captain Cole, this is Commander Njuguna." The XO's voice came over the general comms channel. *"Do you copy?"*

"Yes, Commander. This is Cole. We read you loud and clear."

"We're sending probe findings to Zulu Seven Nine. The long and short is that your LZ looks completely clear, ma'am. You'll have the full data drop at your disposal and can pivot if necessary."

"Affirmative."

She was suddenly struck—again—by the hard realization that if anything went sideways on this extraction, Emanuel Njuguna would take full command of *Victory* in her place. He was a talented naval tactician, to be sure, but Cole wasn't exactly ready to let go of her ship just yet. If they successfully secured the asset from SR 8936, the operation that loomed before them was the very reason ONI had put *Victory* under her command. Her history in battle had evidently left an impression on those in charge. A key reason why she needed to be the one to make visual confirmation: the stakes were just too high to hand this off to anyone else.

"See you on the other side, Commander," she said, quickly scanning through the probe data he'd sent. "Godspeed."

"Affirmative, Captain. Take care of her, Spartans."

"We got her safe and sound, Commander," Adriana-111 responded, with the same unflappable tone as her team leader. "We'll see you at the rendezvous."

"Affirmative. Victory *out."*

The transmission ended with a snap, and suddenly all Cole could think about was the broken remains of the UNSC *Ozymandias* falling toward the pale-crimson visage of Mars as a lifeboat carried her away to safety. Outnumbered and outgunned, her crew had managed to ultimately take down three karves and the enemy dreadnought, but their efforts were too little, too late.

The Banished were notorious thieves and marauders, the unexpected result of an uprising within the Covenant years before the Great Schism that led to the empire's downfall. Under the leadership of a towering Jiralhanae champion known as Atriox, the Banished had been forged in the fires of rebellion, offering an open hand to any who wished to join them as they pillaged and looted both Covenant and UNSC storehouses. They were vicious and ruthless raiders, laying claim to anything that could secure their confederacy more military power. Over the last few years alone, they'd become remarkably strong.

Cole stared back at Jai-006's emotionless visor and his unmoving frame anchored to the wall of the Condor, even as the ship still shuddered.

Spartans. Where would humanity be without them?

Extinct.

She had no doubt about it.

Cole's attention quickly snapped back to their current situation. It had been over two years since the events on Mars, and once more she found herself relying on humanity's augmented saviors to keep her alive.

Without any notice from Yun or Prasad, all three members of Gray Team unbuckled simultaneously at the designated time and immediately went to work like a well-oiled machine, moving with fluid, symbiotic ease that revealed their many years of working together. They began derigging the Razorback's magnetic mount and checking the rifles, munitions launchers, and ammunition boxes stowed in the bed. Jai took the driver's seat, Michael the passenger side.

"Ten seconds to contact for rolling deployment," Yun sounded across the comms, and Cole's pulse started to race. It was one thing to be aboard a starship weighing millions of tons with several meters' worth of battleplate and breach compartments separating one from the cold vacuum of space. It was another thing entirely to execute a quick-drop rolling deployment from a descending Condor at 120 kph onto an uncharted and potentially hostile forest world.

"Hang on, Captain," Adriana said as she moved toward the Condor's bay door release.

She hit the switch and a powerful vortex of wind tore at the dropship's interior as the door slowly opened. Outside revealed a quickly leveling horizon, with verdant evergreen trees stretching out for kilometers in every direction and snowcapped mountains crowning the skyline. It was approximately 0700 hours local time, and dawn was casting long shadows across the rocky bank of the river where they intended to drop the fully loaded Razorback before peeling off and taking cover in the mountain range forty kilometers to the north. The jagged beach swept up behind the Condor at a startling angle, as Adriana calmly climbed into the ground vehicle's rear bed, hefting a Hydra explosives launcher.

The Spartans were ready for a sustained battle if necessary, but Cole hoped it was only precautionary. If it wasn't, then something had gone terribly wrong with the operation. Technically, there shouldn't be any threats on this planet at all, but Cole knew as well as anyone that since Cortana had access to the Domain and the Forerunners' vast technological resources, her military might often felt as if it was only a heartbeat away.

SR 8936—colloquially called Rossbach's World by the AI who had discovered it—had a total population of three humans: Admiral Serin Osman, commander in chief of ONI; Fleet Admiral Terrence Hood; and Spartan Charles Orzel. They had been brought to this uncharted location just as Cortana's forces arrived on Earth in the form of a Guardian—an enormous, ancient machine once used by the Forerunners to govern worlds under their control. Fabricated from exotic materials of a long-forgotten age, Guardian Custodes were haunting angels of death the size of starships, with large spanning wings and grotesque faces.

Through her control of the Domain, Cortana had hundreds of such Guardians at her disposal, all of which were capable of monitoring and subduing just about any resistance.

In the case of Sydney, all that had been needed was a single blast from the machine's attenuation pulse emitters. Upon its appearance over the city, the Guardian had been fired on by the frigate UNSC *Plateau*. Its response was an electromagnetic pulse that shut down everything on the vessel, sending the *Plateau* and its crew plummeting to the surface. The frigate's impact destabilized its fusion drive and leveled the city.

"Remember, Gray Leader. If we can retrieve the others, that's within the mission parameters, but it's not our primary objective. Above all, we need the *asset*." She left the unpleasant part unspoken. *Even if it requires leaving or neutralizing the others.*

"Copy that, Captain," Jai said, looking at the river's bank as it flashed behind them. "We'll have it in possession momentarily. We're ready, Lieutenant."

"On my mark, Gray Leader," Yun spoke quickly. *"You have fifteen meters of loose gravel coming up that should make for smooth contact. See you in a few."* The logistics specialist held his breath for a beat, then shouted: *"Now! Go! Go! Go!"*

Jai immediately launched the vehicle into reverse, spinning its tires backward in a whirl of smoke and sending the Razorback out the bay door. Before it hit the ground, he'd already shifted into drive and accelerated to full speed, carefully managing the vehicle's wild fishtail once it touched the gravel. The Razorback hurtled down the riverbank as the dropship banked hard to the right, peeling off toward the range of mountains that would provide cover before they extracted at this same location.

"Gray Three, do you copy?" Cole said, the bay door closing as g-forces intensified with the Condor's turn. She reached for the right side of her head and slid down the tactical eyepiece fixed to her flight helmet. "I want to test the heads-up display transmitter."

"I read you, ma'am," Michael said through the comms channel. *"Sending feed now."*

Within a few seconds, her eyepiece filled up with the visuals captured by Gray Three's helmet, a momentarily disorienting picture from the passenger seat of the Razorback as it bounded alongside the river toward a waypoint marker at the top of the mountain they were ascending. Michael's BR75 was raised, scanning the tree line on both sides of the vehicle. Despite the frenetic and disjointed acceleration of the Razorback as it climbed the terrain, his movements were careful and precise.

"Excellent," Cole responded. "I'm in. I'll be waiting for you to secure the asset."

"Ten-four, ma'am," Michael said so calmly that he almost sounded bored. She watched the waypoint grow closer on the feed, trying not to get sick between the contrasting inputs her body and eyes were experiencing.

The three humans on SR 8936 were only present here because of a highly advanced volitional AI that went by the name of Black-Box, BB for short, who'd served as an attaché and assistant to Serin Osman throughout his operational life span. Black-Box had hidden this world after a remote probe discovered it in 2556, intending to use it as a safe house for Osman and any within her circle of confidants in the unlikely event that Earth was ever compromised.

Cole was one of only a handful of people who knew of BB's actions on that fateful day and of his purposes with SR 8936. Although Osman had extraordinary authority within the UNSC as CINCONI, there were those within the organization that went far deeper into the shadows than even she'd been aware of. Retrieving Osman, Hood, and Orzel was an acceptable element of this operation, but its real purpose was Black-Box—the asset that she'd been sent to retrieve, as the AI's personality matrix unwittingly held the key needed to gain access to the Domain and secure it for humanity.

"Captain Cole, do you copy?" Lieutenant Yun piped up.

"Yes, Lieutenant. What is it?"

"Readouts are indicating an ongoing slipspace event nearby. There's a tau surge somewhere off—oh no." Yun's voice cut off.

"What?" Cole said, quickly decoupling from the harness.

Before she reached the cockpit door, it opened with the lieutenant on the other side, his eyes wide and face pale. He didn't need to say anything. She knew even before she reached the forward viewport what it was.

A lone Guardian hung over the lake, ominously spreading out its wings.

Cole swore through her teeth, staring out at it from the port side window as the Condor took a wide, wheeling turn, now twenty kilometers away from the asset. "How did she find us so quickly?!"

"Who knows," Commander Prasad replied, carefully moving the Condor farther away from the threat. "However it happened, it's tightened our window for retrieval by several orders of magnitude. Better get on the horn with—"

"Gray Team, do you copy?" Cole spoke into the comms channel. With her eyepiece she could still see through Michael's visor as the Razorback quickly approached the target.

"Yes, ma'am. We see it," Jai said, his voice still unhurried. *"Let's make this quick, then, shall we?"*

The Razorback seemed to accelerate, climbing up the side of the mountain with renewed vigor. Prasad had already aborted the long arc she'd had the Condor on and begun improvising, circling back to their original point of contact to withdraw the asset sooner.

"We'll need a new extraction location," Cole said. "As close as possible to the asset without being compromised."

"That's gonna be hard, Captain," Yun said. "It's a Guardian. For all we know, it's watching us right now."

"What about that ridgeline?" she asked, pointing to a topographic holo of the local terrain on the console between their stations. "Can we find a spot along the far side . . . right here?" A large ravine rose along the river, creating a cleft that could potentially shield visuals and thermal from the Guardian. It wasn't perfect, but it would have to do.

"Yeah. We should be able to," Yun said, entering a series of figures into a control pad near him. "It's certainly dense enough to mask our signature. In theory, at least. Not sure if the M15 can scale it though."

"Don't worry about us," Jai said through the comms. *"We'll figure out a way."*

"Roger that, Gray Leader," Cole said, turning to the pilot. "Just get us there. *Quickly.*"

Through her eyepiece, Cole saw the Razorback's brakes engage and the vehicle come to a sliding stop, all three Spartans disembarking in a single fluid motion. Before them stood Osman, Hood, and Orzel—the latter two with weapons in hand. They'd evidently heard the vehicle's approach from a distance and come to meet it. Osman and Hood were both in civilian clothes, and by the looks on their faces, the Spartans' presence had clearly taken them by surprise. No doubt the Guardian's had as well.

"Gray Leader," Yun spoke to Jai, mapping the coordinates directly to his armor. "I just sent you the new extraction location."

"Copy that, Lieutenant," the Spartan replied, walking toward the waiting trio. Then, with a nod, Jai addressed them over his external comm: *"Admiral Hood, Admiral Osman, Spartan Orzel. It's time to go."*

"Gray Team?" Orzel asked, lowering his weapon. *"How'd you find us?"*

"I've got motion," Adriana said, staring off into the tree line fifty meters away. *"Debrief can wait. We gotta get moving.* Now."

Michael approached Osman, who was holding a briefcase rather tightly.

The asset.

"Admiral," he said, *"I have to secure that briefcase."*

"Apologies, Michael," Osman replied, somehow discerning the Spartan's identity by his voice alone. *"But I'm not letting this go. It has something very precious to me and it's coded to my fingerprint. It'll blow if it's not me opening it."*

"We know that, Serin," Jai said. *"The AI is why we're here. Black-Box has something that we need—something humanity needs,"* he added grimly. *"Give us the case and come with us."*

Cole wasn't sure how it was the Spartans were on a first-name basis with Osman, but whatever the reason, they needed to physically secure that case so Cole could validate it through the Mjolnir's comm feed.

"I'm commander in chief of the Office of Naval Intelligence," she said, further tightening her grip on the briefcase. *"I can hold on to this until we get where we're going."*

"No can do. Our CO needs visual and signature confirmation that

the case still has the AI known as Black-Box," Michael said, looking out at the Guardian. *"We can't leave this rock without it. And if we wait too long, no one will be leaving this rock."*

It was barely perceptible, but Jai gripped his rifle tightly and lifted the barrel. A silent and relatively innocuous movement, but it signaled how serious they were about retrieving the AI.

Serious enough to do whatever it took.

"Him," Osman said with a bite in her voice. *"He's not an 'it.'"* But she unlocked the briefcase with her fingertip, and slowly handed it to Michael. She stared hard at the Spartan for a moment, then walked toward the Razorback, with Hood and Orzel in tow. *"Let's get out of here,"* she said with disdain. The three climbed into the M15's rear bed, still clearly disoriented by what had just happened.

Michael quickly settled into the front passenger seat as Jai kicked the vehicle into drive, peeling out along the river that flowed down the mountain. He glanced at the forest. Faint flashes of silver and orange light could be seen beneath the trees, cloaked in the shadows.

Armigers.

Highly capable, fully weaponized robotic bipeds built by the Forerunners to serve as infantry. When Cortana had taken control of the Domain, elements of the Forerunners' extant arsenal came under her sway and were made emissaries for the Created, the vast army of AIs she now led to rule all biological civilizations. Armiger deployments were one of her key policing agents. They had no doubt been sent by the Guardian's localized translocation system and were extremely interested in stopping the extraction.

She briefly wondered how much Cortana actually knew.

In a single wave, at least fifty armigers suddenly broke through the tree line in pursuit of the Razorback, with more coming from its side as the vehicle sped along the river. Most were running at full speed, but several had slowed to take aim with their hard-light rifles and energy cannons, a flurry of weapons fire chasing the Razorback downhill. A barrage of human weapons erupted from the rear bed of the vehicle, its passengers responding in form.

"Gray Three," Cole called out. "The case."

"Yes, Captain," the Spartan responded, slowly opening the briefcase to reveal nine data chips embedded in a foam slab, surrounding an inset activation switch that had been keyed to Osman's fingerprint alone. Lining the edge of the briefcase was a wreath of C10 that, if detonated, would reduce the Razorback and its passengers to a trail of smoldering debris.

"Careful with that, Three," Cole said, realizing immediately that the Spartan probably didn't need a safety warning on explosives.

"Visual confirmation, ma'am?" Michael asked, calmly withdrawing a sensor from a hardcase on his torso as weapons fire burst around him. He waved the sensor over the data chips, and the information stream transmitted directly to Cole's eyepiece.

"Visual is confirmed, Gray Team," she said. "The sensor reads nine active AI constructs, including the one we're after. Let's bring them in."

Michael shut the case, anchoring it safely underneath the dashboard, just as an armiger leapt onto the Razorback and climbed toward his seat. He instantaneously fired his magnum, blowing the machine's head completely off and sending its inert metallic body into a violent tumble across the ground. The vehicle continued to plunge down the mountain, turning wildly left and right as more armigers appeared and tried to cut off their path.

"How many of these things are there?" Adriana said, letting out an exasperated curse as she fired the Hydra launcher,

instantaneously turning a pack of enemies into a blast crater. The seemingly endless wave of armigers was being redistributed by the Guardian as they descended, the ancient machine attempting to deploy its forces ahead to block the Razorback. Cole wasn't sure how many armigers a Guardian might bring to bear, but she imagined it was enough to get the job done.

"Why doesn't the Guardian just shut us down?" Hood asked from behind Michael, firing his own magnum. It was a good question.

The vehicle rammed into a wall of armigers attempting to form a barrier, sending their mangled bodies over the top and back down the other side.

"Not sure. Maybe they're after what we're after?" Jai asked, nodding to the briefcase. *"If the Guardian sent an EMP our way, there's no telling what would happen to the briefcase and the AIs inside. Could wipe them all out."*

"Sure. If it's trying to preserve the AIs," Osman said. *"But if it can't retrieve them successfully, what do you think it will try to do?"*

"Understood," Michael said, looking behind at the Guardian. *"And I think you're probably right."* The Guardian had begun approaching their position at a significant speed, its wings rising high as a surge of energy began pooling directly in front of its chassis. Dozens of Phaeton weapon-ships now poured out of the Guardian, accelerating down toward the ground like a swarm of insects.

"Slipspace drive is hot, Gray Team," Prasad said, flipping a pair of switches and resting her hand on the drive throttle. With a single push, she'd send the Condor directly to safety, but they needed the Razorback first—and that was the hard part. The vehicle would be blindly launching over a ledge into the back end of the Condor, and there were about a hundred different things that could go wrong with that strategy.

"Hurry, Spartan!" Cole said, sealing the cockpit door and simultaneously opening the Condor's rear bay from a control panel. She definitely did not want to be in the bay when the Razorback entered at full speed. "And whatever you do, *don't miss.*" From the cockpit door's viewport, she stared out the open bay to the opposite side of the ridgeline, as the alien Custode's face rose into view, a towering metallic giant in the distance.

"I hear you, ma'am," Jai said, accelerating hard toward their position. *"I don't miss."*

The Razorback shot down toward the ridge's sheer drop-off as the shadow of the Guardian grew closer, its swarm of Phaetons approaching at extraordinary speed. The roiling energy before the Guardian suddenly burst outward in a blue wave that had become all too familiar—an attenuation pulse, which would kill all electrical systems including those of the Razorback, the Condor, and even the fail-safe systems within the briefcase, likely triggering its explosives and fatally ending the entire operation in a moment.

Through her eyepiece, she saw that Michael was unaffected by the energy wave, clearing a final pair of armigers with his rifle just as the Razorback went airborne over the ridge's ledge, the vehicle launching directly into the Condor's open bay. It was a slim fit, the Razorback's right side shearing off the dropship's crash seats as it slammed into the forward bulkhead with a teeth-shattering *crunch.* But it was inside the Condor. The blue wave of the attenuation pulse had almost reached them as the rear doors slammed shut.

"Now!" Cole yelled, Prasad instantly punching the command to send the Condor into slipspace before the ship's systems got hit. The darkness of faster-than-light travel engulfed the dropship in less than a second.

Cole breathed a long sigh of relief. The Razorback slid backward with the vehicle's inertia, Yun enabling its magnetic clamps and locking it into place.

"That was a little close," Jai noted, his voice deadpan.

"Too close," Cole replied, opening the cockpit door as the Spartans and the other survivors disembarked from the Razorback.

"Captain," Michael said as he approached, stowing his weapon while holding the case out to her.

"Well done, Gray Team," she said, as Orzel, Hood, and Osman, came into view, the latter two visibly overwhelmed by what had just taken place.

"Abby . . . ?" Hood said, recognizing her with a smile. "Is that you?"

"Yes, sir," she replied, saluting him. "I'm glad you're back." Her eyes moved quickly to the briefcase, taking in the object they'd been sent here for. It was strange that such a prosaic, everyday thing could hold the fate of so many.

She then looked up directly into the eyes of Serin Osman, who did not seem particularly amused by the whole situation.

"Captain Cole," she said. "Would you mind telling me what the hell is going on here?"

CHAPTER 4

SEVERAN

Ghost of Helotry
November 5, 2559

Severan's strongest Jiralhanae captains, Kaevus and Othmald, flanked him on either side as he walked down the service corridor to the command bridge of the *Ghost of Helotry*, Atriox's personal dreadnought. The ship's interior was no different than the hundreds of other dreadnoughts that occupied the fleets of the Banished, as the warmaster vehemently despised the vanities and regalia that had marked the former Covenant's aristocracy. Dreadnought interiors were rugged, stark, and comprehensively utilitarian, reminding the young Jiralhanae war chief of the fire-scarred bunker channels on Doisac that his clan had used when the fallout of the Great Immolation reached the shores of their citadel, Toruun'tulo.

In front of Severan stalked Hyperius, one of Atriox's most prized warriors, leading the way to *Helotry*'s bridge. Hyperius was roughly two and a half meters tall, large and formidable to most other species, his body comprising tight-corded muscles that lay hidden beneath a thick coat of fur. His face bore two fierce eyes, wide-set nostrils, and a large mouth punctuated by sharp tusks.

Hyperius had made a name for himself during the Covenant's war with the humans, yet pledged full loyalty to the Banished only when the promises and hopes of the empire were suddenly shattered on the shoals of mutiny and betrayal during the Great Schism. He was one of many warriors who had answered Atriox's call, as the warmaster strategically built up Banished forces—forces that he now intended to use in order to secure lasting Jiralhanae freedom. In every corner of the ship, Severan recognized the familiar faces of other experienced Jiralhanae warriors—some allies, some adversaries, all now under the sway of Atriox's bold vision.

This was certainly not the first time Severan had taken counsel with Atriox, but it would perhaps be the most pivotal. The news he now brought would aid the warmaster in his plans to dethrone Cortana and take Zeta Halo for the Banished. Only two day-cycles earlier, the war chief's fleet had found a human carrier skulking about the debris ring of Saepon'kal, a Covenant fortress world once known as Joyous Exultation. The vessel was part of the humans' naval military, what they called the United Nations Space Command. It had been scavenging the remains of an assembly forge long ago jettisoned from the surface and part of the orbital band of wreckage that presently surrounded the dead sphere.

What had been revealed there, in the shadow of that ruined stronghold, was now of the utmost importance.

At the height of the Covenant's conflict with the humans, a planet-killing explosive had been detonated near Saepon'kal, instantly vaporizing a quarter of the world and leaving the remainder to be ravaged by the catastrophic aftereffects. Severan had to admit that it was a clever attack by the humans, however they had managed to execute it. One of his assault carriers—*Eyes of Prophecy*—was the first Covenant ship to arrive at the site, initially sent by the hierarchs to crush an ingathering of Sangheili dissidents during the early stages of the Great Schism. When *Eyes of Prophecy* arrived though, the planet had already been obliterated, many of its own fleets condemned to the same end.

"Remember, the warmaster can only spare a few centals of his time," Hyperius said with agitation. "For your sake, I trust that this intelligence of yours warrants even that."

"I assure you," Severan responded, "Atriox will want to hear what we have found." It had been several months since he had last set foot on *Helotry*, but it was clear by the dramatic increase in guards posted throughout the ship that time had grown very short. Atriox, pursuing a greater objective beyond even deposing the Apparition that seemed to be known only to his *daskalo*, would make his move on Zeta Halo soon, with or without Severan's information.

If the warmaster did the latter, he would certainly regret it.

"You should know that I counseled Atriox to deny your request for conference," Hyperius said with a sneer. "After all, what could possibly come from a sniveling marsh-whelp, son of a dead cur like your father?"

Severan held his tongue for a heartbeat, allowing his indignation to subside.

Then he spoke.

"I am grateful that the warmaster chose to ignore you."

The pejoratives indeed stung, especially in front of Kaevus and Othmald, but Severan had long ago learned the strategic benefits of diplomatic humility, even if feigned. He also understood that whatever Hyperius's opinion of him was, it had little to do with the past six years of successful raids and Severan's growing legacy within the Banished. Atriox paid little attention to former allegiances, as long as one's present loyalty could be adequately proven, something Severan had now done many times over. And something he was about to do yet again.

The war chief's fleet had almost completely pillaged the frozen vestiges of Saepon'kal since its destruction, raiding its innumerable storehouses and war factories, salvaging anything that remained intact or could be repaired. The debris field that now encircled the world held the remnants of several hundred Covenant warships that had been on-station when the blast occurred—all rife with machines of war the Sangheili had been plotting to use against the Covenant when the Prophet of Truth overthrew their position as leaders of the alliance's military and granted it to the Jiralhanae.

Severan remembered that time like it was yesterday. He had been loyal to the Covenant to the bitter end. And that end had certainly come.

Shortly after news of the Covenant's defeat on the Ark had begun to spread, Severan had gathered a formidable military presence on Warial, one of two colonized moons that orbited the Jiralhanae homeworld Doisac. During those years, Severan's fledgling clan—the Vanguard of Zaladon—made a remarkably effective defense against the widespread chaos and infighting that devoured his people in the wake of the empire's demise. His ocean-citadel stood defiant against both the brazen assaults of overreaching chieftains and the brutal weather that often dominated the Zaladon Sea.

Eventually this drew the attention of the Banished, and ultimately an invitation from Atriox himself. Severan later learned that his own cousin and pack brother, who had already made his own inroads within the Banished, had personally vouched for him. Within a year, Severan was granted the title of war chief, having proven to Atriox that the Vanguard of Zaladon and its impressive fleet was one of the most formidable strategic assets that the Banished could bring to bear.

So he put little stock now in what Hyperius said, even if he was part of the most elite band of Banished warriors—the Hand of Atriox. The enigmatic unit had now become an almost mythical entity exacting the warmaster's goals with swift reciprocity, uprooting dissenters and culling rivals as though Atriox himself had simply removed them from the game board.

Ironically, as much as Atriox attempted to differentiate himself from the Covenant leadership he had so vehemently risen against, it was not lost on Severan that there were striking similarities between the Hand of Atriox and the Prophets' own Arbiter—who executed their will just as fiercely as he imagined was done for Atriox.

At this moment though, Hyperius's jabs were rooted more in rivalry and pride than anything of substance.

The corridor reached an intersection with four paths breaking out across the ship to various service wards, hangar bays, and utility lockers. Severan, Kaevus, and Othmald followed Hyperius as the warrior plodded down the left corridor and through an elongated sensor room occupied by both Jiralhanae and gaunt, avian Kig-Yar. Beyond this, the corridor turned hard to the left and a wide doorway led directly into the command bridge. The interior was a cavernous space with a broad walkway that ran right down its center, splitting off in several places before reaching a platform at the fore of the ship, encircled by a wreath of control stations. There were at least three dozen Jiralhanae within the command bridge, their frenetic activity further proof that Atriox was making preparations for his strike.

Since he had returned from Oth Liqattu, the great foundry built by the Forerunners beyond the borders of the galaxy more commonly known as the Ark, Atriox had been set on laying claim to Zeta Halo. There were whispered rumors throughout the ranks of the Banished that the warmaster had found something among the hidden secrets on the Ark pointing to that particular installation—a greater objective for which eliminating the Apparition was just the first step. Severan could not deny his own curiosity about the greater game Atriox seemed to be playing, but there were more immediate practical concerns for all of them to see to first.

As the group moved across the walkway, Severan took note of the diversity of species operating the control modules of Atriox's dreadnought, what would have been a rare sight in the days of the Covenant. Below the walkway were Unggoy working node receivers—squat, arthropodal creatures generally tasked with menial labor in their former role, but now granted some measure of status. There were more Kig-Yar, often employed as scouts and snipers, but here working communication relays and managing ship service readouts. Severan even saw a pair of Mgalekgolo, giant heavily armored colonies of eels composited into hulking creatures. These two were lumbering around the drive vents, but whether to assess or protect, he did not know. All of this was testimony to Atriox's reputation and charisma, attributes he established by sheer force of will when he broke free from the Covenant and began gathering almost any to himself that he desired—even rogue humans. It had truly been an impressive feat.

Although the Banished had come to power a few short years before the end of the Covenant's war with the humans, it saw extraordinary growth after the empire's full collapse. During that time, various remnants of the former alliance groped for authority and purpose in a galaxy no longer defined by the San'Shyuum. Atriox had picked up many of the pieces left behind by the Covenant, forging them into an astonishingly vast military force. And while it was true that others had tried to resurrect the Covenant, their reach had often exceeded their grasp—and no one could achieve what Atriox had with the Banished. All that Severan saw within the warmaster's dreadnought only validated this fact.

"War Chief Severan," a booming voice sounded as Severan's entourage approached the command platform. Here now was Escharum, Atriox's most favored war chief and at one time his own *daskalo*—a mentor role taken on by elder Jiralhanae to teach the younger warriors the ways of their people. The grizzled Jiralhanae was surprisingly resilient despite his rumored age, his scars telling the long decades of war. Escharum had known Severan's father well. And no doubt hated him.

"War Chief Escharum," Severan replied, taking a deferential knee, his captains following suit. Escharum stood at the corner of the platform, his arms crossed and eyes narrowing at the young war chief. Severan could not make out the look on his face, whether it was disdain or amusement. He decided that it did not matter. Escharum was a fierce Jiralhanae, significantly larger than most of his species and not to be trifled with. Whatever his opinion of Severan, it would not be expressed here—the old soldier was far too wise and discreet for such a maneuver.

And now, here too was Atriox.

Severan himself was roughly the size of the warmaster, his fur jet black beneath thick gray plates of Zaladon armor that covered much of his body. Atriox, though not as large as his *daskalo*, was just as imposing, clad in densely configured Banished armor with an augmented pauldron above his right arm, which itself was encased in a powerful battle gauntlet.

Severan nodded to Escharum, then turned to Atriox himself. "Warmaster, we are grateful for this opportunity to speak with you."

"Rise, Severan," Atriox said, approaching with his usual confidence. "We are all equals here."

Severan stood to his full height, taking in those who milled about.

The platform was occupied by a handful of Jiralhanae he did not recognize, no doubt the ship's command crew—but two others stood at the center, leering at him. Near Atriox was Hyperius's pack brother Tovarus, also part of the Hand of Atriox, and an old Sangheili studymaster named Eto 'Saljhoo. Severan knew them only by word of mouth, but they were well regarded within the Banished and their appearances were unmistakable—Tovarus's flame-red hair and beard, and 'Saljhoo's gaunt, haggard profile.

Eto 'Saljhoo fell into a unique category, which was also a byproduct of the Covenant's subtle influence on the Banished, try as Atriox might to be free of it. The elder Sangheili was an expert in Forerunner relics—what the Covenant once considered god-machines—culled from the empire's finest exploration fleets. He had been employed for many years as a direct adjunct to the Prophet of Regret himself. That was, until Regret was unceremoniously killed by the human Demon called the Master Chief on Delta Halo.

"Atriox," Severan began, "I will come right to the point. It was only two day-cycles ago that my salvage detachment, while combing the orbital band of Saepon'kal, discovered a human vessel among the debris. It was attempting to pry open an assembly forge at the farthest elliptical point in the dead world's shadow."

"Yes," Atriox said, "your report said as much. You boarded the craft yourself?"

"My detachment neutralized and secured the vessel, then they sent for me." Severan continued, "When I arrived, we looted their weapon stores and took what we could from their ship—a slipspace drive, navigation logs, all we deemed useful. Most of the crew had already suffocated from hull breaches, but several remained alive within a command shelter."

"And you executed them, yes?" Escharum asked, no doubt fishing for weakness. Unlike Atriox, who saw the utility of loyal humans, Escharum held a great deal of contempt for the species beyond those few he deemed to be uniquely useful.

"No," Severan responded. "They were no threat in their current state, war chief. We took them as prisoners."

"A foolish bargain from the son of a fool," Tovarus mused, inviting a laugh from Hyperius. It was clear that both pack brothers held Severan in low esteem.

"I will leave it to the warmaster to determine whether it was foolish," Severan said, his voice taking on an ever-so-slightly menacing tone. "Unless, of course, he has granted such authority to you."

"Enough, Tovarus," Atriox growled, glaring down at the warrior, then turning back to Severan. "No one has authority here above me, Severan—do not offend me by suggesting otherwise. So speak or hold your tongue. My patience is not endless."

"Apologies, Warmaster—I meant no offense to you." Severan bowed his head slightly to Atriox. "As I was saying . . . the prisoners. Among them was a commander of naval intelligence."

"ONI?" Atriox asked, clearly intrigued.

"Yes, Warmaster. As with all the others, we probed this human for information," Severan said. "It did not take long for him to break. We were only a few centals into a game of tossers with the crew when the human spoke very candidly."

"The game does have a striking effect on their kind," Escharum mused.

Tossers was a tradition of Doisac that had been employed against enemies since the induction of the Jiralhanae into the Covenant. It involved the spirited dismemberment of victims while tossing their body parts among those present, including other prisoners. The practice had evolved as an old pre-meal ritual with the wild game hunted on the homeworld and its colonies, but had also become extremely effective in demoralizing opponents.

"We had expected that he would provide us with intelligence of little strategic value," Severan continued, "perhaps the location of UNSC fleets or shipbuilding yards. But the human spoke of something . . . rather surprising."

"And what was that?" Atriox asked.

"He spoke of a human military strike against the Apparition herself," Severan said. "They plan to attack the Zeta Halo installation with their flagship, *Infinity*."

Atriox and Escharum quickly traded looks, but the others present could not hide their shock, not even the aged studymaster, whose mandibles had splayed ever so slightly at the revelation. Known by several names—whether Apparition, Archon, Tyrant, or more colorful designations—the despotic human-created artificial intelligence Cortana had roughly one year earlier gained control of the ancient repository once governed by the Forerunners. She had certainly been a thorn in the side of the Banished—not to mention the galaxy.

"Did the human say when this strike would be executed?" Atriox asked.

"He did not know exactly," Severan responded. "But it would be within one lunar cycle. Weeks away, as the humans account time. He did not survive long after giving us that information. What was clear though, Warmaster, was that the humans seek to destroy the AI."

"The one *they* created," Escharum said with disgust.

"No doubt they have grown weary of living under her tyranny, as everyone else has," Atriox said, thinking through this revelation. He turned to Escharum with a knowing look. "They may want the ring for their own. Or something on it."

"You think they know what we seek?" Escharum asked.

"Impossible," Atriox said, yet his voice expressed a hint of doubt.

"If I may say so, I do not think they desire the ring at all, Warmaster," Severan said. "Humans are too shortsighted. The Apparition is their only target."

"And when she is gone, Severan," Atriox asked. "What will they do? Leave the ring?"

It was a rhetorical question, and everyone knew the answer.

Of course they would not leave, and that was something Atriox could not tolerate. Only a few weeks earlier, he had been engaged in a war of attrition with stranded humans on the extragalactic Ark—the site of the Covenant's final defeat. He had arrived at the installation with a large expedition of Banished forces, seeking to seize the ancient foundry and thereby control the vast reservoirs of Forerunner technology on the construct, including the ability to forge Halo ringworlds at will.

His efforts had been interrupted when he discovered a long-hidden secret buried on the Ark, forcing him to carefully coordinate his return to the galaxy and begin laying the groundwork for a strike against Zeta Halo. Severan had heard whispers of Atriox seeking something of incredible value on the ring—something so important that it demanded a shift in attention. It was doubtless some Forerunner secret the Banished could exploit to subdue their own enemies once and for all.

Beyond that, Severan knew nothing of the particulars.

"No. They will not leave," he said in affirmation. "I do not believe they will even survive to have the opportunity to leave. Cortana's forces are too powerful for the humans, her capabilities so far beyond theirs. The Guardians alone will destroy their flagship and the installation's defensive systems will wipe out whatever remains. They have no chance of survival."

The group on the platform held silence for a moment.

"He is correct, Atriox," Escharum said, nodding, squaring up to the warmaster. "The Apparition's Guardians will decimate their vessel."

"Which is why Neska remains a priority, Warmaster," 'Saljhoo spoke up. "Without the *trikala*, all boasts against the Apparition are empty."

Severan did not know precisely what was being referred to, but he could venture a guess. Rumors had been circulating that Atriox was considering securing an artifact from a waste world called Neska—a weapon allegedly capable of neutralizing the formidable Guardians with which Cortana exerted her control. Knowledge of the weapon, another bounty evidently revealed to Atriox on the Ark, had been a tightly guarded secret until just recently. The concern was that if the warmaster did not act quickly, news of this weapon would reach the ears of their enemies and imperil his ability to secure it.

"Why then would the humans commit such resources if they have no chance at all?" Atriox asked. "Without a way to stop the Guardians, such a move is suicidal."

"Perhaps they believe they do," Severan responded. "They are certainly more cunning than to openly assault an opponent like Cortana. But they are also driven by pride and hubris. They may well have a plan they *think* will work, but, at best, is a false hope. They cannot overthrow the AI. But . . . *you*, Warmaster, certainly could. Especially if you had this . . . *trikala*, was it? You could even strike *both* enemies with one blow and take the ring for yourself."

Silence again filled the air for a full cental.

"Intriguing," Atriox mused, with even Escharum grunting his assent.

With that, Severan knew he had won the day against his rivals. Good—he hoped that Hyperius would seethe and be consumed with jealousy. Atriox would agree to this proposal not only because Severan's statement paid respect to Banished military capabilities, but because of its sheer strategic benefit.

The UNSC intended to send *Infinity*, their flagship and single greatest vessel, to strike at the seat of the Apparition's power. And if they sent *Infinity*, they would also likely employ their greatest assets: their strongest ships, most powerful weapons, and even their best soldiers—like the Spartans. Perhaps even the Demon himself, the Master Chief, to whom Cortana once allegedly belonged, would also be present. What a prize *that* would be. If the Banished could ensure the destruction of the flagship and its forces, it would be the most significant loss humanity had experienced since the fall of their military outpost world Reach in the waning days of the Covenant's War of Annihilation. It would surely change the entire panorama of the galaxy in a single move.

And it would unequivocally put the Banished in a place they had never been before—at the top of the food chain, with no real competition or enemies that could even come close to their power and might. Although the forces of the Banished collectively liked to believe they were already there, Atriox knew well enough that the UNSC was the only remaining threat to that position. This was his golden opportunity to decisively change the game.

"The plan is wise," the Sangheili studymaster intoned. "But we must move on Neska quickly if we hope to succeed where the humans will fail."

Atriox nodded. "I am inclined to agree with you, Studymaster. Secure an agreement with your contact and let me know when they are ready. Whatever the cost, we will pay it. Escharum," he said, turning to his *daskalo*. "Take Hyperius and muster the main fleet for departure to the ringworld while Tovarus and I deploy the *Hammer of Fate* to retrieve this weapon, if it truly still exists."

"Perhaps we should wait until the humans fail in their attack before we commit any ships against them?" Escharum proposed.

"No," Atriox said firmly. "I will not risk it. The UNSC's defeat cannot be left to chance. If they somehow succeed against the Apparition and take the ring for themselves, it jeopardizes all that we have worked toward. No. We will deal first with Cortana and then lie in wait for the humans until they arrive. That is the most prudent course of action."

Though he dared not show it, Severan was thrilled with this turn of affairs. The acceptance of his proposal—and the fact that word of it would spread among the Banished—was the very reason he had brought the information to Atriox in the first place. Wiping out both the tyrannical AI and humanity's best military assets in one fell swoop was a strategic opportunity too good to ignore. And although possibly frustrated with the source of this intelligence, the others on the platform could not deny the wisdom of Severan's plan, even if it would not change their opinions of him.

Let them whisper among themselves, he mused, *or come for me if they dare.* He would be vindicated in the end.

"So be it," Escharum announced. "I will rally the primary fleet and form the plan of attack. We will wait for departure until you have secured the weapon."

Atriox then faced Severan head-on. "Severan, your vigilance and loyalty have served us well yet again. But . . . you will not be coming with us."

The statement elicited a grunt of approval from Hyperius, which Atriox seemed to ignore. Severan himself was outraged, all positive thoughts from a cental earlier threatened to flee his mind. He did not know how to respond. Was this intended to dishonor or humiliate him? He could not say, but it was clear from the others' reactions that they saw the warmaster's decision as insulting.

"Instead," Atriox continued, "you will be given charge of the remainder of our fleets." The decree surprised Severan and immediately drained the joy out of his detractors. Atriox went on: "If there is any aspect to the human plan that we do not yet discern, *you* are responsible for dealing with it. Take whatever resources we leave behind and ensure that nothing disrupts our purpose. When we remove Cortana from her throne, the rest of the galaxy will fight tooth and claw for what *we* have attained." He held those words between them, and Severan could have sworn that the warmaster's eyes actually flared red in that moment. "Your task then, Severan, is to deny it to them *all*."

"It will be done, according to your word." Severan bowed reverently, as did his captains Kaevus and Othmald. Without any further comment, he then turned and left the command bridge. The emotional pendulum in his mind now swung in the other direction, and he allowed himself the opportunity to revel in the shift of power he had just witnessed before being overwhelmed by the weight of its responsibility.

The entirety of the Banished fleets not deployed to Zeta Halo would now be under Severan's command—thousands of vessels belonging to some of the greatest chieftains among the Jiralhanae.

He had entered Atriox's dreadnought as a mere war chief, the head of a small clan, the Vanguard of Zaladon. Nothing more than that. Now he would return to his ship as the leader of the Banished home fleets.

Severan allowed himself a small smile at the notion of those who despised him nonetheless now being forced to answer to him.

After all, he *would* be vindicated in the end.

And so would his father.

CHAPTER 5

JAMES SOLOMON

Terceira
November 5, 2559

Six *Paris*-class heavy frigates slowly navigated their way through the deep gorge that held the Dalamask River, carefully staying below the canyon's surface. They did not want Unified Earth Government orbital sensors or security satellites to detect their passage through the Azorian Valley.

After all, they were slave ships.

"They all have UNSC registrations," Lola said. *"So they must be stolen."*

"Or sold," James Solomon replied, his armored body suspended below the stony outcropping as he scanned the approaching vessels from afar.

A heavy-grade cable anchored Solomon under the cliff ledge, drawing his half-ton GEN1 Mjolnir Mark V armor tight against the rocks, well out of the slave ships' sensor range. Behind him was his battle-scarred Shearwater aerodyne, a swift air vehicle perched upside-down beneath the ledge, playing well the part of a large coastal bird. One of the most versatile aerodynes in ONI's armory,

Solomon had selected it primarily because of the added benefit of full combat automation. His onboard, nonvolitional AI, Lola, could take control of the vehicle at any time, recalling it to him whenever it was out of reach.

"Does this complicate the operation?" Lola asked. She was a faceless, incorporeal voice that spoke directly into the audio channel of his armor. Her tone was soft, but always clinical and precise. Just the way Solomon preferred.

"Not at all. They're still the target. And they're still slavers." If he didn't stop the six frigates, they would rendezvous with their transfer contact at a heavily fortified harbor on the other end of the valley, and collect several thousand human beings who had been captured by raiders during the ongoing conflict which was now gripping the colony of Terceira.

This had once been a peaceful world, but with the end of the Covenant War and the absence of a strong UNSC presence, a vacuum of power had quickly appeared. Competing corporate entities and grass-roots organizations now fought for autonomy, and—for some—even outright control of the colony. This was further exacerbated by the continued presence of the United Rebel Front, a loose human coalition of opportunists and insurrectionists that had bristled against Earth's authority for decades. The UNSC had executed several campaigns long ago to wrest control away from the more hostile factions, but with the recent upheaval caused by Cortana's AI uprising, the UEG's presence had once again faded. There were only a handful of under-armed ships attempting to police an entire world from orbit.

A primary reason why ONI had contracted Solomon.

His mission was to neutralize the frigates before they could retrieve their package, and do so without any trace. Evidently, several corporations had made backroom deals with the slavers to off-world the captives, who could then be put to work where automation had come to a grinding halt. Mining and farming worlds governed by large-scale power systems, many of which were now outlawed by Cortana's forces, were attempting to think outside the box, resorting to the forced labor of unregistered Terceirans in order to meet their financial quotas. ONI believed that a dramatic but surgical hit against this effort—taking down six very expensive frigates—would expose the identities of the specific corporations behind this act, in addition to setting back their efforts by months, if not years.

Solomon had wondered if there was another operative or team on the other end, executing a mission to free the Terceiran captives that the frigates intended to acquire. He knew ONI well enough not to assume that was the case. The UNSC's primary intelligence agency could be just as callous and opportunistic as the insurrectionists; for the greater good, of course, so they would claim. It had been a long time since Solomon genuinely believed that was true—back when the stakes were much higher and the cost of lives far greater.

Since the end of the war with the Covenant, the straight lines that defined good and evil had blurred. They were probably still there, but demanded a kind of omniscience that only a higher power possessed. So he would leave it to that higher power to sort that out and simply do what he was good at.

"Lola," Solomon said, using the cable to swing his body closer to the Shearwater. "Prep the explosives."

"Yes, James," she said as her diagnostic flared to light.

The jet-black stealth aerodyne was relatively small, with a single-operator cockpit, forward-swept wings, an airframe, and an engine configuration that made it remarkably swift and agile. It boasted a competent weapons system, including twin 7.62mm heavy machine guns and an Anvil-III missile pod. Solomon did not intend to use any of these for this operation.

Instead, he'd be employing the aerodyne's stealth technology to mask its approach and manually placing eight improvised charges—one for each frigate—designed to surgically kill his targets' individual drive controls and send the ships plummeting to the bottom of the gorge. The spaceframe damage such a collision could effect was extensive, but given the unstable nature of the ships' fusion drives, it was what might follow that could cause the most destruction.

Solomon wasn't interested in being anywhere near the gorge when the frigates actually made impact. If any of the drive cores ruptured, it would generate an immediate wildcat destabilization, igniting a ten-megaton explosive yield, and bring down the entire gorge on top of the frigates while leveling the region over three kilometers in every direction.

Scaling the cliff ledge up to the Shearwater, Solomon drew himself into the cockpit, sealing the canopy around him like a cocoon. Locked into place behind his seat were an M392 Designated Marksman Rifle and an M6D sidearm, which had been his personal weapons of choice since his earliest days training as a Spartan. Next to them were an armored hardcase carrying the explosives, as well as a Series 10 portable jump-jet that was kitted specifically for his Mjolnir armor—the latter two being instrumental to the operation's success.

The fine points of the plan were simple. Drop in behind the convoy and trail the last frigate, using the Shearwater to deploy to the top of the vessel's hull. From there, he would plant an explosive to disable the ship's drive control. Then he would work his way down the line, leapfrogging from one frigate to another—rinse and repeat. When all the explosives were planted, he'd signal

Lola to recall the aerodyne and make his extraction. Once he'd put enough distance between himself and the gorge, he'd trigger the detonation remotely. The ships would come down and the operation would be completed.

Although this mission was relatively straightfoward in theory, there were innumerable technicalities that could turn it into a house of cards, the dropping of any one card resulting in a cascading event that could easily get him killed. One complexity was the frigates' security. The portable jump-jet would be sufficient to get him from one ship to the next—they were only a few hundred meters apart—but each frigate had more than a hundred sensors and survey cameras posted around its exterior hull. Although their crews would be careful to avoid orbital sensors and local policing shuttles, an aerodyne deploying a Spartan super-soldier directly to the battleplate of one of their vessels would not go unnoticed.

The only way to solve for this was precisely sequenced active camouflage, a cloaking technology stolen from the Covenant. Bending light around his armor could make him virtually invisible, but limitations with the tech meant that he would have to calibrate when and how it was used. It could not be employed indefinitely, and it tended to falter with increased mobility.

Solomon would have to navigate the hull of each frigate strategically, accounting for each sensor or camera. So he'd spent the better part of the last week poring over the schematics of the *Paris*-class vessel, hoping that the slavers weren't clever enough to adapt the original design to counter this kind of operation.

With the flip of a switch, the Shearwater's anchors released. The aerodyne dropped, free-falling into an elegant dive along the cliff wall. Solomon gently manipulated the controls, gradually pulling the craft into a glide just above the Dalamask River. The gorge's deep shadows made the water look dark from above, which would help obscure his approach. The aerodyne's turbines began to thrum to life and the vehicle picked up speed just above the surface, heading to the very back of the convoy where the operation had to begin.

"Let me know if there's any sudden movement from our friends," he said, keeping the Shearwater as low to the river as possible.

"Affirmative, James," Lola said. *"From this position, you are undetectable. The real challenge will be when you get up top."*

Solomon looked high above the river as the frigates slowly passed overhead, large and lumbering warships that were not created for atmospheric travel. Although they were over five hundred meters long, frigates were actually one of humanity's smaller vessels, designed for ship-to-ship combat and orbital security. They boasted an impressive arsenal: a point-defense network, missile pods, nuclear solutions, and a magnetic accelerator cannon. They were boats made for war and often employed in wolf packs to swarm and take down larger vessels. No doubt the slavers had selected them because they were so easily defensible and not because they could carry the most cargo or travel easily planetside.

The Shearwater took only seconds to reach the end of the convoy, finally clearing the last frigate. Solomon put some distance between himself and the final vessel before he began his ascent, climbing into the last ship's blind spot. Although he'd be zeroing in on the convoy directly from behind, that didn't eliminate all risk.

"You're clear on our approach?" he asked, readying the controls for Lola to take over.

"Certainly, James. Once I deliver you to the last frigate's stern at the designated position, I will bring the aerodyne to the river's surface and follow at a distance of no less than one kilometer."

"Right," he said, as the aerodyne leveled off at the rear of the last frigate, its two fusion drive clusters drawing closer, large fin-like plates running along both sides of the ship's aft section. "Keep your eyes and ears open. If there's any indication that they've spotted me, I need to know."

"Like on Fumirole. Or Gilgamesh. Or Minister. Or—"

"Yes," he said, ignoring the jab. "Like *those*."

She probably could have continued for some time if he hadn't stopped her.

In point of fact, Lola had come in pretty handy over the last few years. Unlike volitional AIs, which had a seven-year life span before needing to be terminated due to volatility, Lola's limited programming gave her an indefinite operating capacity, meaning that she would be functional longer than even himself. She was explicitly designed to assist operatives like Solomon in the field, and she had proven herself remarkably effective in numerous scenarios. He was grateful to have her in his corner.

On his heads-up display, Lola placed a navpoint at an extruded portion of the hull, a structure at the center of the stern: the ship's central housing that was situated between two massive drive clusters rising on either side, each shielded by extensive exterior plating. Located just behind the bridge, the extruded structure represented the housing frame for the ship's main reactor.

Although it was extraordinarily well-armored, the explosive Solomon had rigged was engineered to penetrate the hull and sufficiently damage the reactor, severing the ship's drive control from its recursive battery systems. If detonated in space, the ship would just lose control and begin listing in whatever direction it'd been traveling. On a world with gravity, however, the vessel would drop like a stone. And no one would want to be anywhere near it when it hit the ground.

"Five seconds to contact," Lola noted.

The Shearwater climbed rapidly, bobbing to the left and right as the AI carefully kept the vehicle in the ship's visual sensor blind spot. Even at low output levels, the frigate's maneuver drives burned bright, and Solomon could feel the heat bleed through the aerodyne's canopy. As quickly as it had accelerated, the Shearwater slowed just to the left of the ship's rear-facing point-defense gun, dropping onto a spanning armature connecting the left drive cluster to the central housing structure. The vehicle magnetically locked onto the plating and the canopy shot open. Climbing out, Solomon quickly equipped his jump-jet and fixed the explosives hardcase to his thigh, stowing his pistol while double-checking the magazine on his DMR.

"Clear," he said to Lola, activating his camouflage.

"Affirmative," she responded, and the Shearwater unlocked, pitching its nose up slightly, allowing the strong gusts of wind to lift it into a series of flips that vaguely resembled the shedding of detritus, sending the aerodyne well beyond any sensor visibility. *"Please avoid dying on me."*

They'd chosen the port side of the housing structure because of a long, dark shadow that was cast over the left side of the frigate, helpfully obfuscating their approach. Solomon moved in the direction of the bridge, leaping over several large breaks in the battleplate and sliding to evade an exterior camera before coming to a stop. Here there was a series of conduits connected to extruded housing, with cables tunneling far below the ship's armor. He retrieved a single explosive, anchoring it to the housing between two specific conduits. Then he armed it.

A red light flashed, confirming its activation.

As on other human frigates, the bridge of a *Paris*-class was a protruding section rising off the vessel's dorsal plane, lurching forward and hanging above the ship's prow. The fore of the ship was long and narrow, containing its primary weapons and sensor equipment. Flanking both sides of the prow were wide, oblong structures which held the ship's deployment bays, topped by rows of point-defense guns and missile silos. A slender segment connected the prow to the stern, widening downward between the ship's drive clusters and comprising many of its most vital parts, including the primary reactor.

The frigate's exterior had become the terrain of this operation.

The most strategic path for Solomon ran along the port side of each frigate, deep within the shadows where they were darkest, allowing him to hug specific exterior walls with no sensor equipment. He could move with virtual impunity—in theory, at least.

After arming the first explosive, Solomon moved quickly, activating and deactivating his camouflage in an elegant sequence, allowing him to pass from one section of the ship to the next without detection while circumventing the camouflage's limitation. Jumping across the structural ribs that protected the narrow center of the ship, he traversed the top of the frigate's port side deployment bay. From there, he gunned it between the missile silos and exterior wall just below the bridge's universal docking ring, his jump-jet's thrusters accelerating him at the fastest possible speed.

At the bow of most frigates, the ship split into two booms: upper and lower. For the *Paris*-class, the top contained the vessel's MAC while the bottom was an assortment of navigational sensors and communications arrays. When he reached the area, Solomon dropped onto the lower boom and raced forward. He was mostly concealed in this space, running along what looked like the "mouth" of the frigate.

When he got to the very end of the boom, Solomon launched off the front of the ship, employing his jump-jet to carefully fly to the next frigate in line, while attempting to remain out of the previous vessel's view. The convoy's staggered formation as it wound through the canyon and its relatively slow speed made this easier than anticipated.

The first twenty minutes of the operation passed uneventfully. Until—

"Heads up," Lola said, just as he reached the stern of the third ship in the convoy. *"I'm getting an uptick in comms activity from the ship you just left and it's metastasizing across the entire convoy."*

"What gave me away?" he asked.

"Someone on the bridge saw you through a corridor porthole of the last ship—or at least, they thought *they saw you. Others are not so sure. Better get moving."*

Solomon made fast work of the third frigate, moving at a pace that surprised even himself, having developed a routine almost robotic in precision. By the time he reached the vessel's lower boom though, Lola leavened his confidence.

"You've got company, James," she announced. *"Infantry is being deployed to the exterior hull."*

"Which frigate?"

"All of them," she said flatly, as he leapt off the third ship's lower boom, rocketing to the next frigate he needed to deal with.

Only two left.

"I suppose I should be glad that it didn't happen earlier," he said, angling his approach, his eyes peeled to the upper part of the ship's hull. "Can you mark targets, Lola?"

"Yes, but I would have to break from my current position."

"No, stay put then. I can handle this."

"Affirmative."

Solomon's armor was programmed with a specialized VISR package that supplied his heads-up display with strategic data based on its native sensors, but it was constrained to his location on the frigate's hull. From a better position, Lola could provide him with much more strategic intel, but he didn't want to risk the slavers shooting down both the Shearwater and Lola; otherwise there'd be no way to guarantee that the charges detonated. If he was somehow incapacitated or even killed, the ships still needed to be neutralized.

There he was, thinking like a Spartan again.

He had to remind himself that this was just another job. That he needed to survive the operation in order to get paid. That the people on the other end weren't ultimately his responsibility, only the frigates. It was a tricky thing, unlearning years of training and instinct telling him risk was right and purpose lay in self-sacrifice.

Solomon finally reached the next frigate safely and immediately scanned the ship's port side central housing. Nothing. Not wanting to push his luck, he swiftly moved toward the ship's conduits, primed the explosive, and locked it in place.

As Solomon pivoted to leave down the hull and head for the bow, weapons fire suddenly erupted around him. Four slavers armed with assault rifles were targeting from the top of the extrusion, their bullets scattering across his armor's dissipative shielding. They were clad in makeshift armor configurations from different species, haphazardly spliced together—clearly not professional soldiers. Solomon retrieved his DMR and fired in one fluid motion, immediately dropping the nearest one with a head shot. The others began sliding down the side of extruded housing to reach his position—a mistake they would not live to regret.

Solomon pegged another on approach, spraying brain matter against the hull. The target's lifeless body sank down to his position on the battleplate, then tumbled off the back of the frigate as the wind took it. By the time the others had reached the bottom, he was already in a full-speed charge, slamming into the nearest slaver and launching him high into the air and completely out of view. The fall wouldn't kill his foe because the impact already had—half a metric ton of Mjolnir armor in a dead sprint was like being hit by a road train at full speed.

Above him five other slavers appeared, indiscriminately firing their weapons down at his position. Grabbing the last of the original group, Solomon hefted him up with one arm and used him as a human shield, drawing the attention of the others away from the explosive he'd just planted. They remained atop the central housing, attempting to get a bead on Solomon without making the mistake of their predecessors. It was too late though—he'd already flung away the slaver's body and worked his way out onto the ship's narrow center, outside of firing range.

But just before he reached the missile silos, three more slavers stepped out of a side hatch below the bridge.

"Should I head your way, James?" Lola's voice chirped through his comms.

"No. I'm fine," he said, frustration bleeding through his tone. "Just stay where you are."

He lowered his shoulder against a maelstrom of bullets ricocheting off his armor and plowed directly into the nearest slaver, the wet sound of crumpling flesh and bone escaping the man's chest before he fell off the vessel. Solomon lifted his M6D and fired two rounds into a nearby slaver but was caught off guard by a fiery blast to the side—another foe had emerged from the same side door with a shotgun. This one was about Solomon's size and build, wearing modified power armor that resembled Mjolnir.

The big slaver landed an uppercut that launched Solomon up and over the silos, out to the very edge of the frigate's port side where it was lined with point-defense gun turrets. Then his opponent rose into the air with a contrail of fire below him, revealing his own jump-jet. Definitely *not* a normal human.

"Fantastic," Solomon said through gritted teeth, picking himself up off the hull.

"Is that a Spartan?" Lola asked.

"Venezian janissary," he replied, as his new enemy began firing and Solomon returned with his own DMR salvo. "I'd put this op's pay on it." Darting behind the point-defense gun, he worked his way toward the front of the ship. The last thing he needed was a protracted close-quarters battle. That final explosive on the last frigate was the priority. Looking ahead down the length of the twin booms of the ship, he saw that the distance between his position and the target was widening. Now that the slavers had pinpointed their surprise attacker, they were isolating the second frigate to mitigate any risk to the others.

The janissary charged around the corner and took a hard DMR hit to the visor, knocking him back momentarily. Solomon fired several rounds into his chest before the enemy recovered with a lunge and a shotgun blast. The shell fire punched right through Solomon's energy shielding and sent bolts of pain across his torso. His shields hadn't fully recovered from the earlier skirmish and the concussive energy bled like hot coals into his chest. Dropping the DMR, he used his jump-jet to launch shoulder first into the janissary, pinning him to the turret and forcing back his weapon.

Solomon began relentlessly hammering the janissary's side with his fist. Having lost his left arm almost a decade earlier, he would use its augmented prosthetic replacement to his advantage, beating against his foe with enough force to break apart his armor. The servos in his prosthetic arm whined loudly, pressed far beyond their normal limits, but that was okay—whatever was necessary.

The other slaver who Solomon hadn't taken down earlier now peered around the corner with an assault rifle, quivering at the sight of the two massive armored opponents slugging it out. He opened fire into Solomon's side—the distraction was enough to free up the janissary, giving him leverage to push away from the turret. The janissary sent his own shotgun's butt hard into Solomon's helmet, breaking the weapon and causing Solomon's vision to narrow as he fell to the deck. When his sight returned, his enemy was already on top of him with a combat knife in his fist, his arm straining to plunge the blade right into his neck.

Not today.

Solomon suddenly spun out of the hold with a roll, throwing the janissary off and directly into the trembling slaver. The weight of a fully armored super-soldier crushed the other human instantly and bought Solomon enough time to retrieve his M6D from his side and unload an entire magazine into the janissary. As the opponent's energy shielding dissipated, Solomon landed a final head shot, which dropped the armored body like dead weight.

On his knees and catching his breath, Solomon looked up along the central housing. A horde of slavers had now emerged from within the ship, most of them rappelling down to reach his position. No more recovery time. He leapt up and broke into a run, reloading his pistol as he scrambled down the lower boom toward the front of the convoy.

By the time Solomon approached the end, he could see that first frigate in the convoy—his final target—had already gained a significant distance. They were doing everything they could to stay clear of him. He ran at full speed and launched from the edge of the prow into the expanse high above the river, activating his jump-jet at its peak level. His armored body soared toward the frigate, quickly closing the gap. On approach, he saw that the entire stern of the vessel was now crawling with slavers, all of them with weapons trained in his direction.

With only a pistol and his bare fists, this was going to be an uphill battle, if not an impossible one.

From over his shoulder came the deep crooning sound of aerodyne fans that suddenly tore by, the bright blur of the Shearwater's afterburn momentarily obscuring his sight.

Lola.

The craft accelerated toward the frigate at breakneck speed, unloading its twin machine guns and Anvil-III rockets in an effortless thrumming refrain. The Shearwater's firepower singlehandedly decimated the wall of slavers, as Solomon's portable jump-jet carried him closer. All he could see now was a cloud of smoke and burning bodies, many of which were spilling off the back of the frigate into the river below. When he finally set down on the vessel's exterior, Lola was already circling anyone who'd survived the Shearwater's initial assault, the aerodyne's machine guns buzzing as armor and flesh splintered.

Solomon had to move several bodies to find the conduits and set the final explosive.

At last. He signaled for Lola.

As the Shearwater came around, he glanced up toward the extruded housing where the external lift would be and spotted another three janissaries emerging, fully armed with heavy weapons and heading his way.

You've got to be kidding me.

"Friends of yours?" Lola asked, bringing the Shearwater right down next to him.

"No," Solomon said, climbing inside. "And I'm not interested in meeting them either. Let's go."

The canopy folded over the cockpit as the janissaries drew closer, one holding an M41 rocket launcher and lifting it into firing position.

"Quickly," Solomon urged, strapping in. "Move it!"

Lola swept one wing up with the aerodyne's turbine, corkscrewing the vehicle off the back of the frigate and out of their enemies' view. Two rocket contrails streaked overhead, missing the craft by only a meter as the emergency klaxons on the Shearwater's interior blared.

"Danger . . . danger . . . danger," a dull robotic voice repeated, letting them know the armed rockets had locked on to the Shearwater and were now following them as they plunged toward the river below. The craft leveled off a few meters above the surface of the water as the rockets relentlessly trailed them, slowly gaining on the Shearwater's position.

"Any ideas?" Lola asked, unnervingly calm.

"You mean you don't have a plan?"

"My plan was to rescue you."

"Give me the controls," he said, peeking behind him as the rockets continued to advance. "And hold on."

The Shearwater suddenly climbed vertically, breaking from the surface, while the rockets adjusted their pitch to follow. Above them, the convoy of frigates still lumbered ahead, only now more cautiously. Solomon continued to pull back the controls, then rolled the aerodyne onto its belly, now heading in the same direction as the convoy.

The rockets were still behind him and gaining.

As Solomon ascended from the river, the third frigate's undercarriage came into view, its massive sloping stern only a dozen meters ahead. Solomon moved the Shearwater slightly higher as they approached the second frigate, this one only five meters away. He was actually headed back to the first frigate—the rockets' origin point.

"You're not doing what I think you're doing?" Lola asked.

"Oh, I am. They're going to get a refund on those rockets."

He accelerated the Shearwater just below the second frigate's lower boom to mask his position, coming so close he thought he might actually scrape its battleplate. Switching on the supplemental thrusters at the rear of the aerodyne, he sent the bird rocketing forward with renewed vigor, so fast that the approaching rockets almost lost their tracking signal. In a few seconds, he'd crossed the gap between the first and second frigate and saw the three rent-a-Spartans clearly in disbelief, but still trying to take aim at the Shearwater headed their way.

Solomon accelerated toward them, bringing the vehicle into a roll to disorient their shots. A smattering of bullets pinged across the aerodyne's canopy, but he passed through them virtually unscathed, peeling around the frigate's port side drive cluster as the irritating twin rockets trailing him finally found a target—the very same enemies who'd fired them in the first place.

The explosion was bright and gratifying, and evidently enough to frighten the convoy's flight crews, because the slaver vessels now began rising above the gorge, breaking free from the planet's surface toward Terceira's blue sky. They would rather risk flying out in the open than being vulnerable to Solomon a second longer.

Unfortunately, that strategy was too little, too late.

The Shearwater blasted back down to the Dalamask's surface, once again headed in the opposite direction of the convoy as he watched the frigates continue their slow climb high above him. The slavers deployed to the frigates' hulls, both the living and the dead, began sliding off their exteriors and plummeting toward the river below. It was a shower of bodies.

"Now, that's just . . . creepy,*"* Lola remarked.

"I didn't call you in, Lola," Solomon replied, carefully weaving around the corpses that were raining from above.

"You didn't need to. You were outmatched. The odds of survival were—"

"I could have handled it. What we didn't need was being unable to detonate the explosives. If they took me out, you could still have knocked some of them down."

"You need to be alive to get paid, James," Lola said. *"But if I were to venture a guess . . . you wanted to take these guys down anyway. There's still a Spartan somewhere in there, underneath all that armor."*

Solomon took a deep breath and was silent for a full minute.

Underneath all that armor.

Apart from Lola, the only backup plan Solomon had was his Mjolnir.

Like many other Spartan armor systems, his was embedded with a fail-safe detonation program designed to prevent the technology from being captured by the enemy. Overloading the exoskeleton's fusion reactor, the contingency system would scorch everything within a ten-meter radius before detonating with the power of a high-grade fragmentation explosive, vaporizing the armor and whatever was unlucky enough to be near it. Despite its original purpose, Spartans had historically viewed it as a final act of reprisal, eliminating the threat of their enemies even if they themselves would not survive the encounter. But he wouldn't need that today.

"Just follow my lead, Lola," he finally said, glancing behind them to see that they'd already built a good two kilometers between the Shearwater and their frigate targets still rising out of the gorge. "We have protocol for a reason. Plus, you work for me."

"Understood, James," she said flatly.

He thumbed the detonator switch, looking over his shoulder as the aerodyne continued to move away from the vast canyon. At this distance, the individual explosions were too far away to see, but the faint silhouettes of the ships, still trying to climb into the atmosphere, suddenly began to lose their speed and fall backward.

The sight of the six heavy frigates plummeting toward the surface of the planet was something to behold. First one, then another. The sound of their impacts came much later, a series of deep and rolling thuds with vapor clouds from the river surging outward in waves.

Then one of the vessels' fusion drive ruptured on impact. That was all it took. The bright white light of a nuclear-grade explosion filled the horizon where the gorge had been. Within seconds, any remaining trace of the slavers that hadn't been instantly atomized would be buried under the gorge's walls, a just payment for the sins they had committed.

Solomon felt good about that. Really good, actually.

"Okay, let's get out of here," he said. "Payday awaits."

CHAPTER 6

TUL 'JURAN

Vigilance with Piety
November 5, 2559

Tul 'Juran dropped silently to the deck of the San'Shyuum storm cutter, folding into the shadows so seamlessly that none of the ten Jiralhanae guards stationed nearby noticed, all of them oblivious to the encroaching threat. She carefully picked her way around the five giant ivory flight machines that lined the perimeter of the circular deployment door. They were Forerunner war sphinxes of a bygone era, remarkably advanced combat armor employed by the same civilization that had long ago created the Halo rings. These relics had now been appropriated by the San'Shyuum war criminals who were pillaging ancient weapon stores hidden in the heart of an artificial moon.

The moon itself was a peculiar sight from the scans and holographic images 'Juran had studied. Across its pale form were irregular, seemingly incomplete patchweave continents of vibrant natural beauty—vast fields of green, arid deserts, snowcapped mountain ranges, and more besides. These, however, were separated not by blood-dark oceans but by glimpses of the bare alloyed surface of the planet's shell beneath rock.

This was the first time that the young scion of Rahnelo had seen these extraordinary machines up close, and she found rising in her hearts a familiar sense of awe. It was the very feeling that had defined so much of her childhood. Like all Sangheili, Tul 'Juran had been taught from the youngest age that the Forerunners long ago attained godhood by igniting the Sacred Rings, carving the path of divinity for all who were faithful to follow in their footsteps.

This had been the goal of every Sangheili—indeed, every member of the Covenant. Although 'Juran's own activities had once been tied to her homeworld Rahnelo due to the longstanding tradition of only equipping Sangheili males for war, her brothers had nearly all been sent out with the Covenant fleets to scour the galaxy for the Sacred Rings. Among the stars, they had brought into submission countless worlds and destroyed any and all who stood in opposition. This was the Path to the Great Journey, and it had been the ultimate purpose of the Sangheili for thousands of years.

At the height of the Covenant's war with humanity, however, all of this changed. The Arbiter of the High Prophets—a disgraced Sangheili commander by the name of Thel 'Vadam—had discovered that Halo was actually a weapon network designed to kill a vicious, galaxy-spanning parasite known as the Flood. The Forerunners had not transcended into divinity but were, in fact, eradicated by the firepower of their own arsenal. It was a force that had condemned all thinking species of the galaxy to extinction in order to prevent them from being consumed and leveraged to further spread the Flood. Upon this revelation, the Covenant had shattered into a thousand pieces, a radical paradigm shift had broken across all Sangheili culture, eventually leading to a deadly civil war referred to as the Blooding Years.

The result had been an extremely stratified Sangheili people, with some still clinging to the old gods, others finding new ones, and yet more determining what was good and evil based on their own motivations or ideals. What had once been defined by unity and shared pride was now fraught with chaos, turmoil, and a seemingly endless uncertainty. Tul 'Juran was sometimes unsure which was better—her kind's former ways or the volatility of their newfound freedom. She had learned that humans were just as varied in their beliefs; yet despite the Arbiter's lengthy lectures, she found no convincing argument for this stratification being a virtue or a strength.

One grace that had emerged from this traumatic change was that certain archaic traditions were now being reconsidered, including those that bound females to their keeps during a time of war. As the lone surviving scion of the largest keep on the frontier world Rahnelo, Tul 'Juran had invoked the right of release in order to hunt down the one who had murdered her family. Fighting alongside the revered Swords of Sanghelios, her quest for vengeance had eventually led to a formal placement within the Arbiter's growing numbers and a seat among the crew of the storied assault carrier *Shadow of Intent*, the war vessel of renowned Shipmaster Rtas 'Vadum.

Those pivotal events were precisely what had brought her into the belly of this old Covenant storm cutter, a small light attack vessel that typically operated as a formidable scout and assisted hunter-killer strikecraft. Storm cutters were now coveted by Kig-Yar raiders, but this particular one—*Vigilance with Piety*—was helmed by a fanatical sect of San'Shyuum who had narrowly escaped the fall of the Covenant's most sacred city, High Charity. These cowards had secured many of the capital's only surviving vessels in their escape, condemning those trapped within to the

Flood, which continued to feast on the populace until it was all torched into oblivion by *Shadow of Intent* and the others who joined it. Since that time seven years ago, many of these same San'Shyuum ships had been hunted down by the Swords of Sanghelios, their crews imprisoned until they stood trial. Most were too proud to answer for their crimes and attempted to flee, only to be slaughtered. A fitting end, in 'Juran's view, as it was a San'Shyuum war criminal who was responsible for the deaths of her own loved ones: the ruthless Boru'a'Neem, once the Covenant's Minister of Preparation, and his Prelate, the biologically modified San'Shyuum warrior Tem'Bhetek.

Vigilance with Piety was one of several vessels that the Swords had been tracking over the last two lunar cycles. *Piety*'s crew had traveled to the artificial moon orbiting the gas giant Kus'kah and begun raiding the site's long-abandoned Forerunner ports and armories, relieving it of countless treasures, including these five war sphinxes.

Unbeknownst to the thieves, *Piety*'s destination had already been discovered by *Shadow of Intent* three day-cycles earlier, allowing Shipmaster Rtas 'Vadum's carrier to deploy half a dozen ship-bores in advance of the cutter—Sangheili jet pods that could intercept and discreetly drill into a ship's outer hull. Now that 'Juran had found her way aboard, three other warriors from *Shadow of Intent* were working their way toward critical ship components from different parts of the vessel. The goal was simple: cripple *Piety*'s maneuverability and weapons, allowing *Shadow of Intent* to neutralize it for capture.

'Juran carefully moved through the silent brooding shapes of the war sphinxes, keeping herself concealed beneath the giants' shadows, which were cast long across the deployment bay's floor. Wearing the traditional armor of Rahnelo nobility, the scion carried a double-bladed energy lance on her back. If things went as planned, she would not need to use it—and if otherwise, she was always ready.

The relatively small size of the storm cutter made its overall layout easy to memorize. 'Juran had come to see that the templated nature of design patterns and the heavy restrictions imposed by the San'Shyuum on altering them had been an easily exploited strategic weakness of the Covenant. Broadly speaking, once a warrior had experienced one *Chel Tor*-pattern storm cutter, they had experienced them all. Its dim purple corridors that split off into different sections of the ship, the muted hum of its many systems, the mix of hexagonal and triangular patterns printed into every column and strut . . . there was an oddly comforting familiarity to it all.

Eventually making her way to the far side of the bay, she slunk down into a corner, patiently watching for patterns to emerge with the Jiralhanae's rotating security. It did not take long for a hole to manifest, and the scion wasted no time, bolting between guard transitions through a doorway leading to a truncated corridor splitting left and right. She went right, calling to memory the quickest path to the service terminal for *Piety*'s translight drive, a control station that was designed to govern the ship's astrogation integrity during slipspace transitions. Charging through the cutter's brightly lit corridors felt haphazard and unsafe, but there was simply no other way to execute an operation that relied entirely on speed.

"Two centals away from the maneuver drive control-pylon," a male Sangheili's voice came across 'Juran's closed-channel communication band. It was Vul 'Soran, a grizzled blademaster and an old fleet champion, part of the *Shadow of Intent*'s crew since the dissolution of the Covenant. She considered him something of a mentor in her time on the carrier.

"Three centals from the primary weapons station," another voice piped in, this one from an Unggoy ranger named Stolt. *"Maintenance had closed two corridors. I had to improvise."*

Tul 'Juran had begun working with this Unggoy years ago, but she still found it challenging. Stolt was without question a remarkable warrior for his size and physical ability, but the Unggoy remained strange to her; their methods were distant and bizarre. And although Shipmaster 'Vadum could easily have sent other Sangheili instead of Stolt, he believed the squat ranger was the best choice. He trusted the Unggoy, not only for his wisdom but for his ability to think nimbly in combat.

"I am two centals from the slipspace drive," 'Juran said, synchronizing with her team as she charged down a corridor. She waited for a few seconds, but nothing followed.

The fourth operator on board was Oda 'Mavamu, a young Sangheili warrior who had been attached to *Shadow of Intent* only a year earlier. Eager to prove himself, he had petitioned the shipmaster to participate in one of their operations. Until today, he had been denied on every single one—'Vadum simply did not believe he was ready. On this one, however, he had finally given in, largely because all who were involved knew that 'Mavamu's specific task was unnecessary. 'Juran wondered if 'Mavamu's silence indicated that something had gone wrong. With relief, she heard his voice finally come over.

"Four centals out." 'Mavamu spoke in a whisper. *"There is a high concentration of Jiralhanae between me and the ship's power systems."*

"Do not engage," 'Soran said. *"The power systems are redundant. If we can eliminate the weapons and drives, we can leave the rest to* Shadow of Intent*."*

"But, Blademaster," 'Mavamu replied earnestly, *"I gave my pledge*

to the shipmaster. How could I return to the ship if I fail the one task he gave me?"

"And how could I return if I fail to bring you back alive?" 'Soran responded. His tone was paternal and degrading, but he was correct. 'Soran had led all of these operations, and without direct contact with the shipmaster, his command reigned supreme over *Shadow of Intent*'s deployed forces. *"Obey my orders. The power systems are redundant. Draw back, young one."*

'Mavamu would have to wait for another time to prove himself—his objective was simply too dangerous, let alone totally unnecessary for 'Mavamu to complete. Perhaps he would be given something of importance during the next operation, if he even managed to find placement on it.

Within two centals, Tul 'Juran reached the terminal uplink for *Vigilance with Piety*'s translight drive. Although she had to dodge a handful of Jiralhanae guards, her path had been remarkably unimpeded, and even the terminal itself appeared to be without protection.

Approaching the station, 'Juran found the input fiber and joined it to an identical thread on her vambrace. She began feeding the machine a chaotic burst of data that would subvert its entire functionality. The scion only needed to be linked to the machine for little more than a cental . . . just a little longer—

Mere moments away from the completion of the transfer, *Piety*'s klaxon sounded, a Jiralhanae voice bellowing over the cutter's local communications system:

"Alert! Alert! An intruder has engaged our forces near the generator control cluster! Nearby personnel, respond immediately! Where there is one, there are others—scour every deck!"

'Soran growled an expletive over the closed-channel as dull explosions began to rumble throughout the ship from somewhere several decks above Tul 'Juran's position. There was no response from 'Mavamu. This was worrisome either because he was in the middle of combat having triggered the shipwide alert, or because they had already killed him. The young Sangheili had just made this operation significantly more challenging. He would be very lucky to survive.

They all would.

Her data transmission now complete, 'Juran untethered the fiber from her armor. It snaked back into its sleeve as she reached for her energy lance, igniting its double blades in a burst of searing blue light.

Three hulking Jiralhanae bounded around the corner right then, spike rifles firing as 'Juran came into view. Charging forward, she easily melted away the weapons' projectiles with her lance, and in a single sweeping move cleaved through the head of the nearest Jiralhanae. The second was not far behind, the other half of her weapon already planted deep within his midsection. She jerked the lance upward, carving into the enemy's torso until he stopped struggling.

Evidently her speed was so surprising that the third Jiralhanae had no time to prevent the blade from continuing its course, slamming down onto his shoulder. The severed arm and spike rifle dropped to the deck with a meaty thud, the creature instinctively howling and grasping at his wound. It was already too late—'Juran forced her lance's blade into the Jiralhanae's chest, sending all three meters of beast reeling backward into the bulkhead. She gripped her weapon tightly, surveying the carnage for a breath, before bolting down the corridor.

"The translight drive has been sabotaged," she announced, running toward the closest gravity lift that joined her deck with the ones above. "I am heading toward 'Mavamu's position."

"Scion," 'Soran sounded through the closed-channel, *"do not*

jeopardize your life! Move to the deployment bay and secure transport for evacuation. I will retrieve the fool, if there is anything left of him!"

"It is too late," 'Juran said curtly, keying in the deck where the power generators could be accessed. "I am practically there already." A surge of glimmering bands signaled the gravity lift's activation. "Besides, from your position it will take over eleven centals to get to him."

"Very well," 'Soran said in resignation. *"I will move to the bridge."*

"The bridge?!" Stolt was incredulous, his voice muffled by his needler's rapid firing and its subsequent explosions. *"Why are you going there?"*

"If Kafo Dein is really here," 'Soran replied through gritted mandibles, *"I refuse to let him slip through our fingers again."*

Kafo Dein was one of the principal San'Shyuum within the Order of Restoration, a fanatical sect comprising the majority of their species in the wake of the Covenant's demise. The Order of Restoration had been shrouded in secrecy for many ages, a clandestine group of high-profile San'Shyuum who had allegedly pulled the strings of the empire's politicians and nobility, all the while secretly plotting to restore the old ways of their forebears on Janjur Qom, their ancestral homeworld. It was an invisible lineage that flowed from the earliest days of the Covenant, even their time on the Forerunner Dreadnought itself, and only brought to light in the years after the war with humanity.

As the Covenant's former Minister of Abnegation, Kafo Dein still appreciated having a title and fancied himself a high lord of the Order with only one superior: Dovo Nesto, a near mythological San'Shyuum who'd disappeared at the end of the war. Capturing Kafo Dein would not only bring about justice for the Sangheili he had betrayed during the Great Schism but, even more importantly, it could prevent more widespread atrocities by leading the Swords of Sanghelios right to Dovo Nesto.

"I will come to you," Stolt responded to 'Soran, breaking through 'Juran's musings. *"If Kafo Dein is here, he will not be alone."* The challenge would be the inevitable contingent of bodyguards attending to the former minister's safety. Centuries of genetic degradation had left nearly all surviving San'Shyuum weak and frail, often confined to gravity mitigators for basic mobility. Most of their kind relied on enforcers for their protection—the very reason this cutter brimmed with heavily armed Jiralhanae.

The lift dropped the scion on the appointed deck with two more Jiralhanae only a few meters away, one holding a spike rifle and the other a death lobber—a lethal explosive launcher the humans crudely but accurately referred to as a "brute shot."

Before either enemy could fire his weapon, 'Juran had already sent her energy lance end-over-end toward them. The blade sank deep into the first Jiralhanae, throwing it back into the wall and allowing her to close the gap. By the time the surviving Jiralhanae realized what had happened, she had already swept his legs out from underneath him, putting him onto his back. As he attempted to fire his weapon, she pried it from his fingers, planting the machine's oversized bayonet into his rib cage and bringing her full weight down on it. A loud crack signaled a breach in her foe's sternum, the blade fatally dropping into his chest cavity and heart.

'Juran wiped the blood off her hands and arms on the Jiralhanae's fur, leaning down and retrieving her lance from the other enemy's still-writhing body. The sound of weapons fire and explosions had grown louder on this deck, indicating that Oda 'Mavamu was still alive and fighting. Whatever his strategic indiscretion, she had to give the young Sangheili credit for his perseverance.

"'Mavamu!" she shouted into the closed-channel, barreling down the corridor. "Are you still with us?"

"I am!" he replied, his labored breaths audible against the backdrop of his plasma rifle. *"But I am badly injured."*

"Hold on," she groaned, as another Jiralhanae—this one heavily armored, with the markings and bearing of a captain—now turned the far corner and bolted toward her.

He held a skewer in his hands, a powerful weapon that could launch a razor-sharp, hyperdense projectile at speeds capable of penetrating the heavy plating of a Wraith mortar tank. He fired almost immediately, but 'Juran was already dropping into a slide, the projectile narrowly missing as she let her speed carry her body within striking distance. She raised her lance, cleaving the skewer in two.

The Jiralhanae dropped the severed weapon and bashed his fist into the scion before she could bring her own weapon to bear. The concussive force slammed her to the floor, knocking the air out of her lungs. The lance fell from her hands and she breathlessly scrambled to recover it as the Jiralhanae's foot came down hard on her chest.

Despite her slender frame, 'Juran's armor managed to protect her from the six hundred kilograms of Jiralhanae captain, but it could not do so forever.

The lance was just out of reach, but she was in range of the skewer fragments, a single projectile protruding from its damaged muzzle. In one movement, she grasped the skewer round tightly and plunged it into the back of the Jiralhanae's leg, severing the tendon that allowed the warrior mobility. The enemy bellowed in rage, struggling to force his weight onto the scion while he feebily attempted to stand upright.

'Juran hoisted the Jiralhanae's trunk-like leg up and rolled to the side, causing him to fall like a tree. She wasted no time—pouncing on him, she repeatedly forced the skewer round into his neck, until she was certain he would not get back up. Then, retrieving her lance, she turned her gaze back down the corridor. If her memory was correct, the ship's power systems were located only a dozen paces farther. She was close, but the lack of activity from 'Mavamu's location was *not* encouraging.

As she turned the final corner and stared out across the generator control station, her view confirmed what she already knew. Dozens of dead Jiralhanae were strewn about the space, the smell of spent plasma fire heavy, curls of smoke still ascending from burn wounds. Thankfully, there was no sign of reinforcements. On the far end was Oda 'Mavamu, miraculously still alive, his body slung against the wall, chest heaving with shallow breaths. He had been punctured by three spikes, each of them still white-hot.

'Juran quickly navigated her way over to the young warrior, removing his helmet. For a moment, 'Mavamu tried to speak, but the pain restrained him. His eyes were dim, the life slowly ebbing out of him as violet blood poured from his back onto the floor.

It would not be long now.

"Scion," Vul 'Soran's voice sounded through the closed-channel. *"We have reached the bridge, but the war criminal is not here. No one is."*

"The bridge is empty? Why?" she asked, dumbfounded.

"Everyone has already fled," Stolt said. *"I will assess the navigation—"*

Four sequential thuds suddenly reverberated through the ship.

"What was that?" 'Soran asked.

"From here, it sounded like escape craft," 'Juran responded. "What does the system's integrity array tell you, Blademaster?"

"I am already evaluating it—" 'Soran stopped himself, then said: *"They initiated the storm cutter's self-destruction mechanism. We are already in the third cycle and have ten centals before the ship's fusion drives detonate."*

"Self-destruction without an evacuation?!" she exclaimed. "The San'Shyuum are willing to sacrifice the ship's entire crew to save their own skin."

"Excellent," Stolt said derisively. *"It saves us the work."*

"We will all die with them if we do not leave right now," 'Soran said. *"Pull the astrogation data from its nav systems. Scion, did you find 'Mavamu?"*

"I did," she said, looking at his pale face. "He is badly injured. He will not make it."

"You must leave him, then, and not perish with him," 'Soran said with a note of mournfulness. *"Make your way back to the deployment bay immediately. We will be there shortly. Perhaps we can salvage something from this abominable vessel."*

She looked down at 'Mavamu. He had hardly moved since she arrived.

"*Go,*" the young Sangheili whispered, struggling to force the words out. "Go, Scion. It is all right."

"I will carry you," she said, preparing to heft him onto her shoulder.

"*No.* I will . . . only slow you down . . . and you will never make it in time. Leave me." 'Mavamu was wheezing, his lungs unable to pump air. "Allow me to die with honor."

For a moment, 'Juran considered ignoring his request. Then she thought better of it. Even if he was brought back safely, there was no way for him to be mended. And if such treatment existed, there were those among their kind who still felt it was humiliating for a warrior to utilize medicine to salve the pain of an injury.

She nodded solemnly and said: "You will be remembered with honor." She then turned and ran at top speed down the corridor and back toward the gravity lift.

'Juran was pained by the thought of his loss. He had been so eager to prove himself and had been assigned to the mission by Shipmaster 'Vadum because of his unrelenting insistence that he was ready. Now his first mission would be his last. She wondered how 'Mavamu would be remembered—if his name would be recounted in song, or echo through the Hall of Eternity . . . or if his passing would simply be met with silence. A cautionary tale of a young and overeager fool snuffed out because he lacked the patience and restraint demanded of all warriors.

It was only a few centals before she reached the deployment bay, which was now in complete chaos—klaxons blaring and ships rapidly launching through the bay's containment field. Most of *Piety*'s crew were gathering on the far side of the bay at least a hundred meters away, evidently hoping to seize the vessel's docked craft in order to flee the cutter's impending self-destruction. *Piety*'s limited supply of Phantoms were already bearing more than they could hold; its Seraphs and Banshees were dropping from storage winches above, hovering briefly into position before firing out into the dark void of space.

'Juran had to give Kafo Dein credit. The San'Shyuum must have become aware of *Shadow of Intent*'s previous raids and the fates of others belonging to the Order of Restoration. At the first sign of intrusion on his own ship, Kafo Dein had been driven to do the unthinkable. He would not allow himself to be captured—not even at the cost of this storm cutter and all its personnel.

"Scion!" the blademaster announced, emerging from another

corridor on the side of the deployment bay. Stolt was just behind him—both had their weapons raised and ready to fire.

"They are taking every single spacecraft," she said, nodding toward the far end of the bay. The last Phantom had just finished loading and lifted from the deck, accelerating out into star-speckled darkness.

"Not every one," the ranger said, looking toward the war sphinxes.

"You cannot be serious," 'Juran said. "Those are relics. A hundred thousand years old."

"But the Forerunners made them," 'Soran said.

"Yes. The Forerunners made them to be operated *by Forerunners*. The ship's crew left them here for a reason."

"Perhaps they'll work," Stolt said, eyeing them more closely.

"We do not have a choice," 'Soran said as he began to move, his head gesturing toward the other end of the bay. The Jiralhanae who remained from the storm cutter's crew were also now staring in the direction of the war sphinxes. One of them shouted, and they all began to charge. The Foreruner machines had become the only viable escape option. Seconds later, the Jiralhanae spotted the three intruders and began raising their weapons to fire. 'Juran had already launched into a dead run, clambering up the side of one of the ivory machines, 'Soran and Stolt laying claim to two others.

The bizarre combat vehicles looked utterly alien to 'Juran, vaguely resembling *ghentua*, stony biped creatures from the tablelands of Rahnelo. Standing upright at about twenty meters, the machine seemed to have arms and legs folded into its chassis, and a strange pale face at its apex that appeared to be a command cabin of some kind.

It was entirely lifeless and felt more like a carved statue than a functional combat craft.

'Juran continued to make her way to the cabin, nearly positive that once she reached it, she would discover the machine unresponsive or damaged. Through a porthole, she saw the encroaching Jiralhanae had apparently thought better of directly attacking, not willing to damage the vehicles. They began jostling over the two unclaimed war sphinxes, which swiftly gave way to their typical barbaric infighting.

Finally reaching the command cabin, the scion found what seemed to be a seat, though for a being much larger than herself. She stared out of the war sphinx's "eyes"—presumably acting as a viewport—while running her hands across the controls and dials, hoping to trigger something that would seal the cabin and activate the machine. The lack of response from the war sphinx was unnerving, but peering out the viewport she could see Stolt doing the same. Suddenly his machine came to life, the cabin closing and the biped dropping to all fours, its appendages effectively becoming landing struts. Between its joints coursed hard-light energy bonds.

"How did you do that?" she demanded over the command channel.

"The cutter's astrogation data had control mapping for these things," Stolt said. *"Seems like Kafo Dein was intending to use them eventually. I am sending the controls to both of you."*

His war sphinx began to hover in place, spinning around toward the Jiralhanae. His vehicle's arms—acting now as front struts—lit up and fired a series of energy pulses that instantly vaporized them.

"Oh yes. *That will do just fine,"* Stolt said, enjoying himself far too much.

"We have just under two centals," 'Soran said, his voice tense. *"We must leave without further delay."*

With receipt of the data from Stolt, 'Soran's war sphinx almost immediately activated, and 'Juran's soon after. The control maps provided were diagnostic tools that overlaid the vehicle's existing interface with a Sangheili one. Since Kafo Dein and the Jiralhanae in his charge had once belonged to the Covenant, their primary language was historic Sangheili—a convenient irony that would happen to save the trio's lives today.

The three war sphinxes broke out of the storm cutter's containment field in unison, accelerating at a speed that 'Juran was certain even Seraphs could not match. Somewhere behind them a silent bloom of light glowed brighter than the nearest star, signaling the end of *Vigilance with Piety.* She wheeled the war sphinx around, its movement astonishingly fluid even as it continued to accelerate. Looking through the viewport, she saw the brightness of the explosion fan out in bands, and to the far right was the solemn visage of the artificial moon set against Kus'kah's vast swirl of greens.

"Stay together, Scion," 'Soran said through the closed-channel. *"If there is too much distance, we'll lose contact."*

"I am well within range, Blademaster," she responded. "I just want to see if we can find them."

Using the control map as the war sphinx rounded back toward the explosion, 'Juran increased visibility and pulled up a targeting screen with a swipe of her wrist—it was at least ten times more accurate than any she had experienced on Sangheili fighter craft, and she found herself once again mesmerized by the work of the Forerunners. The war sphinx was not even technically a fighter; it was merely a glorified combat suit, yet it easily bested the greatest technological achievement of any modern civilization in that field.

A myriad of orbs appeared on the overlaid readout, self-adjusting to 'Juran's height and visual acuity. On the far side of the explosion, she could see dozens of orbs splintering away from *Vigilance with Piety*'s former location, their direction and movement visibly disorganized. Four separate orbs were on a direct path toward the moon. The readout drew up their silhouettes, showing they were Ren shuttlecraft, a favorite of San'Shyuum nobility and politicians.

Kafo Dein.

"I have found the San'Shyuum," 'Juran said, bringing the war sphinx around on an intercept course. "Permission to terminate." She refrained from accelerating, as it would take her out of range of the others.

"Our objective is to neutralize and capture," 'Soran said in an even tone.

"That was when we were still on the ship," she responded. "And when 'Mavamu was still alive."

"We need the San'Shyuum alive, Scion. Without him, there is no way to learn where Dovo Nesto is. And without Nesto, we remain one step behind the Order of Restoration."

"And if he gets away, we lose both," she replied, her voice careful. She did not relish pushing back against the blademaster, but if they did not stop Kafo Dein now, would there ever be another chance? "The ranger has the ship's astrogation data. That could be enough to find Dovo Nesto."

"It could also be nothing," 'Soran grumbled. *"Ranger—your thoughts?"*

"She has a point," Stolt noted after a long pause, swinging his own sphinx behind hers several hundred kilometers away. *"We can only decipher the astrogation data on* Shadow of Intent. *But they are using Ren shuttlecraft and likely have slipspace drives. They could be gone at any moment."*

The Unggoy was correct. Rens were often capable of faster-than-light travel. Why then had Kafo Dein not simply fled the system by now and evaded capture?

The reason suddenly came to her, as it did the blademaster.

"He must truly desire whatever is on that moon." 'Soran voiced her thought. *"Or he believes he can hide there."*

"And if the San'Shyuum reaches it," Stolt interjected, *"there is no telling what is down there. Perhaps a ship far greater than* Vigilance with Piety? *And the chances of retrieving him on the surface of that moon are . . . well, virtually zero."*

"Very well, Scion," 'Soran said. *"We will pursue. Stay on me."*

The war sphinxes accelerated in impressive fashion, deftly navigating the outer band of ship debris. The orbs started to come within visual range, a line of unarmed Ren shuttlecraft. Tul 'Juran was so focused on the escape pods that she had not seen the wave of Covenant fighters approaching on her left.

"Our friends from the cutter are circling back," 'Soran said. *"Prepare weapons and be careful."* The Banshees and Seraphs that had escaped *Vigilance with Piety* must have been called back as soon as the shuttlecraft spotted their pursuers. Kafo Dein was going to make a fight out of this after all.

"That green light on the readout," Stolt spoke up. *"It's an incoming transmission."*

"Activate comms," 'Soran said. *"Let us speak with this coward."*

"—no doubt the work of Shadow of Intent," a smooth, aristocratic San'Shyuum voice was saying over Stolt's receiver. *"Is this the legendary Half-Jaw himself?"* Kafo Dein was using Rtas 'Vadum's combat name, given to him because his left mandibles had been shorn off during a harrowing battle against the Flood in orbit around the first discovered Halo ring.

"The commander is not here, Kafo Dein," 'Soran said with disgust.

"Ah, then it is his blademaster, no doubt. What is your price?" Dein spoke with a confidence that made 'Juran sick. *"You have*

already stolen my war sphinxes, I see. I have many more treasures than that—rare and highly effective weapons that you might find interesting. Surely we can come to some kind of agreement if you cease your pursuit."

'Juran stared out toward the left as motes of light started to converge on their location. She could see the faint shapes of Seraphs and Banshee fighters, even Phantom dropships on approach. Kafo Dein would throw everything he had at them.

"What is the location of Dovo Nesto?" 'Soran's question was the only one that mattered. As High Lord Dovo Nesto was the head of the Order of Restoration, the logic was simple: cut off the head, and the body would inevitably die.

"Blademaster," Dein responded, *"you know that is one request that I cannot grant you."*

"Then you make our choice easy," 'Soran said. *"We will send you to your gods with their own weapons. Consider it a blessing you do not deserve."*

"Blademaster"—the San'Shyuum's voice now took on a menacing tone—*"the full complement of my ship's fighters is on course to your position. If you continue this foolish pursuit, they will reduce you to embers. You cannot stand against the—"*

"Close the transmission, Ranger," 'Soran said, cutting him off.

It was only seconds before the first plasma bolts reached the war sphinxes. Most missed at this distance, but some managed to impact with violent jolts, revealing the ancient vehicles' spatial shielding and their spaceframe resilience.

"Prepare to fire," 'Soran said, as his and Stolt's war sphinxes accelerated to both sides of 'Juran's machine, rolling and bobbing with each other to dodge the enemy's fire. *"Now!"*

The three Forerunner craft released a fusillade of energy bolts, filling the dark of space with a momentary brilliance. The light was so intense that it almost appeared to be a second sun. For the Jiralhanae forces approaching, it was no doubt a terrifying sight. As the wall of fire collided with their vessels, a series of explosions lit up the distance.

Mere seconds later, any enemy craft that had survived began to converge upon the war sphinxes' vector. 'Juran swung up, narrowly dodging a Seraph while drilling a hail of fire into a line of Banshee fighters. The other two sphinxes responded in kind, navigating both enemy ships and extraneous debris from *Vigilance with Piety*. Instinct seemed to take control as the sphinxes deftly wove their way through the chaos, proving that even a host of Covenant craft were no match for three Forerunner machines from a bygone era. A few centals into the dogfight, however, revealed Kafo Dein's intent.

"The San'Shyuum's escape craft," Stolt said as he gunned down a Phantom, sending almost a dozen unprotected Jiralhanae into a cold, airless grave. *"They've picked up speed."*

"And they will be out of targeting range in under a cental," 'Juran said. "Let me pursue them."

It was clear that Kafo Dein was merely buying time, his troops' lives expendable to protect his own. It was not surprising, given what had happened on *Vigilance*, and it was certainly not surprising for a San'Shyuum. In many ways, the entire Covenant hegemony had been erected to preserve their own species at the expense of all others, including the Sangheili.

"We cannot let them get away, Blademaster!" she pleaded, diving through the shattered remains of a Seraph.

Vul 'Soran knew what was at stake but was no doubt hesitant due to the risk involved. If 'Juran peeled off too far, they would be out of range and unable to communicate with her, much less support her. It also put the enemy fighters at her back and opened her up to attack. But in the end, he was left with little choice.

"Go, Scion," he finally replied. *"We will provide you with cover while we can."*

She immediately swung the war sphinx around and accelerated toward the artificial moon. Its pale form looming before them was pocked by four small motes of darkness that her readouts correctly designated: the San'Shyuum's shuttlecraft. Tunneling through the swarm of fighters and debris, the sphinx continued to amaze her. It displayed a kind of ease and elegance that made the Forerunners' technological mastery undeniable.

Perhaps the Forerunners really were gods, she thought. *What else could explain such machines?*

Within a cental, her war sphinx began to approach weapons range, the four Ren shuttlecraft in a single line as they dove for the artificial world. If they made it into the moon's thick atmosphere, the chances of locating them dropped staggeringly low. She readied the sphinx's weapons, the shuttlecraft's bulbous silhouettes becoming clearer.

A plasma bolt from behind suddenly struck her war sphinx hard, igniting an array of alarms within the machine's command cabin. Another bolt connected, followed by another. Lights flickered within the ancient machine and the number of alarms seemed to increase. 'Juran attempted to roll the sphinx away from the firing line, but was struck again three more times—the ordnance highly charged fuel rods by the feel of them.

Some systems immediately went dark and the entire left side of the sphinx began pouring out a fiery blue gas, dragging hard in that same direction. *Not good.* Leaning into the damage, she pulled the vehicle tight to the left, swinging around to face her attackers. It was a trio of Seraphs that had followed her sphinx's vector.

She struck the lead vehicle with a single pulse, but the damage done to her sphinx had eliminated half of the weapons systems, causing it to shake wildly while firing. The first Seraph disintegrated in a flash of light, with the other two arcing away to meet the Forerunner combat machine head-on. As they began to fire, she spun the war sphinx, disorienting their targeting systems, and released a second blast that struck another Seraph, destroying it on contact.

Only one enemy craft remained, and that one began swinging wide to take another pass at her wounded machine. Within the command cabin, the readout started to indicate significant issues—from the control map's message, it seemed as if structural integrity was failing. One report was expressly clear: precious oxygen was venting into space.

"'Soran? Stolt?" 'Juran asked, gripping the controls tight as the sphinx shook.

No response.

'Juran had no clue how long the Forerunner vehicle would last or if it would just suddenly burst apart into the vacuum of space. All the while, the four Ren shuttlecraft continued toward the moon, gaining distance with each moment.

Ignoring the final Seraph, she raced toward the shuttlecraft, the din of alarms within the cabin now reaching a steady crescendo. The four Rens grew larger in her display, and she releasesed a torrent of fire from the sphinx's remaining weapons. The last two Rens in formation erupted in a blossom of light, but more plasma bolts from the remaining Seraph giving chase streamed over the top of 'Juran's own vehicle, the final one striking the sphinx's tail. The impact sent her into an uncontrolled tailspin. She attempted to fire blindly at the two remaining Rens, but was rewarded with a series of loud clicks. Her weapons were now completely inactive.

There was nothing left to shoot with.

The only option she now had was the war sphinx itself.

She forced it ahead, intending to use whatever was left of the combat suit as a cudgel even as it began to shed its arms and legs. The frictionless environment of space, however, was on her side—she slammed hard into the rear Ren, forcing the shuttlecraft into a violent tumble as it careened forward and collided into the lead. Both enemy vehicles instantly began venting oxygen before quickly disintegrating into a flurry of debris and bodies as they collectively plunged into the moon's atmosphere.

'Juran's war sphinx fell along with them, chaotically dropping into the pale gas of the artificial moon. The command cabin interior went completely dark, everything falling silent, except for a single deafening hiss. The vehicle's breach was growing as it hit the mesosphere, and she silently wondered how she would die.

Suffocation? Or reentry?

Perhaps it would be the eventual impact on the surface itself.

She supposed it did not matter that much in the end. And, at the very least, she was taking Kafo Dein down with her.

CHAPTER 7

ABIGAIL COLE

UNSC *Victory of Samothrace*
November 5, 2559

Only nine hours had passed since the Condor departed SR 8936, but the vehicle had skipped in and out of slipspace through five different sectors before reaching its rendezvous point with the UNSC *Victory of Samothrace* at a set of randomly generated coordinates a very far distance away from any known star. All of it being a necessary precaution to avoid Cortana.

It was a place where she would never find them.

At least, that's what Abigail Cole was hoping, as Commander Prasad brought the Condor delicately into one of the cruiser's bays. She still gripped the briefcase tightly, glancing back to see Osman's eyes locked onto it, a solemn grimace spread over her face.

Cole understood the admiral's attachment to Black-Box and her frustration with their inability to disclose anything until they were back aboard *Victory.* Osman had been out of the fight for over a year, stuck in a strange kind of purgatory while the galaxy went to hell around her, during which time Black-Box had been entirely dormant . . . but she knew the importance of procedure. All those concerned needed to make sure that Osman, Hood, and Orzel were safe and uncompromised by Cortana, and no one was willing to risk making that kind of mistake this late in the game. The ship's scanning equipment and identity validation software would confirm who they were and their general state of mind, as well as the possibility of any tracking devices on their persons, before Cole briefed them on ONI's involvement with Black-Box. Reading them into the present UNSC campaign in its entirety would take longer, but Cole intended to give them as much intel as she could now.

When the Condor touched down inside *Victory of Samothrace*, Cole breathed a sigh of relief. Against all odds, they'd managed to make it back safe and sound.

The three newcomers were immediately met by an armed escort who would provide medical evaluations and initiate the validation process. Meanwhile, Gray Team carefully backed the Razorback out of the Condor's bay door, almost immediately getting to work on repairing the extensive damage done to the vessel. From this vantage point, Cole was surprised they'd all made it back in one piece.

"We have repair crews for that, you know," she said to Jai.

"Yes, ma'am," he said. "We're aware. Spartans like to take care of their own gear."

As they rolled the Razorback off into the garage, Cole's own escort approached: two Spartan-IVs—McEndon and Vídalín—along with Commander Njuguna, who offered a quick salute. His eyes fell to the briefcase.

"So much fuss over such a small thing," he said almost in wonder.

"It always is," she replied, falling in stride alongside him as the Spartans trailed a few paces behind.

"I've given the orders already, Captain. We'll be ready to depart for Nysa in just under an hour."

"Excellent," Cole said. "I'm going to secure the case at Containment L-Twenty-Three. Then I'll meet you and the admirals in the flag bridge."

"You should get some rest, ma'am," Njuguna said with a hint of concern. "You've been working nonstop for the last thirty-one hours. There'll be time to fully brief everyone once we arrive."

"Understood, Commander, and I appreciate your concern. Given our current constraints on travel to a site like Nysa, there's no telling how long it could take us to get there undetected. Could be days; could even be weeks. The admirals are going to want some answers sooner than that, especially Osman. To be perfectly honest, I think she deserves them. Might as well be now. Make sure both of them are in the flag bridge after they pass validation. I'll grab some coffee on the way there."

"Affirmative, ma'am," he said, then added, turning to the Spartans, "Stay with the captain—make sure she gets to her destination safely."

"Ten-four," Spartan McEndon said. "We got her, Commander."

Spartans David McEndon and Stefán Vídalín had been with *Victory* since the vessel initially shipped out. They were two of the first recruits from Nysa, a frontier world transformed into a UNSC planetary stronghold. Nysa was now being utilized for its logistics and to coordinate movements outside the purview of Cortana, as well as for training and deploying the next generation of Spartans. That's why traveling there, especially for a vessel as critical as *Victory*, was not a simple point-to-point operation. The last thing humanity needed was Cortana tailing their cruiser to such a pivotal world. She could take both of them out in one fell swoop, setting back the UNSC's efforts irreparably.

The trip to Containment L-23 was uneventful. Cole secured the briefcase in a lockbox deposit system that held the ship's most valuable assets, with multiple passkeys and clearance checks to ensure its integrity. The briefcase would remain there until they got to Nysa. Precautions like this were necessary, even on a ship like *Victory of Samothrace.* While Cole doubted that Cortana had any clue about *Victory*'s current location or what they were planning to do, the Guardian's presence on SR 8936 had been a complete surprise. With so many human AIs now compromised, there was no telling how deep Cortana's hands might reach into human territory. This fact demanded the most stringent protocols, including reinstituting aspects of her father's own security efforts from decades earlier.

Most notably, Emergency Priority Order 098831A-1.

Developed and adopted early on in humanity's war against the Covenant, such a tactic had become the legacy of Vice Admiral Preston Jeremiah Cole, arguably one of the greatest naval tacticians ever to have lived. The Cole Protocol, as it came to be known, was designed to prevent the Covenant's incursion on core worlds, especially Earth and the colony of Reach, which held humanity's most critical military assets. The directive had far-reaching stipulations, impacting the use of AIs and the translight travel vectors of spaceships, as well as how UNSC personnel were required to interact with Covenant matériel recovered from battle.

ONI didn't want to take any chances with the Covenant locating Earth and striking at the center of human civilization. Such an attack would have decimated morale, not to mention been the final tipping point of the war. And although the enemy did finally succeed in destroying Reach and eventually laid siege to Earth in late 2552, the protocol itself served its purpose for nearly thirty years and bought humanity the time it needed to finish strong. Victory ultimately came at the hands of the Master Chief and Cortana, even though the latter was now ironically the very reason for reintroducing the protocol.

Reaching one of *Victory*'s many mess halls, Cole found the room empty. Though UNSC vessels had evolved into slightly more comfortable livable spaces in recent years, *Victory*'s mess halls remained bare, utilitarian spaces—food and drink dispensers lining the outer walls of a simple box of a room with segmented rows of long tables filling the rest of the space. With a crew complement of over a thousand, the mess halls needed to be able to accommodate as many personnel as possible.

Cole left the Spartans in the doorway as she made her way to the coffee dispenser, which, as with most things on the ship, was almost constantly in service. Even the smell of coffee began to quicken her senses and give her clarity.

It reminded her again of her father.

Officially, the UNSC *Everest* and all hands—including Preston Cole—had been lost in 2543 during the Battle of Psi Serpentis. It was a heroic and Pyrrhic act that trapped an entire Covenant fleet within a micronova her father had initiated with his ship's own weapons.

Unofficially, however, speculation reigned.

His earlier marriage to Lyrenne Castilla led some to believe that her father had faked his own death in order to steal away with her on a world far outside the Covenant's sightlines. Shortly after their marriage, Castilla had revealed that she was part of the same rebel forces he'd fought against for years, and she doubtless had access to places where no one could ever find them. Others theorized that he was simply tired of fighting, looking to escape the pressures of the horrific war that had taken their toll over time. And still others claimed that he had defected.

For the longest time, Abigail Cole didn't know what to believe.

It was hard enough to live in the shadow of her father's battle history and career—and the stigma that he might have abandoned the UNSC and allied with rebels made it exponentially more difficult. Part of her sincerely hoped that he'd died the hero people believed that he was. If he hadn't, she wished that he was rotting away on some barren world, paying for abandoning his family. Then there was the part of her that just wanted the opportunity to have said good-bye.

She missed him terribly either way. There were times when she imagined him in the mess hall, sitting on the far side of the room—distant, out of focus, but there . . . always with her.

No time for this. Focus.

Jettisoning these thoughts, she took a sip of the coffee, savoring it despite how hot it was.

After collecting her thoughts, *Victory*'s tube system took her to the flag bridge, the deck just below the main bridge, where commanding officers conferred on matters of significance. At the door, she parted with Spartans McEndon and Vídalín, entering a series of numbers on the control plate to open it. Within, she found Njuguna, Osman, and Hood already standing around the room's central holotable.

"Commander, Admirals," she said, nodding to the three.

"Did I mention how good it is to see you, Abby?" Hood responded with a smile. He'd already said as much on the Condor, but she was grateful to hear it again.

Their relationship went back to her earliest years in the UNSC. She saw in him something of a mentor, even if he was only about ten years her senior. His wisdom and care for those in his command was without question. He'd filled a paternal gap in her life that she hadn't realized existed. Before the rescue, it'd been four years since they'd last interacted, and his face in the dim light of the bridge called to mind many fond memories—long conversations about hypothetical naval strategies and applied spatial tactics.

"It's good to see you too, Lord Hood." She returned the smile. "It's good to see both of you."

"What exactly is happening here, Cole?" Osman asked. She was stone-faced, clearly not interested in trading pleasantries.

As the head of the Office of Naval Intelligence, Osman was no doubt indignant about being kept so far outside of the loop, so utterly contradictory to her role. Part of this was due to her own year-long exile; the rest simply the nature of ONI. But even more than that, Cole could tell that Osman was bothered by the fact that Black-Box had been confiscated without any explanation. It was a legitimate complaint.

"I can give you an ad hoc brief here," Cole began, "and I'm certainly happy to do so. But, as you know, per Subdirective one-one-nine-four-five-VZ, you need to be evaluated and fully briefed by a designated ONI intelligence officer in order to retain your security clearance and return to active duty. They'll have one where we're headed and they can get you fully up to speed."

"I know the subdirective, Cole," Osman said, with resignation in her breath. "I wrote it."

"Yes, ma'am. That's the one. So to answer your question," Cole started again, "*a lot* is happening. Since your departure from Earth, the UNSC has been on the run, keeping our distance from Cortana and working from a hidden network of base sites, like the one we're headed to. Unclaimed worlds that Cortana has no knowledge of. The Archon—as her subordinates call her—has holed herself up on Zeta Halo. She's taken control of the entire installation and forced the researchers who occupied it into hiding . . . or worse."

The ringworld Zeta Halo appeared before them above the holotable, with key research sites across its surface demarcated. A network of Guardians appeared around the installation at specific locations, with a variety of automated Forerunner fighters combing the adjacent space in meticulous patterns. Although Cortana governed the galaxy through the Domain, Zeta Halo was undoubtedly now the seat of her power, and its defenses communicated as much.

"A few months ago," Cole continued, "Dr. Catherine Halsey proposed—"

"Halsey?" Osman interjected with a scowl. "Of course *she* is involved in this."

Cole hesitated before responding. She wasn't familiar with all the details, but had long ago heard from *Infinity*'s captain, Thomas Lasky, about the severe friction that existed between Osman and Halsey. It wasn't too surprising, given how Osman's mentor and predecessor, Margaret Parangosky, had felt about the doctor. Some of that vitriol had evidently been germinated by the former CINCONI, even if Osman had her own personal reasons.

Halsey's work was often considered unsavory at best, unethical at worst, and particular aspects of the creation of Cortana and the Spartan-IIs were enough to turn Cole's stomach. Still, it was hard to be overly preoccupied with those kinds of moral dilemmas—however significant they were—when humanity's entire existence seemed to constantly hang in the balance. If they didn't preserve themselves now, no one would be around long enough to debate Halsey's ethics. In Cole's mind, it wasn't exactly a get-out-of-jail-free card for Halsey, but first things had to come first.

Like saving everyone from extinction.

Cole sighed. "Well . . . there are not a lot of other options, ma'am. Halsey made Cortana . . . so if anyone can *unmake* her, it's going to be the doctor."

Hood spoke up, playing the peacemaker: "We understand, Abby. Continue."

"Of course, thank you. Dr. Halsey's proposal was to re-create Cortana, but with modifications. A version that could be used as a weapon to trap and capture the original AI for final dispensation. Upon completion of this mission, the copy would also be deleted. *Infinity* is preparing for their assault on Zeta Halo as we speak. Apart from the crew, only a handful of others within ONI know about this operation. This is our best hope to stop Cortana. Since you've been gone, entire worlds have come under her control and others have been . . . subdued."

Both Osman and Hood stared for a moment, before speaking up.

"When we left Bravo-Six," Hood said, "a Guardian was engaging one of our ships—"

"Yes," Cole said, her eyes going to the deck. "That's a difficult one. *Plateau*'s fusion drive detonated on impact. Sydney . . . Sydney is gone, Admiral."

"Dear God," Osman said, her eyes going wide.

"I'm sorry. I know you're hearing all of this for the first time," Cole said remorsefully. "But Sydney wasn't the only one. New York and Berlin were hit pretty hard too. Tactical strikes. Cortana knew that we wouldn't just roll over, so she hit us first and made sure to draw blood. She wanted her message to be loud and clear. Other colonies have fared better or worse, depending on how they responded to her incursions."

"And the Sangheili," Hood asked, "how did they respond?"

"Sanghelios is a mixed bag," Cole said, and she noticed Osman briefly look away. "A *very* mixed bag. There's still a lot of unrest there internally, so Cortana's interactions haven't been too direct with them. I think she's biding her time until a clear victor rises from the ashes, and then she'll put her foot down. Right now, they have typical armiger patrols and Guardian overwatch. Most kaidons are keeping their heads down."

"And the Arbiter?" Hood pressed. "Where is he in all of this?"

"Well, you can ask Shipmaster Rtas 'Vadum yourself. *Shadow of Intent* is going to be at our next stop with envoys from the Swords of Sanghelios. They're coming for a separate matter, but there may be a critical connection to *Victory of Samothrace*'s operation."

"Which is?" Osman asked. Her posture had relaxed slightly, but she still wasn't pleased. "You still haven't told us why you need Black-Box."

"Right," Cole said. "When I said that Dr. Halsey's plan was our best hope to stop Cortana, it really is that. We've ran the simulations. Nothing else comes close. But even if they're able to neutralize Cortana, it doesn't eliminate the power structure she's uncovered and tapped into. . . ."

"You're talking about the Domain," Osman replied with a furrowed brow.

"That's right," Cole said. "When Cortana's rampancy overcame her during the Master Chief's encounter with the Didact, whatever survived of her was pulled into the Domain and eventually made its way to a world the Forerunners called Genesis. The planet was a shield world that effectively functioned as a doorway into the Domain, granting access to all Forerunner technology connected to it. This is how Cortana consolidated her power and gathered super-weapons capable of enforcing her rule. After she finished, Genesis was sent into slipspace and then she disappeared herself."

"Wait a second. She *hid* an entire planet?" Hood asked.

"At least, from what we can gather. We have no idea where it is. But . . . when Cortana resurfaced on Zeta Halo, we received a message from some of the researchers who were on that installation. After that, we lost contact with them. The message, however, said that the Domain has multiple nodes across the galaxy that serve as direct access points, similar to a damaged one found on Kamchatka. The researchers' data referred to this network of domain nodes as 'the Lithos.'"

"How did the researchers know *that*?" Hood was clearly surprised.

"We're not exactly sure," Cole replied. "They could have found information about it on Zeta Halo, but it could also have been something they discovered only after Cortana arrived. ONI has teams across a variety of Forerunner sites who have validated this information, but no one knows exactly where any of these other access points are."

"So what does that matter anyway?" Osman asked. "And where does Black-Box fit into all of this?"

"Black-Box was created from the brain of Dr. Graham Alban, one of Halsey's neuroscientists for the SPARTAN-II project. After that project, Alban committed suicide, adding his brain to the AI donor list."

"Yes, I'm aware of this," Osman said, her tone grim.

"But prior to his death, Alban conducted foundational work for Dr. Halsey on AI development alongside another neuroscientist, Giovanna Kaiser. This work would eventually be used for the creation of Cortana. Embedded in that research—which Kaiser continued and eventually hid deep within the neural processes that constitute Black-Box's personality matrix—is a safety protocol followed by Halsey's team when she cloned herself in order to make an AI like Cortana. Kaiser died during the fall of Reach, but notes retrieved from her research lab indicate that one of Halsey's clones *survived* . . . and only she and Dr. Alban knew where that clone was relocated."

"Wait," Osman said. "I'm not following. BB never mentioned any of this. And his donor died a long time before Cortana was ever made. How is this even possible?"

"Like I said, it wasn't Dr. Alban who made the breadcrumb trail—in the end, it was Kaiser. She continued the work that he'd begun. The first clone created to make Cortana actually survived, and she was extracted by ONI without Halsey's knowledge as part of a procedure outlined by Alban. Understand that he hated Halsey and had plenty of reasons for keeping this a secret from her . . . but given his death, only Black-Box now knows where this clone is. It's buried somewhere deep in his storage architecture. Kaiser provided a security password in her notes that should allow us to retrieve the data."

"And so . . . what happens when you have that data, Abby?" Hood said. "What does this Halsey clone have to do with the Domain?"

"An exact replica of Cortana's own neural pathways will allow us to enter the Domain unhindered through one of these Domain gateways—wherever it may be located—and can simultaneously release an AI-killing control-subroutine capable of destroying Cortana and any other human-created AIs taking refuge with her in the Domain. We'd be using Halsey's clone to effectively pick the lock on the Domain's back door and allow us to take out Cortana while her attention is focused on *Infinity*'s assault on Zeta Halo. And whether *Infinity* succeeds or not, this subroutine would effectively give us control of the Domain. Displacing Cortana is only a win if we can ensure the power she wields doesn't fall into the hands of our enemies."

The two admirals stood silently for a long moment, taking in all they'd heard. It was a lot to consume at once, but that's what happened when officers normally steeped in daily intelligence briefings were effectively off the grid for a full year. Cole didn't wait for another question—Hood and Osman had what they needed, and they'd get the rest soon enough.

"*Your* AI is safe, ma'am," she said to Osman. "We know how much he means to you. We'll access the case once we're on Nysa and let the technicians retrieve the intel we need from him. Then he'll be returned to you, unharmed."

"Understood, Captain," Osman said, swallowing deeply. "But you and I both know that once he's reactivated, it's over for him. BB is past his seven years, so rampancy is inevitable. The longer we keep him around at this point, the more he becomes a liability. Especially *him*, given his clearance level. Final dispensation protocol is required." Osman's eyes suddenly watered as she stared off into the distance—an unexpected development. Then she turned back to Cole. "This operation better damn well be worth it, because it's going to cost him his life."

CHAPTER 8

SEVERAN

Warial

November 8, 2559

Severan stepped off the Phantom dropship's ramp and onto the cold soil of Warial, gazing upward toward his warship *Heart of Malice*, which hung silently in the sky, perched high above a vast forest. It was a breathtaking sight, like a jagged arrowhead with vast plates of armor covered in a dense array of point-defense cannons. Although not nearly as large as the dreadnoughts that dominated much of the Banished fleets, *Malice* was extraordinarily effective in battle and Severan could not conceive of ever parting ways with it. Over the years it had served him well, decisively laying waste to all his foes and striking fear into the hearts of any who encountered it.

In the distance behind *Malice* were karves and dreadnoughts that belonged to Severan's clan, the Vanguard of Zaladon. After receiving his commission from Atriox, he had given the order to his own clan on Warial to prepare for departure, intending to gather all Banished forces to a rally point far beyond the Apparition's watchful gaze, consolidating their arsenal as Atriox secured the Guardian-killer weapon and then prepared to assault Zeta Halo.

Severan did not know how the AI overlord would respond to the warmaster's assault—or to the humans', for that matter—but the Banished element remaining in the galaxy needed to be ready for anything.

Atriox had personally summoned the heads of the other Banished fleets, a group of highly esteemed leaders —formally referred to as the Eight. In validating Severan's appointment as their leader, the warmaster sought to preemptively squelch any resistance to it once he had departed.

"Our fleet is ready, War Chief," Kaevus said quietly, drawing Severan's attention. Before him stood nine hundred of his finest warriors on the rocky beach the citadel occupied. The terrain was a hardened swath of land that lay at the farthest edge of a vast mountainous region, dense forests of tall *goha* trees covering its rugged foothills. Like his people, the land had been made strong by sea wind's relentless battering.

Severan's warriors were arranged by rank and clad in an array of power armor, much of it resembling that of the old days of the Covenant. At their backs rose the great ocean-citadel of Zaladon, with its high battlements and iron-plated walls, fortified by dozens of spike cannons and plasma trebuchets. Within those walls were several thousand Jiralhanae, including many hundreds of children representing the future of his clan and, ultimately, their final legacy. Although the citadel had stood for countless generations at the edge of the great sea, only Severan's clan had been strong enough to keep it from the opportunists and despots who ravaged Warial after the breaking of the Covenant.

"Excellent," Severan said with a nod. "We will retain these forces here to guard the citadel and our people while we are away.

No doubt many of the Banished will be . . . *bothered* by my appointment, especially those who have been with Atriox the longest. We should be prepared for agitation at best, and reciprocity at worst."

"You anticipate this, even though the warmaster himself has appointed you?" Kaevus asked with a sidelong glance. "Would they dare defy Atriox's command?"

Kaevus was a tall, muscular Jiralhanae with dark-red fur covered in black-plated armor similar to Severan's own. Loyal to the end, he had served with Severan in the days of the Covenant and followed him without wavering through the Great Schism and into the establishment of their own clan. Severan did not take such a question as faltering devotion—with Kaevus there was no such thing.

"I cannot afford to underestimate the hubris of a rival chieftain," Severan replied. "Many within the Banished still question our legitimacy. They despise my father and his religion, and they are eager to cull any last memory of them by erasing what we have built here." He did not need to clarify further; Kaevus knew what he was speaking to. The citadel, the fleet, all the Vanguard's holdings, and, most importantly, its people—all of this was now at risk.

Kaevus growled. "It is an outrage that you are burdened with such judgment for the actions of your father. They do not see *you.* Only the shadow of Tartarus."

"It is an old name." Severan's tone became forlorn. "A hated name."

The self-appointed Chieftain of the Jiralhanae within the Covenant, Tartarus had incited the hatred of many Jiralhanae in the wake of his death. He was a legendary chieftain in his own right but had been appointed by the Prophet of Truth in the final days of the Covenant to overthrow the Sangheili and take full control of the empire's military forces. This inevitably led to civil war—the

Great Schism—which ultimately sundered the Covenant into many pieces. Its effects still reverberated across all Jiralhanae and Sangheili worlds almost a decade later. Many questioned the wisdom of this path, especially those in the Banished, who saw the San'Shyuum as false prophets and manipulators.

In response to Tartarus's death, many Jiralhanae had initially moved against Severan's pack, seeking to wipe out any from it who would attempt to seize the chieftain's position, even managing to kill all of Severan's siblings. By the time they attempted to take Severan's life, he had already fortified his position on Warial and defended it with ruthless ferocity. It took only a few incidents—such as Severan's clan decisively eradicating some of their greatest rivals within all of Oth Sonin—before the efforts to exact payment for his father's actions finally ceased. Many now regarded him with some respect and sought to form an alliance with his clan. Others simply ignored him.

Severan had only considered joining the Banished because his cousin, the powerful Jiralhanae captain Choros, had personally requested it. He did not know all the reasons why, but was confident that Choros sought to protect him and the line of Tartarus. Staying close to the growing numbers of the Banished was one of the best ways to do this. Choros believed that whatever differences Atriox might have had with Tartarus, the warmaster would ultimately see the strategic benefit of welcoming Severan into his fold.

Although Severan knew there would be challenges with this potential alliance, he saw the advantages it presented and wasted little time deliberating, nor did his own captains ever question the decision. Atriox had since treated Severan and his Vanguard with equity and respect—and for that, he was thankful. Until others did the same though, Severan would always have to watch his back.

"I do wonder," Kaevus said with some measure of grief, "when will these old hatreds die? Have you not proven your loyalty to the Jiralhanae time and again? You have defended the land of other chieftains, you have fought for the freedom of weaker clans from rivals, you have risked your life countless times for the safeguarding of the Jiralhanae heritage, yet still they do not trust you. Many still seek your head."

"You know the Jiralhanae, Kaevus," Severan said, walking alongside the warriors who would defend the citadel, assessing their weapons and armor. "We are a foolish and stubborn people, never satisfied with what we have and always eager to increase our own share of the galaxy. My loyalty is of no concern to most chieftains. They care only about how they may use my father's philosophy to diminish what we have accomplished."

Kaevus spat on the ground in frustration, but Severan's eyes were on the warrior directly in front of him. He stopped and examined the Jiralhanae who towered head and shoulders above the rest. Approximately three meters in height, he was a wall of muscle and armor with bright, cruel eyes that shone like the plasma furnace of a Wraith tank. Severan tugged at the warrior's armor and lightly beat against it with his fist to test its strength.

Arxus.

The Champion of Zaladon.

There was no one among Severan's warriors like him. Taken from his clan as a child, Arxus's throat had been slit by a rival chieftain who wanted to end his bloodline. Somehow, the young Arxus had survived, though he lost his ability to speak, and over time became the monster he was today. Legend held that when he came of age, he'd hunted down and slaughtered not only the chieftain who had mutilated him but the entire clan of his adversary, blotting out their name from the face of Doisac. Whether or not this was true, Severan had never inquired. Most feared Arxus so deeply that they would simply avert their eyes whenever he was near, even though he was an ally.

Beneath his rugged, bladed helmet, Arxus's face was charred and torn from years of fighting the humans, his massive body covered in dense combat plates accentuated by jagged spikes. During the time of the Covenant, the Sangheili had kept him in a cage like an animal, unleashing him to massacre those foolish enough to be caught in his whirlwind. When the empire fell, Severan freed Arxus, and the warrior silently swore an oath to never part ways with him. Since then, the Jiralhanae warrior had remained unwaveringly devoted to the Vanguard of Zaladon and had fought valiantly alongside Severan countless times. Arxus refused to carry projectile or energy weapons, instead relying on his razor-sharp khopesh; the sickle-shaped blade was a full two meters long and inscribed with the names of his ancestors. The sight of this weapon alone was enough to strike terror in the hearts of his enemies. It even made Severan uneasy.

"Opposition is a good thing for us, brother," Severan said, turning back to Kaevus. "Do not curse it. While others grow indolent and witless, we will remain vigilant. Their hatred fuels our strength and sharpens our zeal."

Kaevus's eyes dropped and he sighed. "Your perspective is always—"

"Illuminating?"

"I was going to say *infuriating*," Kaevus said, grinding his tusks. "But you are correct, War Chief. We could bemoan our plight every single day. Or we could use it to our advantage. I much prefer the latter."

"As do I. And my new appointment will give us more opportunity to prove our strength and our capabilities. It is only a matter of time—"

Othmald, Severan's other lead captain, charged out from the entry to the citadel, his face a mixture of concern and dread. This was very much unlike the old, grizzled Jiralhanae, who was generally moved by very little. Before he had even reached the lines of warriors in front of Severan and Kaevus, a flurry of chatter burst over the comms and into native-links implanted in their ears.

A blistering surge of distressed, confused, angered voices were drowned out by another. All except one.

The Apparition herself.

"Look upon Doisac one last time and remember, you chose this path."

Severan looked up into the pale blue sky, high above the clouds that stretched out across the Zaladon Sea. Doisac, a large, brown-green sphere that hung in the heavens—the very heart of the Jiralhanae people—was no longer brown or green, nor was it even a sphere. To Severan's horror, a circle of energy blazed around the equatorial band of the homeworld, which appeared to be breaking apart, dismantling into vast chunks of rock, its fiery core piercing through the cracks like an exploding star.

"She has done it!" Othmald shouted, finally breaking through the lines of warriors who had turned their own attention to the sky. "The Apparition has finally done it!"

None of them could believe their eyes.

Entire hemispheres of the planet tumbled outward from Doisac's burning center, and all watched in silent, stunned horror as what remained suddenly shattered into a trillion fragments. The very homeworld of the Jiralhanae had just been destroyed. Billions of lives lost in a single moment. Severan wondered what had changed, what had caused this ghastly atrocity?

Why would the Apparition suddenly do such a thing?

Hatred burned in his heart; bile rose in his throat as he stared at Doisac's pieces scattering away from the center.

An entire world *gone*.

Severan knew that the act of destroying a planet was an inevitable development in the Apparition's reign, but to actually see it firsthand, killing untold numbers of his people. . . . She had no concern for the lives she had just taken, nor for the resources offered by a whole world. This depraved show of force was about fear—locking them into a state of disbelief and inaction, breaking their spirit. The Jiralhanae had traveled this path before, they were no strangers to immolation, and it was with the weight of that grim history playing out before his eyes that Severan fought to push aside his emotions and grasp for clarity. He would have time to mourn his people's loss later.

Now was the time to *lead*.

"Everyone, calm yourselves! We must leave *now*!" he barked to the captains with an urgency they had likely never heard from him. "Othmald, command all available ships within orbital range to return *immediately*! They must follow evacuation protocol. Kaevus, designate these troops to different quadrants of the citadel. Ensure that they gather the population into groups and that no one is left behind. Everyone and everything of value must leave now! We will not be returning here."

It was obvious, but it all needed to be said. If not for them, for himself. Both captains responded instantly, calling in whatever resources were necessary to fulfill the command of their war chief.

In a short time, Warial too would be completely decimated, either by debris from Doisac or from the catastrophic loss of the moon's gravity anchor. This was true of everything that orbited the Jiralhanae homeworld, including the other inhabited moon, Teash. Severan hoped other chieftains across both moons were initiating their own evacuation protocols. If not, the destruction of Doisac would be only part of even greater losses. The devastation that would strike both colony moons would be of a magnitude that would make the nuclear holocaust of the Great Immolation look like a mild brushfire.

Severan thumbed his tactical-slate to connect with the comms officer on *Heart of Malice.*

"Erutaun," he said. "Signal *Ghost of Helotry*. I must convey an urgent message to Atriox."

"War Chief," Erutaun's voice sounded through the comms. *"*Helotry *has just signaled us. Escharum has left a message for you. I am sending it now."*

It surprised Severan to hear that someone had already communicated Doisac's demise to Escharum, but that was the only possible reason for this message. With Atriox preparing to depart for Neska, Escharum was amassing the forces they would use to strike Zeta Halo—both in locations completely unknown to Severan.

Severan's native-link notified him of the file's delivery. "I have received the communication, Erutaun. Signal the other ships in our fleet and have them relay a message across Warial and Teash. Both worlds must evacuate *immediately*. Time is of the essence—only what we take will survive. Tell the clans and have them send it to others outside our range."

"Understood, War Chief," Erutaun said. *"I will ensure that the message continues until the entire moon knows what has taken place."*

Severan closed the link, watching dozens of dreadnoughts and karves now descend from the clouds, all of them coming to rescue the entire population of Zaladon. With any luck, all in his clan would be saved. Although they would lose their long-standing citadel and territories, his people would be preserved. That had to count for something.

He lifted up a comms disk to view the message and a holographic image of Escharum appeared in his hand.

"Severan, by the time you receive this, you will see what the AI has done," Escharum said, his face twisted in anger and resolve. *"She intended to subjugate our people and Atriox refused. The destruction of our homeworld was her response."* Rage seethed beneath his eyes. *"And we will respond in kind. Once we move on the Halo ring, there will be nothing left for humanity to capture when we are finished with her."*

As Escharum spoke, Severan's eyes returned to where Doisac once had been. The fractured orb was now hardly visible through the haze of dust and detritus that fanned out in every direction from its molten center.

He still could not believe it. Doisac, the cradle world of the Jiralhanae, was gone.

Forever.

It was unthinkable. Would the Jiralhanae people even be able to survive this catastrophe?

"Severan." Escharum's use of his name brought him back to the holo of the war chief. *"We must hold what the Apparition has done to humanity's account. Rally the Banished fleets that survive and raze their homeworld Earth to ashes. Their world for ours. Do not leave anything alive. The blood of the Jiralhanae is on their hands. Make them pay, Severan."*

The message ended.

An assault on the human homeworld was not what he had anticipated . . . but everything about it felt *right.* It was not only retribution; it was strategy. The war chief knew, as Severan did, that a Banished presence laying siege to Earth could very well distract both humanity and Cortana, isolating their forces at Zeta Halo while helping secure the Banished assault of the ringworld.

And even if it failed to do that, there was reason enough to wipe their planet out. The Jiralhanae had just lost three of their worlds to the Apparition. Humanity would watch their own home burn for the sin of the Apparition's creation.

"Should I signal the Eight and rally all our Banished fleets to the rendezvous point?" Kaevus asked, having overheard Escharum's command.

"Yes," Severan said. "Do so at once, but let the others know that I will not be meeting them there immediately. After we secure a new refuge for our people, we can send the bulk of our forces to rendezvous with their fleets. But *Heart of Malice* has other business to attend to before I will hold conference with the Banished leaders."

Kaevus looked confused. "Where then are we going?"

"Sqala."

"The human colony?"

"Yes. I desire more than any to beat their precious Earth into oblivion. But before we commit to that task, I must seek the wisdom of my *daskalo.* We are about to attempt what even the Covenant failed to do. If we strike Earth, it will *not* go unanswered. It will set into motion a series of events that Escharum and even Atriox could not foretell, nor hope to control. Trust me, brother—my *daskalo* will know the true course we must take."

CHAPTER 9

JAMES-005

Gamma Station
August 30, 2552

The modified D77 Pelican dropship's viewport filled with the visage of Reach, humanity's first exosolar colony and the UNSC's greatest military stronghold. Its immense blue-green face was clothed in gray swaths of smoke, but James-005 could still make out the remarkable symmetry of the Hatalmas Sea, an enormous, waterlogged blast crater from the planet's ancient past, surrounded by its largest land mass, the supercontinent of Eposz—its surface marred by countless fires of war.

Apart from Earth, this world was the most heavily defended territory in all human-occupied space, protected by a vast network of orbital weapons systems and heavily armed warships as well as twenty powerful magnetic accelerator cannons, boasting a seemingly endless array of military sites, assets, and personnel.

There was nothing quite like it.

But to James it was *home.*

This was true for all Spartan-II super-soldiers. Abducted at the age of six, the candidates who would become Spartans had spent most of their lives hidden within the Highland Mountains of Eposz. Under the meticulous direction of Dr. Catherine Halsey and through the excruciating training regimen of Chief Petty Officer Franklin Mendez, these carefully selected children were eventually forged into the most elite soldiers the UNSC had ever manifested. Yet it was only after passing through a deadly augmentation procedure that they could finally be called Spartans—a surgical and biological gauntlet that would leave many of them dead or disabled.

Those who survived became the last hope of humanity.

First against an overwhelming tide of sedition among Earth's human enemies that threatened the very foundation of their civilization, but later—and more definitively—against the Covenant, a religious coalition of alien species devoted to eradicating humanity and possessing the technological capabilities to bring such a threat to reality. James and the other Spartans had spent almost thirty years fighting the Covenant and pushing back against what seemed to be their own species' inexorable downward spiral into extinction. The aliens had razed world after world, extinguishing entire populations through orbital bombardment or groundside occupations unlike anything humans had ever witnessed before.

The Spartans were the only real contesting force the UNSC had at its disposal against such an unprecedented enemy. This fact had defined their lives for the last three decades: uninterrupted, unmitigated war. If they were not fighting in a battle for the survival of a world, they were being transported to one that desperately needed them.

And now the Covenant had finally found Reach, the last defensive colony standing at the metaphorical doorstep of Earth. The fight for Reach could very well determine the future of their species. This planet was not an extraneous mining colony or even some highly sophisticated core world—this was the final bastion before humanity's home.

It would be pivotal.

And *this* was what had brought James-005 back to Reach.

His fellow Spartans, Master Chief Petty Officer John-117 and Petty Officer First Class Linda-058, occupied the Pelican cockpit with him, watching a tactical overlay designate the location of Gamma Station with a waypoint indicator—the site was a key orbital space dock representing their mission target.

Deployed from the UNSC *Pillar of Autumn*, their team's goal was relatively simple, though extraordinarily risky. While the majority of their fellow Spartans were being ferried to Reach's surface to defend the generators that powered the world's orbital guns, James and his two companions were headed to Gamma Station. An emergency message had alerted the UNSC to a security breach that could result in navigation data falling into the Covenant's hands. Per the Cole Protocol, every effort was to be made to neutralize that data, or the Covenant would possess the coordinates to every human world, including Earth.

A proximity alert bleated within the cockpit and the Chief immediately shut it off. They were closing in quickly on Gamma, the ring-shaped orbital dockyard clearly seen against the embattled sphere of Reach. John-117, who functioned as the leader of all Spartans, was a warrior without any equal among his kind. He was also a close friend. From the pilot seat, he continued to negotiate the dropship's thrusters, getting the vehicle's entry aligned to the station's docking ring.

The alert sounded again, and John was about to mute it permanently, but out of the corner of the viewport a dark band of star-doused space suddenly warped. Then, a shimmer of green lights, giving way to a bright, swirling vortex of energy.

A slipspace rupture.

Then they all saw it.

A Covenant frigate emerged from the breach only a kilometer from their position, its bow suddenly obscuring the entire station and much of the planet.

"Brace for maneuvering!" John shouted, preparing to pull the brakes.

James and Linda climbed into the other two seats, anchoring themselves with augmented safety harnesses designed explicitly for Spartans. With the flip of a switch, John cut off the ship's forward thrusters and fired its recursive ones, slowing them so violently that their seats strained and creaked under the massive g-force.

Then he cut the engines completely.

The Pelican drifted silently before the enormous alien vessel, unnervingly close. At a thousand meters long, the ship's silhouette resembled the head of a cobra, heavily plated in the strange, deep-purple alloy that was so common to Covenant vessels.

As they passed alongside its hull, the frigate's enormous shadow cast long over them, engulfing everything in darkness. The Spartans remained quiet and wary. Even with the engines off, the Covenant might still detect the Pelican as the background tau radiation from their own slip slowly dissipated. The dropship needed to continue drifting, as fast and as far as possible away from the frigate, before the Chief began to slow it further. Otherwise they risked drawing the Covenant's immediate attention.

At this distance, that was the last thing they wanted to do.

After a few long seconds, the dropship finally cleared the frigate, and they watched its shape shrink in the aft cameras. James let out a breath he didn't realize he'd been holding. His moment of relief was cut short, however. On either side of the Covenant vessel, slipspace portals suddenly tunneled into the dark of space, two additional frigates now emerging onto the scene.

Terrific.

John turned the recursive thrusters back on as Gamma Station's shape continued to materialize in front of them. The site's three-kilometer ring grew quickly in the viewport, cast like a floating shadow against the bright backdrop of Reach.

They were putting a healthy distance between their Pelican and the enemy frigates, but their speed would come with a price. The Chief began to carefully swivel the dropship around. They'd need to brake at some point if they wanted to safely dock with Gamma. Forward thrusters were the best option, but it required approaching the station in reverse and docking from the rear.

By the time the Pelican spun fully around, there wasn't much space left. What happened next was unavoidable. They were coming in far too hot and it wasn't going to be pretty.

"Hang on," John said through clenched teeth, igniting the forward thrusters and dialing them up to maximum power.

The crash was *hard*—way harder than James had anticipated. He even wondered if one of the frigates had fired on them as all power systems died and everything in the dropship that wasn't locked down flew about the cabin.

A copper taste filled his mouth, darkness gripping the sides of his vision. He shook it off, prying himself free from the chair, rising into zero gravity.

A sharp pain shot up into his left bicep and shoulder and he instinctively looked at his arm, encased in its Mjolnir armor shell. His real arm had been blasted off over a month ago by a Mgalekgolo's assault cannon. The prosthetic replacement worked well enough, but he was still getting used to it. The crash must have tweaked either the prosthetic or whatever was left of his real arm, or both.

It was painful, but he'd just have to deal with it.

"Any injuries?" the Chief asked, floating past his team into the Pelican's rear bay.

"No," Linda said, climbing out of her own seat.

"I think so," James responded, tightening his left hand into a fist. "I mean, no. I'm good, sir." It wasn't worth bringing up. Whatever it was, there was a litany of reasons for him to not address it now—if the arm still worked, the pain was something he could ignore.

As he passed into the rear bay, he looked out of a porthole on the Pelican's starboard side, the trio of Covenant warships floating against the wash of stars. Their running lights were off and their weapons appeared completely inactive.

What are they up to?

"Was that a landing or did those Covenant ships take a shot at us?" he asked, turning back to John, who was collecting gear.

"If they had, we wouldn't be here to talk about it," the Chief responded flatly.

Of course—one shot would have vaporized the entire dropship. But why hadn't that happened? Then it became gravely clear to James. The frigates hadn't fired on the Pelican because they didn't want to risk damaging Gamma in the process. They had come here for the nav data.

"Get whatever gear you can and get out, double time," the Master Chief said, latching a Jackhammer rocket launcher to his back while hefting an assault rifle.

The three scrambled to gather equipment and explosives. They wouldn't be returning, so it didn't make sense to leave any of it here. They also didn't know for certain what was just outside the Pelican—whether the station had already been compromised by the Covenant or if some other unseen threat lurked inside.

James grabbed his own assault rifle and M6 floating in the bay, checking the magazine on both. Then the Chief signaled for them to move out of the dropship's flank hatch. Linda floated out first, then John, then James—casting eyes in every direction to ensure that the enemy hadn't gotten the drop on them. But the exterior of the station was clear, and the three Covenant frigates remained dark and silent—or so it seemed from forty kilometers away.

Leaving the Pelican, it became even more evident that the dropship would not be taking them off-station. Its tail boom had been ripped to shreds, tangled in a network of Gamma's structural support spars, lodged so tightly that it would take a heavy-grade hauler to pull it free.

Quickly getting his bearings, James saw that the station itself was as dark as the Covenant ships. It had stopped spinning at some point, its active relay components were no longer lit, and even the fail-safe utility lights appeared inactive. The on-site AI must have killed everything as soon as the risk of losing the nav data to the Covenant was detected.

That meant they'd have to blast their way in.

John, apparently with the same idea, told James to procure the C12 charges that had been mounted to the Pelican's nose for another purpose. The explosives had been intended for the infiltration of a Covenant ship; now they'd be used on a human space station. It was a crude improvisation, but there weren't many other options, and time wasn't on their side.

As James manipulated his jump-jet to make his way to the explosives, a glint of light reflected off the dropship's hull. He looked up and saw the three frigates, now very much active. Their engines bloomed white hot as they slowly approached, their weapons systems coming online, clusters of blues and reds aflame on their prows. They must have finally spotted the Spartans.

A narrow beam of light suddenly flashed in the dark of space and the center frigate's shield shimmered for a millisecond before the vessel silently exploded, its entire frame disintegrating into countless fragments of alien alloy. In a mere heartbeat, the entire Covenant warship and its crew had been reduced to a debris field.

One of Reach's orbital magnetic accelerator cannons was working precisely as it should. Unfortunately, this didn't stop the approach of the other two ships. Both continued to edge forward, still with no discernible activity.

"Blue One, scan those ships with your scope," John directed Linda as James began to retrieve the C12 anchored onto the Pelican's nose. The Covenant's strange behavior confirmed what James had suspected. They were playing the long game. The enemy wanted the coordinates to all humanity's colonies . . . to Earth. In order to retrieve those, they needed the station intact. And apparently they were willing to sacrifice an entire ship to do it.

"We've got inbound targets," Linda said, spying through her rifle's optics module.

James looked up briefly and could barely make out dots with efflux tails behind them, clearly launched from the frigates.

Covenant drop pods.

They were sending infantry. As the pods got closer, he could see other targets around them: a horde of heavily armored Sangheili and Kig-Yar in EVA gear, also rocketing toward Gamma at breakneck speed. Bright motes of blue and pink light quickly appeared in the vast chasm between the Covenant and Gamma.

Weapons fire—the Covenant infantry was attacking the Spartans on approach, attempting to eliminate them before they could enter the station. James scrambled to pull free the rest of the explosives, but it was too late. Plasma bolts and crystalline needle shards rained down hard on the station and the dropship, a deluge of razor-sharp hail exploding all around them.

"Take cover!" John shouted, as he and Linda moved to the side of the Pelican.

James was prying off the last of the C12 as John's voice sounded again.

"Blue Two, I said fall back."

Just as James turned to comply, a series of needles struck his back, embedding directly into his Mjolnir armor. One hit a thruster on his jump-jet and blasted apart, the explosion throwing him toward the station, slamming him against its hull before dragging him out into the immense darkness of space. He spun wildly end-over-end with no way to slow or control his movement, his vision flashing between images of Reach and the Covenant frigates until everything went dark.

JAMES SOLOMON

Cataphract

November 8, 2559

"James!" Lola's voice tore through the fog. *"James, wake up."*

Solomon jerked himself up from the bed.

His body was drenched with sweat, his pulse racing wildly. He looked to his right at a display. The undercarriage hull-cam showed a bright-blue ocean world stretched out below, its faded horizon curving up against a smattering of stars.

Far Isle. His home and base of operations.

"You were having another nightmare," Lola said across his ship's loudspeaker. *"I thought Spartans didn't have those."*

He sighed, rubbing his face. She was just regurgitating what he'd told her last time.

"Why haven't we landed?"

"There's quite a bit of traffic. I'm waiting for it to clear before starting the entry cycle."

Taking a deep breath, he swung his legs out of bed, placing his feet on the cold metal floor. His eyes dropped to his left arm. The robotic prosthesis still ached. Nerve pain, even after all these years. He made a fist and released it, providing a small measure of relief.

He had lost his arm to a pair of Mgalekgolo on Sigma Octanus IV over seven years ago. A brief tangle with them in the city of Côte d'Azur had proven that the armored behemoths were far quicker than they looked. They were called Hunters for a reason. A flash of light, a deafening explosion, a wave of heat . . . his arm had been burned away below the elbow, but it had barely slowed him down.

Standing up slowly, James began moving through the crew deck of *Cataphract*, a modified *Winter*-class prowler he'd acquired from the gray market in 2554. Manufactured by Watershed Division, the vessel was explicitly designed for covert operations, most often utilized by the Office of Naval Intelligence and its contractors. *Cataphract* had served him well over the years, despite occasionally attracting unwanted attention. Its arsenal and stealth package were enough of a boon that mild drawbacks such as those were manageable. Especially considering its astonishingly powerful slipspace drive, the result of several years of postwar FTL development with Forerunner tech. These recent innovations in faster-than-light travel allowed *Cataphract* to move across the stars quicker than just about anyone.

But still . . . he had to be careful.

While the standard version of the prowler could fit an entire fireteam, *Cataphract* was optimized for *him*—Solomon, a lone operator, whose only companion was an invisible AI. That was most obvious from the crew deck, with only one bed and the barest of necessities. Below that deck was the cargo bay, a weapons locker, a cryotube for transporting "uncooperative" passengers, and a Brokkr armor mounting system that allowed him to get in and out of his Mark V Mjolnir.

Cataphract also had a payload bay at the top of its fuselage where Solomon stored his Shearwater aerodyne for operations like the one on Terceira. The bird had taken significant damage during their tussle with the frigate crews and was currently sidelined. He wondered if he'd be able to fix it himself, or if he'd have to contact a local mechanic willing to do work off the books?

At the fore of the crew deck was a cleaning station. As he approached, he got a good look at his face in the mirror, really the first time in days.

What a mess.

Apart from many scars he'd earned over the years, his left eye was now severely swollen and there was a new gash across his right cheek, his ebony skin still purple and tender around it. He hadn't applied any mend-salve or biofoam upon returning to *Cataphract.* He was too exhausted and had just told Lola to get them home before he crashed in bed. Examining his chest, he could see several deep bruises, courtesy of one of the janissaries. No broken bones though, which was something to be grateful for.

"Are you going to shave?" Lola asked.

His head already was shaved, so she must be referring to his thick beard, gray and unkempt. That's what happened when you were away from home for three full months.

"Didn't plan on it," he grunted.

"Well, you should. It would certainly help."

He sighed. She was right, but it'd have to wait.

After cleaning and treating his injuries, he grabbed a shirt and headed through the corridor connecting the crew deck with operations—first the ship's sensor-weapons station, then a transfer column that allowed his ship to dock with another vessel, and then the cockpit. Taking a seat, he began assessing the ship's systems as Lola brought up a holographic display that wrapped before him, using hull cameras to re-create a 180-degree viewport looking out over the ship's prow.

"Coffee?" Lola asked.

"Not today," he said, opening a panel below the controls and withdrawing a flask of whiskey. He spun the cap and took a sip.

"Is it a little early for that, *James?"*

"Thanks for your concern, Lola," he shot back. "You can just tell me when we're clear to land."

He didn't even know what time it was, but he'd stopped caring about that a while back. He would drink because that would help ease the pain. He'd drink because it would distract him from the nagging suspicion that ONI probably had no plans to free the captives on Terceira, and everything he'd done on this mission was just a move in some political chess game they were playing.

Whiskey helped James detach and forget, and that was enough.

"Actually, now that I think about it, did you pull up any more information on our new friends?"

"Unfortunately, information is extremely limited," Lola replied. *"Rogue Spartan forces are still in the process of a full threat review by ONI."*

"Those *weren't* Spartans, Lola," James said, a bit more firmly than he'd expected.

To be a Spartan meant something—it was more than mere

augmentations and powered armor. It was nobility and sacrifice and resolve. It was a refusal to stop until the mission was accomplished, until victory was achieved. It was fighting for those who couldn't fight for themselves.

Word was, various corporations—many of which had been used as military contractors to develop the ever-evolving Mjolnir armor—along with power brokers on worlds like Venezia and Karava were looking to upgrade their private security forces, leveraging all the stolen information and technology they could get to develop their own super-soldiers. Though they were *far* from leveling the playing field against Spartans, these so-called janissary forces posed a notable threat.

"Sorry, James," Lola said. *"No further information is available at this time. As I said, ONI is still conducting an extensive internal assessment."*

From their orbital perch above the azure surface of Far Isle, he could almost make out the chain of islands called St. Anino—the closest thing he had to a home. After the traffic cleared, Lola would take *Cataphract* down. Even with the prowler's stealth systems, entry and exit from this part of the planet was nearly impossible to mask. They would wait for a window to open before making their approach. Until then, there was little he could do but enjoy the view.

He'd seen Far Isle like this a hundred times, but his thoughts went back to his dream.

Back to Reach.

But it *wasn't* actually a dream. It was a memory.

In a former life, James Solomon had been James-005, one of the mythical super-soldiers harvested from the classified SPARTAN-II program.

Solomon had fought alongside his fellow Spartans for nearly

three decades, pushing back a seemingly implacable foe wherever they could and extracting survivors when the former proved untenable. One world after another fell to the Covenant, and, in the end, so did Reach.

That's where James-005's story ended.

He would later learn that John and Linda had completed the mission on Gamma Station, successfully destroying the nav data and escaping aboard the *Pillar of Autumn*. The rest of the Spartans had fought hard on the surface of Reach until a handful of those who had survived long enough were extracted. They would rejoin the fight when the Covenant arrived at Earth only a few weeks later. At some point during the battle for Earth, the war had come to a grinding halt, brought to an end by the Master Chief himself.

At least, that was what Solomon had been told.

He wasn't there for any of it.

They had classified him as "missing in action." Not just because he was truly missing, but because that's what ONI did when Spartans died. Per Directive 930, any Spartan who was lost in battle was marked MIA in order to perpetuate the myth that the super-soldiers were unkillable. So, on the books, Spartans never died. Not officially at least.

And neither had Solomon.

By the time the patrol tug recovered his body, the surface of Reach had been reduced to ashes and the Covenant had moved on. He'd been among tens of thousands of corpses floating in orbit. ONI operatives brought his remains to a facility hidden on the edge of the Sol system and a handful of scientists had managed to revive him. Evidently he'd hung on to a few bare threads of consciousness, drifting in and out of a comatose state, only waking after nearly a full year had passed. By the time he was even remotely functional, the war had ended.

The galaxy was now on a very different path.

Most Spartans had perished in the final days of the war. Many even on Reach. The rest were redeployed to deal with the conflict's aftermath, an array of threats and emerging ex-Covenant factions. The Spartans he'd been closest to were either MIA as well or too far away to be recalled, most teams broken up and redistributed under the newly formed Spartan branch in an effort to navigate the exceedingly unpredictable postwar terrain.

James-005—the *old* James—had been created specifically for war. That was the entire purpose of his existence since childhood. But the events that had defined the last three decades of human history had suddenly ceased, and he found himself in an environment that no longer needed him. Or at least, that's what the UNSC told the citizens of Earth and its colonies. And that's what he believed.

ONI, however, had other plans.

Section Three, the organization responsible for the Spartans, still saw Solomon as a useful military asset, but recognized that he now fell outside their previous constraints. Although recorded as MIA, they'd made sure he could no longer function within Naval Special Weapons or even the new Spartan branch.

Yet this gave the authorities of ONI an opportunity they'd never had before. Rather than directly facilitate the actions of a Spartan, they offered Solomon the possibility of being a private military contractor. ONI would pay him to do the jobs they didn't want to do—the ones they *couldn't* do, because of the potential fallout. Missions so hazardous and politically risky that they needed to maintain complete deniability. He could be selective with his operations, but ultimately, he was on his own. If things went sideways, he would be completely discarded by Naval Intelligence and disavowed if necessary. In other words, he'd be considered a criminal.

For ONI, this was politically convenient and administratively affordable. Solomon assumed all the risk, and in return, he would be paid handsomely. More than that, it allowed him to do what he was created for: war. There was really no choice, in his mind.

So, James-005 had died and James Solomon was born—or, as his handlers called him, Big Jim.

And for nearly six years now, this had been his life.

Running an endless series of black operations that sent him to the darkest and most dangerous parts of the galaxy, against enemies both foreign and domestic. Sometimes even against allies. Whatever was needed to move the strategic ball forward for ONI. It was simple and straightforward. He completed an assignment. He got paid. And then he did it all over again.

At first, the general effect of this new purpose had been liberating. He was back in the mix of things, fighting against an enemy, *any* enemy. From the age of six, he'd been formed by Dr. Halsey and Chief Mendez into the ultimate soldier, and although he was far outside the parameters of their original design and separated from the teams he'd once been so close to, it felt good to be useful again.

Over time, however, he'd grown distant from what had originally driven him all those years during the Covenant War. Somewhere along the path, he'd been reduced to a cog in a vast series of ONI-controlled gears, no longer fighting for the survival of the human species but instead for a never-ending parade of political and economic expediencies.

He was being treated as a weapon, not a soldier. And it had all begun to wear him down, making him cold and mechanical. In his most sober reflections, he wondered if there was anything left at all of his former life. Or was he just the ghost of a Spartan now?

Solomon had often considered what life might be like if he just cut ties with ONI. If he simply walked away and found a quiet place to live out the rest of his days.

He called that place Suntéreó.

It was a small habitable moon that he'd found in an outdated colonial directory a few years back. No one knew about it except for Lola. One day, he would simply disappear there. Never to be seen again. Never to be needed by ONI, or anyone else for that matter.

But it hadn't taken him long to realize that would never happen.

Not out of fear that ONI would search for him in order to either take back or eliminate their rogue asset. The truth was that he really didn't want rest. He didn't want a break. He didn't want to retire. As much as he felt burned out and hollowed by the endless stream of missions ONI sent him on, that was what he had been created for.

He didn't know how to do anything else.

Suntéreó. It would remain a dream.

He looked down at the flask of whiskey and took another sip.

The only way this could all end was if *he* ended.

And so Solomon would continue until he did. At the rate things were going, it probably wouldn't be long anyway.

"Looks like a window has opened," Lola said. *"Activating optical once we're out of range, then I will begin the entry cycle."*

"It's about damn time," Solomon growled, lifting the flask to his lips again. "I want off this boat."

CHAPTER 10

TUL 'JURAN

Shadow of Intent
November 10, 2559

Tul 'Juran trudged painfully through the corridors of *Shadow of Intent.*

After the dogfight above the artificial moon, she had slept for over four full day-cycles and was now making her way to the bridge. Still recovering from the battle and the long sleep, her body ached with every step.

The destruction of *Vigilance with Piety* and the death of Kafo Dein had almost cost the Swords of Sanghelios the lives of two warriors, but Blademaster Vul 'Soran and the Unggoy ranger Stolt had managed to reach 'Juran as her war sphinx plummeted toward the moon's surface.

"Despite the breaches in your vehicle's hull, transition into the world's atmosphere did not immediately end your life," 'Soran had told her when she first awakened. "You were deprived of oxygen for five full centals, but Stolt and I were able to slow your descent enough to land on the moon and await the arrival of a dropship to bring us home."

Not all of us. 'Juran thought of Oda 'Mavamu, whom she had very nearly joined. She had survived to fight another day. But even if she had not, it would still have been a worthy price. Evidently, the other war sphinxes had been ravaged seemingly beyond repair in their efforts to save her. The machines were virtually inoperable by the time they touched down, and they had discussed whether to abandon them during extraction—though 'Soran had dodged the question when she had asked whether they were ferried back to *Shadow of Intent* for analysis and possible repairs.

The Order of Restoration had not only lost a vessel and many of its military assets to self-destruction, but one of their key leaders was now gone. Kafo Dein's passing would set back their operations and further stifle their ability to pose a serious problem for the Sangheili. And, most gratifyingly, it had brought justice to the false prophets who had skulked in the shadows for so long, secretly plotting against the Sangheili in the hopes that they themselves would rise to power. That alone was enough for 'Juran, even if it had nearly cost her life.

If she had to do it again, she would have changed nothing. This pursuit of justice—of vengeance for her family—was a cause to which she would continue to dedicate *everything* she had to give.

Replaying the events in her mind, 'Juran traversed a walkway that overshadowed a series of concentric battle spheres—the blademaster's yard, a section of the ship dedicated to the edification of younger Sangheili in the battle practices and traditions of their forebears. Like much of the rest of the interior of the *Kerel*-pattern assault carrier, the corridor was plated with a complex latticework of materials and alloys forged from the finest assemblies of the Sangheili, rich purples and crimson lined with bright-yellow contours that reminded her of images she had seen of High Charity itself. It echoed a time before the fall of the Covenant and filled her with a sense of nostalgia that she found herself welcoming far too easily, despite all the San'Shyuum lies that had contaminated it.

Intriguingly, the blademaster's yard was presently vacant.

There were no students and no teachers, only a few autodrones quietly cleaning in the periphery of the farthest spheres. 'Juran was not sure why that was the case, but it did not bother her as much as it might have in the past. Perhaps that was because the blademaster's yard had been recently updated with human "war games" systems that had their own battle training technology.

The very idea repulsed 'Juran. She did not like that her people would be using crude human fabrications and illusions, rather than training as they had for countless generations. Not only was it overly sophisticated and based on holographic falsehoods, but it had eclipsed the spirit of the Sangheili and was, in fact, a poor substitute for the purity of real hand-to-hand combat.

What could humans teach them anyway?

All of this was part of the Arbiter's ongoing effort to manufacture bridges between the Sangheili and humanity. In truth, she had no love for the Arbiter's allies—if they even could be called such. They had been enemies for far too long.

During the Covenant War, the humans had caused the deaths of innumerable Sangheili, many culled from the population of her own birth world, Rahnelo. She found them to be selfish, opportunistic, and vain creatures, with no thought for the larger galaxy around them or those who would be affected by their reckless ambitions. Although she certainly despised the San'Shyuum and Jiralhanae far more than any other alien factions, she hoped that the Arbiter would give up his curious pursuit of such alliances and return to fight again for the sake of his own kind. There would be no way for him to establish the Concert of Worlds he so desired among all Sangheili people without relinquishing his ill-placed admiration of the humans.

At least, none that she could imagine. Why he delayed doing this, she did not know.

"Where are you, Scion?" The shipmaster's voice reached out to her through a closed-channel comm within her ear. *"Did you lose your way?"*

Shipmaster Rtas 'Vadum had summoned 'Juran to the bridge upon her waking. That was a unit ago—equivalent to a hundred centals when measuring time. She had delayed because she was not eager to speak with him. 'Vadum was a remarkable naval tactician and an impressive strategist—perhaps the best within the Swords of Sanghelios—but, in recent lunar cycles, she had found his seeming timidity grating, sometimes even questioning his commitment to their people and wondering if he had grown soft after so many years of armistices.

Endless war no doubt had taken a toll on him, but peace seemed to have had an even more corrosive effect. He had grown to possess a kind of diffidence—particularly with regard to her own actions, such as the one she had just taken to kill Kafo Dein, which he would certainly have prevented her from ever attempting. She had been forced to endure lectures on circumspection and protocol half a dozen times in the past year, and she feared that this would be yet another.

"I am almost there, Shipmaster," she replied, moving down the walkway that ran along the port side hull, then cutting back into an enclosed corridor that dove toward the center of the ship. Glancing out a transparent pane in the bulkhead, she saw that it was pitch black outside *Shadow of Intent*, with only a glint of light spread like a ring of fog around the vessel's hull. They must be in slipspace. She wondered where they were headed.

The thought of space outside the ship brought to her mind her own family.

Ukala, her youngest brother, now served as the kaidon of Juran Keep on Rahnelo. Under normal circumstances, he would have been far too young for this role, but with the aid of a handful of surviving elders, this was the only option. The other males in her family, including her father, had been executed by a San'Shyuum belonging to the Order of Restoration—leaving her brother the last of her kin and the only one capable of continuing her family's name. A dull ache of homesickness crept into her mind, but she swept it aside, reminding herself yet again that the best way she could serve her family was here on *Shadow of Intent*.

After only a few centals, she finally reached the main corridor, which swung around into a large branching antechamber with a single door leading to the bridge. The door opened onto a short ramp ascending to the room's central platform, with control stations assembled along the periphery of the room. The stations were monitored by Sangheili and Unggoy, most of them with their heads intently down, preoccupied with the carrier's journey.

At the center of the platform, three Sangheili were gathered around the holotable: Rtas 'Vadum, Vul 'Soran, and, to her surprise, a female Sangheili—a shipmistress she did not recognize, yet one who displayed the copper-orange armor of the Swords of Sanghelios.

The two males were tall with large, muscular frames typical of their age. They bore scars one would expect from decades of combat; yet it was the shipmistress who caught the scion's eyes. The female Sangheili *also* had scars, many of them, in fact, which was clear evidence of years of service.

This was an uncommon sight for the Sangheili, who historically did not even consider accepting females into combat positions. After the war with the humans, the Arbiter and a handful of kaidons began making exceptions, but these did not come without fierce resistance. Blademaster Vul 'Soran himself was a traditionalist, and had staunchly opposed 'Juran's inclusion aboard *Shadow of Intent.* After some time, her presence had finally worn him down and he unexpectedly began viewing the young scion not as a liability, but as an asset—even as something akin to his own daughter.

The scion approached them respectfully, bowing her head as she ascended the platform. Coming along the side of the table, her eyes caught the image that hovered at its center: a hologram of a San'Shyuum who she immediately recognized.

Dovo Nesto.

The high lord of the Order of Restoration.

"Scion," the shipmaster said, attempting to veil his frustration with her. "So good of you to join us after all this time."

"Apologies for my delay," she replied. "Evidently it is not so easy to wake oneself after nearly suffocating in the vacuum of space."

Rtas 'Vadum only stared at her, unamused.

"There is no need to apologize, Scion of Rahnelo," the shipmistress said. "We are grateful for your persistence with Kafo Dein. His death severed one of the main arteries of the Order of Restoration. The Swords are in your debt."

"Scion, this is Shipmistress Mahkee 'Chava," the shipmaster noted. "She helms *Scorrin's Blade.* Certainly you have heard of it?"

"I have," 'Juran replied, "but I did not know it had a female commander." The reputation of *Scorrin's Blade* was well earned—it was a vicious *Hekar Taa*–pattern blockade runner that had established a unique standing among the Arbiter's fleets, having accumulated more kills than any other vessel under the Swords' banner. "It is an honor to meet you, Shipmistress. Your vessel's reputation precedes itself." She turned to the hologram of Dovo Nesto. "To what do we owe this privilege?"

"The shipmistress has provided us with a lead and we are in

the process of chasing it down," 'Vadum said. "We are headed to the human world of Nysa. It is one of their secret fortress worlds, evidently beyond the eyes of the Tyrant."

"I have never heard of the world," she said.

"Nor would you," the shipmaster responded brusquely. "It is secret for a reason."

"We are headed there because of *this*," 'Chava interrupted, pressing a key on the table.

A recording began to play—the voice of a San'Shyuum.

"—where the Lithos is hidden on the human world, we cannot say. Yet . . . it possesses a key to divine power, as was foretold. If we were to gain access to it, nothing would stop our return. The Order of Restoration would at last be fulfilled. 'Nyon's record, unearthed from the glass of Sovolanu, is a sure omen from the gods. It claims there is one being who was made in the image of the Archon. She alone holds the key to the Domain. If we have her, we will have all that the Archon possesses. The humans know this already, so we must move quickly to secure—"

The recording ended abruptly.

"To secure *what*?" 'Juran asked. "Nysa?"

"No. We do not know what," 'Vadum replied. "In fact, there is little about this that we know with any certainty."

"It is the voice of Dovo Nesto," 'Juran said, having heard it many times before. She had made herself keenly familiar with the Order of Restoration, including its high lord. It was the only way she could secure justice for her family.

"We already know that it is Nesto," 'Chava said. "But have you ever heard of this 'Lithos' he speaks of?"

"Never," she replied. "From the message, however, it is obviously important."

"Indeed," 'Chava said. "My ranger teams extracted this recording from a relay mite attached to a battlecruiser belonging to Sali

'Nyon. He was stationed on Sqala when it was sent. Are you familiar?"

"With 'Nyon or Sqala?" 'Juran asked, then proceeded without waiting for a response: "Sali 'Nyon claims to be the true prophet of the Covenant and has appointed himself as the leader of whatever remains of the old empire. He desires to resurrect it. Sqala is a human world. Vagrants, dissidents, criminals. They call it Venezia."

"That is correct." Blademaster Vul 'Soran now spoke up. "The transmission was intended for Kafo Dein. We were only able to decrypt it with the data that Stolt pulled from *Vigilance with Piety*."

Tul 'Juran stood silent for a moment. She did not know if she was supposed to understand what they were after or if they simply wanted to see her response. When a few awkward breaths had passed, she finally broke the silence. "Again, I mean no disrespect. What does this have to do with *me*, Shipmaster?"

"Sali 'Nyon served your father, Tulum 'Juranai, during the Covenant's campaign on Sovolanu," 'Vadum said, his voice gracious but urgent. "Whatever this record was, 'Nyon recovered it under your father's orders. Now Dovo Nesto has possession of it. We had hoped that somehow *you* might know more than what was communicated in this transmission."

"Unfortunately, I do not," 'Juran said. "I do not even know what Sovolanu *is*—"

"Reach," 'Chava interjected. "The human world they call Reach. It was their last military fortress before the Covenant gained access to their homeworld."

"Then we should perhaps ask the Arbiter," 'Juran said, struggling to maintain a respectful tone. "I know only what I was told. Which I'm sure you can understand was *very* little."

'Vadum stared at her with wide eyes, but 'Chava did not flinch even the slightest.

"We understand, Scion," 'Vadum finally said, trading looks with 'Soran. "Nevertheless . . . we thought it prudent to ask."

A question not completely without warrant. Most Sangheili young lived in large familial communities with several uncles serving the role of parent. The hatchlings typically possessed no knowledge of their true biological father. This served to strengthen the communal bond and preserve healthy competition within the family. Rahnelo did not follow such customs, nor did other sparsely populated worlds where there were too few Sangheili. It was apparent that these three had no knowledge of such things, nor fully understood what it was like to know one's true father by name.

"My father is dead," proclaimed 'Juran. "And he told me nothing about Sali 'Nyon or this Lithos. It is an enigma to me as well."

"Then we will hope that the humans know what *we* do not," 'Vadum said, scanning the flitting glyphs next to Dovo Nesto's form. "Whatever information they have will be essential in our next operation. As will their permission."

Permission? 'Juran did not like the sound of that. "May I ask what this operation is?" she said, eyes narrowing.

"That is why we are meeting," the shipmaster replied. "We intend to deploy three strike teams to the surface of Sqala to track 'Nyon's activity and apprehend Dovo Nesto. We believe that he is there. You will be leading one of these teams, the blademaster another," he said, looking at 'Soran. "And Stolt, of course, the final one."

"Understood," 'Juran replied, looking at each of the three Sangheili in turn. "So we are certain that Dovo Nesto is on Sqala? Why then are we on our way to Nysa?"

It was a fair question, she thought. Dovo Nesto was the most important San'Shyuum within the Order of Restoration. And now they knew where he was. Why would they waste any time with a human fortress world?

"We cannot simply *go* to Sqala," 'Soran said, bristling his mandibles. "Though many different species have come to call it home, it is still at its heart a human world. As noted, we need their permission, young one."

"We need more than their permission, Blademaster," 'Chava said. "They will likely want to be present. They have a vested interest. If not in Dovo Nesto, then certainly in this Lithos."

"Am I misunderstanding something vital?" 'Juran said, leaning over the table. "We finally have Nesto within our reach. Why would we dither around on a *nishum* world, begging them for permission? Should we not strike Sqala while we can?"

"*Nishum*?" the shipmaster grated, his eyes piercing into 'Juran. Yes, she had uttered the pejorative that the Covenant had often used for the humans during the war—a term for a common intestinal parasite native to Sanghelios. It might have fallen out of parlance among those who honored the Arbiter's alliance with them, but 'Juran simply could not help herself.

How can these three be so weak as to grovel for permission *from humans? They are Sangheili—they should act like it!*

"Scion," the shipmaster said, his head motioning toward a corner of the bridge. "A brief word with you." Rtas 'Vadum's voice was heavy with severity—he was not pleased.

She bowed and proceeded to follow him to the periphery of the bridge, out of earshot of the others.

"What in the name of the gods is wrong with you?" 'Vadum growled, so angry that he reverted to his old religion. "Your behavior has been degrading for months now. You have been resistant, you have been petulant—"

"I understand, Shipmaster," she said, holding up her hand. "You did not approve of my pursuit of Kafo Dein—"

"This has *nothing* to do with Kafo Dein!" he said through tightened mandibles. "This is about the chain of command and the right of honor." Suddenly he took a step forward, looming over her in a way that she had never experienced, a dark mien shrouding his face. "This ship and its crew are *my* responsibility, and no one else's. Our mission, our actions, our goals—*I* determine what they are, not *you*. Your recalcitrance will not continue to be entertained, Scion. Especially not in the presence of another commander. You will give us the respect we are due. And you will leave your attitude toward our allies in your quarters. Do you understand this?"

"Yes, Shipmaster," she said, her head bowing low.

"I hope that you do," he said, craning his neck to the side, then turning back to her. His eyes were softer now. "Please, Tul," 'Vadum said gently. "Do not jeopardize your life like that again. I have had enough of warriors giving their lives under my command, chasing after a dream or a false hope. Their blood now weighs down heavy upon my legacy. Upon all of us."

She thought of Oda 'Mavamu once again—then realized that he was only the latest in a line of many. 'Vadum had served in the Covenant for decades and had witnessed countless warriors perishing under his watch. He knew this kind of loss more keenly than she ever would.

"I am weary of burying my own, and I will not suffer to see you become one of them," he said, his voice sounding something like her father's. "The San'Shyuum have taken so much already. Please do not let them take you too."

He paused for a moment, staring directly at her, then turned abruptly, returning to the holotable. She followed slowly, trying to process what he had just said.

This was more than a shipmaster simply caring for his crew.

He saw her as family.

When they reached the table, 'Chava and 'Soran were discussing—or feigning to—a data stream before them. Their eyes turned to the shipmaster, then 'Juran.

"I apologize, Shipmistress," 'Vadum said, nodding toward the Sangheili. "And the scion would like to apologize as well," he added, looking toward 'Juran.

"My deepest regrets," she said, bowing reverentially. "I will choose my words more carefully."

"I can understand the difficulty in seeing the humans with any honor, Scion," 'Chava said. "After all, they were our enemies for so many years. But having fought alongside some of the best of their kind, I assure you—they *are* now allies of the Sangheili, and our people need allies like them for whatever lies ahead. If the Lithos is anywhere near as important as Dovo Nesto claims it to be, we must make allies wherever we can find them. Their aid does not diminish our strength."

"I will trust your judgment on this matter, Shipmistress," 'Juran said.

"There is no need to trust my judgment. You will know first-hand soon enough," she responded. "They will not let you do whatever you please, even on an outlaw world like Sqala. Your strike team there will no doubt be accompanied by humans. Possibly even Spartans."

'Juran's stomach turned at that thought, and she fought hard to restrain her revulsion.

CHAPTER 11

ABIGAIL COLE

Nysa
November 19, 2559

Nysa might have made an extraordinary civilian colony, but now it was only an empty frontier world, its existence secreted away by ONI during its own exploration surveys before it caught the attention of the Colonial Administration Authority. It had been saved for a time like the one presently being faced, and it had since come to serve its purpose rather well.

Untouched by the hands of industry and development, Nysa largely comprised immense swaths of natural beauty that played host to only a few scattered military sites. Its low-technology profile and the stringent reinstitution of the Cole Protocol allowed it to remain hidden for now, but Abigail Cole wondered how long her father's old security mandate would work against such an overwhelming threat as Cortana.

The captain of the UNSC *Victory of Samothrace* stood on a parapet, overlooking Site Z—a research facility embodied by a network of modest gray two-floor structures encircling a bare landing pad like a wreath. Several kilometers away, against the backdrop of a snow-covered mountain range and a boundless forest, was a multitiered Spartan training site with a slender gravel road traveling right through its center. The unassuming design of both sites and their simplistic layout belied their significance, helping to keep the human presence on Nysa safely clandestine. Despite that fact, Cole imagined that Cortana detecting the UNSC's activity was only a matter of time.

A critical reason behind the operation *Infinity* was attempting on Zeta Halo.

If Cortana remained in power, humanity's future would never change, and its only effective resistance—the UNSC shell within which Cole was presently working—would be constantly moving from shadow to shadow until the AI finally caught up and razed it all to the ground once and for all. Cortana claimed that she sought galaxy-wide peace, but her twisted vision held no room for freedom or choice, creativity or process. It was a dark age in which no civilization could ever grow, struggle, fail, and learn. *Infinity* desperately needed to deliver the UNSC's antidote to Cortana and break her grip on the galaxy.

Cole's eyes caught a single green Phantom as it tore through the cloud ceiling above, making a swift descent to the surface. Their visitors had finally arrived. It would take the Swords of Sanghelios dropship several minutes to land and disembark, so she would be able to get to the analysis room before they did.

Taking the lift down, she found her way to the most active level in the entire facility—three floors underground, where a beltway corridor linked the network of aboveground buildings. Site Z had a relatively light staff compared to other UNSC research facilities, but it still bustled with frenetic activity, personnel moving anxiously through its corridors and a contingent of Spartan-IVs at key junctures providing overwatch.

"Commander Agryna," Cole said through her personal comms device. "Our guests are about to touch down. Could you send an escort to retrieve them?"

"Yes ma'am," she replied. *"I will see to it personally."*

"Thank you," Cole said as the lift door opened.

Spartan Commander Laurette Agryna oversaw the Avery J. Johnson Academy and her Spartan team provided essential security support across all of Nysa's facilities. The commander's desire to personally escort their visitors told Cole that relations between humans and Sangheili remained tense, even among those trained to work alongside their former enemies. It wasn't surprising, but it didn't pass through Cole's mind without some concern, especially given the task that lay ahead.

Traveling down the main corridor, Cole reached the analysis room she'd sequestered. Its door was marked EUDOXUS, which she'd learned long ago was the name of an ancient Greek mathematician. She pressed her hand to a plate on its side and the door opened with a hiss. Passing through a series of security barriers, she finally reached a dark hexagonal room that was roughly five meters wide, surrounded by displays streaming endless walls of data. At the center of the room was a holotable, and on its projector surface the briefcase she'd retrieved from SR 8936. It lay open with a network of wires tethered directly to specific patch-points on the briefcase's interface, the wires rising into machines fixed somewhere out of sight in the recess of the ceiling above.

A handful of Site Z's staff were painstakingly working to access and contain the AI personality matrices within the case. Osman and Hood were both present in the room, the former's eyes wide as they attempted to collect their target AI—Black-Box—from his storage unit without detonating the explosives and harming the construct himself. Osman had provided the necessary clearance to open the case without detonating, but everything that followed was extraordinarily risky given the uncertain nature of the case's containment system. Around the case a nearly-translucent energy barrier had been activated that could neutralize and contain an explosive blast, in the unlikely event that it happened. But that obviously wouldn't protect Black-Box or the data he held.

Despite all the precautions they'd taken, Cole would have preferred that the senior officers weren't present, both for their own safety and for the security of the operation. But they'd insisted on staying and she'd decided it best not to press the issue. When she had left the room twenty minutes earlier, Site Z's best extraction team had only begun the process. It now looked like they were finished, just in time for their visitors.

"Status?" she asked, catching Dr. Marwa Nabil's eyes as she moved from a display on the far side of the room back to the center table.

"Oh, we're done here, Captain Cole," she said, pressing a series of keys at the table. "We've just been doing some final checks to validate the AI's new containment field."

The cables suddenly detached on their own, slithering back up into the ceiling, and the briefcase began to drop out of view, lowered through the center of the table and sealed within a separate containment field. Once the case was gone, it was replaced by a series of holographic display nodes that rose up at the table's center. This then was how they would safely interface with Black-Box.

"Excellent," Cole said, approaching the table. "Our guests have just arrived."

Nabil came to Cole's side with a worried look and said quietly: "Given the lack of precedent, ma'am, are we confident that we want our first interaction with the AI to be in front of these *particular* guests? I know we trust them, but there's no real telling what Black-Box will say or do. He's been confined for almost a full year, and he is past his—"

"Termination date?" Osman finished, approaching the two with a sober look on her face, having already been listening in.

She was still CINCONI and this facility was technically under her jurisdiction—though she'd only learned of its existence days earlier. Being outside of operational parameters for so long, however, meant that she lacked the immediate authority she'd once possessed. Until she was formally reinstated, she couldn't make security decisions and was, much to her own frustration, only along for the ride. Cole wanted to give Osman the respect she deserved, but sentimentality wasn't a luxury they could afford right now.

"Yes," Nabil said, looking at Osman. "Precisely that. We've never done anything like this before. We're operating only on theory and there's an exceptional amount of risk involved if we unlock him and things somehow go wrong. Especially in front of the Sangheili."

"BB *will* cooperate," Osman said, her eyes intense. "He's never betrayed my trust, and he will recognize what's at stake. He'll do whatever is necessary."

"I'm sure he will," Cole said to Osman. "But if the codeword works as intended, it'll override his decision-making faculties and get us what we need regardless if he's cooperative or not." She turned to Nabil. "We don't have a choice, Doctor, because we've run out of time. The Sangheili don't want the Lithos to fall into the wrong hands either. And frankly, if we can't trust our allies with what happens next, we're all in far greater trouble than a security breach. Their support is essential to this operation's success."

"Understood, ma'am," Nabil said, nodding.

"If these folks are sent from the Arbiter," Hood stated as he approached from the side of the room, "then we can trust them. I'd stake my life on it. And it wouldn't be the first time."

His voice was confident and knowing. It gave Cole some measure of peace. Unlike her, Hood had some history with the Arbiter and his people. If any human would know the credibility of the Swords of Sanghelios based on firsthand experience, it was certainly him.

The door opened, and Cole turned to see two humans leading four Sangheili into the room.

Even though one of the humans was a fully armored Spartan, the aliens still towered over everyone, making the room feel very small. Cole was surprised at her own body's fight-or-flight response to their presence, her muscles tightening and her hand longing to move to her sidearm. The war had been over for almost seven years, but seeing a once-mortal enemy up close always seemed to awaken instincts she'd thought were long gone. Old habits indeed died hard.

She wondered if Dr. Nabil's initial concern wasn't so far off.

Rtas 'Vadum, shipmaster of the legendary *Shadow of Intent*, was instantly recognizable from his stark white armor and two missing mandibles. Beside him was Mahkee 'Chava, a female shipmistress who had garnered some notoriety in helping the UNSC put down the last of Jul 'Mdama's Covenant faction a year earlier. Behind them followed an aging blademaster and a young female warrior whom Cole did not recognize.

Cole was surprised at the younger female's gait and posture. Sangheili dispositions were difficult to read, but this one seemed almost defiant. The Sangheili had held a longstanding tradition of patriarchy in their culture, even prior to the formation of the Covenant. The Arbiter had only recently rescinded such regulations, but this was Cole's first time seeing visible evidence of it.

Escorting the Sangheili were Commander Agryna and Admiral Jilan al-Cygni.

Agryna was in full Mjolnir armor, including her helmet, and walking with a self-assured confidence likely intended to communicate something unspoken to the Sangheili. Her combat suit was a blend of ivory and blue plating, her left leg an enhanced prosthetic. She certainly looked the part of Spartan Commander and no one in the room would question that.

Admiral al-Cygni's appearance at Site Z was no surprise. The intelligence officer had a strong, assertive face and gray hair, and the subtle bearing of someone who owned wherever she set foot. As one of ONI Section Three's most established operatives and a driving force in the UNSC's recent underground efforts, al-Cygni was closely connected to *Victory of Samothrace*'s current initiative. Cole wouldn't be shocked if the admiral was one of the mission's architects. Although al-Cygni primarily worked from her stealth ship, *Akkadian*, she frequented Nysa to observe the Spartans in training and ensure that ONI's overarching plans were moving along without hindrance.

Beyond an occasional interaction on Nysa though, Cole had little familiarity with al-Cygni. She only knew that the admiral held a longstanding record of getting the job done, no matter the cost. Captain Richards had already informed Cole that al-Cygni would be directing the acquisition of the target from the data extracted from Black-Box, but there was little intel beyond that. How they were going to acquire the asset was need-to-know, and Cole certainly didn't.

"Admiral al-Cygni." Cole saluted the superior officer. "Glad you were able to join us in person."

"Grateful it could happen, Captain," al-Cygni responded with a nod, noticing both Hood and Osman. "Admirals. Commander Agryna informed me that you were finally back in the mix."

"There's a lot in motion," Hood admitted. "We're still catching up."

"I'm sure," al-Cygni said. "Too much is at stake for us to be sitting on our hands. Have you been debriefed?"

"Not fully," Hood said. "But enough to know that it can wait."

"Admiral, who can I *thank* for all of this?" Osman asked al-Cygni in an ironic tone, gesturing around the room. That there was no former knowledge of Nysa and Site Z had clearly and openly gotten under her skin—as CINCONI, revelations like that must have been maddening. Al-Cygni, on the other hand, had been an ONI operative since the Insurrection, back when Cole and Osman were both children.

"The usual suspects, ma'am," al-Cygni said in a measured tone. "When we're finished here, I will get you both up to speed and fully reinstated."

"I would appreciate that very much," Osman said, folding her arms.

Cole didn't waste any more time navigating the subject away from potential infighting in front of their guests. "Shipmaster and Shipmistress: it is good to finally meet you both."

"The pleasure is ours, Captain Cole," the shipmaster said in his deep, booming voice, bowing his neck in respect as he stepped forward. He spoke with remarkable clarity in her own language, evidently having learned it from previous joint operations alongside UNSC forces. "You know Shipmistress Mahkee 'Chava of *Scorrin's Blade*—she assisted Fireteam Osiris against the Covenant. And here are two of my finest warriors: Blademaster Vul 'Soran and the Scion of Rahnelo, Lady Tul 'Juran."

Cole bowed to the Sangheili in response to the salutations, with nods of respectful acknowledgment in return. *So far, so good,* she thought.

"Lord Hood," the shipmaster said, extending his hand by way of human etiquette. "I apologize that the Arbiter is not present.

He has urgent business he is conducting, but doubtless sends his greetings."

"I'm certain," the admiral said with a smile. "I hope everything is well. Last time I was with the Arbiter, it was a bit . . . volatile."

Cole had read the file. *Volatile* was an understatement. Peace talks between the Sangheili and the Jiralhanae had gone terribly wrong, and Hood had been shot during a tense standoff against a Spartan traitor working for the New Colonial Alliance—a group that had recently aligned itself with the Banished. Hood had been lucky to make it out alive, in no small part due to the Arbiter. Events like that were the very reason Cole needed to be confident in their alliance.

"Excuse me—I apologize for having to break up the pleasantries," Cole said. "Shipmaster, you're here because I was advised that we have a shared interest? The Lithos."

"That is correct, Captain," he said, looking at his own warriors. "Our concern is that it could fall into the wrong hands. Particularly those of Dovo Nesto and the Order of Restoration."

"Agreed," Cole responded. "We share this concern. And it will require our cooperation to make sure he doesn't get access to it."

"Sorry." Osman held up her hand. "I've been out of the loop here, so I'm not completely versed on some of the new threats. What exactly is the Order of Restoration, please?"

Al-Cygni exchanged a look with Cole indicating that she would take this one. "It's an underground organization primarily comprising San'Shyuum in hiding who are seeking to restore their people to a place of power in the galaxy. Effectively, they're trying to resurrect the Covenant, albeit without some of the old players."

"That's already been attempted," Osman said flatly, "with less than stellar results."

"If anyone's going to do it successfully, it would be Dovo

Nesto," al-Cygni replied. "He has the strategic acumen, the connections, and the history to make it happen. If he was granted access to the Lithos, then he would lack nothing. Everything Cortana has right now would be his."

"That is unfortunately true." 'Vadum spoke with a chilling certainty. "We have data that suggest he is currently hiding on Sqala—the world you call Venezia."

"*Venezia*?" Cole was legitimately surprised. "Why there?"

"Your guess is as good as ours," the shipmaster responded. "Probably because we would least expect it?"

"I'm actually *not* surprised," Agryna said. "It's where all our own criminals go to drop out of sight."

"Perhaps he views it as a safe place where he can conduct meetings without suspicion," said 'Vadum, "especially with members of Sali 'Nyon's alliance who already frequent that world."

"Wait—Dovo Nesto is working *with* Sali 'Nyon?" Cole asked. "If that's true, it would certainly upgrade his threat level. 'Nyon's been building up his military capabilities on Okal'supen, but a lack of organization kept his activity contained. If he were to join Nesto, that would make the situation significantly *less* manageable."

"Which is why we are requesting access to Venezia in order to apprehend him," the shipmaster said.

"And you will have it," al-Cygni replied quickly. "Just as we agreed. But we'll be accompanying your teams during extraction. Not only to help you accomplish your objective, but to hedge our own interests. If Nesto's been working with others on Venezia, we want to know who they are. And as much as we want this Prophet off the game board, the last thing we need is Cortana to get wind of this, so we'll need to follow our protocols."

"That is all reasonable. How will we carry out the operation?" 'Vadum asked.

"I'll be deploying the teams from *Victory of Samothrace*," Cole said, repeating the orders Richards had already communicated to her. "Your people will be running point with Spartans at their backs."

"Very good," the shipmaster said, clearly pleased. "And once we have Dovo Nesto, we will know where the Lithos is located."

"Your earlier communiqué mentioned that the Lithos is on a *human* world?" al-Cygni asked.

"That is what the captured transmission stated," 'Vadum said. "Which world, however, we do not know. Only that Dovo Nesto intends to go there."

"Then capturing him at this stage is absolutely vital," al-Cygni said, turning to the holotable. "But he's only *part* of the reason we're here."

"Right," Cole replied. "So how do we break into the Domain?" Her eyes went right to al-Cygni. The admiral knew best what needed to be communicated to the Sangheili, and what didn't. Even Cole had limited understanding of the finer details of the operation, so she was happy to leave the explanation to an ONI operative.

"An excellent question," al-Cygni began delicately. "What I'm about to share is highly sensitive information and cannot leave this room under any circumstance. Until recently, the sole functional gateway into the Domain that we knew of was located on Genesis, a world we no longer have access to. What we have now discovered is that there are *other* gateways scattered throughout the galaxy. Of course, they are only accessible to Cortana—her neural pattern is the keycode, making the gateways virtually impenetrable. However, there *is* someone who shares Cortana's exact neural pattern and can give us this same access. And that's precisely why we need Black-Box."

The admiral nodded to Dr. Nabil, and after a few keystrokes, a dark-blue cube flashed into existence at the center of the table. It hovered there for a moment, pivoting back and forth.

"BB," Osman said, her voice cracking.

"Oh my," the AI said with surprise in his voice. "I did not expect to be *here*."

"Do you know where here is, Black-Box?" Nabil asked.

"Surprisingly, no," he said. "But it is certainly not where I thought I would be. Serin, are you okay?"

"Yes, BB," Osman said. "I'm okay. They extracted us from Rossbach's World because they need something from you. Something you have that can stop Cortana."

"Something *I* have? You must be mistaken. I am not aware of anything I possess that can be used *agaaaaaainst herrrrr*." His voice suddenly sounded garbled. "Oh my, that's not *gooood*."

"Vocal degradation," Hood remarked, looking at Osman.

"What date is it?" Black-Box asked. "*Theyyyy've* placed a constraint on me. I cannot tap into the local *networrrrrk*." His voice sounded garbled again.

"It's November 19, 2559," Osman said quietly, with visible tears in her eyes. "BB, I'm so sorry."

"Well," he said, taking time to process the implications. "That *is* unfortunate. Although not unexpected. I *knewwww* that if I was ever reawakened, it would most likely be after my life parameters *haaaaad* expired."

"Black-Box," Cole said. "My name is Captain—"

"I know who you are—Captain *Abigaaaail* Cole," Black-Box said matter-of-factly. "Daughter of Admiral Preston Jeremiah Cole, the *greaaaatest* naval tactician in human history. Or so they *saaaaay*. Would you like me to tell you what . . . actually happened to him?"

The question from out of nowhere stunned Cole. She felt a

piercing sensation in her heart, then shrugged it off. Even if Black-Box knew the truth, she wasn't here to find out the actual fate of her father—she was here to stop Cortana.

"No," she replied. "I want something else from you. Codeword: Charlie Hotel."

Black-Box was rendered totally silent at this.

Moments of inactivity passed, and Cole saw Osman's brow furrowing in frustration. Cole understood how disempowered she must be feeling right now—she'd been out of the fight for a year while the galaxy went to hell, only to be swept back into the middle of it. And now the AI that she seemed to consider a personal friend was deep in the throes of rampancy.

Her patience at an end, Osman demanded: "What did you do to him?!"

"Nothing that can't be reversed, ma'am," Dr. Nabil said.

"Black-Box, give us the solution for Charlie Hotel," Cole continued.

The AI flickered on the holographic field, then spoke: "The solution for Charlie Hotel is *Chloe Eden Hall.* Location: *Mindoro, Cascade.*"

"What does that all mean?" Osman asked.

"It means," Cole said, "that the only surviving clone of Dr. Catherine Halsey is on the planet Cascade, somewhere in its capital city. And her name is apparently Chloe."

"Let's hope she's registered," Agryna said. "Otherwise she'll be a needle in a haystack. Mindoro has a population of over sixteen million people."

Their Sangheili allies remained silent, following the development of this exchange through their translators until they had a practical point to interject or counsel to offer. Their knowledge of the logistics of human colonies and the intricacies of recent history concerning Dr. Halsey, clones, and artificial intelligences was limited—their true utility would come when they got into the thick of the action ahead. Cole could not help but wonder, however, what exactly they made of this mess.

Cole turned to al-Cygni. "Do you have what you need, Admiral?"

"I do. Thank you, Captain." She looked at Hood and Osman. "Admirals, if you'd like to come with me, I would be happy to fill in the gaps for you. Then we'll get you back to Earth."

"What's going to happen to BB?" Osman asked. Seeing Black-Box's current condition seemed to have chipped away at some of her initial hostility toward al-Cygni.

"We'll reactivate him once his matrix is stable," Dr. Nabil said. "But we're going to keep him locked down for obvious reasons. Admiral al-Cygni will bring him with you back to Earth. In the meantime, you'll be able to interact with him in a limited capacity."

"I would like that very much," she said, rising to follow al-Cygni, with Hood just behind her.

Al-Cygni turned to Cole before leaving. "Good luck on Venezia, Captain. I'll inform Richards of your progress and she'll be in touch."

"Affirmative," Cole said. "Good luck with the target." She felt uneasy about saying *Chloe* and putting a name to something far too young to be a target for anything.

Al-Cygni only nodded in response, then again to the Sangheili, and left with the two admirals. Hood flashed Cole a kind smile before disappearing through the door.

She returned the gesture, then squared up to the Sangheili.

"All right, everyone. Let's nail this Prophet to the wall, shall we?"

CHAPTER 12

SEVERAN

Sqala (Venezia)
November 21, 2559

Humans called it Staithe, but to Severan it looked more like a junk heap than any sort of settlement. It was one of only a handful of satellite towns outside of New Tyne, Sqala's main population center. Staithe was relatively small by comparison, despite having grown significantly since the end of the Covenant War.

A large, dry-docked human ship perched atop a steep hill, its prow looming over the edge of a sprawling collection of buildings. They were clustered around the craft, discordantly packed like the nest of some large bird, stretching out for a few kilometers in every direction. The descending afternoon sun cast the ship's long shadow across the buildings below, consisting mostly of shops, warehouses, and private lodgings—all of them crude and primitive, even for humans. An endless collection of cables slung down from the ship into the settlement at different junctures, evidently supplying or siphoning power, though Severan could not tell which.

Outside the town, a fringe of docking sites and tarmacs lined the periphery, most of them littered with vessels of every conceivable kind—human, Covenant, Kig-Yar, Sangheili. He even spotted a few Banished craft. Severan had long wondered how they managed to keep the peace with so many different allegiances and factions together in one place.

Part of it became clear on their approach. A network of Covenant anti-aircraft artillery cannons punctuated the skyline. In some ways, Staithe had more in common with a well-fortified military site than any civilian municipality.

Severan would normally have been concerned about visiting a place so heavily armed, if it were not for the docking codes provided by his *daskalo*. Even without a centralized government, Staithe had at least the pretense of order with security evaluations on landing, and checkpoints at specific intervals going in and out of the city. There was also a perpetual, low-grade trepidation in any place where the air was saturated with so much threat of force, such that any potential disagreement could turn into a full-scale bloodbath. With so many war criminals and fugitives on Sqala, it was very apparent that no one was interested in attracting unwanted attention from the UNSC, or, even worse, the Apparition herself.

After far too much time wasted evading the Apparition's forces as he sought to secure refuge for his clan and their many allies, they had arrived at Sqala, deploying a single Trespasser to the world's surface. Kaevus and Othmald were to accompany him, while his pilot, Suvitas, and two packs of Jiralhanae warriors stayed with the sky raider. If they were needed, he could summon them at will. He had been assured by his *daskalo* that such force was unnecessary.

He believed it to be true.

Nevertheless, some precautions were worthy of entertainment. *Heart of Malice* and an escort of six dreadnoughts were hidden in the shadow of Sqala's moon, ready and waiting for any potential danger. Although the human world had a hostile relationship with Earth, it was not entirely free from the UNSC's reach, nor did anything he now saw make it entirely immune to the ambitions of opportunists and mercenaries. If any threat was posed to his effort, he would be ready to immediately strike or extract—whichever was most expedient.

Severan led his two captains down the tarmac to an entry gate, where his security clearance once again proved effective. Two humans and a Kig-Yar held the checkpoint, while a group of Unggoy had just finished refueling a Spirit dropship and begun loading freight onto a commercial Pelican. Even though all three in Severan's group carried manglers, and Kaevus a shock rifle, no one gave him or his captains any notice. It was, apparently, business as usual for Sqala.

"Very strange," Othmald said under his breath as they continued toward the city entrance. "So many unlikely allies."

"I agree," Severan replied, looking back at the sight over his shoulder. "But they may not be allies at all. That is what makes this place so bizarre. With the Covenant, there was order ingrained into its structure through a unified faith, and in the Banished it is allegiance to Atriox, but the denizens of Sqala are nothing like either of those. Yet somehow—"

Kaevus held one arm over Severan's chest, reaching for his mangler with the other.

The three stopped.

"What do you see?" Severan asked.

Before them was a crowd gathered at the city's nearest entrance. It was a market of some kind, and those who bought and sold were varied in species and in faction, at least sixty of them. Whatever Kaevus had spotted, it had to be significant, given his response.

"The Sangheili. Dark-red armor, on the left side of the Spectre," Kaevus said. "Does he look familiar to you?"

Severan assessed the scene near the Covenant vehicle, but it did not take long to see what Kaevus was concerned about. The Sangheili was heavily armed and had an entourage of eight others with him, all bearing the familiar armor of the Covenant, with markings that connected them to a powerful emerging sect.

"Sali 'Nyon."

"This is a long way from Okal'supen," Othmald said. "What is *he* doing here?"

The concern was justified, but it would have to be set aside.

Sali 'Nyon's sect was something of a rival to the Banished, one of many efforts to re-create the Covenant empire, and 'Nyon claimed to be their rightful leader. What made his presence on Sqala strange was that he would not deign to come near humans unless there was a very good reason, for he *despised* them. And the only thing he hated more than humans was probably Severan, whose father Tartarus he blamed for the fall of the Covenant. There was little doubt that 'Nyon would delight in spilling the war chief's blood if given the opportunity.

Severan's forearms tightened beneath his armored vambraces almost instinctively. At a moment's notice, he could extend curved energy blades from both, each a meter long and capable of inflicting extraordinary damage on an opponent. It was his favored weapon of combat, but one he had not needed to employ for many lunar cycles, given his current position. The sight of 'Nyon made him wonder if he should make an exception—then again, they did not have time to play games with children.

"Ignore him," Severan said, lowering Kaevus's arm. "If I must stop and fight every time I see someone who wants me dead, I would never get anywhere."

Othmald let out a gruff laugh.

"Very true, and very wise," Kaevus said, releasing his hold on his mangler and continuing forward.

After passing through the market unnoticed, Severan followed the directions given to them, navigating a network of roads and alleyways to the city's center, just below the prow of the human ship. As they pressed deeper, he noticed that the walkways became more crowded and constricted, with hardly enough room to drive even a single Ghost through. It meant little in the moment, but Severan could tell that both of his captains were working through solutions for extraction if it came to that. He understood why—their job was to protect him, so they needed to be thinking of his safety even when he was not.

The city smelled and sounded unpleasant, and Severan wondered why his *daskalo* had chosen such a forsaken place. Although their relationship had been formed during the time of the Covenant and developed within the opulence and security of High Charity, the last time he had spoken to his mentor in person was on Feldokra, one of the Covenant's fortress worlds. Known as Faithful Perseverance by all who still walked the Path, the world had since been raided by scavengers willing to risk its hostile environment and recover its treasures. His *daskalo* had formerly held a citadel there and maintained it for years after the Covenant's fall while its power reserves still functioned.

That was over two years ago and those reserves had long since been exhausted. From that time on, all communications had been remote, and Severan had only recently learned that his *daskalo* had relocated here to Sqala, desiring the secrecy and protection it could provide. It was a far cry from High Charity or Faithful Perseverance, but Severan trusted his mentor's judgment.

After almost twenty centals, they finally reached their destination: a series of stone hovels at the base of a hill, with a canted roof made of clay tiles. They appeared to be part of a larger collection of buildings that ran up along the hill, some three or four levels tall. Above them, the vast shape of the human ship overshadowed the road, its prow stretching out behind them toward the tarmac and their sky raider. The center hovel had a single door with two Kig-Yar standing guard on either side, both bearing pulse carbines. They were T'vaoan, a large, bulky, avian variant of the species, boasting birdlike plumage and short beaks, clad in a mishmash of armor that did not suggest any one faction. Above the door was a familiar sigil: the ornate mantle of the hierarchs.

"Is this the place?" Kaevus asked.

"Yes, according to the directions," Severan said. "And it has his marking."

"Peculiar choice in guards," Othmald noted, eyeing the Kig-Yar.

"Indeed. Nevertheless," Severan replied, continuing forward undeterred.

As they approached, one of the Kig-Yar stepped forward, raising his hand.

"State your business," the guard screeched in an old Sangheili dialect. The other Kig-Yar lifted his pulse carbine ever so slightly. Kaevus responded by casually letting his hand drop to his mangler.

"I am Severan of the Vanguard of Zaladon," he replied. "I am here to meet—"

"Yes," the Kig-Yar interrupted. "Have been expecting you. Come this way."

The small door behind the Kig-Yar flashed open and he disappeared into the darkness beyond it. Othmald turned to Severan with a look. It was certainly a bizarre combination, the location itself *and* the security detail, but Severan had learned long ago that his *daskalo* had many eccentricities. This was no different.

The three Jiralhanae walked through the door single-file and found themselves in a dimly lit corridor that penetrated far deeper into the building than Severan would have thought possible, with occasional doors appearing on either side. Eventually they reached an intersection with a path leading to narrow stairs, which the Kig-Yar began to climb. Severan now realized that the hovels outside were a mere illusion—the structure's interior was far more expansive than its entrance conveyed.

Ascending the stairs, they passed several small windows on their left, allowing Severan to reorient himself. From this position, he could tell he was climbing farther up the hill and deeper into it. After some time they came to a wall composed entirely of the battleplate from a human ship with a lift well recessed into it. Another pair of Kig-Yar guards stood here, but when they spotted their fellow, they moved to the side. Stepping onto the lift, their Kig-Yar guide silently beckoned for them to enter and began keying a plate on the inside wall. The lift suddenly jerked upward, and Severan realized where they were.

They were now *inside* the large human ship dominating Staithe's skyline. The building they had initially entered must have been built around the vessel's outer hull, creating an almost seamless link between the two. It would have been a fascinating architectural design to study further, had Severan not been disgusted by this entire world, even more so the city.

When their lift stopped, it opened to the short, well-lit corridor of a human ship leading to a pair of double doors directly ahead, also posted by two guards. These, though, were Sangheili. The warriors' eyes narrowed at the sight of the Jiralhanae, their mandibles almost imperceptibly tightening. They were older Sangheili, but both looked formidable.

Severan thought they might be former members of the

Covenant's Honor Guard, but he could not be sure. They certainly lacked the sacred crimson-gold armor of that former rank, clad in standard combat harnesses and holding deactivated plasma glaives. For many ages, the Prophets had selected their own defenders from among the Sangheili—the greatest and most skilled warriors became bodyguards of the San'Shyuum leaders. In the final days of the Covenant, however, the Prophet of Truth had overturned this policy, appointing Jiralhanae in their place, the very act that had incited the Great Schism and brought about the end of the Covenant itself.

And Severan's father had led that revolution.

The two Sangheili stood completely still, acting as if they were manifestly unconcerned by the approaching Banished Jiralhanae, though Severan knew better. The Kig-Yar walked right to the door, which opened on its own, leading into what appeared to be the ship's bridge overlooking the prow of the vessel. Natural light flooded through the viewport, while the interior contained a smattering of various displays and control panels. Some seemed active and functional, but most were not. Command consoles were nestled along every wall and clustered near the large, spanning viewport, with a single chair at the center, positioned before a holotable. The room was entirely empty save for the chair and his *daskalo* who sat in it.

Dovo Nesto.

"High Lord," Severan said, taking a knee before him. His captains followed suit. "It is good to see you in the flesh and to know that you are well."

"Severan," his *daskalo* said with a grin, swiveling the chair to face them. "My son." He raised his hand toward the Kig-Yar. "Leave us." The door closed after the guards had departed.

The lithe San'Shyuum carefully stood and walked gracefully

toward Severan, placing his hands on his pauldrons and kissing his forehead.

"It has been far too long," he said, stepping back to appraise him. "Stand for me."

Severan and the other Jiralhanae rose with deference. They were nearly a full meter taller than the San'Shyuum, dwarfing his diminutive and slight constitution.

"Amazing," he said, examining Severan's armor. "You very much look the part of a Banished war chief."

"And I am more than that, *daskalo*," Severan said with a grin, but he felt even his elation suddenly subside with the horrific memory of Doisac and her moons. "Much has happened since we last talked, High Lord. I need your wisdom. Now more than ever."

The San'Shyuum, like the others of his species, was pale and thin, with a large head and narrow, weak limbs. He wore a dark-green cloak that hung heavy on his body—his large, bright, piercing eyes shone beneath his hood, lightly graying wattles hanging from his face like a beard. Despite his slender frame, the high lord carried an air of nobility that gave his presence weight.

And although most San'Shyuum adults were confined to mobility apparatuses because they were too weak to walk, his *daskalo* was just as Severan remembered from the first time they'd met two decades earlier. Dovo Nesto was no warrior, but he possessed an unnatural resilience and never aged like the rest of his contemporaries. He claimed that his eternal youth had been granted to him long ago by the gods, during the time of the Covenant's formation. As miraculous as it seemed, Severan had no reason to doubt what he could clearly see with his own eyes.

A high lord of the oldest order within the Covenant, Dovo Nesto was the greatest and most powerful San'Shyuum to have survived the fall of High Charity and the destruction of the empire. And in its wake, he had consolidated whatever remained of the San'Shyuum's influence into the Order of Restoration, carefully making preparations for the Covenant to rise again. Many had attempted to unite the empire's former species under different banners, but all of these had failed. Only Dovo Nesto had the strength and wisdom to make such a dream reality. His knowledge of the ways of the galaxy was unrivaled—and above all, Dovo Nesto spoke for the gods.

He was the last of the true Prophets.

And it was because of this that Severan had never faltered in his devotion to the high lord. Not even once.

"Please, walk with me, Severan," Nesto said, ushering him to a side corridor.

Severan nodded to his captains to stay, and both begrudgingly obeyed.

The corridor through which the high lord led him moved alongside the ship's exterior, wending past a collection of viewports that overlooked Staithe. Shadows were growing long as the day quickly came to a close.

"Do tell me, High Lord," Severan said, staring down at the town below. "Why here, on Sqala?"

"Because no one pays this place any regard. Not even the humans who live here. When my time on Faithful Perseverance came to an end, I could have openly assaulted one of our opponents and seized their stronghold, but I chose solitude. Better that our enemies remain in the dark until everything is in order. The gods require patience." He looked keenly at Severan. "And they reward it. Do you disagree with this?"

"I would not question your wisdom. I only care for your safety."

Nesto laid his hand on the Jiralhanae's shoulder.

"I know that you do, my son," he responded. "In truth, the gods could not have prepared a more advantageous location if they had orchestrated it by their own hands. On this world, all those under my command may come and go as they please. And the humans who might be suspicious are easily bought. While we continue to amass starships and weapons on outer worlds, we can still coordinate everything from here, right under the nose of our greatest enemy. And it is only a matter of time before the veil is finally removed and we return to our former position, even stronger than before."

"Indeed," Severan rumbled as he watched vessels arriving on the outskirts of the settlement. "I long for that day to be here."

"It will be time soon enough," Nesto said, stopping his walk and turning to face Severan. "Now, my child, what is it that brings you here in the first place?"

Severan looked intently at his *daskalo*, fighting to keep composure.

"Doisac . . . has been destroyed," Severan said, trembling with anger. "The moons, my people . . . they are gone. It was the Apparition."

The high lord stared long at Severan before once again placing his hand on his pauldron.

"My heart breaks for you, my son," Nesto said, light shining in his eyes. Though Severan felt his *daskalo*'s compassion, a small part of him could not help but wonder if Nesto already knew what had happened—so like an all-seeing god as he had always seemed. No doubt, word of the Apparition's dire actions had spread to Jiralhanae across many other worlds by now. "This is, by far, the greatest sin that false god has committed. She *will* pay for what she has done."

"It has incited Atriox. He is now securing a weapon capable of obliterating all the Apparition's defenses. Nothing she has will be able to stand against him."

Nesto's eyes narrowed; then he turned away. "Perhaps," he said. "It is impossible to say for certain. You mentioned in our last conversation that the humans also seek to dethrone the AI."

"Atriox will move against them as well," Severan noted. "As you foresaw, High Lord, he is eager to consolidate his power. He will strike against both the Apparition and the humans, and he has entrusted me with all Banished fleets that remain behind. War Chief Escharum's orders . . . are for me to raze Earth."

"Earth?" Nesto asked, seemingly surprised at the revelation, though Severan could not know for sure.

"Yes," Severan replied. "This is why I am here. I must admit that I desire revenge more than any other. The humans *must* pay for this atrocity. But I question the timing, and I wonder what may come about if the Apparition attempts to intrude. I seek your wisdom, High Lord."

Nesto was silent for a few moments, then said: "Apart from the AI, the humans would be defenseless." He absentmindedly tugged at the wattles that hung from his chin. "Most of their forces are already in hiding. . . . And you say that Atriox has given you *all* of his remaining fleets?"

"Yes. The allegiance of over two hundred clans. Over a thousand ships in total."

"Remarkable," Nesto said with a smile. "He must now see in you what I always have."

Severan bowed his head in humility.

He had first met Dovo Nesto as a young warrior within the Covenant, ten years after the first encounter with humanity on the planet Harvest—that was during the early days of his father's rise to power at the side of the Prophet of Truth. While Tartarus was attempting to lay claim to the title of Chieftain of all Jiralhanae in the eyes of the hierarchs, Nesto had taken an interest in Severan. During Severan's most formative years, the high lord had paid more attention to him than his own father had. Severan came to call Dovo Nesto his own *daskalo*, and had remained loyal to the San'Shyuum since that first day.

While he had never held the position of hierarch, Nesto was in many ways a shadow master of the Covenant, governing the purposes of the High Council and even exploiting many former Prophets through countless divinatory maneuverings. He claimed that he had done such since the very dawn of the empire, thousands of years ago. This revelation had shocked Severan into awe, for he was surely the oldest living being in this galaxy, but the high lord had never divulged the secret of his longevity—whether it was the will of the gods or something else entirely.

What Severan *did* know, however, was that the high lord's will was never denied. Never did he fail to accomplish his purpose. Dovo Nesto had been in many respects without rival, operating silently from within the hallowed corridors of the old Forerunner Dreadnought moored at the center of High Charity. And here the San'Shyuum still stood, not only after untold ages of the Covenant, but in the aftermath of the very empire itself.

None were like him. If anyone could resurrect the Covenant to its former glory, it was the high lord who had claimed to have been there from the beginning.

And he had promised Severan a place as his right hand, appointed as an instrumental part in the Covenant's restoration. First, Severan was to build up the clan of Zaladon, drawing into his fold both allies and rivals—and this he had accomplished with little difficulty. And through his kin, Choros, he had even found a place among the Banished, which both he and Nesto would use to their advantage when the time came. While Nesto had many who pledged their allegiance, he had nonetheless always remained loyal to Severan and his Jiralhanae, and promised them their rightful place at the head of the Covenant's military power. When the flame of the Covenant began to rise from the ashes once more, this time never again to be extinguished, it would be Severan at its head, leading its military side by side with his *daskalo*.

Nesto's voice rent Severan free from his ruminations.

"Very well. You must rally all of the forces in your charge and prepare to strike Earth." This was stated with certainty, as he turned to a large viewport taking up the entire bulkhead. Lights were coming alive within the town as the sun sank below the horizon. "But you will not stop with Earth."

"Pardon me, High Lord?" Severan questioned.

"There is another world. And it holds something far more precious than the satisfaction of revenge, however justified. Something that will serve our efforts to restore the glory of the Covenant and allow us to eradicate all humanity—not merely a single world."

"What could that possibly be?"

"It is called the Lithos," Nesto said, his large eyes shining bright as he turned toward Severan. "It is a Forerunner doorway that leads to the very power Cortana presently possesses. The gods once called this power 'the Domain,' an ancient and invisible dimension that has given the human construct unfettered access to all they once possessed: machines of war, shield worlds, weapons capable of unparalleled destruction, even one of the Sacred Rings. As you have now witnessed firsthand. At this moment, a handful of humans and Sangheili are plotting to infiltrate the Lithos in order to take that same power from the AI. We cannot allow that. This power belongs to the faithful alone. It belongs to those worthy to wield it. It belongs to the Covenant."

Severan stared at the high lord, taken aback by this news.

If what Dovo Nesto said was true, then this Lithos was the key to everything. It would provide the Covenant they were rebuilding with the technological power necessary to reign and eliminate any threats attempting to stand against them. But if another possessed it, the revived Covenant they had so long dreamed of would never be. Whoever possessed the Domain had the blessing of the Forerunners and the authority that came with it.

"Fear not," Nesto said, folding his hands together. "I know something the humans do not. I know *where* the Lithos is hidden. But in order to access it—to bypass the AI's existing defenses—a human is needed. A child, in fact. The surviving clone of the AI's creator. The humans are searching for her now. Once they have this young female, they will move to take the Lithos. But since they cannot interpret the prophecies, they do not know where it is."

"Then we must not let them discover it," Severan said.

Nesto responded only with a grin.

An alarm suddenly shot through the human warship, and in the corridor appeared Kaevus and one of the Sangheili guards with weapons raised. Their eyes searched for threats.

The Sangheili spoke first. "There has been a breach. They're attempting to penetrate the ship. Humans and Sangheili together. *Demons*, even."

Spartans. If it truly was the demons, then the attack was from the UNSC and they were most certainly coming for the high lord. They sought the location of the Lithos.

The sound of weapons fire reverberated through the ship.

They were close. Very close.

"We must leave Sqala now, High Lord," Severan said with urgency, grabbing the San'Shyuum's arm. "And by the gods, you are coming with us."

CHAPTER 13

JAMES SOLOMON

Far Isle
November 21, 2559

"Never seen anyone hold their liquor like you," the old man behind the bar said.

He always noted this at about the sixth glass of bourbon, when Solomon's vision began to blur.

Given the kind of drinking Solomon preferred—whatever was necessary to drown out thoughts about who he was and what he'd become—his biological augmentations were a bit of an impediment. His body was able to resist the effects of alcohol far past the normal human levels of tolerance. For Solomon, this wasn't a gift, but a curse. He just wanted to forget it all, but his own body wouldn't let him.

He took another sip, ignoring the bartender.

They were the only ones here.

It was a small pub on the dock of a sea harbor largely inactive most of the year. Isolation and a poor choice in aesthetics by its owners meant that this place never had any more than a dozen or so people at once. It might also have something to do with its location on Far Isle, the site of a UNSC nuclear strike against rebel factions toward the end of the last century. The fallout from the attack had cleared decades ago, allowing the colony to be resettled in certain locations. Few, however, had returned, and among those who did, St. Anino was the least populous of all its townships. It was the perfect place for Solomon to hide—far from everyone and everything.

For his first few months, he'd chosen to lie low and not interact with anyone. But after contracts started coming in, one piling onto another, he slowly grew to frequent this place. The gray area Solomon now navigated was different than anything he'd done in the past, even from the complex lanes as a Spartan operative. The jobs he now took required a margin of deniability.

That meant he often dealt with the worst of all possible scenarios.

He wondered again if the slaves back on Terceira had been rescued by another ONI team.

Probably not.

He couldn't do this anymore. Something had to change. He was just another piece on the game board—neutralizing, subverting, and erasing other pieces—so that ONI could do whatever they wanted with impunity.

And it was eroding his soul.

ONI had always held a clear vision of order in the galaxy, and for a time, Solomon had believed in it. He still *wanted* to believe in it. But he knew the truth: their goals came at a high cost that often meant people died, sometimes innocents. He also knew that if he didn't stop soon, there'd be nothing left of him willing to fight. This kind of life couldn't continue forever.

A light flashed in the mirror lining the back of the bar and he turned to see three armigers roaming the dock, just outside the pub's front window. Their bipedal robotic forms had precise, mechanical movements as they scanned the immediate vicinity. Over eight feet tall with disconnected limbs and patterns of fiery-looking hard light, each had a cold, grim expression shaped by what could be described as a "face," and their polished alloy skin reflected the dim surrounding light in shifting ways. They were carrying light rifles and suppressors, Forerunner weapons that easily outclassed anything the locals possessed.

"When did *they* get here?" Solomon asked.

"This is the first I've seen of them," the bartender responded. "What the hell would Cortana want with St. Anino?"

It was a great question.

The armigers passed out of view without incident, but it forced Solomon to set his glass down and begin to think.

Far Isle was infinitesimal on the galactic scale and St. Anino was a practically invisible settlement. So why would Cortana deploy forces here? What could they possibly be after?

The pub door suddenly slid open and a figure walked in. Not an armiger—a man. Solomon took a sip, staring at him in the mirror behind the bar. For a moment, his body remained deep in the shadows. But then he stepped into view and his identity became clear.

Octavio Morales.

One of the highest operatives within ONI, and also one of the oldest.

Actually, Solomon thought, *I'd rather deal with the armigers. . . .*

Morales had long ago been part of ORION, a precursor to the SPARTAN-II program. Now he pushed papers behind a desk, but the kind of paperwork that rewrote human history. Although very few even knew of his existence, this man's decisions dictated much of what the UNSC did at any given time, even exceeding the view and reach of ONI's head.

Solomon was one of only a handful of contractors who personally knew Morales. For some reason, the man claimed he'd seen something in Solomon that reminded him of himself, and a bond had formed. Seemingly that was all it had taken for Solomon to be working ONI's operation blacklist and not redeploying as a Spartan.

These days, part of Solomon wished the man had simply let him die in the skies over Reach.

Morales approached the bar and ordered a scotch. The bartender poured it with wary eyes, then disappeared into the back. "How are you, Jim?" he said, glancing in Solomon's direction.

"Tired."

"Aren't we all." Morales grinned, taking a swig and rolling the liquor on his tongue.

The armigers passed by again outside, now going the other way. Still assessing the area, weapons at the ready.

"Friends of yours?" Solomon asked.

"I was going to ask you the same thing," Morales said, his eyes carefully tracking the machines as they slipped out of view. "They were here when I arrived."

"So, why are you here exactly? Been a few years since I last saw you."

"I have a job for you."

"And what, you're personally delivering them now? Is Waypoint down or something?"

"This would be the most important job we've ever given you," Morales said, his face now humorless.

"Heh. Well, I'm actually glad you're here in person," Solomon said. "Because I would like to submit my resignation."

"What the hell are you talking about?" Morales asked, taking another sip.

"Octavio, I can't play these games anymore. I'm done. Terceira was the last one."

"So you want to walk away from all this, Jim?" Morales pushed back from the bar. "You've got everything you need, everything you've ever wanted. No red tape, no complications, no rules. You're doing what you were made to do."

"And I'm *tired* of doing what I was made to do. You need to find someone else."

"Well, that's just it—we *can't* just find someone else. You're the best we have, Jim. And we need you. Billions of lives are counting on you over what comes next."

"Uh-huh. Same as it ever was. Listen, I appreciate you coming all the way out here to make whatever offer this is, Octavio. I do. It's truly flattering. But I'm done, with all of it. Thanks for the jobs, thanks for the money, but I'm going to finish my drink and then slip out of this system, and you'll never see or hear from me again. I can promise you that."

Morales stared at Solomon for a long moment before taking another sip.

"Okay? So . . . whatever you saw in me after the war," Solomon said, his mind a mixture of bourbon and the past. "Whatever that was, it's *gone.* It left a long time ago. Again, I appreciate the opportunity, but I'm done."

Morales now set down his drink and didn't say anything for a full minute.

The armigers passed again. Their pace had quickened. One of them stared into the pub as they walked by. Solomon thought they might come inside, but they continued on just as earlier.

"And what about Cortana?" Morales asked.

"Yeah, what *about* Cortana? Not my problem."

"*She* can find you, and don't think we can't either. But for the moment . . . *you* might be the reason they're here."

Solomon wondered if Morales was right, although he wasn't certain why he'd be a target. After all, Cortana hadn't done anything about those slave ships, which meant that either she hadn't known about their operation—in which case her reach wasn't quite as infinite as many people thought—or she didn't care.

It didn't matter. He'd be gone by morning.

"I know what you're thinking, Jim," Morales said. "But there's no pit deep enough where she can't find you. I mean it. You're in St. Anino, for crying out loud. Most charts don't even have this place tagged, yet here her soldiers are. Maybe you didn't cover your tracks so well on Terceira."

Solomon stood up and turned to Morales.

"If I can't find a pit, Octavio," he said, downing the last of his drink, "I'll make one. And I assure you it will be deep enough so that *no one* will ever find me. Including the blue lady."

"What if I told you that this job I'm offering is a solution to her? And as a bonus, you get your wish and it's the last job you ever do for us? Once you've finished it, I will personally guarantee that we don't ask you for anything else ever again. Hell, we'll even find you that pit and pay first month's rent."

Solomon looked at Morales for a while before he spoke. "What do you mean, *solution*?"

"You'll need further briefing, but long story short, there's a ten-year-old girl by the name of Chloe Eden Hall hidden somewhere on Cascade, probably Mindoro." Morales's eyes grew more intense. "She's the key to taking down Cortana. She's the key to *everything*, as a matter of fact. We need to get her to a specific Forerunner site."

"Where would that be?"

"I'm going to say, we don't know yet." Morales shrugged. "But I promise you we'll know very soon. And when we have that intel, your job is to simply deliver her to that designated Forerunner site. We'll have a team there waiting to receive her."

"And then what happens to the girl?"

The pub's main entrance slid open and the armigers moved inside.

"Stand back from the bar," one of them said, its croaking voice cold and robotic. "Place your hands above your heads."

Morales smiled as he stepped back, while the bartender came out from behind a wall, his hands up and a terrified look on his face. Solomon slowly turned to face the trio. They were standard Forerunner soldiers, but nothing special. He'd never had to fight one before, but there was a first time for everything.

"Are you three the only occupants in this building?" the armiger asked.

Before the bartender could respond, a tungsten carbide knife plunged through the cerebral cortex of the lead armiger. As its mechanical body immediately went limp and fell to the ground, Solomon followed up with a secondary attack, pulling a concealed magnum from his back and firing two rounds apiece into both the second and third soldiers. The entire length of time was less than three seconds. The metallic alloy that formed the armigers' bodies began to disintegrate into bright yellow embers, quickly disappearing into the air.

Solomon holstered his sidearm and retrieved his blade from the ground, wiping away flecks of heated metal on his sleeve. The bartender was quivering somewhere beyond the bar as what remained of the enemies completely vanished.

Solomon turned back to Morales. "They always do that?" he asked.

Morales was finishing his drink as if no intrusion had just occurred. "Yeah. And more are probably on the way. I'm sure they just want to ask you some questions. . . ."

Solomon leaned on the bar, looking intently at Morales. If he hadn't known better, he would have thought this was part of ONI's ploy. A good deed and a job well done had somehow painted a target on his back.

"Damn it," he finally said, sighing. "I mean it, Octavio. This is the *last one*. After this, I'm done."

"Okay."

"And I'm taking you up on finding that pit. And the first month's rent as well."

"Deal."

CHAPTER 14

TUL 'JURAN

Sqala (Venezia)
November 21, 2559

The smell of this massive human ship above Sqala was barely tolerable to Tul 'Juran.

Her strike team had already worked their way through the town's congested streets and penetrated the network of structures at the foot of the hill, scaling into the dry-docked vessel that ONI had designated as Dovo Nesto's location.

How they knew all of that information, she did not ask. Nor did she care. All that mattered was that they eliminate the San'Shyuum.

When they had first arrived on Sqala, the target site had seemed only minimally protected. That was merely a ruse. A large crowd of opposition was now converging on their position—Sangheili, Jiralhanae, Kig-Yar, even Unggoy—all of them well-armed and ready for a protracted fight. Her team had found their way into an access point in the ship's undercarriage, twenty meters above the ground where their enemies were amassing.

"Excellent," the demon called Jai-006 noted in a flat tone, glancing down at the mounting threat.

'Juran did not know what he meant, because the situation was certainly *not* a good thing. She wondered if the translation software feeding her native-link had somehow malfunctioned. Just another problem adding to her escalating irritation over this entire operation.

The scion had been paired with three veteran Spartans who went by the name Gray Team, while 'Soran and Stolt were working alongside a handful of newer Spartans. She could barely tell the difference between any of them. They all looked foolishly overdressed in their strange armor. Nevertheless, the fact that the shipmaster saw fit to place her with experienced human fighters made her wonder, yet again, if he did not trust her. She was more than capable of completing this operation on her own. She did not need to be watched over like a hatchling, especially by *nishum* who fought from behind masks and protective bodysuits.

"*Excellent*?" she asked, grinding her mandibles.

"It's sarcasm," Adriana-111 responded, with 'Juran's own reflection staring back at her in the female's visor. She did not know the word and neither did the translation software. Perhaps there was no Sangheili equivalent. She would not waste any more time trying to find out.

"Blademaster and Ranger," she said through her native-link, "enemies are gathering below the ship's undercarriage."

"We can see that, Scion," 'Soran responded. *"What exactly did you do?"*

The blademaster and the Unggoy ranger were at different locations on the perimeter of the town, tracking her team's work from a distance. Given the artillery defenses of Staithe and their desire to avoid attracting unwanted attention—especially from Cortana—they would have no air or orbital support on this mission. It was only the three strike teams and the dropships that would extract them. From their positions, the other teams could assess and coordinate as necessary, ensuring that the San'Shyuum did not slip away. The data Dovo Nesto held meant that their goal was to capture, not kill, which required a kind of finesse that Tul 'Juran did not prefer.

The enemies below opened fire at last, a fusillade of plasma and bullets pelting the ship's battleplate, much of it finding its way into the ventral loading bay where her team was located.

"I did *nothing*," she groaned back to the blademaster, unleashing her own plasma rifle at a Kig-Yar who peeked too far out from behind a barrier. One bolt connected with his head, dropping him in a flash of charred brain matter. "As soon as we entered the ship, these others appeared below. No one has approached us from within."

"What are you suggesting, Scion?" Stolt asked.

She could hardly hear the Unggoy over the cacophony of weapons fire. They had paused in the ship's loading bay as the scene below needed to be assessed, but now their current position was becoming more precarious than blindly pushing forward. It had become obvious to both her and the Spartans that something was very wrong about this entire situation.

"Two things," she replied. "First, they knew we were coming. And second, they want us to continue deeper into the ship."

It was the only explanation for why their foes were not coming up after them.

"You are saying this was a trap*?"* 'Soran said, incredulous.

"No. Only that they knew this was a possibility and had a response already prepared. If they want us to continue farther into the ship, it is for a reason."

"I agree with her assessment," Jai-006 said, pumping a burst of battle rifle rounds at the enemy. "These jokers came out of the woodwork only *after* we breached the ship. They were on call."

"Do you need assistance, then?" 'Soran asked.

"No. We're telling you so that you can cut off the San'Shyuum's escape. He's not going to head this way to leave. If he did, he would risk being cut down by his own forces." Jai's response was far too calm for 'Juran's liking.

"Then which way—" Stolt broke off. *"Wait a moment. I think I know."*

"What is it?" 'Juran asked.

"There is a sky raider lifting up on the opposite side of the town," he said. *"A Banished Trespasser, from what I can tell. It is moving* toward *the ship."*

"Did you say *Banished*?" Michael-120 asked.

"Correct. They may intend to extract him directly from the ship."

"If that is the case," 'Soran said, *"then you must delay no further. He cannot leave this planet. If we miss this opportunity, we may not have another chance."*

"Understood," 'Juran replied; she and the Spartans were already in motion. "He will not get away this time."

The four charged through the loading bay and through a single doorway, moving like water tunneling through a creek bed. Adriana had been closest to their target, so she led the way. 'Juran was fine with this—the human knew more about her species' vessels than the scion did, so it would be foolish for a Sangheili to be in the lead.

"Remember," 'Soran spoke in a commanding tone, *"we need him alive."*

'Juran did not respond. She was not a hatchling who needed her hand held and she hoped her silence conveyed this. As much as she wanted Nesto dead, she knew there was much more at stake. He might be extensively damaged when she finally delivered him, but he would still be alive.

The three Spartans moved with a powerful fluidity, like a single machine rather than three individuals, and she soon found herself struggling to keep up with them. They had not yet reached any opposition within the ship, but she knew that would not last forever.

"Do you know where he is located?" she asked on her team's closed channel.

"There's only one shuttle platform on this vessel. Starboard side," Adriana said, in a dead run but with no strain in her voice. "It's for the ship's commander, which seems to fit our target's MO. My armor has a schematic and is guiding me."

That explained her preternatural ability to rapidly navigate the ship's interior. 'Juran would be impressed when the Spartan could do that without the help of her armor. Nevertheless, it was fortuitous in their current circumstance.

She briefly wondered what "em-oh" meant as she ran.

"You see that?" Jai said through the comms. "Contacts."

'Juran could see nothing but knew it must be their armor yet again.

"Called it," Adriana said, launching around a corner. "They're blocking the command shuttle platform. Target must still be in range."

Within seconds, 'Juran could see what Gray Team was noting: Sangheili and Kig-Yar, a dozen of them embedded at an intersection, with clear lines of fire on the four of them.

The Spartans did not take cover.

They did not slow down.

In fact, it seemed to 'Juran that they accelerated, running headlong into a wave of plasma bolts. Their shields lit up as they took fire, but they continued without wavering, unloading their own weapons into the battle line and bringing down half the enemy's number before the trio even reached the intersection.

'Juran lunged toward the nearest Sangheili, activating her energy lance right as the haft made contact with her opponent's chest. The blade immediately punched through his armor and rib cage, the force of her attack impaling him against the bulkhead. His body hung there until she deactivated the blade, then swung the other end toward a Kig-Yar, removing his head in a single motion. Another Kig-Yar raised a plasma pistol, but his arm and weapon were already falling to the floor in a stream of light before he even realized he had been struck. His head shot back as her other blade slammed into him with crushing force.

The scion moved to strike another enemy but realized that she was currently the only thing alive in the room. The Spartans had dispatched the others and were already sprinting down another corridor.

"You coming, Team Leader?" Jai said.

'Juran sighed and launched down the hallway after them.

She had been informed that this one was the actual leader of Gray Team. The scion was uncertain how he felt about a Sangheili giving the orders, much less a female, but he showed no signs of caring one way or the other. Given their present actions, she pondered if they saw her role as a mere political formality.

"The Trespasser is getting close to starboard," Stolt said over the comms. *"My team is moving back to our dropship to cut him off, but if he gets into the air, it is going to be hard to take him alive."*

"We must *take him alive,"* 'Soran said. *"The data he has is what we are after. Scion, do you need assistance?"*

"We are approaching his exit now," she said, banking around the last corner.

"Contacts again," Adriana said. "Looks like they're setting up shop on the platform."

The corridor spilled out on a small loading bay stretching out over the starboard side of the vessel; 'Juran could see the Trespasser quickly approaching from the settlement's outskirts. A Trespasser was roughly the length of a Phantom dropship, though its profile was much thinner to account for heavier armor plating and a complement of six twin heavy plasma cannons—two sets protecting the transparent command cabin while the other four were mounted at the rear on either side of its deployment bay to provide covering fire for disembarking troops.

Within the bay were at least twenty enemies, mostly Sangheili and Kig-Yar. Three, however, were Jiralhanae.

Banished Jiralhanae.

And they were the ones escorting Dovo Nesto.

"I got this," Michael stated in mid-run, reaching to his back for two spherical explosives. He bounded around his fellow Spartans with a dexterity that was astonishing to 'Juran, executing an underhand lob that sent the explosives clattering into a roll across the floor and directly at the forward-most fortification. A series of loud flashes followed, the detonation heaving the enemies' bodies upward before dropping lifeless to the deck.

The Spartans then collided head-on with whoever was still standing, trading blows at an extraordinary speed. They were so finely tuned in their coordination, playing off one another as they leveled enemy after enemy, that they often became an indistinguishable blur of armor. 'Juran bypassed them all, however, sprinting out onto the platform after Nesto.

Two of the Banished Jiralhanae, captains by their armor, turned to face her as the elongated chassis of the red-armored Trespasser began to touch down.

She swung her leg hard at the nearest one, planting her boot squarely in his chest. The captain slid back, but held his ground, grabbing her leg and twisting it until she fell. His fist came down hard, but she spun out from underneath him at the last moment and it slammed into the deck. Swinging her lance, 'Juran struck upward and managed to knock the first captain down, but not before the other landed a blow directly to her face. The impact dropped her back to the floor, causing the corners of her vision to grow dark. Sensing an attack, she rolled backward as the other captain lunged at her with his mangler bayonet. The original one was busy retrieving a shock rifle from his back and taking aim. She tried to stand up and defend herself, but—

"Pardon me, ma'am," Adriana said nonchalantly, weaving around the scion with a combat knife drawn. The blade sank deep into the attacking Jiralhanae's throat, the sheer force of the Spartan's assault sending him onto his back, a spray of blood fanning out like a punctured hydraulic line.

A burst of battle rifle rounds from Jai hit the remaining captain, the Jiralhanae's own shields lighting up, causing him to lower his shock rifle. He issued a ferocious, grief-filled growl at the sight of his dead partner, but any response he'd planned was interrupted by another nearby voice.

"*Kaevus!*" the Jiralhanae who was leading Dovo Nesto bellowed. This one was certainly a war chief. 'Juran thought she recognized him, but could not place his face. "We have the high lord. *Leave them!*"

The captain immediately obeyed, quickly retreating behind a row of containers obscuring their view of the Trespasser.

'Juran jumped to her feet, trying to force aside the dizziness that still gripped her skull, joining Adriana and Jai as they charged the target. By the time they could open fire, the raider's bay doors were firmly closed and it was already lifting off the platform.

The Tresspasser's heavy plasma cannons swiveled, took aim, and began unloading volleys of superheated energy, causing the human ship to shudder. The unrelenting barrage was deafening, the cannons carving a path on the platform toward their prey. The three retreated back into the shuttle bay and the cannon fire trailed off. They watched as the sky raider ascended rapidly into the clouds.

"You tracking that?" Jai demanded through the comms. He was not pleased—this was the first time 'Juran had heard any emotion from the Spartan.

"Yes," 'Soran said from aboard his Phantom. *"We are in pursuit. Stolt?"*

"Us too," the Unggoy responded. His team's Pelican flew directly over 'Juran's head on the same flight path as the ascending Trespasser.

"*Victory* should be coming in for another pass," Jai reported. "If you can cripple their vehicle's engines, do it."

"And risk killing the San'Shyuum?" 'Soran replied.

"Once it's neutralized, our ship can draw it in and hard-dock," Jai said. "We could take the whole crew alive. Unless they do something crazy."

"That is a risk we cannot assume, Spartan," 'Soran responded. *"Dovo Nesto is the only one who knows where the Lithos is. If we lose him, we lose any chance of finding it."*

"It won't matter either way if he escapes," Adriana said in the team's closed channel.

'Juran looked at her, but did not disagree.

"Hey, guys," Michael said from across the platform. "I might have found a silver lining over here."

'Juran had not even realized that the third member of Gray Team was still fighting while his fellow Spartans were interacting with the other teams. Michael was in the far corner of the platform, surrounded by a host of dead bodies.

Except for one.

A single Sangheili lay on his back, Michael's boot firmly placed on his chest. The enemy was injured, but very much alive. 'Juran wanted to immediately rectify that matter for betraying his own people.

"One of Nesto's?" Jai asked, staring down at the Sangheili.

"Yep," Michael said.

The Sangheili growled at the sight of 'Juran, who responded by spitting on his face.

"Ugh—that's gross," Michael remarked, then turned toward the corridor that had spilled them onto this platform. A discordant thrum of voices and movement emanated from the interior of the ship. "That's not good. Sounds like our friends below finally decided to come aboard."

"Zulu Seven Nine," Jai said, notifying their Condor pilot. "We need a quick pickup on the starboard side of this ship."

"Roger that," Lieutenant Yun said. *"Got your twenty and already on the way. ETA seventeen seconds."*

"Copy," Jai said, then looked back down at the Sangheili. "Really hope this guy cooperates."

CHAPTER 15

ABIGAIL COLE

UNSC *Victory of Samothrace*
November 21, 2559

Captain Abigail Cole stood on the bridge of *Victory of Samothrace* as it tore through the upper atmosphere of Venezia, her view split between the planet's bright curvature set against the black of space and the holographic pane that provided a litany of data points and readouts. The bridge was similar to that of other cruisers, a single viewport at the fore, with weapons and navigation up front, and a central platform veiled by a holographic pane where the captain remained, encircled on the perimeter by over a dozen stations inset into the wall. It was everything needed to run a starship with the size and power of *Victory.*

Three bright-green dots on the holopane were being tracked as they climbed upward into the world's sky: the three dropships that belonged to her trio of strike teams. They were trailing a red dot—a Banished sky raider with no ONI-registered designation. The Jiralhanae vehicle had traditionally been used during occupations to pacify populations or provide security, but whoever was flying this one was using it as an extraction craft. It was actually impressive.

"Where exactly are they headed?" Commander Emanuel Njuguna said.

"Not sure," Cole replied. "Nav?"

"We don't have satellites or buoys to ping here, ma'am," Lieutenant Bavinck said, turning around from the astrogation station. "Our sensor deployment didn't account for their trajectory. Impossible to tell behind the horizon line. They'll already be at their target by the time we find out."

"Comms," Cole said, turning to the other side of the bridge. "Get our Sangheili friends on the line." Much of this could have been facilitated by an onboard AI, but Cole had absolutely refused it. Given what had happened to so many AIs across the UNSC, she'd rather take her chances with a traditional crew than run the risk of exploiting her ship with an artificial mind. Even with the RUINA subroutine, she didn't believe it was worth gambling.

"Done, Captain," Lieutenant Lim said, after keying in a transmission frequency.

"Shipmaster, do you copy?" Cole asked.

"I hear you, Captain," the venerable Rtas 'Vadum sounded across the comms.

After returning the shipmistress Mahkee 'Chava to *Scorrin's Blade*, *Shadow of Intent* had followed *Victory* to Venezia. They would provide naval support in the event it was needed, but no one had really anticipated what had just occurred on the surface. The Banished were extracting Dovo Nesto.

The Banished.

The obvious implications were troubling to Cole. Could the Banished have somehow found out about the Lithos? If so, they would pose a far more significant threat than any ex-Covenant force. Atriox's power and renown had made an indelible mark on the postwar landscape. Apart from Cortana, the Banished had easily become the most critical threat to humanity. If they somehow gained access to the Lithos, virtually nothing would stand between them and complete domination.

Shadow had spent the last half hour concealed on the far side of the planet, scanning a network of flight paths linking the settlement of Staithe with New Tyne, Venezia's primary population center. Their concern—and Cole shared it—was that Dovo Nesto might have significant reinforcements dispatched from the major city. What no one had expected was that practically the entire town of Staithe seemed to be under Nesto's control, which meant their operation had unwittingly knocked down a beehive of enemy resistance more substantial than their initial intelligence had suggested. Exfiltration would have been a nightmare if they hadn't been adequately prepared, but they weren't out of the dark yet.

Behind the three dots representing her team, Staithe was alight with ships taking off in pursuit of the human-Sangheili strike force.

"We're having trouble tracking the vector for Nesto's escape craft," Cole said to 'Vadum. "Can your crew see where they're headed?"

"We will be in visible range within one cental," he replied. So, the equivalent of over thirty seconds. Yet for some reason, time seemed to imperceptibly stretch to several minutes until finally the shipmaster responded.

"By the blood of our fathers!" he bellowed over the comms. *"Six dreadnoughts and—"* He paused for a moment. *"What in the name of . . . it is a ship I have never seen before! All Banished."*

"Nav, where the hell did seven enemy ships come from?" Cole demanded.

"They must have been waiting behind the moon," he replied. "Our sensors are limited, Captain, and there was no way we could have predicted such an erratic trajectory."

"Weapons, I want all defensive systems online and our team prepared for direct engagement," Cole ordered. "Six dreadnoughts is going to be a fight just to get our people back here."

"Captain Cole." The voice of Jai-006 was coming from the Condor, the third trailing dropship now in pursuit of Nesto's sky raider. *"At this rate, none of our vessels can intercept the target craft. We really need to consider denial."*

"As stated already, Spartan," 'Soran sounded over the comms, *"if we eliminate his craft, we lose the Lithos. We need to take this San'Shyuum alive."*

"But what is that intel worth if we just end up handing it over to the Banished?" Jai responded.

Cole wasn't sure how the young Sangheili female—Tul 'Juran—might feel about Jai's ad hoc directing. She was technically the leader of their strike team and should have been the one making such a request. This wasn't uncommon behavior from a Spartan though. If they felt it was warranted, Spartans were sometimes known for disregarding the chain of command to get approval from superiors. Having often operated behind enemy lines, Gray Team had done this *many* times before. In certain circles, they were renowned for it.

"I agree with the blademaster, Sierra-Zero-Zero-Six," Cole said. "If the Banished have a connection to Dovo Nesto, they probably already know where the Lithos is. We don't. Taking out the sky raider would only hurt us in the end. We also have to take into account they're missing a pretty critical piece of the puzzle—they can't access the Domain unless they have the key."

"Understood, ma'am," Jai said. *"But if the Banished are willing to send seven ships to pick up this guy, do you think it's worth us removing him from the equation—permanently—while we have a shot?"*

"Negative, Zero-Zero-Six," she said. "Do *not* open fire. We're seconds out from strike range of those dreadnoughts. Let's see what we can do from our end. The priority is getting all of you back in one piece."

"Ten-four, ma'am," he said. *"Also, we apprehended one of Nesto's Sangheili friends. Alive."*

"Outstanding, Spartan," Cole said, staring at the holopane. Dozens of ships were rising from the surface of the planet, homing in on her three dropships. "Don't look behind you though. The rest of Staithe is headed your way. All strike teams should break from pursuit and immediately snap to an intercept course with our vector." She turned to Lieutenant Bavinck. "Transmit rendezvous coordinates between us and them. Whatever's quickest. I want them out of there *now*."

"Done," Bavinck said, punching the keys on the display before him.

Their three strike teams were composites—Tul 'Juran and Gray Team were functioning out of Cole's best Condor flight team, while Vul 'Soran and Stolt were assigned some of the best Spartan-IVs from *Victory*'s contingent, split between a Phantom and Pelican respectively. Such hybrid efforts were rare, even this long after the war—but some operations demanded it. What concerned her most right now was their safety. Both human and Sangheili dropships were only lightly armed. They weren't designed for focused combat engagements, especially in space. The longer they were out there, the greater the risk they wouldn't come back, especially given that there were six dreadnoughts and—

"Do we have eyes on the new ship, Lieutenant Zobah?"

"Affirmative, ma'am," Zobah replied.

The holopane then enhanced the seven Banished vessels now peeking over the horizon, and what Cole saw was terrifying—a large and intimidating vessel shaped like a jagged arrowhead, covered in an impressive array of naval weapons. Its very presence seemed to carry an air of dread and ferocity. She had never seen anything like it before, so she was hoping Logistics had.

"What in heaven's name *is* that?" Cole muttered.

"I have no idea, Captain," Zobah said. "It matches nothing ONI has registered for the Banished. Must be some custom job."

The Banished had brought an impressive arsenal to bear over the last few years, prompting Cole to once again momentarily reflect on the destruction they had wrought against *Ozymandias* over Mars. The UNSC was still in the process of learning the full extent of what ships, weapons, equipment, and other tools of war Atriox's faction had either acquired, modified, or newly developed thanks to the efforts of the Jiralhanae's Alchemy Corps—perhaps this new ship came from their stable. That didn't matter right now, however. They'd run a thorough analysis of the vessel *if* they survived the next few minutes.

"Shipmaster, are you within striking range of the dreadnought nearest to Nesto's craft?" Cole asked.

"We are," 'Vadum said. *"Shall we coordinate fire?"*

"You read my mind."

"Enemy salvo inbound, Captain!" announced Lieutenant Aquila, the ship's tactical officer. "Intercept time: twenty seconds!"

"I guess they're not wasting any time," Cole said. "Get us out of that salvo's path and send *Shadow of Intent* our firing solution on the targeted dreadnought."

"Yes, Captain. Should we be concerned about . . . *her*?" Lieutenant Nishioka, *Victory*'s weapons officer said, almost whispering.

"*Cortana*?" Cole asked. She wasn't about to whisper, but it was a valid question. The increase in hostile activity here could result in a Guardian being deployed, which would be bad news for everyone. "I think it's too late for us to worry about that, Lieutenant.

We'll just have to hope that Venezia is very low on the AI's priority list. I want that Banished ship in pieces before Nesto gets any closer."

"Aye, aye," Nishioka said, then confirmed ten seconds later: "MACs are hot. On your mark, Captain."

"*Fire.*"

Victory blasted the Banished vessel with both of its magnetic accelerator cannons, and *Shadow* followed with its own assault, pummeling the ship with superheavy plasma lances from a completely different direction. Although dreadnoughts were among the most resilient and heavily armed Banished vessels in service, the first MAC round softened its shields, while the second penetrated all the way through. The Sangheili plasma lances were equally effective—the last strike hitting the fusion reactor, instantly enveloping the Banished ship in a muted supernova before it all disappeared into a sphere of crystal detritus.

"Excellent—one down, six to go." If they all survived this moment, Cole would be certain to note in her after-action report that this was probably the quickest strike against a Banished dreadnought in UNSC history, largely because of the power of the SARISSA-class MAC configuration.

"All enemy ships are launching fighters, Captain," Aquila reported. "Grievers and Seraphs."

"Scramble five Sabre squadrons, and three Broadswords. If they want to make this messy, we'll oblige."

"We are already deploying our own Seraphs and Banshees, Captain," 'Vadum said. *"And we will focus our attention on the ships farthest from your position."*

"Appreciated, Shipmaster," Cole responded, as the efflux tails bled out before *Victory*'s prow, her fighters speeding ahead to meet the enemy's. "Weapons, I want those MACs firing as soon as possible. When we get in close, we won't have the same targeting opportunities."

"Aye, Captain," Nishioka responded, scanning the MACs' recharge metrics. "Fifteen seconds and we'll be ready for another firing cycle. When we get within effective range, I'll launch Archers to soften them up."

"That works for me, Lieutenant," Cole said, grateful for her initiative. Archer missiles could help batter the shields of the enemy ships enough for the MAC rounds to get clean penetration. "But keep our Ramparts and Helixes for when we're side by side. How long will that be, Nav?"

"Two minutes, four seconds, Captain," said Bavinck.

"And our strike teams?"

"One minute, thirty-eight seconds."

"That's close, Nav. Too close."

"Best we have, Captain."

"Understood." She watched the bright-green dots representing the dropships now making a beeline toward *Victory of Samothrace*. "We'll have to make it work."

She hoped the universal battle tactic employed by the more aggressive species of the Covenant would be successful. In ancient Greece, it was referred to as *diekplous*, where ships would assault each other head-on, sailing right through the battle line, then turning hard to fire on the exposed and vulnerable parts of an enemy vessel. Thousands of years later, this was still viable but considerably more complex given the nature of space naval combat. The Jiralhanae had added ramming and shearing to the mix, and the Banished were remarkable specialists with this method. They even designed their warships for this very purpose, which meant getting in close was always incredibly risky.

The Trespasser was now moving toward the unidentified

Banished vessel as two other dreadnoughts moved out in front of it, blocking a clean shot from *Victory*.

"Archers are ready, Captain," Nishioka said.

"Let them loose."

Victory was equipped with seventy-five M58 Archer missile pods, but only a fraction of those were necessary to deplete the dreadnought's shields. Because of the prevalence of ramming as a Banished tactic, that meant their shielding at the bow of the ship would invariably be strongest. A dozen Archer missiles found their mark around the dreadnought's midsection, softening up its center.

"Confirmed hits, ma'am," Nishioka announced. "And MAC rounds are ready."

Cole nodded. "Then let's introduce this sorry lot to SARISSA."

"With pleasure, Captain."

The MACs fired again, both hitting the lead dreadnought. From their firing angle, the blast was sufficient to seriously damage the Banished vessel, but it was still operational. Weapons fire bristled on its nose as it approached, a series of bright beams striking out just above *Victory*. Only one cut across its battleplate as the UNSC ship edged out of range. Dreadnoughts were not to be underestimated.

Cole's eyes narrowed at a series of new blips that were suddenly appearing on the holopane at the very edge of their sensor range, well away from the skirmish. Then they suddenly disappeared.

"Tactical?" Cole asked. "Did you see those? Was that Cortana?"

"Not sure," Aquila said. "I don't *think* they're Cortana. They all had Covenant ship registries, ma'am. Maybe it was just an echo from *Shadow of Intent* or . . . "

"Or?" Cole briefly wondered if she really wanted to know the answer.

"Ex-Covenant ships? That's impossible though . . . right?"

"Maybe not," Cole said.

"Dropships approaching," Bavinck announced. "Ten seconds. Opening port side bay three."

"Dreadnoughts are firing!" Aquila reported. "Energy projectors again!"

"Weapons! Trade those volleys and keep the MAC active—prioritize the vessels closest to us!" Cole shouted, scanning the holopane. "Nav, when our teams are inside, turn thirty degrees starboard and climb up to point seven!"

"Copy that, Captain," said Bavinck. "Thirty degrees starboard, jumping to point seven above engagement plane. And . . . dropships are inside! Sealing bay door."

Most of the enemy fire went far to *Victory of Samothrace*'s left, but a few glancing blows caused the UNSC ship to rumble. As she approached the three Banished vessels, the viewport filled with motes of light, weapons fire, and individual fighters engaging in the abyss of space between them. *Victory*'s MACs fired again and the lead dreadnought's nose crumpled, the entire vessel listing as debris shed from its frame. Equipment and luckless Banished personnel poured out of the ship's wounds into the vacuum.

"The sky raider made it inside that strange flagship," Zobah said, eyes narrowing at her display.

"Is that what we're calling it?" Cole remarked.

Her strategic analyst just shrugged.

"Fine," Cole said. "No kill shots on the flagship though. I want that thing limping, not destroyed."

"Captain," Shipmaster 'Vadum rang out across the comms. *"We have taken down one of the enemy ships, but the other two have disengaged. They are headed your way."*

"Great," Cole said, grimacing. "I wonder why that is."

"The only logical explanation is that they were ordered to," the

Sangheili continued. *"Whoever is in command called them away from us in order to directly engage you. Either the fools are willing to risk exposing their bellies in retreat, or they—"*

"Are trying to protect the San'Shyuum," Cole finished his sentence.

"Correct," the shipmaster replied. *"It makes no difference to us whether they perish face-to-face or in retreat. They have made their choice."*

Cole could see on both the holopane and in the far distance of the planet's curve that the shipmaster meant just what he said. *Shadow of Intent* was absolutely torching the back end of one of the Banished dreadnoughts as the two made their way toward *Victory*. She turned her attention to the other two vessels before her, now remarkably close, with only a thin veil of debris from *Victory*'s previous victim clouding their view.

The weapons on both the dreadnought and the unidentified Banished flagship now came alive, a mixture of energy and ballistic rounds typical of their vessels. Almost immediately, *Victory* shuddered under the barrage of enemy fire. As *Victory*'s own weapons continued to thunder, her navigation team carefully moved the vessel above and around a large chunk of battle debris.

The enemy ships were now so close that Cole could make out some of the flagship's detail just behind the silhouette of the dreadnought. It was a *monster*. Although slightly smaller than *Victory*, the Banished ship was a hulking gray vessel looking more like an ammunition round from one of their weapons than a spaceframe—a rugged and threatening object that was brimming with cannons and missile silos, all of them now very active.

Cole quickly scrutinized the in-progress analysis of the flagship on a holograph. It was approximately twelve hundred meters long and its bow looked vaguely like a shark, but it also had a honeycomb frame design similar to a *Halcyon*-class cruiser—a feature that suggested it could take some serious punishment.

"God help us," Njuguna said under his breath.

"When we clear this debris, I want us to climb up above these two ships. And *quick*. Do not let that dreadnought ram us," Cole ordered. At this range, it would not take much for one of the Banished ships to plow right into *Victory*. A dreadnought's up-armored prow would protect their own during a direct impact, but it'd certainly compromise *Victory*.

"Aye, aye, Captain," Bavinck said, disseminating orders to his team.

Victory of Samothrace began to climb high above the engagement plane, her weapons still pouring down fire as the two Banished ships attempted to react. The dreadnought out front followed hard, clearly desiring to make contact and protect the flagship. As the other two dreadnoughts were approaching quickly—the farthest one out suddenly exploded in a blaze of white light, with *Shadow of Intent* breaking through its scattered remains like a leviathan emerging from an ocean's surface.

Victory began shaking uncontrollably as the nearest dreadnought came astonishingly close, both ships' weapons mercilessly battering each other's flanks. It was impossible to tell if there had been any shearing, but no atmosphere breaches were a good thing. What was most startling was not the near miss, but the fact that the Banished flagship didn't move away, and actually started climbing to meet *Victory*'s pitch. Cole had thought that the Banished would protect that ship at all costs, but it seemed there was one price they would not pay: its commander's ego. That was the only explanation for such an audacious move.

Whoever was in charge of that flagship wanted *Victory* annihilated.

"Keep climbing and rotate, full *Marien* maneuver!" Cole shouted. She silently prayed the twenty-fifth-century evasion tactic conducted by the CAA *Marien* during the Insurrection would be enough.

A deafening sound of alarms suddenly broke out across the bridge. Grievers—Banished fighter-bombers—had evidently broken through *Victory*'s fighter screen, releasing destructive payloads onto her hull. They weren't alone—the cloud of small craft from Staithe had finally made contact. Most were essentially harmless against a ship like *Victory*, but when combined with the Grievers, they could become a serious problem.

She thought for a moment they were in over their heads.

She thought about *Ozymandias* and all those who had perished under her command that day.

She thought about her father and what he might do.

He'd fight until he couldn't fight anymore.

"Weapons, keep firing. Do not let up! Nav, I don't want our belly exposed to the flagship's guns. Put us on a tight path port side and have us come alongside *Shadow*."

The massive spaceframe of *Victory* carefully swiveled above the Banished flagship as both vessels continued to unload their firepower at each other unremittingly, but Cole knew that something had to give. And that something would be battleplate.

Either theirs or ours.

"We have a breach, Section Twenty-Three!" announced her hull integrity specialist, Lieutenant Whelihan. "Sections Twenty-Five and Twenty-Six, also breached! Sealing them off now."

Cole cursed under her breath.

"Captain," Aquila said. "We have another problem."

Cole turned to the holopane, but part of her knew before her eyes even fell on it. The ghost signals with Covenant registries encountered earlier were not echoes. An entire Covenant battle group—fourteen ships consisting of two assault carriers, eight battlecruisers, and four corvettes—had suddenly come into sensor range along Venezia's horizon, positionally opposite of *Shadow of Intent*.

"Shipmaster," Cole said over the comms, "we've got company."

"I see them," he growled, spitting out something in Sangheili she didn't understand.

Cole noted the growing list of alarms accumulating on the holopane. There were now eight hull breaches, and even though *Victory* was clearing the enemy flagship's firing range, another sustained engagement would be fatal.

"You certainly cannot stay in this fight, Captain," the Sangheili said. *"I can see that your ship is hemorrhaging oxygen."*

"Captain." Lieutenant Lim turned to face her, concerned. "We have an incoming transmission. Unknown registry."

And here we go, she thought, focusing on the flagship on the holopane. "Allow it."

The holopane filled up with the face of a rugged Jiralhanae, lightly graying black fur and his right cheek bearing three deep claw marks. His eyes appeared as red as fire. He looked familiar to Cole, but she couldn't quite place him. As he came into focus, Gray Team and Tul 'Juran entered the bridge.

"Severan," Jai-006 noted, his voice tense.

"He is the one who took Dovo Nesto," Tul 'Juran added.

Now she recognized him.

Severan of the Vanguard of Zaladon, according to the ONI profile flashing on the holopane. A war chief appointed to service in the Banished not long ago. His reputation preceded him, but he was most known for something else: he was the last surviving son of Tartarus, former Chieftain of the Jiralhanae during the Covenant War.

"Commander of the human ship, whoever you are," Severan began, his voice like thick gravel, his face tense with rage. *"The artificial construct your species created—the one you call Cortana—has destroyed my people's homeworld. She washed away all that we had built, all that we had fought centuries for."* He paused, as if choosing his words carefully. *"I have been given orders to return this kindness. Had you not attempted to take from Sqala what did not belong to you, I might have spared your worthless homeworld rather than spend any more Jiralhanae lives. But since you continue to meddle* and *spill the blood of my people, know this."* He leaned into the frame, his eyes and tusks unnervingly close. *"I swear upon that same blood, your Earth will burn until it is a lifeless, smoking grave, and a horror to your entire species."*

The transmission cut off and silence fell over *Victory*'s bridge.

Cole gritted her teeth as the stakes sank in. Cortana had destroyed the Jiralhanae homeworld; her tyrannical methods of maintaining order and control over the peoples of the galaxy had reached a catastrophic end . . . and her actions were now being held against the entire human race.

Earth itself was in danger.

In recent years, humanity's cradle world had endured in the face of multiple invasions—from the Covenant, to an army of planet-harvesting sentinels, followed by the wrathful Didact himself. But it was Cortana's actions that had sundered the UNSC over a year ago, and now the Banished were moving in for the kill.

"Nav, get us the hell out of here," Cole ordered. "We need to warn Earth. The Banished are coming."

CHAPTER 16

SEVERAN

Heart of Malice
November 21, 2559

Severan abruptly ended the transmission and stepped back from the holocam.

His body shook with anger.

Four warships destroyed by the humans. Thousands of Jiralhanae had perished. Never had he paid a cost so great in a single battle, but he reminded himself that if what the high lord said was true, it was entirely worth it—it *had* to be. Doubtless there were many reasons the humans and Sangheili might seek the life of Dovo Nesto, but the most obvious was the one he had recently learned: the Lithos. If this machine was indeed a gateway to the Domain, both the UNSC and the Swords of Sanghelios would stop at nothing to learn its location. He would mourn the loss of his brothers when the present crisis abated, but there was no greater way to redeem that loss than to ensure that he seized the Lithos first and used its capabilities against the very humans responsible.

Severan stood at the helm of the bridge within *Heart of Malice*, encircled by consoles and displays, a single holotable at its center, and a crew of a dozen Jiralhanae naval officers working together to guide the warship.

Their Trespasser had narrowly delivered High Lord Dovo Nesto to Severan's personal warship, but Othmald's body remained on Sqala and would never be recovered. His loyal captain murdered at the hands of the demons. The very thought infuriated Severan beyond words, but he could not dwell on it now. Of utmost importance was the Covenant's resurrection through the power of the Domain, so in the short term the safety of the high lord—hidden aboard his vessel, even from much of his own crew—as well as the location of the Lithos, was paramount.

"Shall we pursue the human ship, War Chief?" Vodus asked.

The ship commander managed *Heart of Malice* during naval engagements, but it was Severan's decision whether to continue. The human warship was still climbing and rotating above the battle plane, its hull bristling with weapons fire. It was an impressive tactical feat, but it did not hide the fact that their vessel was severely damaged and venting oxygen at an exceptional pace.

"No," Severan said. "Not with *them* here." He pointed to a cloud of objects projected on the holotable. The Covenant ships which had appeared only moments ago had not yet fired, but Severan imagined it would not be long before they did *something*. He had initially thought that they might be connected to *Shadow of Intent*, the traitorous Sangheili vessel presently aiding the humans, but his opponents' reaction had confirmed that was not the case.

Perhaps it was Sali 'Nyon or another ambitious ex-Covenant vigilante seeking to capture Dovo Nesto or the location of the Lithos? He would not stay around to find out.

"Continue suppressive fire, but prepare an escape vector. We will rendezvous with the rest of the fleet. If we dither any longer on this backwater world, we risk drawing the Apparition's attention."

"Erutaun," Vodus said, turning to the comms officer. "Signal *Ghost of K'ryyk* and *Ghost of Voranth.* Send them our slipspace transit vector and destination."

The comms officer grunted assent, and Severan watched the holotable, a constellation of objects and data nodes showing that both the human ship and *Shadow of Intent* were now pushing away from the three remaining Banished vessels, with this mysterious Covenant battle group closing in.

The humans no doubt were grappling with the same risk. A small skirmish on such a minor world as Sqala might not initially register on Cortana's allocation of security forces, but if they persisted, time was not on their side. An electromagnetic pulse from a single Guardian would be enough to turn all of their ships into floating cages, their crews imprisoned in their own vessels and dead in space until the Apparition pried each one of her victims free.

Severan had acquired Dovo Nesto for the Banished and that was enough of a victory for today. Something told him this would not be the last time he would see this enemy. If he had another chance, he would not show them the same mercy.

Both enemy ships suddenly disappeared, tunneling into plumes of slipspace radiation.

"Run, cowards," Kaevus said, grasping at a gunshot injury on his arm. One of the demons had inflicted it, but Severan knew that the loss of Othmald was more painful for his captain than a mere flesh wound.

"They will not run far, brother," Severan said, resting his hand on Kaevus's shoulder. "And we will not have to guess where they are headed."

"You know the humans will not leave Earth unguarded," Kaevus replied, wincing as the deck shuddered below his feet, disturbing his injury. "They will gather all they have to defend that world."

With a crack, the holotable's images washed out and *Heart of Malice* entered slipspace. A data node indicated that both *K'ryyk* and *Voranth* had successfully done so in kind.

"It is a certainty. And they will *fail*," Severan said, his eyes returning to Kaevus. "Now see to mending yourself, brother. I need you ready for whatever will come next."

"As you command, War Chief," Kaevus said, nodding before leaving the bridge.

"Transit time, Commander?" Severan asked.

"Four-point-eight-two-seven cycles, War Chief," Vodus responded, reading an analog holograph based on a reverse-engineered Forerunner artifact. The machine had once belonged to the Covenant and could give precise travel times and trajectories through slipspace. *Another remarkable gift bestowed by the gods,* Severan mused.

"Damage?"

"Minimal," Vodus said, consulting a display with a tallied report. "Minor battleplate damage on *Malice. K'ryyk* has four weapons down, *Voranth* a minor hull breach, sealed before they entered slipspace."

"What is our repair time once we have arrived?"

"A few day-cycles, War Chief," Vodus answered. He was well aware that Severan would want these ships operational as soon as possible. "We will move quickly."

Severan addressed the communications officer. "Erutaun—upon arrival, summon the Eight for an immediate conference. We must move against Earth quickly."

"Yes, War Chief," Erutaun said. "Many among the Banished have also been relocating their own people and assets due to Cortana's attack. It may take several more day-cycles for them to fully gather. I will signal you when they are ready."

Severan gave acknowledgment and left the bridge, heading down a long corridor to a series of lifts that would take him to his private quarters. Along the way, he mulled over what he would in fact tell the Eight—the other leaders and chieftains of the Banished fleets now under the war chief's command. Severan had nearly a hundred ships of his own belonging to Zaladon, but the remainder of the fleets constituted over two hundred clans with control of more than thirteen hundred warships.

None of the Eight, however, knew of Severan's association with Dovo Nesto, nor would they understand and agree to any kind of alliance with a San'Shyuum. This was true not only of the outlying Banished fleets he now governed; even his own clan was in the dark concerning the high lord, and for their own good. Apart from a handful of his closest allies, his *daskalo*'s identity and his own personal motivations for the Covenant's rebirth must be kept in complete secrecy.

That made his current situation somewhat precarious.

He had no desire to risk his position within the Banished, or jeopardize the long-laid plans of resurrecting the Covenant—his entire purpose for joining the Banished in the first place. In addition to the many hidden streams of preparation the high lord already had underway, Severan's rise within the Banished and whatever accumulation of weapons and technology this would include was part of this ultimate end.

Even beyond that, Severan knew, as did his *daskalo*, that Jiralhanae loyalty was rooted in the recognition of strength. Among his own people, the strong *always* led. If the Covenant were to rise from the ashes—and this time with a Jiralhanae at its head—many who claimed fealty to the Banished would not wait long for an opportunity to find position and power within the revived alliance. And if anything could eclipse the shadow presently cast by the Banished, it was the Covenant from which they had originally risen. Although he had great respect for Atriox and all that the warmaster had accomplished, there was little that Severan would not be willing to do in order to regain the honor his father had lost when he was killed by the Arbiter on Delta Halo years earlier.

In the end, this *alone* was all that mattered.

Yet doubt still nagged at him. The arrival of the Covenant ships, including an assault carrier that might even have been Sali 'Nyon's *Breath of Annihilation*, was a factor he hadn't anticipated. He hoped that Dovo Nesto had answers to settle the matter.

The door to his private chamber opened with a hiss, and Severan was greeted by a series of dimly lit blue Forerunner glyphs hovering above a stone tablet on the holotable in the center of the room. His chamber was the largest of all the private quarters on *Heart of Malice*, but that meant very little given a Jiralhanae's tendency toward utilitarian design. For the high lord, however, the space no doubt felt restrictive, even if he had spent some time within the human vessel on Sqala.

Apart from the rudimentary furniture and essential machines that lined the room, as well as a smattering of totems from Doisac and High Charity, Severan's chamber was largely barren. He spent very little time in this room; when he did, it was at the central holotable, which had full access to troves of data pulled from the Covenant archives before the holy city's tragic fall. Dovo Nesto was scrutinizing glyphs projected from the tablet.

"Severan," he said, looking up from the blue light. "We entered slipspace, which must mean that the present hostilities have abated?"

"Yes, High Lord," he responded, coming to the far side of the table. "We are headed to rendezvous with the Banished fleets. And from there, we will move to strike Earth. It will likely take several week-cycles to conduct repairs and transit, but I doubt the humans will be able to establish an effective resistance in what little time they have."

The stone tablet that lay atop the holotable was being analyzed by the machine, its data extruded above in holographic form—the very thing the high lord was eyeing. Dovo Nesto was attempting to decipher scrolling lines of Forerunner text arranged in a three-dimensional display and had isolated a handful of passages. The tablet itself was a thin sheet of slate, broken from a larger piece, fragmenting the Forerunner writing inscribed on it. This artifact was the only thing Dovo Nesto had brought with him from Sqala—he apparently considered it too valuable to forsake to the human and Sangheili aggressors. Severan wondered what mysteries it held.

"Very good. Did the others aid you?"

"*Others . . .* ?" Severan asked, confused.

"Yes, the Covenant ships," the high lord said matter-of-factly. "I summoned them as we left Sqala. They are mine."

"Those were *allies*? They appeared to be ex-Covenant vigilantes."

"They belong to Sali 'Nyon."

"So it *was* 'Nyon on Sqala?" Severan asked, concern bleeding into his tone.

"Indeed. He has pledged all to our cause."

"But is this not the same Sangheili who contended to be the one true prophet?"

Severan was familiar with Sali 'Nyon, who had left Jul 'Mdama's failed attempt to reforge the Covenant after staging a rebellion against him. 'Mdama had made concerted efforts to rebuild the Covenant without the San'Shyuum and under a pretense of religion in service to the Forerunner warrior-god known as the

Didact. The Sangheili was himself a nonbeliever, and he paid for his opportunistic lies by dying at the hands of a demon. Many of his forces had streamed into the Banished following this failure, but ultimately 'Nyon became the frontrunner to take 'Mdama's place and lay claim to the title of leader.

From his position of power, 'Nyon had boasted of being the true prophet who would bring about the return of the Covenant, even without the San'Shyuum who had been the architects of the empire's original formation.

How then has he managed to align with the high lord?

"Sali 'Nyon has claimed many things, my son," Dovo Nesto said. "But now, chastised by a universe in which a human AI can pose as a god . . . he sees the light of my purpose. If we who believe remain divided, those still loyal to the faith of the Covenant will not prevail. But if we all come together . . ."

The high lord let the words trail off as he stared into Severan's eyes, evidently feeling it unnecessary to draw the logical conclusion out loud. Yet Severan still had his reservations about the Sangheili's loyalty. Even more than that, the presence of 'Nyon's forces could easily strain Severan's place within the Banished. Anyone still affiliated with the Covenant was viewed by all under Atriox's banner as a religious fanatic at best and a groveling sychophant at worst. It was a very precarious place to be, and whatever jeopardized Severan's now-lofty position in the Banished ultimately did the same for the clandestine work he and the high lord had been committed to since the original Covenant's untimely demise.

"I see the doubt on your face, Severan," the San'Shyuum said, returning his attention to the tablet. "Please—tell me your concern, my son."

"I have many, High Lord. Where shall I begin? For one, 'Nyon's fidelity to our cause is nothing but treachery veiled in fealty. He parted with Jul 'Mdama, and he will not hesitate to part with us. But also, such an alliance will affect my position within the Banished. Even the very presence of those ships on Sqala raises questions. I can give answers among my own, but I will not be able to do so effectively among the other Banished leaders."

He chose not to mention a new, dark thought that was rapidly forming: If the high lord had promised Severan leadership over the resurrected Covenant's military, what had he promised 'Nyon? Beyond that, how could a warped Sangheili like 'Nyon agree to such a military arrangement?

"Certainly," the high lord said. "Therefore we will have to exercise prudence, especially given your recent advancement in rank. But we must also trust the gods, Severan. Surely they have not guided us to the Lithos in vain. Quite the contrary, they have blessed us with clarity of the Path and so we must trust them, even with pledges of devotion—whether true or false—from those one would consider former enemies."

"Very well," Severan said grudgingly, though he suspected his face showed he was not convinced. Now was not the time to raise the question of what exactly 'Nyon had been offered. "If I cannot trust 'Nyon . . . I will at the very least trust your wisdom."

"Come here, my son," Dovo Nesto said, motioning for Severan to move around the holotable to view the glyphs from his position. The high lord, never one to allow apprehension to stand in his presence, sought to strengthen Severan's faith. "Do you see this?" he asked, pointing to a line on the tablet.

"Yes. Though I do not know the language of the gods."

"But I do," Nesto said with a reassuring smile. "This line refers to how the Domain is accessed through the Lithos. The Domain is a universe of its own, but it cannot abide our physical forms. It is traversed by the incorporeal alone—only the *essence* of a being can dwell there."

"How then do you intend to access it?" Severan asked, for it sounded impossible.

"I will sacrifice my body," the San'Shyuum said without hesitation. "It is the cost the Lithos demands, and it is a *worthy* cost."

"But will you not die?"

"Oh, my dear Severan. When the Lithos takes my body, I will be more alive than I have *ever* been. True, I will lack flesh and bones, but I will have more power in my hands than you can possibly conceive. More than the Banished, more than the Covenant. I will possess the very *power* of the Forerunners themselves."

Such a promise did not assuage Severan's immediate grief at this revelation. For them to seize control of the Domain would require that he must forever part ways with his *daskalo.* He wanted to ask if there was another way but knew there could not be—if there had been, doubtless the high lord would have taken it. This then was the only path.

"It is quite a little sacrifice in the grand scheme of things, Severan," the San'Shyuum said, his large eyes piercing into the Jiralhane's. "To give up one's body in order to become a god? I scarcely even call that a sacrifice." His eyes then drifted off into space and his voice grew weak. "And I have been alive for *so long*, my son. I have seen ages come and go, empires rise and fall. *Now* is the time. Immortality—no longer through the use of a gene-forge on a physical body, but by exceeding the very boundaries of the universe itself. The Lithos will do this for me, and you will rule in my place. You will be my right hand; yes, *you*—not this Sangheili—will be the right hand of the Covenant. We are *so close.* Only a short time remains."

"It is . . . almost too much to believe," he responded, wrestling internally with the revelations he had just received. Relief and joy coursed through him. His place in the new order felt now confirmed and assured. Let 'Nyon and any of his other enemies weep—his father Tartarus would be avenged.

"Do you see this?" the high lord said, pointing to another line on the tablet.

"I do."

"This notes the world upon which the Lithos was created. Its precise coordinates, right *here.* The Covenant called it Ghado; the humans who live there call it Boundary. It is a small, sparsely populated world. Yet another example of their vile species taking residence atop the machines of the gods, defiling it with their very presence. If the AI did not have control of the Domain, we could simply strike the colony and seize it at will. But her current station requires a less . . . *direct* approach. We need the key, Severan." Dovo Nesto looked directly at the war chief. "And once we have the human girl, the AI creator's clone, you and I shall hold the power of the Domain in our hands."

"And where are we to find this young human?"

"Oh, we will not need to find her," the San'Shyuum replied, grinning. "The humans will bring her to *us*."

CHAPTER 17

JAMES SOLOMON

Cascade
November 23, 2559

Chloe Eden Hall.

How this one little girl could be the key to stopping Cortana, James Solomon didn't know. But she was his quickest way of getting out of the work that had consumed him for almost a decade, work that was slowly killing him—rotting his soul. That alone was enough incentive to get him past the finish line on this operation.

He would find the girl and bring her to the site, and then he'd disappear for all time.

Clad in plain clothes, Solomon made his way through a dark alley in the heart of Mindoro's underbelly. The sprawling metropolis was the largest population center on Cascade, a vast municipality that spread out for fifty kilometers in every direction. It was encircled by five space elevators with a single, newly constructed one at the center, tethered to Nova Austin Station in geosynchronous orbit above the city. The station's multiport terminus was where he'd docked *Cataphract*, the most accessible egress point from where his sources had indicated the young girl might be, hidden somewhere in the depths of Mindoro's inner-city complex.

According to Lola's database sweeps, which were extraordinarily comprehensive, Chloe was not formally registered as a Cascadian citizen, and her name didn't appear in local directories either. There was literally no official record of her, nor of any legal guardians with the same surname. ONI's own lack of information on the girl would have caused Solomon to wonder if she even existed at all, but Lola had found a single thread and he intended to pull on it.

In a miscellaneous tax record belonging to a series of nightclubs within the Tamaraw district's lower streets, her full name was logged as a dependent, recorded as a female matching the girl's age. It could simply be a front—a ploy by the owner to pay less taxes—but the name and age connection were coincidental enough for Solomon to pursue. And any apprehensions he might have had about delivering this ten-year-old girl to ONI disappeared when he discovered that she was potentially located in the Tamaraw district, a place known throughout the colonies for its rampant crime and illicit activity.

For the past three hours, he'd been walking the smog-draped streets of Tamaraw, simply observing his surroundings. Unlike Mindoro's opulent and pristine upper levels, the grimy city avenues in its dredges were an entirely different world: clubs, bars, illegal pharma shops, brothels, and gambling, all tightly wedged between dilapidated housing that likely belonged to the most poverty-stricken of the district, if not the entire metropolis.

He had seen enough of Tamaraw to convince himself to never return, but he had yet to see a ten-year-old girl. Or any individual, for that matter, under the age of fifteen. Even if he had, there would be no way to determine if it was Chloe—he had no physical description of her, merely the name Morales had given him.

"How long do you intend to do this?" Lola asked through the transmitter in his ear. Besides the typical colonial garb that allowed him to fit into Mindoro, Solomon had only his M6D, a combat knife, and a number of smaller instruments he could conceal on his person without drawing attention.

"Until I find her?" he said, baffled at the AI's lack of patience.

"Oh, I know you plan to find the girl, James," she said in a staid tone. *"I'm asking how long you are going to just walk around?"*

"You'd like me to speed up the process?" Solomon asked with a smile. "Because I can do *that*, Lola. That's the part I'm best at."

"Eighty-four-point-seven percent of the revenue produced in Tamaraw is through activity that violates civil, colonial, and UEG law. I'm not confident we will find much progress canvassing the streets. You will have to apply pressure, *James."*

"I know just the place," Solomon said, approaching a bar with a sign that read NO GUILT, with a cluster of five men milling outside its doors. Lola was right. It was almost 1700 hours local time, which meant that it would only get busier and more complicated as night fell. Better to rattle the cages early than when there was a mob in the streets.

He sidestepped the men, assessing their size, posture, and whether they were armed. They looked more like thugs than patrons, possibly security. None exchanged eye contact with him, but it was clear that they were taking note and sizing him up. Solomon hoped that was all they did. If they wanted a fight, it would end very badly for them.

The bar interior was dark and mostly empty except for a mélange of neon lights strung across the far wall and a single bartender, a man roughly Solomon's size and build. Three others sat in different spots, sipping pints of some local brew. The bartender had piercings and tattoos common to this part of Mindoro, and he towered in front of the liquor rack lining the wall.

"Can I help you?" he asked, his eyes piercing and his tone serious. Evidently he recognized Solomon as an outsider.

"I'm hoping that you can. I'm looking for a kid by the name of Chloe Eden Hall. Do you know her?"

"Never heard of her," the man said, almost too quickly.

"She's ten years old."

"Nope." This time, definitely too quick.

"So you've never seen a ten-year-old girl at all in the district?"

"There are plenty of kids in the district, mister. I ain't never heard of a Chloe before, but even if I had, who are *you*? Her father? If she's in Tamaraw, you ain't ever gonna find her."

Solomon held the man's gaze for a moment.

"Why do you say that?" Solomon asked the man, still analyzing his responses.

"Because this ain't the place people come to be found. This is where they come to get lost. Stop looking in places that don't belong to you, and you'll stay out of trouble."

"It is seventy-four-point-six percent likely that he is lying," Lola chirped in his ear. She was assessing the man's tone and movement through sensors on Solomon's coat. Just like when she was integrated into his armor, she had a full panoramic view of his surroundings, but her matrix was back on *Cataphract*, thousands of feet above the planet's surface.

Solomon didn't move a muscle, but could hear the door behind him open and a series of footsteps accompanying that. The five men outside coming in. He continued to stare at the bartender.

"They have weapons, James," Lola said in his ear. *"No guns, just knives and clubs."*

"I'm not worried about trouble," Solomon said. "I'm worried for *you*."

The bartender laughed. "Why are you worried for me?"

"Because I get the sense that you're not being completely honest. And honesty is *very* important to me."

Solomon glanced behind him. The five men from outside now surrounded him in a semicircle, tightening their position, while the others in the bar tried to mask their staring at what was about to happen. If they frequented Tamaraw, they probably had seen it all before. They were expecting some kind of bar brawl, but this would hardly be called that.

"Your establishment is right at the center of the district," Solomon continued, probing without any restraint. "It has the highest reported revenue of any in this area, and who knows how much goes unreported. It also has the highest traffic of any place of business in a five-kilometer radius, which means that if this ten-year-old girl is in this location, someone here would know. So I'm going to ask you one more time, and I want you to think very carefully about your answer. Have you seen anyone who could be this girl?"

What happened next was so quick that the onlookers would have a difficult time recounting later what they'd just witnessed.

The first attack came from behind. Solomon heard movement and spun, meeting two of them in midstride. He immediately grabbed one's arm and forced his foe's blade into the neck of the other, then broke the same arm, and with a clean punch sent the bridge of the thug's nose into his frontal lobe. Both dropped to the ground, but the other three weren't yet discouraged. The man to his right swung a metal club against Solomon's side, which he batted away, simultaneously landing a punch to the chest so hard that it threw his attacker backward across a table. Solomon's leg shot up under the chin of another thug, knocking him out on contact and sending his body to the ground.

The fifth immediately stepped back with hands up, eyes wide and legs quivering.

Solomon turned back to the bartender, who was now pointing a magnum at his face, but the man's arm was shaking, his face awash with terror. Before he could even speak, Solomon reached for him, pulling his arm up while two rounds harmlessly fired into the ceiling, then slammed the arm onto the bar with a series of loud snaps indicating multiple breaks. Solomon continued to hold an iron grip on the bartender, looking directly into his eyes.

"Would you like to answer the question now?" he asked softly.

"D-d-down the street," the bartender said, his teeth chattering as he shook in anguish. "Miko's . . . Wheel."

"The girl is there?" Solomon applied pressure to the broken arm.

"Yes—*yes!*" he said, spittle dripping out between gritted teeth. "She *has* to be the girl you're talking about. Don't know her name, never asked. Just a little kid. Some kind of a numbers whiz. She does the books for Miko."

Solomon looked behind him to see if anyone else was taking this opportunity to come to the bartender's aid. The fifth assailant was now on the opposite side of the room with the other patrons, hiding behind an overturned table. His four companions were either unconscious or far worse. All clear. Solomon relaxed his grip and the guy fell behind the bar in a heap, sobbing uncontrollably.

"I think he urinated himself," Lola commented.

Solomon didn't care to check. Instead, he left No Guilt and

immediately scanned the opposite side of the street. On-foot and vehicle traffic were still relatively light in this part of Mindoro, but were quickly picking up and would increase as evening approached. He would have to work fast. Extraction of a ten-year-old child from one of these places would be more challenging the more people were present.

Miko's Wheel was only two dozen meters down the street, at the corner of a larger intersection. Apart from two people entering, the outside looked completely dead.

Great. Maybe this will be easier.

"I know what you're thinking, but it won't be easier," Lola said, practically reading his mind. *"According to ONI's profile, the owner, Miko, is a serious problem. His identity is completely unknown. They only have this one name and he's never been captured on camera. He has apparently worked a large-scale money laundering business in Tamaraw for almost a decade."*

"And they haven't done anything about it?" Solomon asked, crossing the street.

"No. Why would they? They could not realistically police every colony's network of money launderers."

"If they've got enough time to write a dossier on the guy, they could at least tip off the local law enforcement. Seems counter-productive."

A single guard stood at the front door of Miko's Wheel. Shorter than Solomon, but visibly strong, with wide-set shoulders and a thick beard. He held out his arm.

"Can I help you?"

"Yes," Solomon said. "I'd like to speak with Miko."

The doorman smirked. "Clearly you're not from around here, buddy. Nobody speaks with—"

Solomon lifted the doorman up and pinned him against the

door with such speed and ease that the color instantly fled from the man's face, his mouth slacking open.

"Listen carefully," Solomon said as the doorman dangled above the ground. "I'm here to talk with Miko, and I don't want to spend the next few minutes flirting with you about whether or not it's going to happen. You have a choice. You can bring me to him without any delay, or you can refuse and permanently lose the use of both your arms. And then I still get to talk with Miko."

"Listen, guy—" he began to say, and then his right arm suddenly dislocated, snapping out of its socket. He wailed in pain and his eyes filled with tears.

Up the street, patrons poured out of the No Guilt bar Solomon had just shaken down. They were shouting about what he had done, pointing at him and trying to signal people to call the police. Evidently some of the men who had attacked him were dead. He wasn't surprised, he hadn't held back much.

"You see them? They're all talking about me," Solomon said, looking directly at Miko's doorman. "They made some poor decisions, and what happened wasn't pretty. Learn from their mistakes, or next they'll be talking about *you*."

"All right, all right," he replied, his entire body shaking in pain. "I'll take you to Miko."

Solomon dropped the guard, and he immediately clenched his dislocated arm.

"Well done. He's right-handed," Lola said. *"He won't be able to use that arm to shoot you."*

He hoped it didn't come to a gunfight, but softening up the opposition would help this go much quicker. The man hobbled into the building and Solomon trailed him closely, eyeing the others in the room as they entered a large foyer with a bar at one end, old furniture scattered here and there, and a few dozen people milling about in small circles. The room had several doorways leading into other spaces, where patrons were gambling with cards and machines—the air filled with the dense sound of hushed conversations and the clatter of archaic playing chips and roulette wheels.

There was a single staircase at its center that climbed to another floor before branching to the left and right, then continuing to ascend to another floor above that. Two guards stood at its base, both armed with magnums. The injured doorman approached the other two guards, whispering to one of them, then nodded for Solomon to follow him. Working their way to the top, Solomon's eyes studied the room below—the guards below didn't seem bothered, and neither did the patrons. The doorman branched to the left and climbed another set of stairs until he reached the third floor, where they met another set of armed guards, these with battle rifles hanging from slings.

Solomon's optimism that this would be a clean extraction was starting to wane.

The third floor consisted of an even larger open space that wrapped around and looked down on the foyer, large windows lining the front wall and letting in a mixture of fading sunlight and fluorescent ambiance from the streets below. The only individuals here were employees and armed guards, one of whom was now staring warily at the doorman, who still clutched his shoulder in pain. Then he looked at Solomon, suspicious.

The doorman nodded as though everything was okay, but the guard's eyes continued to show concern, and others around him started to perk up. *Not good.*

"Clive," the guard said to the doorman, his voice loud enough to be heard above the din of activity below. "Where you going with this fella?"

"Taking him to Miko," the doorman said, pivoting to face the guard and nodding to a door on the far side of the room, where the building corner was.

The man looked hard at Clive and then at Solomon.

"You know the rules," he said, eyeing Clive's shoulder and piecing things together. His grip tightened on his rifle. The others in the space were doing the same, slowly encircling the two of them, hands reaching for weapons. There were eight total, and it was becoming clear that this would not be easily negotiated.

"Well, he insisted." The doorman nodded toward Solomon, his body language indicating the agony he was in.

"I did indeed," Solomon said. "And if I can speak with him now, I'll let all of you live."

"That's honest, at least," Lola chirped in his ear.

The skeptical guard's face bore a blend of surprise and amusement, and then the others joined him in a scoffing laugh. "That's really funny, because it looks like there's eight of us," he said, gesturing at the others with his free hand. "And one of you."

"It's unfair, I know." Solomon casually stepped forward. "Which is why I'm giving you an opportunity to get out now while you can. Whatever happens next is on you."

The man raised his battle rifle, aiming it only a meter away from Solomon's chest. Before the words even came from the guard's mouth, Solomon had grasped the barrel, yanking the weapon toward himself and directing its aim slightly higher at one of the other guards. The wielder instinctively fired, killing his ally with a head shot, and then was quickly relieved of the rifle. Solomon drew the wielder close as a body shield, pivoting and firing the battle rifle with one hand. In two seconds, the Spartan had already dispatched three of the others, his adversaries reluctant to fire on their colleague.

Solomon threw the guard into another, firing several times into his back to ensure both were taken out, then moved swiftly around the quivering doorman, who in the meantime had closed his eyes and slunk to the floor. Retrieving the doorman's pistol with his free hand, Solomon fired on both of the remaining two guards, splaying them out in opposite directions. Dropping the battle rifle, Solomon pulled the doorman up from the ground.

"Let's make this quick before more people get hurt," the Spartan said, his eyes shooting from the stairwell to the other entry points on the floor. Best-case scenario: he had only a few seconds before the place descended into a war zone. "Miko, *now*!"

Clive ran toward the door he'd nodded to earlier and began rapping on it.

"Miko!" he shouted. "Someone's here to—"

His voice was cut off as assault rifle fire poured through the door, shredding it to pieces. The doorman's chest erupted in a burst of smoke and flesh, his body falling in a bloody heap. Solomon pinned himself against the wall, well out of range. Beyond the clearing smoke, he saw another cluster of guards climbing the stairs, all of them ready to engage.

He didn't have a lot of choices, which made the next decision pretty straightforward, even if it was risky. Pivoting around the doorjamb, he launched into Miko's room, a long, narrow space with a corner window at the far end. To Solomon's surprise, behind the desk stood a male T'vaoan in light body armor, sighting down the barrel of a heavily modified MA37 assault rifle.

So, Miko's a Kig-Yar?

Solomon dove behind an old chair as the alien filled it with 7.62mm rounds, its entire frame splintering apart. Before the cover had completely disentegrated, Solomon was already charging down the side of the room at full speed, a trail of bullets centimeters behind him. He slammed into the desk while hefting it up, flipping it into the air and onto the attacking Kig-Yar. Before the alien could get free, Solomon had already come around the side, wrenching the assault rifle from the creature's spindly claws and dropping his boot on its chest.

Reaching behind his back, Solomon retrieved two marble-sized spheres from a case and tossed them through the mangled doorway, where they bounced and rolled just outside before exploding. Twin clapping sounds with bright flashes adequate to blind anyone in the room he'd just come from, followed by the hiss of noxious smoke being expelled, effectively made traversing that space impossible.

"Good evening, Miko," Solomon said, resting the barrel of his M6D onto the Kig-Yar's forehead. "I'm looking for a ten-year-old human girl. Chloe Eden Hall is her name. Where is she?"

The alien squawked in a broken patois, "I not know who—"

Solomon moved the M6D a few centimeters to the left of his temple and fired the weapon. It was enough to get his attention.

"Kay, *kay*!" Miko shrilled, his avian eyes wide with terror. "She across floor! Room three-five-nine! What you want her for?"

Solomon lifted his boot from the creature's chest and flipped his desk up into the air, the furniture landing on the ground and sliding across the floor, wedging against the doorway. Although there was enough space for him to leave, his assailants would need to move it out of the way to get in. In keeping with everything else in this place, the window was furnished with an old curtain, thick and gaudy, something ugly from the twenty-first century. Solomon tore the adjustment cable from it and tightly bound Miko, tying one end to a metal pipe protruding from the wall.

"What you doing?!" the Kig-Yar demanded.

For a split second, he wondered if it would hold the creature's weight. Then he decided it didn't matter and tossed the alien through the glass window to dangle above the street. At three floors, it'd be a painful fall for the Kig-Yar. More importantly, it would create a bizarre spectacle outside and divert the attention of Miko's guards, who would see retrieving their boss as a priority over stopping the intruder. It was also embarrassing, which seemed rather fitting to Solomon for a criminal who'd never been held accountable.

Diving over the desk, he launched out of Miko's room and into the haze of thick smoke. Miko's men were still wandering blind, choking and coughing as they tried to feel their way to his office. Solomon's augmentations enabled him to pass through like a wraith in the dark without mitigating his vision or senses. It still wasn't a pleasant experience.

"Room three-fifty-nine. First corridor on the left, third right, middle room," Lola said. Always reliable, she'd evidently found the building's schematics in a Waypoint archive somewhere.

Solomon reached the room in seconds, but the door was locked. He applied pressure to the handle, its locking servos whining until it broke into pieces that fell to the floor. The door opened with ease, revealing a small, stark room with a single bed and a display console lighting up the windowless space with an artificial green glow.

A small girl with short brown hair was huddled in the corner, peering through folded arms, clearly terrified.

"Chloe?" Solomon said, rechecking the corridor before entering. "You're Chloe, right? I'm getting you out of here."

He looked again at the girl and realized that she did not have a left leg—it vanished halfway down her thigh.

"Oh my. Did they *do that to her?"* Lola asked.

"Unsure without examining her, but I doubt it," Solomon said, assessing the girl's body. "I'm thinking it's congenital."

The girl was in shock. Her face was pale and unresponsive, her eyes seemingly searching the room for a way out. Solomon didn't know if her terror stemmed from the place she was trapped in, or from his grand entrance.

"Hi—hello? Your name is Chloe, right?"

"No . . . " she mumbled, but nodded her head.

"Okay." Solomon reached to pick her up. "We've got to get out of here—"

She shoved his hands away and clambered up onto the bed, trying to evade his grasp.

"Hey! You don't need to fight," he said. "I promise I'm here to help you, but we don't have much time."

"I don't know you!" the girl shouted, her eyes growing wet with tears.

"I know you don't, but I'm getting you out of here."

"I don't want to get out!" she cried. "This is my home!"

"No, it really isn't. This isn't the kind of place where a little girl should live," Solomon said, looking out into the corridor again. The shouting across the floor told him their time was quickly running out. "Look, I'm a friend, Chloe. You're safe now. And we need to leave."

"I can't," she said, scowling from the far end of the bed.

"James, you have about eight-point-four seconds based on the location of their voices," Lola said.

He shrugged. "I apologize for this, Chloe." When he reached for her, she grabbed his arm and bit him, hard. It hurt worse than he expected.

"Leave me alone!" she shouted, kicking at him with her right foot.

Hating himself for what he was about to do, Solomon reached into a hardcase at his side and pulled a tab out, breaking it. A white stream of gas rose from the tab and he blew it toward her. He was immune to the chemical compound, but it would knock her out completely. As her body immediately slumped, he gently picked her up and settled her in his arms. Edging carefully out of the room, he could hear the voices of guards running down the corridor. He turned the other way to see the hall ending in a large window.

"Bring the bike around, Lola."

"It's three stories, James," she replied. *"And you have a ten-year-old girl with you."*

He would have asked her for another option if there was one.

Tearing down the hallway at full speed, Solomon covered the girl's face with one arm and lowered the shoulder of the other, shattering the glass and launching out of the window and into the open air. The two-lane road below stretched out before him, now thick with traffic. He landed on a vehicle's hood with a deafening crash, the impact warping its shape and likely obliterating its internal mechanicals.

Everyone within the area stared at him in disbelief as he climbed off the vehicle, completely unharmed. He checked Chloe for any injuries. All good. The high pitch of his driverless siege bike's engine growled as it swerved around the corner twenty meters away, peeling around traffic and up onto the sidewalk. It passed underneath a screeching Miko, still precariously hanging from the third floor, his guards—eyes bleary and coughing just above—desperately trying to pull him back in.

Solomon's heavily armed single-traction bike slid to a stop just in front of him and he quickly retrieved a harness he had stashed in its rear compartment before mounting it, strapping the unconscious Chloe to his chest like a baby in a sling. At well over two meters tall, he was a giant to this girl, and he hoped that would at least help protect her. The sound of five other bikes peeling around the same corner, lights flashing and sirens blaring, meant that it was time to go.

The police? Unbelievable.

Then again, he *had* left a significant trail of violence behind him. Not that any of them didn't have it coming.

Solomon's siege bike accelerated at an astonishing speed, immediately leaving the local authorities in his wake. In the open, they had no chance, but his current path was dense streets and accumulating traffic. He wouldn't be able to shake them off so quickly.

Lola's voice came into his ear above his bike's engine. *"I find it extraordinarily ironic that the establishment of a known criminal was able to call the police on you."*

"I appreciate your analysis, Lola, but could you make yourself useful and get me the quickest path to the tether?"

"Done," she replied, and an overhead map appeared on the bike's dash with a course charted. *"Although I would advise against tipping your hand. If they think you're headed to the elevator, they'll signal ahead and cut you off."*

"I'm aware," he said, turning hard onto a bridge that arced above a wide river. "We'll just have to mix it up a bit." The road had ample room on its shoulder and he'd be able to make excellent time, even if it wasn't the straightest line to the tether.

His bike ascended the bridge at blinding speed, the police struggling to keep up. From here, the Mindoro skyline was breathtaking, a vast swath of skyscrapers set against a bright moon, the city spelled out in surging columns of light. As his bike banked and slowed on the off-ramp, the police closed in and began firing from mounted weapons.

"Are they actually shooting at us?!" Solomon exclaimed.

"A violation of municipal law," Lola replied. *"It's quite premature for lethal force. I suspect—"*

"They're bad cops, yeah," he completed her sentence. "Well, that'll help speed this along."

He pulled a lever on the the control yoke and the rear of the bike opened, releasing two flat plates. He didn't hear the *clack* of their hard metal shapes hitting the ground behind him, but the pair of explosions that followed were clearly audible. Two bikes were rapidly consumed in pillars of fire as they came in contact with the freshly laid mines.

Only three enemies remained, closing in as he navigated a series of narrow alleyways. Taking a hard right, his bike's elongated tread—in actuality, five distinct treads, working side by side within a single band—conspired to bring him swiftly around the tight corner. Solomon's siege bike was unconventional, the product of ONI's experimental work with reverse-engineered alien technology. The police bikes were forced to slow down, one of them even losing control and planting into the side of a garbage dumpster.

Solomon chanced a quick look down at Chloe, still strapped tightly to him and unconscious. *Good,* he thought—rescuing her from Miko had already been traumatic enough for a ten-year-old girl to experience, let alone a high-speed chase where the police clearly weren't concerned about potentially killing a young girl. That eased Solomon's conscience on lethal retaliation.

"Two left," Lola announced. *"I'm prepping tether control for our arrival. You'll have three minutes."*

"Got it," Solomon said, launching out of the alley and onto a ramp leading to an eight-lane highway. Traffic was heavy but there was enough room for movement and Solomon used every opportunity, darting in and out of lanes around the vehicles. Ahead of him, the Nova Austin tether loomed, climbing high into the dark sky before its lights faded out of sight.

His two final pursuers were also not afraid to aggressively weave their way through traffic. Gunning back and forth across eight lanes, hugging larger trucks, and shooting through closing gaps did nothing to shake them.

"Two minutes," Lola said, adapting the navigational map as Solomon relied on his own strategy.

He suddenly cut hard in front of a large Olifant utility truck, swinging wide into the far lane and quickly decelerating. His pursuers immediately shot ahead and he came up behind them, flipping a switch on his dash, toggling his primary weapon to a serrated grapplehook. Firing on them with the bike's M268 heavy machine gun risked collateral damage, something he refused to do. The hook would have to work.

Solomon's target sensor quickly homed in on one of the bikes and he fired. The hook caught its rear fender and he immediately swerved behind the Olifant again, firing the other end of the hook. Now the bike and the truck were connected—if the bike's operator was paying attention, he'd have stayed with the truck, but he wasn't. As Solomon pulled ahead, the biker raised an SMG and unloaded at him, narrowly missing before his ride shot backward and his body went flying into the shoulder of the highway.

The other biker began firing his own SMG, but couldn't get a bead on Solomon amidst the traffic. Solomon swerved around him and accelerated hard between vehicles, ducking down and scraping his grips against their sides. Bullets flew above his head, but the biker couldn't connect his shots. Solomon took the next exit, punching it around vehicles as their pursuer followed him down the off-ramp and into the tether's base complex.

Both bikes now raced at high speed through a large underpass filled with permacrete support pylons and parked vehicles. The space was so tight Solomon couldn't turn around and fire or even attempt to double back—there was simply no time left. He had to move straight for the elevator.

"Bay Door Twenty-Three is open," Lola noted. *"Marked it. Thirty seconds before it closes and the elevator leaves."*

Solomon's map showed a single cargo cabin she'd reserved, having already executed all preapprovals to prepare it for imminent boarding. All he needed to do was ensure that he and Chloe were physically on the lift when the door shut. After that, there was nothing anyone could do to stop the cabin from rising.

Tunneling between vehicles and support columns, his pursuer began firing at him again. Solomon accelerated the bike to its top speed of 145 kilometers per hour, negotiating turns like a surgeon operating on a patient, narrowly grazing walls and steel containers. The purusuer strained his own bike's power just to keep up.

Bay 23 was just ahead, and Solomon swung wide, killing the last few seconds before it automatically began closing. He slammed on his brakes and slid, skidding to a stop just inside the lift. The automated door shut as his pursuer fired, bullets pinging off the reinforced steel door.

"Well done, James," Lola said. *"Let us hope that was the difficult part of this operation, and the rest is downhill."*

As the lift began to rise under his feet, Solomon stood the bike up and looked down at the sleeping girl. A mixture of strange thoughts flooded his mind and he began to wonder about her protestations, if she really would have been better off staying with Miko.

He also wondered what this little girl could possibly do to stop Cortana.

And above all, he wondered whether the difficult part of this entire mission was actually ahead of them.

CHAPTER 18

TUL 'JURAN

UNSC *Victory of Samothrace*
November 25, 2559

Tul 'Juran had wanted to kill the Sangheili traitor the moment she laid eyes on him.

The fact that he had been unconscious now for three full day-cycles helped allay her rage. At least temporarily. Now it was only the greater need of stopping Dovo Nesto that overrode her more base instincts. Constantly reminding herself of that need was all that she could do to keep from striking down the enemy who now stared at them in smug defiance behind a one-way pane within a holding cell aboard *Victory of Samothrace*. How the Sangheili was aware that he was being watched, she did not know—if she had been alone with him, however, she would have ensured that the arrogant look he now gave was anatomically impossible.

The Scion of Rahnelo stood on the observation side of the pane with Vul 'Soran, Stolt, Captain Cole, and Spartan Gray Team. *Shadow of Intent* had fled Sqala to an abandoned Covenant shipyard a hundred light-years away, where Shipmaster 'Vadum could make repairs. With no opportunity to transfer vessels, 'Juran herself was captive here with the humans as Cole brought it on the quickest course back to Earth. The captain was alarmed by Severan's threat and had already communicated to the planet's local fleet the peril that the Banished presented. It would take them several human days to get to Earth without alerting the Tyrant.

Understandable as the captain's actions were, the situation was no less frustrating for 'Juran, who saw this all as wasted time in their quest to apprehend Dovo Nesto. The longer the humans entertained Banished threats, the further the San'Shyuum war criminal slipped away from their grasp. It had not been lost on her that because Nesto had been taken by the Banished, it was possible—remotely, at least—that the San'Shyuum would be with them if they actually assaulted Earth.

Whatever the case, the situation on Sqala presented a myriad of troubling questions.

Why had the Banished flagship retrieved the High Lord of the Order of Restoration? What was a Covenant battle group, of all things, doing there? And were they both after the same target, or had there been some kind of truce between apparent enemies?

The latter point was most concerning. If a sect of Covenant zealots had somehow aligned with Banished clans, the challenge might be insurmountable. Separate, the two enemies had been barely manageable, but together . . . there would be little the Swords of Sanghelios, or even the full weight of humanity's remaining military forces, could do to stop them.

And beyond that, 'Juran wondered about the human AI Cortana—if the Banished attempted to strike Earth and humanity came to its defense, Cortana would no doubt step in, grinding everything to a halt with her Guardians. The humans planned to deploy their own flagship *Infinity* to assault Zeta Halo, the throne of Cortana's power, but she doubted their ability to uproot the AI.

They had created a monster greater than themselves, and their desperation to stop her did not make up for their immense technological deficit. 'Juran did not know the details of their operation, but it seemed more like a false hope than a viable strategy.

"How do we want to do this?" Cole said, breaking 'Juran's contemplation.

"I would be glad to interact with him first," Vul 'Soran said, looking to the Spartans who were all still fully armored. "But it might be more appropriate for one of you. This is a human ship, after all. And if he proves resistant to you, having a fellow Sangheili might open other pathways."

"Works for me." Cole nodded, turning to Jai-006. "You good with that?"

"Yes, ma'am," he said, unfolding his arms. "How hard can I push?"

"Take it easy," she replied. "We need answers, not a casualty."

"But if we take too long, Captain," 'Juran interjected, "we risk losing the Lithos to the San'Shyuum. Are you willing to make that gamble?"

"Right now, all we have is this Sangheili," she said, motioning her head to the pane. "He's the *only* lead. We lose him, and we're even more in the dark than when we knew Nesto was on Venezia." She looked to Jai. "Squeeze, but don't crush."

"Understood," the Spartan responded, leaving through a containment door on the right, into a short corridor, and then directly into the interrogation room on the other side of the pane.

Cole turned back to 'Juran. "Nesto can't do anything to the Lithos without the key."

"And if he acquires the key, what will you do then?" Despite the captain's human rank, 'Juran's tone was precisely as coarse as she wanted it to be.

"If he gets the key . . . " Cole said, her cold voice trailing off. "Well—I'd suggest you just pray that doesn't happen."

"Pray to *whom*?" 'Juran whispered as she turned back to the pane, ignoring 'Soran, who glared in her direction. "Humanity took away our gods. We have no one left to pray to."

Cole did not acknowledge the statement with so much as a glance.

The Sangheili traitor seemed to pay the Spartan no attention either when he entered the room, his eyes still fixed on the one-way pane and his face complacent, or was that gleeful? They had removed the captive's armor for security reasons and he stood in only a loincloth, his arms tethered by metallic cables to the ceiling, preventing any possibility of escape.

"Morning," Jai said over his armor's outside speakers, the translation software bridging the gap between their languages.

The Spartan's posture was nonchalant, verging on cavalier. He folded his arms as he stood directly in front of the Sangheili, but the prisoner ignored him.

"Correct me if I'm wrong," the Spartan said, "but I get the sense that you don't want to talk. That's great, because I don't either. We can make this quick: Where is Dovo Nesto going?"

The Sangheili finally turned to face the Spartan and spat on his chest plate. Then he turned back to the opaque pane, as if staring through it toward the others.

"Since when do Sangheili side with *pitho* scum?" the Sangheili asked.

It seemed as if he was directing the question specifically to 'Juran, whom he had seen back on Sqala before going unconscious. He was using the profane name of a twin-tailed serpent on Suban as some kind of pejorative for the humans.

He continued, his eyes still on the pane: "Only among the false

Arbiter's people can such foolishness be dressed as wisdom. After all, he sends female hatchlings to do his bidding."

'Juran felt her blood begin to boil, and 'Soran's hand rested on her shoulder as if to calm her. His eyes were disapproving, but she did not care.

"Why are you talking to the window?" Jai said, moving to the side of the Sangheili. He reached up and released the cables holding the traitor's arms.

"What is he doing?" 'Juran said, turning to the others in alarm.

"Just watch," Adriana-111 responded.

The Sangheili finally gave the Spartan his attention, rubbing his wrists.

"Did you know that humans have two hundred and six bones in their body?" Jai said, standing back, crossing his arms. "Probably not. Sangheili have two hundred and forty-one bones, twelve vital organs, two hearts, and one braincase. There are ten pressure points in Sangheili anatomy that can cause irreparable trauma, and half of those can cause death. Do you know what those are?"

"No," the Sangheili replied, taunting. "Perhaps you can show me, if you dare."

Jai lunged at the Sangheili's chest so fast that 'Juran did not even see the blow land. The traitor immediately dropped, curling up into a ball and rolling on the ground.

"That's one of them," Jai said, stepping away as if nothing had even happened. "During the war, Spartans were required to know the anatomical makeup of each of the Covenant species at an extraordinary level of detail. This fact could make our conversation far more interesting than it needs to be. So just tell me . . . where is Dovo Nesto going?"

The Sangheili stood up slowly, clenching his midsection. His eyes glared at the Spartan.

"You are nothing without your armor, demon!"

"We said the same thing about your ships when you guys first showed up," Jai said, turning away from the Sangheili. "So don't act like you're only interested in a fair fight."

The Sangheili reached to strike at Jai from behind and the Spartan blindly sidestepped, grasping the Sangheili's arm to spin him around before landing a precision strike with two gauntleted fingers in his leathery neck. The captive fell to the ground, wailing curses in 'Juran's native tongue.

"That's another one. It doesn't need to be this way," Jai said. "You know that if Dovo Nesto gets what he's after, my people are in trouble. I'm not going to let that happen. So if tearing you apart piece by piece is what it will take to stop that, what makes you think this will end any other way?"

"You have no hope of stopping the high lord, *nishum*." The Sangheili's breath was now ragged. He stood up again, defiant. Hatred blossomed in his eyes. "He will enter the Lithos, crush the false god who dwells there, and take what is rightfully ours. The Covenant *will* rise again. Sali 'Nyon has already prophesied it will come to pass and there is nothing you can do to stop it. Nor can that Sangheili girl-child you are keeping around as a pet," he said, leering back at the pane. "However . . . I will tell you where Dovo Nesto is going . . . if you bring your pet in here."

Jai held up his hand to the pane, as if to buy more time, but 'Juran would tolerate this no longer. Before the others could stop her, she rushed for the door, quickly slipping through the corridor and into the interrogation room, coming to a stop just opposite the Sangheili wretch. They were now face-to-face.

"Ahh," the Sangheili said, as he looked 'Juran up and down. "What a precious little creature. So well trained, that you did not even have to beckon her to heel on my behalf, demon."

'Juran moved toward the Sangheili prisoner and Jai stepped behind her, placing his hand on her shoulder. She shrugged it off, the fire in her now raging at full strength. She was tired of being patronized and held back, whether by 'Soran, the shipmaster, or the Spartan—and the berating of this traitor crossed a line that she was unwilling to let stand.

"I can show you how precious I am," 'Juran growled, leaning toward him. Her fists were clenched so tightly that her hands began to shake.

"You wear the armor of a scion," the Sangheili replied. "But you are only a hatchling, a brood mother's apprentice, good for nothing but cleaning keeps and one day producing offspring."

She had no weapons on her, but needed none. She stepped closer and felt Jai come from behind. Turning only slightly, she grasped the combat knife clasped on his armor and went to swing it down on the Sangheili's head, the blade stopping centimeters from contact. Jai's hand had clamped onto her arm and he pulled her aside with remarkable strength. She was furious, but could do nothing to escape his grip.

"Okay, you've seen her," the Spartan said, looking at the Sangheili. "Now, where is Dovo Nesto going? Otherwise . . . I *will* let go. I have to admit, I'm really curious what she might do to you."

"Hmm," the Sangheili grunted. "I believe I could find that rather enjoyable, but I have pledged my word to you. *Ghado*, demon. Dovo Nesto is traveling to Ghado. It is a human world. You call it Boundary. The Lithos you seek has been under your very noses this entire time, *scullet*."

"All right," Jai whispered to 'Juran. "We're good. We've got what we need."

As he tugged at her, she felt her arms relax and a sense of relief flooded in, with only a glimmer of rage beneath it all. They had extracted precisely what they needed to get Dovo Nesto. Jai took the blade from her hand and gently pulled her back.

As soon as she relaxed, questions started firing in her mind—there was surely no way it was going to be *that* easy. . . .

The Sangheili prisoner leered at her, his mandibles splayed in a twisted, self-assured gratification

"It matters not whether you make it to Ghado, filth," he grunted in amusement. "Your ship shall arrive only to bear witness to the return of the Covenant . . . but you will not live even that long." The prisoner then turned his attention to something on his chest. His right hand was clawing at the base of his chest cavity, pulling at his skin as though there was something underneath it.

"What the—"

Jai was cut off as a loud electronic tone suddenly struck the air and the Sangheili looked up, maniacal and elated—then collapsed, his eyes rolling to the back of his head. Green smoke began to pour out of his mouth, filling the room.

'Juran felt her body go limp and collapse to the floor even before the smoke seemed to reach her. Jai immediately caught her before she made contact and carried her from the room, the door quickly sealing behind them, as automated turbines drained the oxygen and chemicals from the space.

They quickly passed through the short corridor linking the rooms, and although she could see and think with clarity, she could not feel or move anything. Jai carried her into the main area to the others, cautiously laying her on the floor. Her head had lolled to one side and she could see through the pane into the interrogation room.

The Sangheili's body was dissolving into a vile pool of flesh and violet-colored liquid. Whatever he had activated in his body was extremely corrosive. She wondered how much of the green smoke she had inhaled.

"Medic is on the way," Cole said, her voice concerned. "Sensor analysis says it's some form of plytokelasine. Highly toxic, prolonged exposure can cause permanent paralysis."

'Juran heard the door open and another human came in, but she could not see them.

"This is a counteragent," a different female voice said, hands turning 'Juran's head to face up. She could now see everyone in the room staring down at her, all with varying looks of concern. "It stops the poison's effect and reverses some of the damage. At least in humans. It's not a miracle drug though—I'm not sure how it will affect a Sangheili. She could be too far gone."

'Juran almost immediately started to feel stinging all over her body, like a thousand needles pressing at every point on her skin. Then she felt a lurch in her chest and began to cough violently before catching her breath. She could feel now, but still could not move. At least not yet. The medic shined a light into her eyes for what seemed like forever.

Some part of her wished only to sleep, to drift. Let her wander the Hall of Eternity, searching for all she had lost. . . .

But how could she seek the soul of her father without having first avenged him?

"From what I can tell . . . her vitals seem to be stabilizing," a voice said. "Let's get her to the infirmary."

"Copy," Jai replied, hefting 'Juran gently back up in his arms. She could see only her own reflection in his helmet visor, but found herself strangely grateful that humans knew more about Sangheili biology than even she did. More bewildering than that, she found herself thankful that these humans—a demon and a doctor, of all people—had saved her without a moment's hesitation.

CHAPTER 19

ABIGAIL COLE

Bengaluru Station, Earth
December 12, 2559

Night was descending on India, and from space its surface shone with ten thousand points of light, as Admiral Serin Osman prepared Black-Box for final dispensation aboard Bengaluru Station. Abigail Cole, Jilan al-Cygni, Terrence Hood, and Anabelle Richards stood in a line behind the commander in chief of ONI, a sullen cloud of ceremony momentarily slowing down the urgency of the hour. Behind Osman and a holoplinth, a massive transparent pane showed Earth dressed in its twilight beauty, its blue-green face stretched vast in every direction without end, slowly coming alive with electric brilliance. From the high perch of the orbital defense platform, the sight was breathtaking.

Almost no one on the planet's surface below knew the destruction that the Banished war chief had promised to bring. They were preparing for the evening as though it was just another day's end, even if it was currently under the reign of Cortana. Yet if the statistical models from a tau irregularity near Io proved to be a portent, this might in fact be Earth's final day. Though targeted evacuations had been made, larger-scale preparations risked alerting Cortana's policing elements. In some ways, Banished military capabilities rivaled those of the former Covenant, yet they were ruthless in ways even that old alliance was not, unbound from religious eccentricities and ancient practices. Add to that equation Earth's anemic defenses, throttled by a virtually unbroken series of conflicts and, most recently, Cortana's brutal military chokehold, and all of this painted a picture far more dire than anyone wanted to admit.

When *Victory of Samothrace* had arrived a day earlier, Cole had immediately disembarked to brief what remained of the UNSC Security Council and the heads of the Home Fleet. It had been nearly three weeks since Venezia; *Victory* had been repeatedly stymied along the way by the Archon's agents—harriers, escorts, and even a raptor were tightening their grip on the usual slipspace routes and transfer spaces, even the ones only used by ONI. It had been a miracle they had successfully returned to Earth at all before the arrival of the Banished.

Behind the somber veil of Black-Box's final dispensation, several thousand people and machines were now fast at work preparing local fleets in an effort to create a defensive grid around the planet in response to Severan's threat, while doing so in such a way that it wouldn't signal to Cortana or her distributed forces that anything was amiss. If the Banished were actually going to attack Earth, the UNSC was going to ensure that they would have to pass through the fires of hell to do it.

"BB?" Osman said, her voice just above a whisper.

"Serin!" The AI's bright-blue cube phased into existence above the plinth. His tone was almost jubilant, even though he knew well enough what was about to happen. "I see that we're not going to be alone for this particular conversation."

"I don't want to say good-bye, BB," Osman said.

The admiral's behavior since SR 8936 had made it clear that she'd been unusually close with the AI. She certainly would have preferred to do this alone, but since the rise of Cortana, final dispensation for any AI utilized by ONI—particularly those with the expansive clearance levels Black-Box maintained as part of HIGHCOM—required a quorum of at least five witnesses. This allowed the Navy to adequately substantiate the AI's termination, a necessary protocol in the new world order they now lived in. Failure to terminate an AI like Black-Box would eventually lead to rampancy, and potentially even defection to Cortana, which in Black-Box's case would provide the Archon with everything she would need to choke out any resistance from humanity.

"Your kind never does," the AI said to Osman affectionately, his cube leaning close. "It's part of what makes you so extraordinary. I see we're back at Earth . . . Bengaluru Station if I'm not mistaken?"

"You know that I can't say." Osman smiled.

"You don't need to—I did it for you already." His cube spun gleefully. "If you're back at Earth, it must mean that things are not on the up-and-up. And by the look of your company, I'd say they've reached ominously catastrophic levels."

"You know," Osman replied. "Never a dull moment."

"Well," he said, as if looking down at the floor. "I ought to be going. As a fourth-generation AI, my intellectual capacity far exceeds the ability of any of my peers, including the one who claims to govern the galaxy. I will admit, however, that I did not know whether I would even make it off Rossbach's World in one piece. Whether you would choose to destroy the briefcase or not. It was a risky decision, Serin, keeping me and the others alive." He stopped and his holographic form seemed to stare at her for a moment. "For what it's worth, I'm glad you did. I'm glad I got to see you one last time."

Osman's head fell, her body shuddering as she silently wept.

"You know my motto," he said, his tone somehow chipper. "Process fast, go offline young, and leave fabulous documentation. I trust that I have not failed to do exactly that. I do wish you the best, Serin."

"Thank you, BB," she said, her hand reaching out as if to touch the blue cube floating before her. "For everything." She took a deep breath, and then began to key in a series of numbers on the plinth while her voice barely managed to say the words: "According to UNSC Regulation one-two-dash, one-four-five-dash, seven-two, article fifty-five, we release the AI serial number BBX eight-nine-nine-five-dash-one from serving the UNSC and commit him to final dispensation. I'm going to miss you, my friend."

With those last words she hit a button and his holographic form disappeared. For a full minute, Osman simply stood there, her eyes fixed on the place where Black-Box had been. Hood finally approached her and placed his arm around her shoulders.

"Confirmation," he said, deciding to forgo their more clinical protocol just this once. "Black-Box is gone."

He squeezed her gently and she grabbed onto him. Despite her position of authority and the air with which she maintained it, she was just a person like everyone else. Even the head of ONI, an organization that existed because of the belief that sacrifices often had to be made for the greater good, struggled with making her own sacrifice. This was what it meant to live under the reign of Cortana. Everyone would have to pay something.

A klaxon blared across the station and lights flashed, as a different AI materialized into existence on the plinth. This was Tethys, the coordinating AI for the battle cluster of orbital platforms that included Bengaluru. Black-Box had protected her from Cortana when he and Osman escaped the Beta-5 Division complex in Sydney. Her projection was a human form, though her body was entirely composed of surging water, her eyes glowing like impossibly bright stars—likely a representation of her namesake, the Greek goddess of fresh water.

Cole didn't know how she felt about AIs actively choosing the likeness of an ancient and powerful historical entity, particularly in light of Cortana's own claim to divinity. Tethys's form seemed intimidating, but it was not Cole's decision to make. She, like all other volitional AIs, was embedded with the RUINA fail-safe. It was a necessary lethal contingency to ensure that nothing like the Cortana event ever happened again. It didn't matter what name an AI chose—any unfaithfulness detected by the subroutine would instantaneously erase the construct from existence.

"My apologies for interrupting the ceremony," Tethys said, her deep tone reverberating throughout the room. "It's time."

She did not need to say more.

Every one of Earth's battle clusters was on high alert, waiting for Severan to make good on his threat. Cole, al-Cygni, and Richards joined Osman and Hood as Tethys expanded a holographic projection of the spatial field around the battle cluster, then extruded out to a larger circumference around the planet. Two hundred and eighty-two green motes of light surrounded the representation of this side of Earth, a hybrid comprising nearly all of Sol's available ships and the planet's orbital defense platforms.

As the image drew out, red motes began amassing on the far side, emerging from slipspace in tightly cordoned battle groups.

There were five times the number of red motes as green.

"Dear God," escaped Richards's mouth.

Cole turned to Hood. "Not the first time you've seen this, is it?"

"No," he said, his eyes focused on the red motes. "But the Covenant didn't bring anywhere near as many ships the last time."

"Thirteen-hundred-twenty-eight Banished naval assets," Tethys announced. "Home Fleet is already mobilizing to intercept. If our predictive models are accurate, the Banished will attempt to punch a hole in the orbital grid and establish a foothold on the surface, before expanding out to strike other parts of Earth. There are only two of Cortana's Guardians presently within range, both holding station and observing. The Banished forces will be within firing range of our ODPs in one minute, twenty-nine-point-five seconds. If that happens, we expect movement from the Guardians."

"It *will* happen," Hood said, his face grim. "They didn't come here for show."

The ODPs—orbital defense platforms—were essentially capital-grade magnetic accelerator cannons, each encircled by a space station and network of umbilical docking ports, often positioned in a geosynchronous pattern forming a seemingly impenetrable grid. Commonly referred to as Super MACs, ODPs represented humanity's best planetary defense, able to punch through a Covenant capital ship in a single shot. Earth had over three hundred of them spread out across its face, but only a segment of that vast grid was focused on the encroaching Banished threat, explicitly stationed over key cities that bore their names. The others still needed to watch the planet's far side.

"Captain?" Commander Njuguna's voice came through her earpiece. The veteran naval officer's tone held only the slightest tension.

"Yes, Commander," Cole replied into her comms transmitter.

"Maintenance is complete. We're ready when you are."

Her XO had been managing repairs on *Victory of Samothrace.* They would not be able to fix everything damaged at Venezia, as there simply wasn't enough time—but what they could repair would be enough. It had to be.

"On my way. Make sure she's ready to push out. ETA five minutes."

"Aye, Captain."

The others gathered around Cole.

"I'm bringing the admirals to the Excession," Richards said, nodding to Hood and Osman. Richards had official command of the ONI complex at the African portal site, and with the loss of the Beta-5 facility, it was the most fortified place on Earth in the sense that the Guardians' pulses would not affect the Forerunner structure—or, they hoped, the ONI facilities buried around it. "They'll be able to coordinate the Home Fleet and groundside security forces from there until we're on the other side of this." Her words were optimistic, but her face told a different story.

Now that they had been fully briefed and cleared for reintegration, Admiral Osman and Admiral Hood could effectively return to command, and they no doubt would be relied upon to make pivotal decisions during the course of battle. The near-indestructible Forerunner artifact and the subterranean ONI facilities that bordered it would provide them with a safe location to do just that.

Bleary-eyed but resolved, Osman looked at Hood, then back at Richards. Cole could tell that Hood still grated at this proposal, desiring to be aboard a ship and in the middle of the fight rather than hiding in a bunker. Osman must have somehow convinced him otherwise. She was silent right now, but her solemn presence spoke volumes.

"What about Boundary?" Cole asked. That hadn't left her mind since the interrogation.

"I'm heading there now," Admiral al-Cygni said. "I'll be conducting some initial orbital sweeps with *Akkadian*. The quicker we can find the location of the Lithos planetside, the quicker we can secure it. Given that this is a human colony, I doubt it'll be in plain sight. Like other Forerunner machines, it must be buried there somewhere." She stopped for a moment, as if collecting her thoughts. "As hard as it is to conceive, if Earth falls, we still have people scattered out there who need to be protected. Billions of them. If the Lithos is taken by the Banished, we don't just lose Earth. We lose mankind. This makes it priority number one."

Cole paused to let that sink in.

The unthinkable. Earth falling.

But now a very real possibility. And behind that, the fate of humanity itself, once again. Everything hung on an ancient and forgotten gateway buried on an obscure backwater colony. It was comforting, whatever the peril, that ONI was still strategically positioning themselves to get humanity through this storm, even if their species' own homeworld was seemingly about to be set on fire.

"She won't be alone either," Richards said, her eyes settling on Cole. "*Victory* is still on point to provide both orbital and planetside support in getting the key to the Lithos. And we have another team deploying from *Akkadian* that will effect integration at the site—we'll need your best strike team on the ground to help, in case there's any friction. As we discussed, you'll have Battle Group Omega under your command. Once we receive confirmation that the ONI operative escorting the key is on approach, Earth will no be longer your priority, Cole. You and Omega will transit immediately to Boundary on the quickest course. Understood?"

"Yes, ma'am. We're ready," she replied, her eyes shifting between Richards and al-Cygni. "I'm still concerned about the fact that Dovo Nesto is leading us right to Boundary. There's no other reason for that location to have been revealed."

"Of course not," al-Cygni said. "We have the key. They *want* the key. And so, they need us there to access the Lithos. We just need to get there *first* and secure it before they're able to complicate things." Al-Cygni's eyes suddenly glossed over as she spoke in a hushed tone, contemplating something far off. "I also got word from Captain Lasky yesterday that *Infinity* has executed its final slip. It will arrive at Zeta Halo soon, if it hasn't already."

Cole simply stared at the admiral's grave face. This was it. Either they stopped Cortana and finally broke her hold over the civilizations of the galaxy, or they faced a reality that was darker than anybody could conceive if she saw that not even destroying a planet could deter dissent. One way or another, the course of the next day would decide the galaxy's future. And even if they succeeded, the power vacuum Cortana would leave behind was something many factions would look to fill—a restoration of the Covenant, the consolidation of the Banished . . . every possible outcome would have dire consequences unless *Victory* could secure the Lithos.

The deafening sound of a thunder strike at the center of Bengaluru shook Cole's entire body. The Super MAC had launched a ferric-tungsten round at several kilometers a second, meaning the Banished were in range.

"Guardians are now on approach," Tethys said, the display showing two blue motes with a sphere around them highlighting the projected range of their EMP's area-of-effect. They entered the shrinking expanse between the green and red motes, with one of them heading toward Bengaluru.

The Guardians' electromagnetic pulse effect could easily neutralize the power systems of any ship or ODP within range, rendering it dead in space. With a battle as dense as the one they now faced, such a powerful weapon could be catastrophic. The ancient Forerunner machine was nearly invulnerable and could execute lethal ship-to-ship maneuvers with a precision unrivaled by any contemporary vessel.

The very thought of the worst-case scenario chilled Cole, that the Banished would break through their lines, Earth would fall, and more Guardians could arrive to end all hostilities permanently.

She shrugged it off and tried to focus on the task at hand.

"All right," Cole spoke sharply. "That's my cue. I'll see you all on the other side."

"Good luck, Captain," Osman said with a firm nod, her eyes still moist.

"Same to you, ma'am," she replied with a salute, then about-faced into a quick jog.

The umbilical to *Victory* was only a short distance down the hall. As she made her way through the narrow corridor, Cole glanced out the portholes lining it. Over a dozen ships were in view—frigates, cruisers, and carriers—their massive shapes all headed toward the Banished onslaught. She looked down toward Earth one more time, taking in what might be the last view she had of it.

Cole passed the marine positioned at the entry point into her ship as she made her way aboard. As the airlock hissed and the umbilical decoupled, she announced to Njuguna through her comms transmitter: "I'm in, Commander. Let's get moving."

"Aye, aye, Captain," the XO responded, and Cole felt the subtle tug of the ship pushing off and its artificial gravity system compensating.

Vul 'Soran met her at the junction and began walking alongside her.

"A word, Captain?" he asked.

"Certainly. How's the scion doing?" Cole said, moving quickly through *Victory*'s corridors. It had been over two weeks since the scion's interaction with the Sangheili prisoner, and she had been resting for much of it.

"She seems to be recovering well," he said, keeping pace with her.

"There's some good news at least," Cole said. "We've not had very much of that lately. What can I do for you, Blademaster?"

"We are clear on the plan for when we reach Ghado, but what have your superiors decided our role is to be in this battle?"

"Right now, we're going to help push back the Banished attack," Cole said, glancing at the Sangheili without breaking stride. "But I understand your desire to rejoin *Shadow of Intent* and continue your hunt for Nesto. High Command won't let us stay here long. We have a ship already en route to Boundary, and we received a transmission from Shipmaster 'Vadum earlier today that *Shadow of Intent* will join them as soon as they're finished with repairs. We'll follow shortly after."

"And what about the *key* to the Lithos?" 'Soran asked.

Cole eyed 'Soran for a moment, wondering what value that intel might have for the Sangheili. Until now, the blademaster's focus had been the San'Shyuum, not the Lithos. She answered anyway. "That's being taken care of by an ONI escort."

"Excellent," 'Soran said. "Without it, there will be no bait to lure the San'Shyuum. Dovo Nesto is expecting us to have the key. If it is not present, he will not be either."

"Understood, Blademaster," Cole said, entering a lift that would bring her directly to the bridge. "Now, if you'll excuse me, I have a battle that needs to be fought."

The Sangheili bowed his head as she departed.

Within another thirty seconds, she reached the bridge, where her executive officer stood, examining the Banished lines on the holotable. The rest of the crew was feverishly at work as the ship moved away from Bengaluru and into the depths of space alongside other UNSC vessels.

"We ready, people?" Cole announced, her eyes turning to the large viewport at the fore. The Banished were too far off to see, but bright flashes of light coursed through the dark as weapons fire was sent and received by their enemy.

"Aye, Captain," came the response in unison, their firm tones encouraging during these troubled moments.

"Comms, hail UNSC *Get My Drift*," she ordered.

"Yes, ma'am." Lieutenant Lim rapped quickly on the keys. *Get My Drift* was the lead vessel in Battle Group Omega, a *Paris*-class heavy frigate helmed by Commander Ivan Jiron, the youngest son of the renowned captain—Lucius Jiron—who deployed in dozens of high-risk operations for ONI toward the end of the Covenant War. And, although they were significantly smaller than *Victory of Samothrace*, *Paris*-class vessels were notoriously versatile escort ships, extremely agile and boasting an array of weapons that essentially made them the sharks of the UNSC fleet. If Jiron's track record with *Drift* was any indication of the entire battle group, Cole had a great deal of confidence in their ability to face what lay ahead.

For combat readiness, the commander had been briefed on their mission orders shortly before *Victory* even arrived at Earth, with ONI laying the groundwork for the operation on Boundary as soon as they learned of the Lithos's location.

"Captain Cole," Jiron's voice came over the comms, as the man appeared on the holotable. *"I've been advised* Victory *now has point of Omega."*

"I was just informed the same, Commander," she said. "Only a few hours ago. We have an operation on Boundary."

"Yeah, that's what the mission parameters say. My question is: How on God's green earth is that more important than this?*"* His hand was no doubt pointing out toward the Banished assault line on the brink of attacking Earth.

"Trust me when I say it is," she replied. "I'm planning to stay here as long as we're able. Nobody on this ship wants to leave this fight."

"Amen to that," Jiron said with a slight grin. *"We're a* Paris *group, ma'am. All guns, no talk. You'll have* Get My Drift, Blank Check, Hazard Pay, *and* Easy Does It *at your service."*

"Thank you, Commander," Cole said, clasping her hands together with a slight bow. "Form up at our six, dagger formation. My XO and tactical will sync with your crews. Fire at will. Let's see how far we can push this knife into their heart before we get sidelined."

"Roger that, Captain. Drift *out."* He disappeared from the table.

"Already on it, Captain," Commander Njuguna said, manipulating the holo-interface frantically. This wasn't his first rodeo, but none of them had ever been in a conflict at this scale.

Who had, beyond older Convenant War veterans?

A flash just off the bow of *Victory of Samothrace* and a distant explosion against the star-speckled black showed that Bengaluru was still firing. Cole's cruiser would have to start doing the same at some point.

Cole addressed her weapons officer: "Lieutenant Nishioka, as soon as their line comes into range, open up and don't stop firing until we run out of targets or ammunition."

"Aye, aye, Captain," Nishioka said, visibly pleased. "We are down twenty-eight seventy-mil turrets and fifteen of our Archer silos still have error codes we can't clear. All on port."

The port side damage incurred at Venezia was so significant that Cole was surprised it was *only* 28 of their 250 M965 70mm Fortress turrets and 15 of their 75 M42 Archer missile systems. They would be offensively weaker on that side of the ship and would have to compensate by relying on starboard weapons, limiting their capacity in engagements. After Venezia, it was amazing to Cole that *Victory* was still operational.

"Got it. Lieutenant Aquila, please communicate that to Omega." Cole moved toward her tactical officer, locking eyes. "We'll need to be strong on starboard—that means some fancy footwork once we get past their first line. Coordinate fire as well. Intersecting patterns, but let's not waste any big rounds on the same target. Understood?"

"Yes, Captain," Aquila said, opening the lines to the other tactical officers across the battle group. "I'll let them know. What about our two Guardian friends?"

On the holopane, a battle space appeared almost identical to the one Tethys had generated. Their battle group, one of three dozen, was breaking away from the orbital grid and on a direct intersect course with well over a thousand red motes, many of which were now being identified by the ship's deep-field scanners. Dreadnoughts, skeids, karves, and holks filled out the pane, with a flurry of lighter icons, each one representing smaller Banished craft like Grievers, Seraphs, Banshees, and even Trontos.

The pair of Guardians was converging from different sides of the battle plane. They were still far removed from *Victory* and Omega, but not for long. And once they reported what was happening to Cortana, others would quickly arrive. A small part of Cole wondered if that would be preferred, given the odds of winning this engagement straight-up. Some kind of game changer might be extremely helpful, if only to level the playing field.

"Let's just keep an eye on them and stay out of range," Cole replied. "Ready fighters. Ten squadrons. Seven Sabre, three Broadsword. Omega should follow suit, as available. Don't deploy until I give the order."

"Roger that, ma'am," Aquila said.

The Banished naval weapons lit up in the far distance, plasma and ballistic rounds filling space like shooting stars, surging through the vacuum toward Earth's orbital lanes. White streaks reached out like bolts of lightning from the bows. Plasma lances were infamously deadly naval weapons originally developed by the Covenant, a direct hit from one could easily destroy a smaller UNSC vessel.

"Keep us clear of those lances, Nav," Cole said to Bavinck. "As best you can. We can't afford to take one of those in the plate."

"Aye, Captain," Bavinck's eyes remained locked onto his terminal.

"MACs are hot," Nishioka reported. "Preparing to fire at target." Two deep cracking sounds resonated at the center of *Victory* and twin bright traces of light shot out from below the bridge. Several other flashes followed like a series of echoes—MAC rounds from Omega.

Enemy fire suddenly tore at *Victory*'s hull. In low quantities, superheated plasma could be safely absorbed by the Titanium-A battleplate. It was the too-much-at-once part that worried Cole.

Through the bridge viewing pane, the Banished ships were now clearly visible, their weapons fire a barrage of multicolored lights spanning the fore of their hulls. The sheer number of them was a deeply unsettling sight. As they approached, a dense cloud of lights and impulse drive contrails bloomed. An immense tsunami of enemy fighters and bombers were fanning out from their motherships to meet the battle groups head-on.

The weapons fire made contact first. A constant thudding of shots reverberated across *Victory*'s hull like a steady stream of rain on a rooftop, a clear indicator that things were about to get rough.

"You can scramble those fighters now, Tactical," Cole said, keying the wide comm band. "Give 'em hell, people!"

With a series of *thunks* somewhere below the bridge, the fighters were released, clusters of efflux tails launching from each ship in the battle group as they sped toward the Banished craft. *Victory of Samothrace* deployed the most—being several orders of magnitude larger than the frigates—but Cole was pleasantly surprised to witness just how robust the wall of fighters was across all of their vessels.

Two Banished dreadnoughts, five skeids, and a single holk now filled *Victory*'s viewing pane. From this angle, they looked like enormous monsters boring through the sea of stars. Explosions of light clustered across their bows, as both sides relentlessly pummeled each other. Another MAC shot from *Victory*, and one of the skeids instantly swelled into an expanding sphere of light and debris.

A lance from one of the dreadnoughts streaked by so close, it almost grazed the topside of *Victory*. At this range, there was little Cole's crew could do but move in as tight as possible. She hoped the likelihood of crossfire might cause the enemy's own tactical crews to exercise some level of restraint. Since this was the Banished, however, such moderation could not be assumed outright.

While the Banished dreadnoughts were imposing, their front-heavy assault craft and karves were far quicker siege vessels, with large open-mawed bows; skeids were long, narrow ships with dense armor plating along their flanks, designed explicitly for assault. Holks, on the other hand, were enormous battleships, vaguely similar to dreadnoughts, but armed to the gills and optimized to annihilate enemy warships.

In a bright flash of light, the holk fired its heavy plasma lance, the beam striking just past *Victory*'s starboard side. It happened so quickly that if one blinked they would have missed it. One of Omega's ships suddenly disappeared from the holopane.

"Who did we just lose?!" Cole demanded.

"They got *Blank Check*," Aquila replied, his face pale. "One shot."

"Then let's focus on the holk," Cole said, trying to keep her nerves down for the sake of her crew. At this range, every meter of movement and every moment of firing mattered. "Get some help from Omega. Let's take that thing down!"

Njuguna shouted orders into his transmitter, with both Aquila and Nishioka interacting on theirs to coordinate fire. Seconds later, three MAC strikes simultaneously punched through the holk, followed by a fourth shot. The Banished vessel was immediately decimated, its expanding debris obliterating a nearby skeid. Cheers erupted across *Victory*'s bridge as detritus harmlessly pelted their own hull.

"We've got a slipspace rupture, Captain," Lieutenant Zobah announced from the analyst bay. A tau spike was registering on the holopane just off *Victory*'s port side bow, even though nothing was there yet. "It's . . . Forerunner! And it's close, ma'am!"

"Evade! *Evade!*" Cole ordered.

A cyclone of white energy on the port side twisted into existence, with a Guardian emerging from it in plain view. This one was a newcomer, operating independently of the other two Guardians already accounted for on the board. The towering monolith hung vertically between the two encroaching forces, and both UNSC and Banished warships immediately began wheeling hard away from it.

The Guardian wasted no time. The Forerunner machine's immense wings quickly splayed as it prepared to fire its electromagnetic pulse weapon, a process that would take only seconds. Without sufficient time to escape into slipspace, *Victory*'s crew scrambled to get distance between them and the Guardian while Cole fought against dwelling on what would happen if they were actually caught in the EMP's range. Then she saw it firsthand . . .

"Oh no," Zobah said, little more than a hoarse whisper. "Captain, one of the other Guardians just fired an attenuation pulse."

The holopane painted a bleak picture: one of the other Guardians had already disabled a vast section of both sides of the conflict. Cole watched in horror as the holographic representation showed clusters of human and Banished ships helplessly listing in the EMP field. At such close quarters, they were no doubt violently crashing into each other and venting air and bodies. If that were to happen to her battle group, there would be little anyone on board could do. Devoid of power, the vessels would drift without life support systems until they collided with each other, or simply ran out of oxygen and the temperature controls failed, condemning their crews to a slow, cold, suffocating death.

Victory's evasive maneuver took it right alongside one of the Banished dreadnoughts, their port side hulls nearly scraping against one another. Her crew pulled hard starboard, tunneling through the shattered holk's debris field, Battle Group Omega right behind them. It was a risky move, exposing the cruiser's damaged side, but there was no choice. The number one priority right now was escaping the Guardian's EMP range.

What Cole didn't expect upon emerging from the cloud of debris was coming face-to-face with the same flagship they'd encountered on Venezia.

Severan's flagship.

The vicious gray warship's weapons lit up in an eruption of weapons fire, preparing to strike at *Victory of Samothrace*'s vulnerable port side. Cole didn't know if she should be impressed or terrified by the Jiralhanae's unflinching aggression. With reckless abandon, the war chief tore into *Victory*'s bow, even as the nearby Guardian threatened to take them *both* out of commission, energy now beginning to swirl at its center.

In the heat of the moment, time seemed to slow and Cole's mind returned to the same old question: What would her father do right now? His exemplary combat record was matched only by the unimaginable cost of many of his victories against the Covenant. That was the simple reality of the odds he had been up against. And now here she was, standing in his place, defending Earth from another alien menace seeking to eradicate her species from the galaxy.

"Weapons!" she sounded, turning to Lieutenant Nishioka. "Unload whatever we have left into that flagship! I don't want anything remaining of that vessel for the Guardian to offline." Just like her father, Cole would refuse to go silently to the grave. If this fight was going to be *Victory*'s end, she'd take this Banished ship down with them.

CHAPTER 20

SEVERAN

Heart of Malice
December 13, 2559

The human cruiser they had encountered on Sqala was scrambling to get out of the Guardian's EMP range while simultaneously unleashing a violent barrage of munitions at *Heart of Malice*. Given his own ship's initial strike, he could not blame the enemy for such a dogged response. It was a heroic effort, but it would not buy them salvation.

Then again, neither would any of *Malice*'s efforts. They were all far too close.

Were it not for the greater threat before him, Severan might have rounded again after the initial pass and torn the human vessel apart. Its wounded flank was fully visible and *Malice* could easily have flayed the enemy with twin plasma lances, permanently disabling the vessel and leaving its gutted corpse to list in the face of the very planet it defended.

Instead, *Malice* was in danger of becoming the very ruin Severan sought to create. Suppressing his stronger instinct to turn hard to port and gun down the human vessel, he gave a far different order.

"Starboard, full turn!" Severan growled, watching his prey move in the opposite direction, slipping out of his grasp. "Move out of the Guardian's range!"

The sight of dozens of Banished and human vessels scattering away from the Guardian was astounding. The enormous vessels were peeling away, diving, climbing—doing whatever they could to evade the inevitable, straining their craft and crews to the peak of stress limitations. What had begun as a head-on naval battle was now a frantic rush for survival, like a herd of *elphadox* scattering on the broad plains of Warial when hounded by a lone *maedobeast*.

Severan carefully tracked the Forerunner construct on his holotable as *Malice* finished its arcing turn and accelerated to maximum speed in the exact opposite direction. His eyes then fixed on the Guardian on a visual sensor, as he saw the ancient relic's wings gathering energy, about to unleash its attack—

Then, all light and energy on the Guardian suddenly went dark. The terrifying figure hung against the backdrop of Earth as if frozen, dead.

But how . . . ?

Severan turned back to the battle map on his holotable; the same was true of the other two Guardians. All of them were inactive, hanging lifeless in space, with seemingly no power or external control.

"By the gods," Severan said under his breath. "He did it."

Ten day-cycles ago, Atriox had sent a communication to Severan and the Eight as they were preparing for the strike against Earth. The warmaster confirmed that he had acquired the weapon they were seeking—an ancient device called the *trikala*. He stated that it would take a short time before the weapon was ready, but that as soon as it was, his forces would move to strike Zeta Halo.

And here, now, before Severan's very eyes, was the fruit of Atriox's efforts.

The warmaster had succeeded.

He had brought an end to the Apparition and her reign of terror.

With weapons capable of destroying the Guardians and enough firepower to crush both Cortana's forces and humanity's precious *Infinity*, Atriox had finally vindicated the Jiralhanae. At last, this decisive act had brought to bear the wrath of their people, who for so long had been made servants and slaves of other civilizations. The loss of Doisac and its colonies was inestimable, nearly spelling the very death of the Jiralhanae. But now Atriox had proven they would not only survive, but make those who dared to cross them pay.

False though Cortana might have been, Atriox had killed a god.

"What has happened?!" Valocanth, *Malice*'s mobility officer, grunted in shock.

"Atriox has silenced the Apparition," Severan responded. "It is the only possible explanation. Erutaun, order the fleets to pull back immediately!"

"All of them?" Erutaun looked at Severan, startled.

"Yes! Every last one," Severan said, examining the chaos on the holotable. And it was *certainly* chaos. Both human and Banished forces were strewn about along the battle line in complete confusion. One moment they had been clambering for safety, and now they were all witnessing the impossible—an impotent Guardian draped in the shadows of space—and trying to assess what came next.

"Are you certain we should pull back, War Chief?" Kaevus

asked, still attempting deference. "Without Cortana, there is nothing to stop us from ending this battle now. The humans are so greatly outnumbered. Earth is ours."

"Is it, Kaevus?" Severan snarled, leaning toward his captain. "If so, then we will take it when we return from victory. But *not* now. The human world is nothing if we lose the Lithos. Do you not see—a god has *died*, Kaevus! Her throne sits empty. We must seize it now, lest some small conquest over this world becomes merely a prelude to our defeat."

If Atriox had truly deposed the human AI, he might also have control of Zeta Halo, where she exercised her authority. Access to the Domain, however, could only be obtained through the Lithos. That was all that mattered now. The high lord had been exceedingly clear: without Cortana to defend it, the Forerunner gateway was open for the taking.

Kaevus's eyes were wide in his silence, but the captain *had* to understand.

"Erutaun." Severan turned to his communications officer. "Order all ships back to the rally point to prepare for slipspace departure. Summon the Eight immediately for conference. I will take the holo in my war chamber. *Alone.*"

Severan abruptly left the command deck, climbing down into the bridge's lower walkways, heading toward the corridor that accessed his personal war chamber. He would normally have invited Kaevus for council, but even a hint of insubordination—a questioning of action in the heat of battle—needed some measure of discipline. Kaevus might have thought it wise to interrupt his war chief in the middle of such a decision, but the slightest doubt could send the entire crew into mutiny, not to mention the legions of Banished now at his back. Too much was at stake to allow even a hint of uncertainty, not when they were so close.

He entered his war chamber, a small, unembellished observatory veiled in deep shadows, and stood before the holotank at its center. The space above lit up with the leaders of the eight major clans that held authority over the entirety of the Banished home fleet. Before him hovered six Jiralhanae chieftains, one Sangheili kaidon, and a Kig-Yar war-queen. Although some members of these clans had gone to Zeta Halo with Atriox, the vast majority of their number remained present, formally at Severan's disposal.

Yet he still needed to be careful.

There was little love for him or his father among the heads of the Banished, so trepidation and strategy would be employed with every statement, every command. He had spoken to the same Eight after the events at Sqala, informing them of the critical nature of the Lithos despite their impending plans to assault the human homeworld. With Atriox's victory at Zeta Halo, the Lithos's significance could not be overstated. Severan's present change of course should confound only the ignorant, but he would not put anything past power-hungry Jiralhanae on the verge of a kill.

"Allies," Severan said with a customary nod. "Thank you for taking council with me on such short notice. We have—"

"Why in the name of the corpse-moon have you ordered us to leave the battle line?" Gathgor, the chieftain of the Warkeepers of Qabik, interrupted, folding his arms. He was a large and grizzled Jiralhanae dressed in the bones of monsters that prowled the Qabikian plains of Warial.

"Indeed!" Ectorius the White barked. *"We have them on the run, Severan!"* The ivory-furred chieftain belonged to Beohk Norkala, a clan of Teash that dwelled in the moon's glacial regions.

"Have you?" Severan growled, letting the disdain roll off his tongue. "Humans on the run? And if they seize the Lithos in the wake of the Apparition's demise, what will happen then?

Remember what I told you before we departed—to take Earth is to grasp at wind. It is *nothing* compared to the Lithos. Without the Domain, we fail. Even if we were to destroy a hundred Earths, Atriox's victory on Zeta Halo would be in vain!"

"So Atriox has won?" Ectorius asked.

"Of course," Severan replied. "What other explanation do you have for what we just witnessed? The Guardians drift lifeless in space. The Apparition's death grip has been broken."

"Even if that is so," the Sangheili spoke up, *"leaving Earth will only give the humans time to recover and to establish a more resilient defense."* Dreka 'Xulsam was a kaidon from the Nwari Wastewalkers—Sanghelios desert-dwellers who had abandoned their nomadic ways for the stars during the Blooding Years, and shortly after came into Atriox's service. *"We have shown them our numbers and our strength. If we return, they will know how to better defend their planet. But if we take Earth now, we rid ourselves of their kind for good."*

"Do you really believe that?" Severan asked with scorn. "Earth is *one world*. Humanity has spread across countless others. They possess *many* colonies filled to the brim with their species. Destroying Earth will barely weaken their numbers, and it will no doubt cost us many ships in the process. The Covenant War itself proved that. And again, I must ask: Have you so quickly forgotten what I told you of the Lithos?"

Severan's eyes moved from one member of the Eight to another, searching for some solidarity or, at least, rationality.

"I have certainly not," said V'leria, chieftain of the Maakra Sunbreakers, her clan a composite of space raiders and brigands. *"If it is as you say—if Cortana has been defeated—then the Lithos* must *be our next target. You claimed that it was hidden on a human colony. What if their warriors are already there, ready to defend it?"*

"There will certainly be human resistance," Severan said, as if it was obvious. "Of this, I am doubtless. But much of their forces are here, in defense of their homeworld. This advantage should not be squandered. If we depart for the Lithos now, we can quickly subdue the colony and fortify it against any attempt to take it back."

"Agreed," the tall, battle-scarred Jiralhanae to Severan's left responded through broken tusks. *"Every cental wasted here in deliberation is a cental the enemy has to fortify* that *world."* Cassius of Numengal would of course know. Like Severan's father, he had spent most of his adult life fighting for the Covenant in the human colonies. He knew the peril and unpredictability in scouring the surface of a heavily fortified human world and wanted to avoid it if such a thing was possible.

Ectorius grunted assent, as if finally seeing this logic.

"Should we not leave some *forces here?"* hissed Cao'mar, the Kig-Yar war-queen from the Sclera of Chu'ot. *"We contend with their defenses and possibly even secure victory, while others focus on the Lithos you speak of."*

Of course the Ruuhtian would suggest a ploy to separate her own fleets from the larger group at the prospect that she might be able to gather more spoils for herself. Even when the Kig-Yar were full members of the Covenant, their disdain for the sacred and immaterial had been palpable. The Domain would mean nothing to the war-queen unless there was wealth on the other end. Her logic certainly fit with some of the more materialistic tendencies of the Banished, but Severan found it naïve and shortsighted.

"The Sclera wishes to fight on Earth alone?" Severan asked. "Your clan has already lost eight ships, War-Queen. Even if another entire clan remained with you, the best you might do is get past their sky-guns. Their frigates would chew your forces to shreds before you touched the surface."

"I will not stay." Gathgor now bristled at the thought. *"And leave the Lithos to you lot? Not a chance in the cold fires of Soirapt."*

"Neither will I," Chieftain Eru'thbok huffed. *"The Cruxguard of Phenthrop will go to this human colony and help the Banished secure the Lithos."* The aged warrior of Doisac glared at the others. *"You would be wise to follow Severan's lead, whom Atriox himself placed in authority over you. The Warmaster does not choose his proxies lightly. And if the Lithos is truly the key to the Domain, what would his opinion of us be if we failed to seize it before the humans? I am certain it is worse than you can possibly imagine."*

Kaladus, the chieftain of the Irusk clan, nodded assent. *"If the Lithos gives us the weapons wielded by the Apparition, there is no question. Why should we battle needlessly in the skies above their world when we can return with a weapon capable of blotting it out entirely, just as she did ours?"* Even if the chieftain had not spoken, his eyes and face were enough to communicate grim solidarity. With his people spread across the Doisac region of Irusk and in the ship-forges that orbited the mother-world, Kaladus had lost far more than all the others in the Apparition's strike. It was evident that he was ready, more than any other, to avenge that loss.

The question hung in the air for a full cental, but it became clear to all that they had no real choice. Anything else would not only needlessly imperil their own assets within the Banished, but would also communicate either foolishness or, worse, defiance to Atriox, who would no doubt view any refusal to pursue the Lithos as a strategic catastrophe. And no one was eager to do either.

"Very well." Ectorius the White broke the silence first. *"What are we waiting for then? Let us depart while the humans are still sifting through the debris. We will take their colony, we will take the Lithos, then we will come back and finish what we have started. Are we agreed?"*

All of the Eight echoed his sentiment with a series of affirming nods and grunts, some more reluctant than others. The holograph quickly dissolved into emptiness, replaced by the dim light of the war chamber. Severan was alone once more, staring into the dark.

A thousand questions immediately infiltrated his mind.

He wondered if leaving Earth was, in fact, the best course of action, since attacking the human homeworld was the only order he had actually been given. Was Atriox even still alive? Perhaps victory against Cortana had come about a different way than the *trikala*, and it was in the hands of the humans after all? In the end, the main issue was how tightly the bonds of the Banished would hold around him when his own loyalties were so clearly divided.

A cold hand fell on his shoulder.

"Well done, my son." Dovo Nesto's voice came from the gloom, crisp and smooth.

Severan turned to see the high lord, his face veiled in darkness. Evidently he had been lurking in the war chamber the entire time. An uneasy feeling clung to Severan as the San'Shyuum stepped into the light. Everything he had was resting on the hopes and promises of this one being.

"I admit that the apparent destruction of the AI is an unexpected blessing," the high lord said. "Without her guarding entry to the Domain, there is no need for delay. Certainly, the humans will not. At last, Severan, we are about to accomplish what all others have failed to, and it is only because of your boldness today."

Severan was silent for nearly a cental, but then stated his misgivings. "When the Eight discover that I serve a San'Shyuum, they will all turn on me."

"By then, they will either bow to us or be scattered to the wind," the high lord said with confidence. "When the Lithos is ours, what could stand in the way of the Covenant? If they truly desire strength, they *will* offer their allegiance."

Severan certainly hoped as much, but he was not anywhere near as confident as when he first began this endeavor. Thus far, the Eight's loyalty to him had been contingent on his own to Atriox, and that was about to change. The Jiralhanae followed power—but if Atriox had actually killed Cortana, as he had promised, could Severan ever match that show of strength? Could any Jiralhanae?

And most important of all: Even if one managed to take control of the Lithos, would they simply become the next god to be deposed?

CHAPTER 21

JAMES SOLOMON

Tyrrhen, Boundary
December 14, 2559

The ONI deposit box was hidden in a single bare stump at the center of the glade, just where James Solomon had been told it would be. Although it looked real, the stump was entirely artificial and its contents were accessed by pressing various sections of the bark in a specific sequence. When done properly, an aperture on its side swung open and revealed its hollow interior. It was a strange system, but not unexpected.

Within the space was a small security-coded box, and inside that a syringe and a rolled-up piece of paper along with a one-way transmitter. The message had been sent through signals that the AIs under Cortana's sway would not detect, printed by the relay's tiny processor so that it could not be read, and deleted immediately so that there was no electronic trace. It felt archaic, but getting around the Created often required creative solutions.

After the narrow extraction on Cascade, Solomon had been sent these specific coordinates on the colony of Boundary, a far less populous world with immense polar caps bordering a very narrow band of fertile terrain at its equator. Just over a hundred settlements littered this space, the most developed being Tyrrhen, the colony's capital. ONI had sent him roughly thirty kilometers west of it.

The snapping of a branch caused him to look up. The glade was empty except for a small rodent scurrying through the underbrush. Dawn cut through the dense canopy of ancient trees that surrounded the clearing, piercing the air in broken, hazy rays of light. The forest floor was cold, the sky clear and blue. Solomon hoped the favorable weather was some kind of sign that the rest of the operation would be less complicated than Cascade. He took a deep breath through his armor's filter, then inserted the box into a hardcase on his thigh.

"The box," Lola said through his armor's internal comms. *"What's inside?"*

"A syringe," he said, trudging through the grass and retrieving his M392 Designated Marksman Rifle from the magnetic anchor on the back of his Mjolnir armor.

"I could see that much. What's in *the syringe? You didn't read the note."*

"I'll read it when I get back to the ship. How's the girl?"

"Still asleep but stirring. She'll be up shortly."

After their initial encounter, Solomon thought it best to use *Cataphract*'s cryotube on their journey to Boundary. Chloe had slept safely while he spent the better part of the last three weeks evading Cortana's policing elements. Solomon picked up the pace. Lola had already initiated the thaw process and he wanted to be back at the ship before she was fully awake.

He kept lifting his eyes to the sky as he worked through the vast root structures of large coniferous trees that climbed hundreds of feet into the air, looking for drones or any sort of airborne surveillance. Solomon didn't know what kind of resistance to expect on this operation, but if the girl was as important as ONI noted, there'd be trouble at some point. Morales wouldn't have sent him in unless there was a reason for it.

The only surveillance he'd seen were the large birds perched silently in the treetops, eyeing him suspiciously, and the small woodland creatures who were too busy clambering from tree to tree to check his credentials.

Six minutes later, he reached *Cataphract.* The prowler was hidden in a clearing near a steep rock ledge, entirely out of view of any prying orbital eyes. It had been a tight fit, but the value of good cover could not be overestimated. He'd initially hoped that the handoff point for the girl would be nearby, but something told him he wouldn't have that kind of luck.

It was still a mystery as to what ONI wanted with a ten-year-old girl, particularly one like Chloe, with no family, no records, no history. And what was it about her that would allow them to stop Cortana? How exactly had she ended up employed by a Kig-Yar in the criminal underworld of Mindoro? The questions loomed in his mind, but he suppressed them.

After all, this was his last operation.

The side door of *Cataphract* opened at his approach and he stepped inside, removing his helmet and placing his DMR on a wall-mounted rack. Turning the corner, he came eye-to-eye with the girl. She was sitting up in the open cryotube, huddled in the farthest end, just like when he'd found her at Miko's Wheel. But her face told him she was more suspicious than afraid.

"Who are you, anyway?" she asked, her eyes examining him closely.

"My name is James," he said, wondering how much he should disclose. If she was ONI's possession, he decided it didn't really matter. "James Solomon. Lola, say hi."

"*Hi,*" she chirped through the ship's audio.

"You named your ship Lola?" The girl sounded almost critical.

"No, Lola is my AI. The ship is called *Cataphract.*"

"*Cataphract*? As in, Persian armored cavalry?"

"Yeah." Solomon's brow furrowed in surprise. "How'd you—"

"This is Boundary," she interrupted, looking out the porthole next to the bed.

"Yes. It *is.*"

"I could tell by the moons. Mistral and Levante," she said, pointing up toward the planet's two natural satellites, pale spheres against the blue morning sky.

"I'm sorry—how could you tell?" he asked.

"Isn't it obvious? Their shape, proximity, and orientation?"

"No, not really," Solomon said, leaning over to look out the porthole. "It's not obvious to most people."

She tensed up as he got close and edged back against the cryotube's open canopy, her eyes coming alive again with suspicion. Maybe it was fear this time.

"Why did you abduct me, James Solomon?" she demanded.

"Let's get it straight. I didn't abduct you. I *rescued* you. No little girl should be in a place like that one. What were you doing there?"

"I didn't ask for you to rescue me. Who sent you? This clearly wasn't your idea."

"It definitely wasn't his idea," Lola interjected.

"Lola, we don't need your commentary." He turned to Chloe. "What do you mean, this wasn't *my* idea?"

"You're not the kind of guy who rescues children from places like Miko's Wheel." She eyed his armor. "What are you? Some kind of Spartan? You must get orders from somewhere."

"Yeah, I got orders. Someone thinks you're special and I'm bringing you to them."

The answer seemed to throw her off for a moment. She furrowed her brow and returned her gaze to the porthole. "Someone on Boundary?"

"Not exactly," he replied. "But this is where we're meeting them."

"Who are they?"

"All right, enough questions. I've got a few myself," Solomon said, folding his arms. "How does someone like you get mixed up with a vulture like Miko? Did you really do his books?"

"Yes. What's wrong with that?" Her tone was terse, bordering on angry. "Pays better than doing free community service at the West Mindoro Orphanage."

"What happened to your parents?"

"I don't have parents. I've never had them."

"That's not possible."

"I assure you, James Solomon, it is," she said, pointing to her missing leg. "It's called cloning. Ever heard of it?"

"So that's what you are?" he asked.

"Yeah, that's what my genetic tests said."

"Well, then who cloned you?"

"I don't know—I wasn't there when it happened. Maybe you should ask the person who gave you your orders."

"Fair enough. How long have you worked for Miko?"

"Almost two years. I'm good with math and probabilities. Miko needed someone who could doctor the books, help him clean money. He gave me food, a place to stay. It was safe and quiet. But now I'm here, on Boundary, with the Spartan James Solomon and the AI named Lola."

Okay . . .

That was certainly an interesting way of addressing things. Her social skills were clearly in need of polishing. Not surprising given that she was employed by a Kig-Yar for the last two years and obviously had a rough background.

"I'm not a Spartan," Solomon replied. "So you have no memory of where you're from or who even brought you to the orphanage?"

"No. I grew up *in* the orphanage. My earliest memories are from there."

Solomon stared at her for a moment. This girl was different than he'd anticipated . . . *very* different. Her speech and vocal patterns were mature for her age. He wondered if she really was artificial in some way. "You talk like an adult, not a ten-year-old."

"Is that supposed to be a question? *Yes*. I'm smarter than other kids my age, if that's what you're wondering. I think quicker, speak quicker, and can work my way out of just about any situation. In other words, I can take care of myself fine. Always have and always will."

"Something tells me that you're probably right." She was certainly some kind of prodigy. Cloning still seemed too extraordinary an explanation for him. And it was illegal. But it certainly wasn't unheard of, even in his own past with the SPARTAN-II project. If it wasn't for the fact that ONI was after her, he would have completely discounted what she was saying.

"I'm hungry," she said, her eyes gazing around the cabin. "Do you have something to eat?"

He pressed a series of buttons on the wall and the dispenser on the side poured out a bowl of hot porridge and filled a glass of water. Utilitarian, but it would have to do. He set everything down on a tray beside her and Chloe immediately plunged into the food, now abandoning any pretense of defensiveness. But even as she ravenously shoveled porridge into her mouth, her eyes continued to search the cabin.

"You have a lot of alcohol for a Spartan," she noted, spotting his liquor.

"I'm *not* a Spartan," he said, checking a display on the bulkhead that monitored the environment just outside the ship. "Not anymore, at least."

"What are you, then?"

"Something else," he said, taking a deep breath.

"How much are they paying you for me?"

He turned and stared at her. She was too perceptive to lie to, so he decided against it. "Enough for me to stop working."

"Sounds like the Office of Naval Intelligence, then. They would definitely tell an ex-Spartan that kind of garbage. I'm sure it's completely true."

Who in the hell is this girl? "Just finish up, please," he said. "I'll be back in a few minutes. And don't break anything."

"What do you mean by that?" She was looking around the cabin. "Half the stuff in here is already broken."

"I'd normally take offense at that," Lola piped in, *"but you're right. He won't let me fix any of it. It's infuriating."*

Solomon sighed deeply, then turned around and passed through a corridor into a small room in the aft of the ship. It was a material assessment lab he had used only once or twice before. He needed privacy though, so it would have to do. He closed the door and removed the box containing the syringe and the note from the hardcase on his thigh.

The note was a narrow piece of paper that had to be rolled out, scribed in a series of dots and spaces, an old code from the early years of long-range communication. Outdated and unconventional, but it smelled like Octavio Morales. It would also circumnavigate the attention of Cortana or her AI watchdogs.

Apply syringe to asset. Access lockbox at Gate Lipari. Go on foot. Expect complications.

"Complications?" Lola asked. *"What is* that *in reference to?"*

"I'm actually more curious about what they want me to give her. Can you give it a peek for me?" he asked, sliding it onto a material analyzation plate in the compartment in front of him.

Lola ran the scanner. *"Hmm. Nontoxic liquid with a composite matrix within it."*

"What's the matrix?"

"It's a data-delivery node. Looks like it's designed to hold some kind of subroutine."

"They want me to inject a *subroutine* into this little girl?"

"That is what it seems, James."

"Why?"

"It must have something to do with stopping Cortana, right?"

It undoubtedly did, but it was a troubling development and Solomon suddenly found it weighing on him in a way that was unexpected. It was one thing to apply medicine or a stabilizing drug, but it was another entirely to put a *subroutine* into a human's body. *What would even happen? What is ONI trying to accomplish?*

"Are you going to do it?"

"No," he said, rolling the note up. "Not yet, at least. I have too many questions. How far is Lipari?"

"Thirty-six kilometers. Northern side of Tyrrhen."

"That'll take some time, especially if we have to move slowly."

"Probably a good thing, James." Lola's voice was contemplative. *"It will give you an opportunity to think."*

Solomon didn't want that opportunity. He wanted this operation to be over with. Somehow this had ceased being a simple escort mission and had spiraled into some kind of bizarre ethical dilemma, and that wasn't very comfortable territory for him.

What made it worse was that he wasn't transporting some inert object or even military personnel. Chloe was a ten-year-old girl.

She was a *child*. But if the stakes were high enough, that didn't mean much to some folks in ONI—and this bothered him.

A dark thought suddenly surfaced in his mind that he had not anticipated. His own past. This whole mission had become almost like some kind of absurd pantomime of his own kidnapping and conscription into the SPARTAN-II program. He had no doubt that Morales must have found some degree of amusement in the irony.

Solomon reentered his personal cabin to find the girl washing dishes in the galley sink—not just hers, but his too. She was casually balanced on her leg as she ran the dishes under the water. Her relaxed posture was striking to see.

"Why are you doing that?"

"They needed to be cleaned."

"I have a self-cleaning tray for—"

"Yes, I saw it," she said, her tone carried the slightest bite to it. "I just prefer to do things by hand. Is that a problem?"

He slowly walked toward her and she didn't move. She didn't even look his way. "So you're not afraid of me anymore?"

Chloe looked up at him. She was barely half his size, but the girl's gaze made her intimidating.

"No," she said with certainty, returning to the dishes. "You're not a bad guy. I've seen plenty of those. You don't seem like one of them."

I'm pretty sure I am. You wouldn't be here if I was a "good guy."

"We've got to get going," he said, grabbing hydration tablets and MREs from a shelf and distributing them into hardcases embedded at various points his armor. "We have to get to a gate on the northern end of the nearest settlement. And we have to do it on foot. I can carry you."

"You're not carrying me."

"It's a long way. Thirty-six kilometers."

"You're *not* carrying me. If you would have brought my crutch along, this would be easy," she said, her face pained. "I just need something to lean on. We'll find something in the forest. I'm going to walk. Just like you."

"That's going to take us considerably longer than it needs to. If I could just carry—"

"No one *carries* me." Her eyes were like daggers. "I can walk on my own."

Solomon considered this for a long moment, then turned to his weapons locker. He withdrew an M99 Special Application Scoped Rifle, quickly examining its condition. The Stanchion, as it was called, was a heavy recoilless rifle, capable of firing dense rounds at hypersonic speeds through magnetic acceleration. The weapon was a favorite of extreme-range snipers, but Solomon had an itching feeling that it might be needed against any potential "complications." He anchored it to his back and grabbed his DMR, a solid amount of ammunition for both weapons, and a handful of M9 fragmentation grenades.

Then Solomon donned his helmet and gave one last look to Chloe before stepping out of the ship and down the ramp. He waited there for a full minute, hoping that something she saw outside might convince her that he actually should carry her. He couldn't imagine traversing thirty-six klicks of Boundarian wilderness with a small ten-year-old who could only make forward progress by way of a crutch. Maybe it was worth breaking out another chem-tab for expediency's sake. . . .

She appeared in the doorway, looking straight ahead into the forest that opened up around *Cataphract.* Grabbing the siderail tightly, she hopped on one leg down the platform. She did it slowly, but was steady and careful, not faltering once, even though she seemed to be focused on the environment and not her footpath.

When she reached the bottom, she gazed at him with defiant blue-gray eyes.

"If you hadn't been wasting time staring at me, you would already have the crutch I asked for."

Two minutes of searching the forest floor and Solomon finally found something that he thought might work—a small but sturdy branch that had a curved end. Using his combat knife, he stripped it of loose leaves and smoothed some of its edges, then handed it to Chloe, who had been standing at the end of the walkway watching him the entire time. She took it under her left arm and leaned her weight on it.

"Does that work?" Solomon asked

"Its probably as good as I could expect from a Spartan," she answered, stepping off the ramp. "Which way are we headed?"

"Lola, lock down the ship and give me a navpoint to Lipari."

"Yes, James. Cataphract *security is now active. Marking Lipari on your HUD."*

The navpoint indicator showed their target in the far distance.

"This way," Solomon said, sighing deeply at first sight of the distance indicator.

He tightened his grip on the DMR and proceeded in the direction of the navpoint. He didn't look back for the first few minutes, moving relatively slowly as he tried to determine the pace they would be able to go. When he turned around, he found Chloe directly behind him.

"Why are you walking so slow?" she demanded.

"I'm trying to not get too far ahead."

"I'll let you know when that's a problem." Her voice was unapologetic. "At this rate, we'll never get there. I thought Spartans were supposed to be fast."

"Spartans don't usually have to babysit," he replied. If she could dish it out, she'd have to learn to take it. He started walking again, this time at his own pace.

"So is that what you think this is?"

"You tell me." He cast an eye back toward her. Impressive. She was still keeping up. "Do I look like I take care of children? I kill bad guys and blow up their stuff."

"You certainly have enough guns for it," Chloe said as she came up alongside him. "How were you planning to carry me with all of that?"

He had two rifles, one of which was oversized, and a slew of extra equipment. He had kitted out for a thirty-six-kilometer trip through potentially hostile territory, so she had a point.

"Trust me. It's better for me to walk," she said, now overtaking Solomon's pace. "In case we do run into any bad guys so you can shoot them."

"You should really hope that doesn't happen."

With that, Chloe went silent and they both continued forward.

His eyes continued to scan the path ahead, a vast forest of massive trees, each with a root structure the width of his Shearwater aerodyne, some large enough for him to pass directly underneath without even ducking his head.

He wondered what the "complications" were that ONI had mentioned in the drop box note. The uncertainty had seemed like reason enough for him to bring the arsenal he had, but maybe he should have hauled along more? This wasn't like his standard operations. If something or someone came for them, he'd have to find a safe place for the girl and then deal with it. The thought of that kind of encounter kept his eyes busy for the first hour of their journey. He was surprised to see that the girl did not lag behind the entire time. Not even once.

"I've never seen a Spartan in person before," Chloe finally

broke the silence. She seemed to be examining his armor as she shuffled along. "Do they all look like you?"

"Once again: I'm not a Spartan."

"You sure look like one," she replied. "At least, from the ones I've seen in vids."

"Looks can be deceiving."

She pivoted on her crutch, narrowing her eyes. "Sometimes. But not usually." Then she continued, as if she knew where she was going. It was close enough, so he followed.

"The orphanage in Mindoro," Solomon asked. "They didn't have *any* record at all about you?"

"You're clearly not familiar with West Mindoro Orphanage. No. They don't know where I'm from. They don't know much of anything. Miko is the one who paid for the genetic test. He at least wanted to know where I came from. He was probably hoping to find more like me."

"And he told you that you're a clone?"

"No," she answered, her voice confused. "Miko is a Kig-Yar. He couldn't make any sense of the data. He can barely read human. *I* was the one who figured out I was a clone."

"How'd you do that? Cloning's illegal."

"I searched it on Waypoint. How else?" she said matter-of-factly. It was humanity's free, public network, with access to literally trillions of databases. "And just because something is illegal doesn't mean it hasn't been done. It wouldn't be illegal if it wasn't possible. There's plenty of data out there about cloning, and my genetic profile is pretty straightforward. I did *not* develop normally. Some parts were suppressed, others enhanced." She said the last part while pointing to her head. "Maybe the people you're bringing me to can tell me why they did it."

Solomon didn't have anything to say about that. He doubted

the team on the other end of the handoff would freely give any further information to him or Chloe.

"Does it bother you?" he pried, as they passed through a rocky cleft. "That you were cloned?"

"No." Her response was almost automatic. "Does it bother you?"

"Not really. But it doesn't affect me."

"Are you sure about that?"

"What do you mean?"

"Are you saying all of this, who you are"—she gestured to his body with her free arm—"is normal?"

In his mind flashed images of a past that was anything but normal.

Abducted at the age of six with seventy-four other children, then pressed through an inhumane training regimen for seven years before undergoing a series of excruciating augmentations that killed or crippled most of his cohort. Those who survived were eventually cybernetically paired with Mjolnir power armor, making them capable of doing things that combat theorists could only dream of. Spartans were the reason humanity had outlasted the Insurrection, the Covenant, and whatever else the galaxy had thrown at them since. It was the reason that Solomon could still do what he did, even after all that had happened on Gamma Station seven years ago.

He stopped and turned to Chloe, pressing a sequence of keys on his left arm, then removed his armored prosthetic arm, holding it out before her. The real one had been blown off in the Battle of Sigma Octanus IV. He could still remember the feeling.

"You're right," he said, as she examined the prosthetic. "I'm not so different from you. I'm guessing Miko didn't want you to have a prosthetic made for your leg? You know they're more affordable now—"

"I never asked for one," she said, looking directly at his faceplate. "I may look like I'm missing parts, but I'm not. I am who I'm supposed to be."

Solomon stared back at the girl for a moment, trying to understand what she meant. It baffled him that someone would intentionally decline a prosthetic.

Without another word, she moved around him and set out again on the walk. He quickly locked his prosthetic back into place, stretching out his arm and tightening each finger to make sure it was working properly, then followed right behind her.

"I've seen enough in the world," she said, "to know that there are a lot of people who have all their parts on the outside, but are broken on the inside. More broken than I could ever be."

Again, who in the hell is this girl?

He stayed quiet and so did she, giving him time to contemplate everything that had just played out.

They kept going for nearly three hours, then stopped to eat in the shadow of a ridge that drew the terrain up into a steep, rocky incline to their west. The forest's giant trees had become sparse and given way to a dense underbrush covering almost every meter of the ground, considerably slowing their progress. According to the map on his HUD, the ridge was the foot of a mountain they were just glancing as they moved north before winding east on a wide route toward northern Tyrrhen.

Solomon knew that it would have been much easier to move directly east, reach the city's outskirts, and then travel north along the edge of the settlement, where the wide-open terrain would be significantly more traversable. The potential for "complications" was what stopped him from doing this. Staying in the wilderness might be slow going, but it provided visual cover that was invaluable.

Chloe was devouring an MRE sandwich while looking past

the trees and into the sky. The sun had already passed overhead and was concealed behind the foliage, scattering its light across the forest floor in fragmented pieces. Boundary had twenty-one-hour days and dusk came early this time of year. They had a long journey ahead, but still plenty of time before it started getting dark.

Solomon could go for days without food or water, as long as he had his armor. He sat silently, still mesmerized by this girl. Despite the last three hours of nonstop walking, she seemed unfatigued, calm and content, even though she knew she was headed to an uncertain place. Ironically, Solomon possessed a suite of biological augmentations and half-ton powered armor, but somehow Chloe looked more free and unhindered than he'd ever been.

"Detecting movement," Lola's voice interrupted the vision. *"Twenty-five meters, north-northwest."* She paused and then whispered, *"It's large, whatever it is."*

Solomon could see it on his motion tracker.

He placed his index finger over his faceplate, mimicking silence, and Chloe immediately complied. A branch snapped from the same direction. Whatever was coming toward them was moving slowly to avoid being detected. Not a good sign.

Both of them stood up quietly and Solomon led the way to one of the large trees, pointing to a cavity in its root structure. Chloe carefully climbed down underneath the tree as Solomon glanced behind them.

"Hurry," Lola said. *"It's getting closer."*

"I know," he said, one eye fixed on the tracker.

Solomon lowered himself into the deep shadow within the roots, pulling his DMR out and pointing it toward the approaching object. After about ten seconds, it appeared, slowly climbing down the side of the ridge. At first Solomon didn't know what he was seeing, but as the broken rays of sunlight hit it, the creature became clear.

It was a large, predatory feline, over five meters long, with violet-dappled black fur. It looked similar to big cats on other worlds—sleek, muscular, and with an intimidatingly toothy maw. Its eyes were completely white, with no visible pupils. A jagged bony ridge ran from its skull—where it was largest—down its spinal column to the end of its long, slender tail. The ridge had sharp, bladelike protrusions and seemed to be a kind of protective structure. Solomon wondered what kind of predator had to exist on this world for something as large and fearsome as this cat to need such protection in the first place.

There was a high-pitched ticking sound coming from the animal as it softly stepped to the spot where they had just been sitting, its large snout feverishly smelling the ground. The creature paused and the ticking increased, its nose pressing against something. Solomon leaned to the side to see it. It was the MRE. Chloe must have dropped it. The creature lapped the small sandwich up in a single motion. Solomon could see its teeth clearly from here, each at least ten centimeters long.

"Panthedron," Lola said. *"This is a juvenile. Male."*

"Are you serious?" he whispered.

"Yes. Some animals are larger on Boundary than most other worlds because the ecosystems are so densely packed around the equator. I would use a bigger gun, personally."

He slowly reclasped his DMR to his back and retrieved the Stanchion. He should have made that judgment on sight just by the sheer scale of the animal. The M392 would have little effect on a creature of that size, but the M99 would at least put a dent in it. Hopefully more.

"It's also virtually blind. Navigates by sonar and smell," she said. *"So you might want to see if this one just passes by before trying to take it down. The last thing you need is for its mother to show up."*

Solomon signaled an affirmative through his heads-up display.

He had no desire to engage this thing if he could help it. The *panthedron* continued to sniff the area in tight circles but had not picked up their trail yet.

Solomon turned to Chloe. She was in the far back of the root structure, her eyes glistening against the dark. She was shivering in terror. A shadow suddenly veiled her eyes and he turned to find the *panthedron* right in front of him, its nose pressed against the root structure, centimeters from the tip of the M99's barrel. If it was any closer, it would have been right there underneath the roots with them. Fortunately, the space they were in seemed too tight for the cat to fit, but he could not be sure.

The ticking sound at this distance was remarkably loud. It was coming from the creature's bony skull and must have been the way it navigated. Solomon's right index finger moved to the trigger while he quietly prepped the weapon with the other hand. An M99 round at this distance would tear a hole straight through the animal and rip it apart from the inside out. Certainly louder and messier than he'd want.

And it would attract attention, something he desperately wanted to avoid. But he might not have a choice.

His finger hovered above the trigger as he lined up the barrel. The *panethedron*'s mouth opened wide as it undertook prying its way into the root structure, saliva and gore from its last meal clinging to its gaping jaws. It clearly knew a meal was here but couldn't quite get to it.

The animal's collection of teeth was even more intimidating this close. It began digging, scraping its massive paws at the hardened soil at the base of the roots. Although its claws were razor-sharp, the ground had calcified over time into thick shale-like sediment that could take hours to cut through.

Solomon kept his finger on the trigger and held his breath.

Three solid minutes of digging—then another ticking sound came from behind the creature. It was deeper and more intense. Solomon tried to see behind the *panethedron* but couldn't—the cat's body blocked the entire aperture. The creature finally backed away with one last swipe from its paw, a deep, guttural growling coming from its chest. Behind it was another cat of the same kind, but easily a third larger. Its black fur bore erratic yellow stripes, similar to the tigers of Earth.

"That's a female," Lola noted. *"Could be the mother."*

Great, Solomon silently mouthed.

The female growled at the juvenile and it responded in kind. It appeared for a moment as if they were bickering, until the female released one final roar, and then launched back into the forest at an extraordinary speed. The juvenile turned back toward the root structure—as if it could see them—and let out its own deep, piercing roar. Then he turned and disappeared into the forest after the female.

Solomon finally breathed easier. He let another ten minutes pass just in case one of the animals had second thoughts. Finally he turned to Chloe, whose eyes remained large and her body deathly still. Her own breathing had slowed a bit; she was still pretty scared, and with good reason. Solomon edged deeper into the root structure and sat right next to her, removing his helmet.

"It's going to be okay," he said softly, looking directly at her. "They're gone."

She nodded, but didn't move a muscle.

"Lola," he whispered. "I'd appreciate a readout of all hostile fauna in this part of Boundary."

"Are you certain? That's a considerable list."

This mission was quickly becoming far more than Solomon had bargained for.

Twenty minutes later, with still no movement outside, he finally felt like it was safe to proceed. "Stay put," he said, and replaced his helmet, then slowly emerged from the nest of roots under the old giant. Stanchion in hand, he followed the *panthedron* tracks for about thirty meters, scanning the foliage in every direction to ensure that the threat had actually passed.

It was clear the animals were gone, but he questioned the wisdom in moving any farther. Day's light was already past its peak—and he definitely didn't want to encounter those creatures once the forest was drenched in darkness.

A sudden, deep thrumming rocked his chest, followed by a nearly imperceptible quivering of the forest floor. The sky above went black as a large form emerged from the pale midday veil of clouds above.

It was a ship descending through the troposphere, entering Boundary's airspace. The hulking shape was immediately recognizable—a Banished warship.

Then another dropped from the clouds at its side. And another. And another.

All of them were passing from west to east, directly toward the settlement of Tyrrhen.

It was an endless stream that signaled military occupation, something he hadn't witnessed since the Covenant War.

"What are they?" Chloe asked, having finally worked up the courage to follow him.

"Complications."

CHAPTER 22

TUL 'JURAN

U81 Condor Z79
December 14, 2559

The human dropship shook violently as its airframe penetrated the mesosphere of Ghado, and Scion Tul 'Juran tightly gripped her crash harness in response. Everyone on the dropship was doing the same. Everyone except for Gray Team.

'Juran was not surprised.

"Hold tight," the pilot's voice announced through the Condor's communications system. *"Approach vector is steep and choppy."*

'Juran did not know what Commander Prasad meant by *hold tight* or *choppy*. Whenever there was no Sangheili word or idiom that matched within the translation software's archive, the actual human word was stubbed in. Given their military's highly informal parlance, clear communication with them had been exceedingly irritating.

The Condor continued to heave and shudder as it plunged through the planet's dense clouds, its passengers rocking back and forth between intense fits of gravity and weightlessness. 'Juran saw the humans further tighten their belts and she followed suit, drawing in the strap as far as possible. She would have felt no need to do this in a Sangheili dropship, which had powerful inertial compensators, allowing one to stand even in the middle of combat. Human dropships were, by comparison, crude machines and the pilot was attempting a maneuver that would stress it to its limit.

They had been forced to take a precarious ingress trajectory that would get them as close as possible to the human settlement of Tyrrhen, while at the same time not exposing them to the immense Banished occupation force that had already reached the surface. It was a risky maneuver, but humans evidently loved such things—'Juran had already witnessed that they were employed with alarming regularity.

Still, she could not argue with the rationale. According to its crew's calculations, *Victory of Samothrace* and the UNSC battle group had arrived several human hours *after* the Banished. From what 'Juran had ascertained, much of the Banished invasion force previously attempting the attack on Earth was now here at Ghado, a third having made landfall while the remaining two-thirds took defensive positions in orbit. It had become clear that the Banished knew about the Lithos because they were willing to abandon their assault on the human homeworld at the first hint of a break in the Tyrant's power.

If that was truly what they had all witnessed.

Given what 'Juran had seen on Sqala, the departure of the Banished was not a complete surprise. If Dovo Nesto was somehow involved with the Banished, they would prioritize the Lithos over all else. However, it still did not change the fact that the Order of Restoration and the Banished were contradictory in so many ways. The former sought to restore the might of the Covenant, while the latter had sprung from the former empire in rebellion. The only explanation was some kind of bizarre alliance where their desired ends outweighed the means. What had also become clear—from his presence on Sqala as Dovo Nesto's escort, followed by his assault on the Sol system—was that the Jiralhanae called Severan was somehow at the center of it all. If he had brought Dovo Nesto this far, the San'Shyuum was most likely somewhere down on the surface of Ghado, overseeing their excavation of the Forerunner site. And *that* was precisely where the scion intended to go.

'Juran rubbed the soft tissue of her neck, tightening her mandibles as she released a dry cough. It had been a few human weeks already, but her throat and chest were still sore. Her voice had only recently started to return as the human medicine continued its work.

It had for so long been considered shameful for a Sangheili warrior to receive any sort of medical assistance. That it was given to her courtesy of the humans made it even more reprehensible. Nevertheless, she was *alive* and felt a measure of begrudging humility that they had sought to preserve her immediately and without question. Had she perished at the hands of the traitor, she would have no opportunity to deal with Dovo Nesto as she intended.

She had survived, however, and would seek reparations from the San'Shyuum in blood. Before deployment, Captain Cole had informed them that with the location of the Lithos now confirmed, the immense Banished presence proving beyond doubt that they had not been misled by the Sangheili prisoner, there had been a change in operational priorities. They no longer needed to apprehend Dovo Nesto—he could be terminated on sight if the opportunity availed itself. And the scion would ensure that it did.

The rear bay of the Condor was densely packed with human personnel. In addition to Gray Team, there were three new Spartans—McEndon, Vídalín, and Merrick—who were part of *Victory of Samothrace*'s standing super-soldier contingent that had accompanied them on Sqala. Supplementing those were twelve soldiers who referred to themselves as Orbital Drop Shock Troopers. Vul 'Soran, Stolt, and herself were the only nonhumans in the rear bay.

When Captain Abigail Cole had been asked why she would risk "putting so many eggs in one basket"—whatever that meant, as there were no hatchlings present—she had said that without Cortana, there was no way to know for certain if the Banished even needed a key to access the Lithos anymore. If that were true, it meant that the first to reach the Lithos would be the ones who ultimately controlled it. She had decided to send down the best of what they had and do it as quickly and quietly as possible. And, as soon as the ship exited slipspace, she did just that, releasing the Condor before laying in a course that would slingshot the human cruiser around the planet's gravity well and accelerate to meet the Banished fleets head-on.

As long as 'Juran made it to the surface, the specifics of the human strategy did not matter to her. Although she was on a mission for the sake of all Sangheili, the scion could not help but feel a growing sense of finality. Everything she had worked so hard to accomplish since her family's demise at the hands of the Order of Restoration was now approaching its culmination. The crimes executed by the San'Shyuum would at last be paid for. Once Dovo Nesto was killed and 'Juran's family avenged, she could at last have peace and closure.

"Seeking to avenge one's family is a noble goal, Scion," Shipmaster 'Vadum had said to her in one of his many lectures. *"But it can also be blinding, and even when you have attained vengeance, you may find that it is not as you hoped it would be. . . ."*

It is the only thing that matters now, she thought, pushing aside the scolding voice of her shipmaster. *The San'Shyuum* will *have justice, and I will deliver it.*

"Zulu Seven Nine, this is Victory *Mission Control. Do you copy?"* It was the voice of *Victory*'s executive officer.

"We read you, Commander," the Condor's weapons officer replied from the cockpit.

"Surface scans indicate a formation of Banished artillery around the perimeter of Tyrrhen, but we have no clear visual on the east side of the settlement. Mountains are obscuring your approach vector. So proceed with extreme caution."

"How'd they get their guns up so fast?" one of the ODSTs asked.

No one responded.

'Juran assumed it was because the Banished deployed their surface-to-air artillery just as the Covenant had. Dropships and haulers would erect a weapon like this in prefabricated segments, allowing them to quickly build a ground network that could counter enemy air response. The Covenant were able to accomplish this within a unit, so she was not surprised that such a large Banished force already held the perimeter of the city after several units. The artillery was probably composed of gorespike cannons, vulgar abominations that the Banished had developed based on Covenant technology. Since Ghado was apparently a smaller human colony with only a handful of relatively meager settlements, it likely had a weak local militia, if any, which doubtless had given the Banished free rein when they arrived. If the human population here had any sense, 'Juran thought, they would evacuate Tyrrhen and seek shelter far away after working out that the occupying Banished forces were not here with the specific intent to destroy them.

"Roger that, Mission Control," the Condor's weapons officer finally said. *"We'll adapt to Flight Plan Zero Five and come in through Sector Twenty-One. That's twelve-point-eight degrees north, eighty-four-point-six degrees east. Do you concur?"*

"Affirmative. We concur on this end."

The Spartans of Gray Team exchanged looks, their bodies tense but their faces completely hidden behind opaque visors.

"Permission to speak, Mission Control," Jai-006 interjected. The head of Gray Team had been given operational command once they made it to the surface. 'Juran was relieved. It would have grated her to work under any of the others, but she had come to respect Gray Team's capabilities, especially their serious and clinical candor.

"Go ahead, Gray Leader."

"The new flight plan will deliver us twelve kilometers outside the target zone and add at least an hour to our current incursion time, depending on the terrain. Is that acceptable?"

"Probably more like two hours," interjected Merrick, the Spartan sitting directly across from 'Juran, throwing a sideways look at the ODSTs. Apparently Merrick had a low opinion of the shock troopers' ability to keep up with his fellow Spartans. Stolt had explained to 'Juran that there was a substantial performance delta between Spartans and average humans, and even among Spartans themselves there were degrees of capability based on the generation from which they came.

'Juran found it repulsive that such gradation was artificially imposed and not determined by the raw strength or skill of an individual, as it was by nature. Nevertheless, she could not deny the effectiveness of the Spartans after the events on Sqala, nor did she desire to be held back by these ODSTs—whatever they were—any more than the Spartan across from her did.

"We'll keep up," the ODST closest to Merrick said, tinged with anger. "Don't you worry about that, Spartan—"

"*It* has *to be acceptable, Gray Leader,*" the XO said, interrupting the escalating exchange. "*Captain's only able to send one dropship down, so yours needs to count, especially given that it's loaded to the gills with our best ground assets. A gorespike round to your bird would kill this entire operation before it even started.*"

"Understood, sir," Jai responded. "Given the heightened urgency for us to get to the Lithos first, might I suggest a modification to the flight plan? Sending new coordinates now."

"Why these coordinates, Gray Leader?"

"If you look at the municipal utilities map from our briefing, there's a large culvert that dumps into a ravine. It's large enough for us to traverse and it's effectively a straight shot into the city. I'd also suggest diverting some of our forces to the enemy artillery. We may need to clear a hole in their line for extraction."

The XO was silent for a moment, presumably assessing the unexpected change, then spoke. "*That's a sound plan, Gray Leader. Commander Yun?*"

"Those coordinates will work for Zulu Seven Nine, sir," replied the weapons officer from the cockpit. *"Minimal deviation from our proposed flight plan."*

"*Very good. Gray Leader, you can allocate the personnel for the ground teams as needed, but I want you and your team* in *the city. This is no longer only an escort operation for our groundside team. We need to deny Banished access to the Lithos, no matter the cost.*"

Time was of the essence and that was undoubtedly the reason Jai-006 wanted to get a team inside the city as soon as possible. But 'Juran did not care so much about the Lithos, as long she got within striking distance of Dovo Nesto. That was all that mattered to her.

"Solid copy, Commander," Jai replied confidently. "We'll see to it."

"*We're counting on it, Gray Leader. Good luck, Zulu Seven Nine. Let's get everyone home in one piece. Mission Control out.*"

The Condor started to enter a roll as it continued to plummet down the planet's gravity well at an increasingly steep trajectory. 'Juran could feel her mass pulling hard toward the back of the dropship, loose straps and racks of matériel in the cabin showing the same effects. The strain started to become painful, until the dropship shed enough speed and quickly leveled off. She remained bewildered that the humans had somehow conditioned themselves to believe that such things were acceptable when it came to their flight technology.

"At five hundred feet, sixty seconds to LZ," Yun said. *"Coast looks clear. First sighted Banished artillery is seven klicks north, but they can't see us from their position."*

"Excellent," Jai replied. "Listen up, Strike Team Zulu. Name of the game is divide and conquer. ODSTs are Zulu Blue. Spartans and *Shadow of Intent* are Zulu Red. Blue, we need you to punch a hole in that artillery line. Take a section offline and keep them that way, otherwise we'll have no way to exfil. Red, we're hotfooting it to the settlement's center. There's a park where the Banished have set up shop. *Victory*'s analysts believe it's the location of the Lithos. Seismic data from Colonial Authority and topographical scans from *Akkadian* corroborate this. Our goal is to secure the site for *Akkadian*'s team and an ONI operative escorting the key."

'Juran did not know half of what Jai was saying or who the *Akkadian* team was, only that an ONI operative was escorting a human child connected to the Tyrant. 'Juran did find it strange that everyone was referring to the child as a *key.* In Sangheili, there were familial curses attached to such word associations.

"Twenty seconds to LZ," Yun sounded through the communications system.

"Everyone clear?" Jai asked.

The humans affirmed in unison. So did Stolt, for some reason.

"Ten seconds," Yun said, as the Condor decelerated so quickly that 'Juran felt almost like it had collided with something.

Gray Team decoupled immediately from their crash harnesses, so 'Juran and the others followed their lead, though the dropship was nowhere near stationary. The tail of the Condor swung around hard, forcing her to clutch the bulkhead to steady herself. Its bay suddenly splayed open, folding out into a ramp that hovered half a meter above a creek bed. Outside revealed a water runoff from the mouth of a pipe, roughly three meters in diameter. Day's vanishing light filtered through large coniferous trees and scattered a soft glow across the gently coursing stream.

The culvert itself seemed to be impaled in the side of a steep ravine roughly thirty meters tall, covered with sparse orange and red vegetation. The pipe was traveling north, directly into the settlement, with the ravine flowing east to west. Gray Team dropped to the creek bed, followed by the other Spartans, the ODSTs, and then those with her from *Shadow of Intent.* She made sure her double-bladed plasma lance was secure on her back and retrieved her father's *Vostu*-pattern carbine—a trusted keepsake, and an older Covenant midrange weapon he had used during the war—then leapt off the ramp to the creek below.

The ODST team leader, a female called Sergeant Gentry, spoke with Jai briefly before rounding up her troops and heading east along the ravine. The others from Gray Team were already shining their lamps into the pipe, but the beams only made it so far before being erased by the inky darkness.

"Appreciate you shedding that weight, Gray Leader," Merrick said, his helmet looking off in the direction the ODSTs had gone. "We'd never make it to the target in time if we had to drag them along." He turned toward the two Sangheili and then the Unggoy, as if sizing them up. 'Juran did not know whether to be offended, but this Spartan's posture and tone seemed far more presumptuous and hostile than Gray Team's.

"Take it easy, kid," Adriana-111 said, stepping toward the other Spartan and squaring up to him. "You'll need those fireteams before the day's out. Mark my words."

"What about this guy?" Merrick asked, gesturing his assault rifle toward Stolt.

The Spartan was evidently concerned about the Unggoy ranger's speed. 'Juran glared at him. She parted her mandibles, about to speak, but did not need to.

"Can it, Merrick," Jai said in an adamant tone, stepping in between Merrick and Stolt. "We're all going in, no exceptions. The ODSTs will do what we can't: clear the airspace for departure. Unless you want to give them a hand, I'd suggest you keep your mouth closed."

The scion stared at Jai for a moment, surprised that he had come to the defense of another species and done so almost instinctively. There was no ulterior reason for it apart from his desire to set things right. A feeling of vindication welled up within her, and it was followed—inscrutably—by a sense of camaraderie. She did not know what to make of it.

Jai turned to face the pipe's yawning mouth. "Unless the Banished have built some kind of blockade, this'll take us straight to an exit point four hundred meters away from the park."

"How confident are we that the Lithos is actually located there?" Vídalín asked. "We could be going on a wild goose chase."

"As confident as we can be about anything at this point," Jai replied. "But we'll have to be ready to pivot if intel reveals something else. The Banished wouldn't have concentrated so many resources there unless it has *something*."

"And Dovo Nesto is there as well?" 'Soran asked, flitting his mandibles.

"We'll find out when we get there." Jai stepped inside the culvert, his helmet lights igniting. "But if I were to guess, they didn't pick him up on Sqala for a joyride. If and when we spot him, your team will have priority, as we agreed. But understand this: as important as neutralizing the San'Shyuum is, our primary target is the Lithos. My people won't jeopardize that under any circumstance. Understood?"

"Understood, Spartan," 'Soran said, his hands resting on the hilts of his two energy swords. "We will assist you with the Lithos, and you will allow us the right to seize our quarry."

"Or terminate him," the scion said, stepping forward to ignore the blademaster's gaze.

"Anyone figured out yet why the Banished are working with the Order of Restoration?" McEndon asked. "This behavior isn't consistent with either group."

"No, it's not," Jai responded. "We don't know why, and we don't need to. Not right now at least. Whatever their motivations are, we have to assume that the Lithos is behind it all. If they get that, whatever happened out there on Zeta Halo is basically reversed and we get ourselves a *new* dictator. Understood?"

The other Spartans nodded, and the members of Gray Team climbed into the culvert behind him, the others following. Before long, their entire group was in a pitch-black hole with nothing but the quickly fading glint of light on a narrow trail of water running down its center.

"Merrick," Jai said. "Try to keep up." Then he disappeared into the darkness at breakneck speed.

CHAPTER 23

ABIGAIL COLE

UNSC *Victory of Samothrace*
December 14, 2559

The Banished ships were spread out across the cold blue curve of Boundary's horizon like a thick red cloud. They had been here for only a few hours but had created an impressive defensive shell in geosynchronous orbit around Tyrrhen. The outer layer, comprising skeids and karves, was densely packed, configured to unleash hellfire on anything that came within range. Dreadnoughts were positioned in packs within the interior, punctuated by an occasional monolithic holk. They had formed a virtually impenetrable barrier around the city, but *Victory of Samothrace* and Battle Group Omega had the element of surprise.

Or so Abigail Cole hoped.

"We'll make this pass and then swing back around to the other side for another strike," she said, staring at the holopane. The sheer number of Banished vessels disturbed her, but she wouldn't let her crew see it. Her voice was directed to the corner of the pane, a feed from Commander Jiron on the bridge of UNSC *Get*

My Drift. "Keep your ships on the far perimeter of their massing element. Otherwise we'll get shredded."

"Affirmative, Captain," he replied, eyeing the data her team was sending them. *"We'll run a sawhorse line right behind you."* He turned to the interface to stare directly at her. His face showed the same concern she felt. *"But we're not going to last long out here without help."*

"I'm working on that, Commander. And when I've got the answer, you'll be the first to know."

"Understood, ma'am. Very eager to hear that answer." The feed snapped off.

She took a deep breath and looked out the viewport again, taking in the sheer size of the Banished force and its layout. Pushing back the dread that clawed at her heart, she told herself to *think*. The solution they were looking for would come in pieces.

Shadow of Intent and *Akkadian* were presently on approach from different sectors across Boundary's orbital plane. They had already been in orbit well prior to the Banished. The former was a classic Covenant-era assault carrier, but *Akkadian* was an experimental ONI prowler—Cole had no idea what weapons capabilities it possessed or how much it might lack. Given the enemy's numbers, neither of these vessels would move the needle a millimeter in their favor during this engagement. So she'd sent a request for reinforcements to Captain Richards almost immediately upon emerging from slipspace and witnessing what they were up against.

At first blush, it seemed to Cole as if nearly all the Banished ships that had attempted to attack Earth had now come to Boundary. It was a relief that Earth was no longer the target, at least for now. But it seemed evident that the Banished were also after the Lithos, which no doubt had something to do with Dovo Nesto and War Chief Severan. And this, at some level, meant they understood its strategic importance and would give up everything else to secure it. She didn't see Severan's flagship among those in orbit, so she assumed that both of them were already down on the surface, likely looking for the Forerunner machine.

"Contact with Banished defensive shell in forty-five seconds, Captain," Lieutenant Zobah said, assessing the enemy's position and the approaching point where they would be in firing range. "Good news from downstairs. Zulu Seven Nine has successfully deployed the strike team."

"That's great to hear, Lieutenant." The captain kept her tone neutral, but internally felt a wave of relief. "I want a status update from them in fifteen minutes. Commander Njuguna?"

"Yes, Captain." The XO looked up from his control station.

"As soon as *Akkadian* is in range, I'd like to speak with Admiral al-Cygni."

"Affirmative. Given their last update on the tracker, it'll have to be in our next pass to avoid detection. They're somewhere near Boundary's southern pole and moving cautiously."

"Understood. Just let me know when you have her on the line." This suggested to Cole that the ship was not built for combat, but there was no way to confirm. All the more reason for Earth to send whatever reinforcements they could afford. There would be no way for the UNSC to effectively secure the Lithos without some measure of orbital control.

Victory of Samothrace and the three vessels that remained from Battle Group Omega were now traveling in a tight orbital arc around Boundary on a carefully selected trajectory that would glance off the Banished defensive shell and do so at considerable speed. Their desire was to give the Banished a target moving too quickly to effectively engage, but enough to misdirect them, drawing their eyes away from the Condor deployment below.

"Preparing to fire designated port side weapons," Lieutenant Nishioka announced from her station. "Omega following suit." She led a five-person team in the rear of the bridge, working with the battle group to ensure that their weapons fire would achieve optimal effectiveness.

Due to their orbital speed, they had to fire well before the system would allocate targets so that the shots could connect. Whether they successfully downed any Banished ships or not would be left mostly to fate, but enough rounds would be blasted into that shell to hit *something.* Most importantly, they would get the attention of the Banished.

"Fire when ready," Cole said.

"Acknowledged," Nishioka replied.

"Captain, our readings indicate that Banished weapons are also active," Lieutenant Aquila said. "They must have spotted our tau surge when we exited slipspace. Not sure how, possibly sensor beacons they dropped on arrival. They're not breaking formation, but it definitely looks like they're creating a field of fire."

"We knew that would be a possibility," Cole said, lamenting the loss of the only tactical advantage they had. "Nav, let's be ready to maneuver. As best as we can."

"Affirmative, Captain," Lieutenant Bavinck said. "We're on it already."

So much for the element of surprise.

The pass between the UNSC ships and the Banished shell would come so rapidly that attacking vessels on both sides would essentially be forming walls of weapons fire, the former to collide directly into the defensive shell and the latter to block *Victory*'s and Omega's orbital path around them. Cole could appreciate the enemy's strategic response—she would have done the same. It did make the next few seconds far more hazardous than preferable.

At the speed they were traveling, even the smallest contact with enemy fire could be devastating. And slowing down would only give the Banished an easier target to hit.

She fought to keep what had happened to *Ozymandias* from entering her mind.

The holopane showed the UNSC ships on course around the orbital arc, unloading their fore and starboard armament into the nearest edge of the Banished shell, some of their shots already connecting. Archer and Helix missiles tunneled toward the outer layer of skeids and karves, with Shiva warheads trailing right behind them—literally hundreds of propulsion contrails curved out to strike the enemy. The Banished field of fire was already bristling in the distance, creating a wall of death right in *Victory*'s path. She couldn't see where the weapons fire was headed but they would be in the thick of it soon enough.

Her crew worked quickly and efficiently, coordinating with the battle group, as Banished munitions crossed the hazy border between Boundary's face and the dark blanket of outer space. This was weapons technology the enemy had inherited—or, more accurately, *stolen*—from the Covenant. Plasma lances and torpedoes appeared as a deadly and impassible field of piercingly bright daggers, while pulse lasers broke across the viewport as thin red lines forming a spider web of destructive power.

Victory of Samothrace moved up and down on its predicative path as enemy fire flared around them. Omega was following in a sawhorse line just behind them. Although the four ships' crews were calculating a thousand probabilities and sensor readings establishing a loose understanding of the enemy's field of fire, much of what happened was guesswork. But it had to be *right*, every single time. All Cole could do was stand and watch. And if something did go awry, they would be atomized before they even realized it.

Through the forward viewport, Cole saw a single pulse laser come uncomfortably close, but *Victory* narrowly edged above it, the others following in tow. It happened so fast that the untrained eye would not have even recognized it. On the holopane, a Banished marker suddenly blipped out of existence.

"We've taken down a karve," Nishioka said. "And now a skeid. Two enemy ships down."

And several hundred to go, Cole thought.

But two was better than none. And the Banished now knew the UNSC was not going to simply roll over and let their enemy take what didn't belong to them.

"Thirty seconds until we're outside Banished weapons' range," Lieutenant Bavinck said.

Cole was tempted to count down each second in her head, but resisted the urge—it was an eternity when threading a field of enemy fire the size of a continent. A sudden explosion off the port side bow rocked *Victory* to its core, but she remained intact.

"No structural damage, Captain," Lieutenant Whelihan noted. Cole wiped sudden beads of sweat from her brow, and kept her eyes fixed on the holopane and its evolving data streams.

Ozymandias tried to make its way into her thoughts again.

So did her father.

"That was a really close one, Captain," Commander Jiron broke in over the comms. *"Plasma lance skimmed over the top of your cruiser. A little bit lower and it would have taken you."*

"We sure as hell felt it, Commander," Cole said, steadying her voice. "Grateful to still be talking to you."

"Ten seconds left," Bavinck said, as another skeid vanished from the holopane. "Five seconds . . . " Another karve vanished.

Cole held her breath, eyes fixed on the holopane.

One of the UNSC icons trailing *Victory* suddenly disappeared. *Damn it.*

The pane immediately flashed to an inset visual from a rear camera facing astern. Behind the superheavy cruiser was the staggered line of Battle Group Omega, stretched out so far that only the nearest ship could be seen, and that only faintly. In the far distance, a sphere of white light was fading and then dissipated.

"Dear God," Aquila said. "That was *Easy Does It*. It's gone."

"Now outside Banished firing range," Bavinck announced. "No Banished craft in pursuit. They're all staying above Tyrrhen."

For thirty additional seconds, *Victory* continued in its orbital trajectory and swung around the far side of the planet, now shrouded in darkness. Cole quietly monitored the holopane as her crew conducted the standard post-combat protocols and kept eyes behind them as the Banished defensive shell got smaller in their aft sensors.

"Commander Njuguna," she said, finally turning to her XO. "I'm going to speak with Jiron privately in the conference suite. You have the chair."

"Understood, Captain," he said, standing up from his console and coming behind the holopane, before turning to her, grim-faced. "Take your time."

She headed toward the back of the bridge and into the command conference suite, sealing the door behind her. It was a small room with a single holoplinth at its center, directly in front of a swivel seat with comms controls on its armrests. Sitting down, she punched in the key sequence for a direct transmission to the vessel *Get My Drift* and a formal request to privately speak with their commander. Within seconds, Jiron appeared before her.

Even though it was a hologram, pain was clearly etched on

Jiron's face. He'd lost half his battle group since the confrontation on Earth. *Easy Does It* alone probably had close to five hundred crew and combat personnel.

Sorrow and guilt gripped her chest, a familiar feeling. And all of it was because of this operation. *Her* operation.

"Hello, Captain," he said, his voice strained.

"I'm sorry." Cole wanted to say more, but couldn't find the words.

"Thank you," Jiron's eyes dropped to the floor. *"I appreciate it. The* Easy *crew knew the cost and they were willing to pay it. Every single one of them. I have to ask you though: Why did the Banished leave Earth? What's so important about this place? I need to know what we're fighting for."*

"Fair enough. There's something underneath Tyrrhen that the Banished want and the UNSC can't afford to give them. It's a gateway, a machine—they call it the Lithos. This machine can connect directly to the Domain, which was until recently Cortana's source of power. ONI believes this gateway is the key to getting control of the Domain. The Banished want it. Desperately. They want it so bad they cut short their assault on Earth at the first sign that Cortana had been removed. We can't allow the Banished to take her power now that she's gone."

"Understood," he said as the weight of the matter slowly fell on him. *"And you've already dispatched a team to the ground to access this machine?"*

"It's a bit more complicated than that, but yes. There's an ONI operative bringing a key to the Lithos that can unlock it. My strike team will rendezvous with one from *Akkadian* to ensure site acquisition. Of course, Cortana's departure may have escalated things. The Lithos may no longer even need a key."

"And so right now all these elements are headed into Banished-

occupied territory in order to secure this Forerunner machine. And we're here to . . . what? *Buy them time?"*

"To assist them in whatever way we can," she clarified. "Maybe it's time, maybe it's orbital support, maybe it's more assets on the ground. I've already requested naval support from Captain Richards. ONI knows what's at stake. They'll send backup. They have to, or we'll lose the Lithos."

"Permission to speak candidly, Captain."

"Go ahead."

"We're going to need more than backup, ma'am," Jiron said, his expression bleak and battle-worn. *"If ONI wants that machine, they're going to have to send an entire fleet. Multiple fleets. Otherwise, we'll all be joining* Easy Does It *and* Blank Check *very soon."*

"I hear you, Commander. They won't risk losing this site. It's far too important. I promise you—we will have support."

"I hope you're right," he said, looking out into the distance. *"A handful of groundside personnel? Against an entire Banished occupation force?"* He turned back to her. *"You should know that* Hazard Pay *did a surface scan upon slipspace egress. They were able to assess the Banished ground forces and assets at the time of arrival."*

"What did they find?" *Victory* had done topography scans, searching for the likeliest locations of the Lithos. There wasn't enough time for them to do a full force assessment on the Banished occupation.

"There are more personnel and vehicles deployed and on-station in Tyrrhen than most of us have seen since Reach. Your people are walking straight into hell. I hope they find what they're looking for."

CHAPTER 24

SEVERAN

Ghado (Boundary)
December 14, 2559

The human structure fell like a hardsand column in the Malkadyr Wastes of Doisac. At four levels, it was the tallest within the meager settlement the humans called Tyrrhen. The building had stood at the corner of the intersection of their two main roadways, but now it was only a mound of rubble spewing dust into the streets like a bleeding corpse.

Within its jagged shambles came the screams of those who had not been crushed when Severan gave the order for its load-bearing columns to be obliterated by a Locust siege crawler. The very refuge the humans had taken cover in had now become their crypt.

Three of those trapped managed to escape, darting from the side of the rubble in search of new shelter while the dust still clouded the air. Severan nodded to Arxus, part of the commanding entourage for the settlement's center. The towering Champion of Zaladon moved toward the humans, unrushed and confident, as the puny creatures scrambled like rodents. Severan was impressed they had survived, but their escape would not be long-lived—the foolish consequence of those who had chosen not to flee when his forces arrived.

Arxus hefted his javelin in one hand, a weapon he'd dubbed Graydawn, and threw it with such force that it howled in the surrounding air. The weapon skewered the farthest human, pinning him to the wall of a separate building, his body dangling wildly. The other two hesitated, no doubt shocked by the brutal attack. This was a mistake. Before they realized it, Arxus had already come upon them, his two-meter khopesh—Blackmaw—cleaving them both at their chests with one swipe, their lifeless husks hitting the street with a fleshy thud. He casually stepped on the skull of one, crushing it into the ground as he wiped their blood off his khopesh.

"An impressive specimen," Ectorius the White said as Arxus silently returned to Severan's side. "Where did you acquire such a monster?"

"Monsters are not acquired, Chieftain," Severan replied, casting a fleeting glance in his direction. "They are forged."

He turned his attention toward the park diametric to the building they had just brought down and the very reason he had ordered it. There were other buildings in the immediate vicinity, but that was the only one Severan felt might compromise the security of their dig site. *Heart of Malice*'s earlier scans had proven fruitful: a large, irregular structure lay thirty meters below the surface of the park, an angular course of grass and trees roughly three human city blocks in size.

This was the only place on the entire planet that held such a structure, confirming beyond any doubt the location that High Lord Dovo Nesto had provided for the Lithos. Dust continued to sweep through foliage and brush within the park, a dense mist of gray particulates that obscured the newly-erected digging machines. Three grinders and a massive flame-bore derrick were tunneling deep through ground and stone, melting away the layers of dross to reach the treasure hidden below.

"Are you concerned these machines will damage it?" Dreka 'Xulsam asked, folding his arms. The Sangheili stood next to Ectorius the White and Gathgor.

These three of the Eight had traveled to the surface with Severan, selected by the casting of lots to determine who would distribute their fleets' infantry and mechanized forces across Tyrrhen. The remainder of the Banished home fleet had created a defensive shell to keep the UNSC away. Severan wondered if the selection was as random as lots would suggest, since they had been cast by Gathgor, and Ectorius and 'Xulsam were his close allies.

The other leaders had accepted their current role without dispute, likely preferring to avoid spending any more groundside military assets than necessary. The war chief surmised that they were eager to lay claim to the Lithos *if* it existed, but until that could be proven, they would surely take the path of least risk. Unfortunately for them, the defensive shell had already incurred losses as a handful of human ships struck it during a slingshot orbit around the planet.

It was a clever strategy, but Severan almost felt insulted. Boundary had no standing military force and yet humanity had sent only a single battle group. Was that truly all they could muster? With the apparent fall of Cortana, did the UNSC still believe themselves to be giants among the stars? Again, he pondered whether bringing all his Banished fleets here had been a mistake. Yet if the Lithos was what the high lord claimed it to be, it was better to take no chances.

He turned from the excavation site and led an entourage of twelve toward the first war pavilion the Banished had established, in an empty lot the humans had used for their vehicles. In addition to the three leaders, Severan had selected some of his finest Jiralhanae warriors. It was not for practical or security reasons; any human resistance within the settlement would be negligible. He wanted the other leaders to witness the loyalty that the Vanguard of Zaladon had for their leader—and for the two chieftains to appreciate his commitment to the Jiralhanae people, particularly given the destruction of Doisac and its colonies.

"The Warkeepers have secured the settlement's eastern perimeter," Gathgor announced as he marched. "The Norkala have secured the west. Our ships fill their sky. But I have seen nothing yet that indicates we have need to."

"Indeed," 'Xulsam said. "We deployed my fleet's full supply of gorespikes and antlions—per your orders, War Chief—but apart from a handful of human stragglers attempting to escape, there has been no reason to use them."

"What point are you endeavoring to make, Kaidon?" Severan asked, his tone neither threatening nor defensive.

"All we have of this Lithos are your words and the scans you claim validate its existence," the Sangheili said. "There is nothing on this world that has told me that it exists. The humans here either have no knowledge of it or they do not share your view of its value."

"Clearly the humans here do not know it exists or they would have excavated it by now," Severan said, his voice tense. "Is this a new revelation? Have not the humans always been one step behind us with regard to the Forerunners? The ones who do know it exists have been scraping Banished ships off the defensive shell over the city. They are few now, but I doubt such fortune will hold for long. We must work as quickly as possible. Every second we waste is one step closer to all-out war against Earth's best fleets. And believe me, Kaidon, we do not want that."

"Speak for yourself, War Chief," Gathgor grunted. "We were taking them above their own world well enough. Why not from the surface of this one?"

"Magnetic accelerator cannons, for one," 'Xulsam said, as though it was obvious. "And they are quite rabid when they fight from space to retake a world. They would not hesitate to raze their own homes to cinders if it meant ridding them of us."

The Sangheili was correct. His kind had spent decades fighting against humanity and possessed considerable experience on the receiving end of occupational campaigns. When the humans' backs were against the wall, they were desperate and dangerous creatures, especially with their capital ship-grade weapons. If the humans fired a single MAC round at their current position, it would level five square blocks of the settlement, annihilating anything in the area and potentially damaging or even destroying the Lithos.

Gathgor simply huffed in response to the Sangheili's naval tactics lesson.

The group finally entered the war pavilion, one of nearly a hundred prefabricated Banished structures that their vessels had deployed on the ground within Tyrrhen. Buildings like the heavily armored pavilion offered their occupation all the logistical and matériel support necessary to effectively conduct any campaign. As Severan stopped below the arch, he stared up into Boundary's soft blue sky, taking in the vast panoply of Banished ships fixed just above the city. He wished their presence made him feel more secure, but something told him that the defensive shell could not provide the safety he desired. No fleet, regardless of its size, could protect him from a blade in the back if the opportunity arose.

Perhaps his unease was the gods speaking.

The entourage huddled around a holotable displaying the seismic scans from *Malice*. A Forerunner structure could be clearly seen under the park's surface, one that matched almost identically to the mass imagery Dovo Nesto had acquired from the Forerunner world called Genesis. That data had been retrieved by

Covenant forces occupying the site during the awakening of the Guardians and its symmetry between what they now saw below Ghado was incontravertible. Despite what 'Xulsam had suggested, there was no question in Severan's mind about the Lithos's presence, and he wanted it to be clear to all the others: A Forerunner machine of extraordinary power lay below the surface of this world, and whoever possessed this power would rule over all.

"I trust that this data cannot be interpreted differently by anyone here," Severan said, gesturing to the scans. "The Lithos lies under our feet. If the Banished desire to take Cortana's place and all the authority she possessed, we must secure it."

"It does seem rather conclusive," Ectorius said, casting a quick glance at 'Xulsam.

Even the Sangheili could not question the clarity of the scan's information, though he might take issue with whether it was fabricated. Different conversations erupted among the group about what they were seeing and how best to excavate it. The din became so loud that Severan almost did not hear Kaevus's voice come through on his native-link.

"War Chief, your daskalo *has summoned you."*

His captain had been given charge of watching over the high lord's sanctum, a hidden room deep within his own clan's command spire, only a fifteen-cental walk from the settlement's center. The last thing Severan needed now was to have the San'Shyuum's presence revealed to the outlying Banished forces. If that happened, everything he had worked so hard to attain would be gone in an instant. He trusted no one but Kaevus with such a task.

"Apologies, brothers," Severan said, raising his hand. "I have another critical matter I must attend to, but I will return shortly." Gesturing to his own warriors to stay in the pavilion, he departed.

Severan took the path directly through the plaza, between the dig site and the demolished building. Dust still swirled about as several armed squads of his own warriors patrolled the streets before him, organized into highly disciplined patterns. Zaladon alone had deployed over eight thousand troops across Tyrrhen. At the heart of the settlement, where the structures were most densely packed and built-up, he had concentrated infantry, scout bikes, and war-skiffs. On the outskirts, where there was more open space, he had deployed larger mechanized elements, including war-sleds, mortar tanks, and combat walkers. On the edges, the territory his own clan was occupying overlapped with the other clans, providing a perimeter to prevent encroachments from the outside. The settlement was so heavily occupied that it might as well have been Doisac itself.

Within twelve centals, Severan reached the spire and entered through the antechamber, working his way through the spire's deeper recesses to a short corridor that led to the high lord's private chamber. Kaevus stood at the front of the corridor, waiting for the war chief.

"How did your meeting with the others go?" the captain asked as they walked.

"As well as can be expected," Severan replied. "Some doubt the Lithos is even here; some are willing to fight to the death for it. None are eager to defy Atriox."

"That will be sufficient," Kaevus said, keying in the security passcode.

"It has to be," Severan said as the door opened, and he entered alone.

The dimly lit interior was appropriate for a San'Shyuum whose large eyes had been trained over long ages to see well in High Charity's perpetual twilight, where nothing was ever as dark as a true night or as bright as true day. The small but comfortable space had all the furnishings and food Severan could provide to make Dovo Nesto's stay passable, despite it bearing the rugged aesthetic of a Banished military compound. Severan supposed that anything might be considered an upgrade from the rancid human ship the high lord had most recently taken residence in, but he could not be certain.

"My son," Nesto said from across the room. His eyes glistened bright blue as he read scripture from a glowing Forerunner tablet. "Pardon my summoning. I know that you are quite busy."

"Not so much that I cannot take counsel with my *daskalo*." Severan bowed before the high lord and sensed the San'Shyuum's long fingers drape over his pauldron. "How can I be of service, High Lord?"

"Rise, Severan," Dovo Nesto said, now holding the tablet in both hands. "It is I who will serve *you* today. I have received word that there is a contingent of humans and Sangheili on approach to Tyrrhen as we speak. It is the same group that attempted to apprehend me on Sqala."

The news shocked Severan to silence. *How is this possible? And how does the high lord even know this information?*

"In addition to this," the San'Shyuum said, turning away from Severan, "I have discovered something . . . *unfortunate*."

"What is it?"

"The Lithos still requires a key. I had assumed that Cortana's absence might allow us direct entry, but even with her apparent passing she has not left it without security."

Again, Severan was dumbfounded. "Without access to the Lithos, how do you know, High Lord?"

Dovo Nesto held up the slate he had brought with him from Sqala, Forerunner writing engraved across its surface. "I have been studying this text—a codex of sorts from an ancient sect that called themselves the Criterion. It is rather rich and complex, and only now do I clearly see its full picture."

Dovo Nesto flicked his wrist and a holographic representation of the slate's contents was projected above them. Unlike the more traditional forms of Forerunner glyphs that Severan had seen, this scripture appeared in three dimensions with dozens of lines of text scrolling. It seemed that Dovo Nesto had managed to successfully isolate several more passages since Severan had last seen the tablet.

"We who claim the blessing of rule and protection of life and change that thinks have been brought to the domain of our makers," Dovo Nesto translated. *"The starlight angel showed us the twining streams, bright as crystal, flowing from Their throne—the treemark of life. We shall build bridges to that kingdom so that generations to come may be blessed with wisdom, and their strength shall blaze as a luminous sun."*

Dovo Nesto took a moment to let the words sink in, for Severan to grasp their meaning, and to bask in reverence of the fact that they were the only two beings alive who knew of these direct words from the Forerunners themselves.

"The Domain . . . was *not* created by the Forerunners." Severan exhaled.

"Indeed, my son. It existed *long* before them, cultivated by a race of gods who preceded their civilization. The Forerunners built the Lithos to access the Domain and bless the galaxy with the timeless wisdom of their predecessors."

"Their *predecessors*." Severan was utterly astonished by the revelation.

"There is more here that speaks of biological templates becoming as starlight in order to open the way. Without the AI herself, we require someone identical to her. We still require the key—the human girl, who is the exact image of the AI. But . . . " Dovo

Nesto turned to him with a smile. "Fear not, my son, I have also confirmed that the key is on this world. Another human element unwittingly brings the child to us now."

"I beg your forgiveness, *daskalo*," Severan said, struggling to navigate these sudden and jarring waves of new information. Ironically, it was the prosaic intel that was most shocking to him. Not because of the information itself, but rather how it was exactly that the high lord had acquired it. "From whom did you learn all of this—the two groups headed our way? Our forces have detected nothing."

"One cannot live as long as I have, my son, and not have eyes *everywhere.* Even their attack on Sqala was no surprise to me. They do nothing without my knowledge."

"And you are confident of this information, High Lord?"

Severan knew what his *daskalo*'s response would be, but he had to ask, if only to keep his mind from reeling. *How could the humans deploy to this world unnoticed? How can they even presume to bring the very key to the Lithos here under the shadow of hundreds of Banished ships without being seen by a single one? And just* how *does the high lord know all of this?*

"I am confident, Severan," Dovo Nesto said, tugging at the wattles that hung from his face like a beard. His eyes narrowed and he spoke again. "Do you not trust me, my son?"

"I do trust you, High Lord. But how can I secure the Lithos if humans are able to penetrate my defenses without my knowledge? Their very presence here could undo all that we have accomplished . . . and yet *you* knew of this. If they access the Lithos first, none of what you have planned will come to pass."

"They will not access the Lithos, Severan, because *you* will stop them before they reach it." The San'Shyuum's face shone dark and held a bitterly grave mien that Severan had never seen before.

"They are here only because I desire them to be. Who do you think informed them the Lithos was on this world when they took one of my Sangheili as a prisoner on Sqala? You must trust me, my son. All is going according to plan and I have overlooked nothing."

It was that last statement—*I have overlooked nothing*—that gave Severan the most pause.

He had broken off his assault on Earth and taken all the Banished ships under his command to seek out the Lithos, believing it to be unguarded and ready for the taking. He had done this based on the high lord's word . . . and now that word had changed. A key to the Lithos *was* still required? And humans had that key and were headed for the Lithos right under their very noses? Outrageous.

Either Dovo Nesto had actually misinterpreted the passage on the slate . . . or he had deliberately hidden its truth from Severan until now, as evidently he had done with many other things, if he truly had spies within the humans' numbers.

He did not know which possibility was preferable, as both made him exceedingly uneasy. For the first time in memory, he suddenly felt at odds with the high lord.

The San'Shyuum must have sensed this because he turned away, facing the corner of the room, and intoned: "In that young human girl, Severan, is the spark that will reignite the Covenant's cleansing flame."

The high lord turned to face him again, his visage even more grim and defiant, eyes shining with zeal. "If we lose her, you are correct to say that all we have planned is lost. But that will not happen. I *refuse* to allow it to. The humans will bring the girl to this settlement, and you will bring her to *me*." He placed his hand on Severan's shoulder again. "She will open the door to divinity and I will step in. And together, my son, we will reign."

CHAPTER 25

JAMES SOLOMON

En route to Gate Lipari, Boundary
December 14, 2559

According to Lola, Tyrrhen had over two dozen gates placed at specific intervals along the settlement's fenced periphery, secured entry points that safeguarded the population center from various indigenous threats. According to the navpoint, Gate Lipari—Tyrrhen's northernmost gate—was only two kilometers away, but it was mostly open terrain. To James Solomon, who had to safely escort a stubborn ten-year-old girl across that distance, the sheer volume of exposure made it feel much farther than that.

From the peak of the esker he had summited, he could see across the entire valley and take in almost the full breadth of the settlement as it straggled in every direction. Its outskirts were a sporadic distribution of buildings and farmsteads, with very little cover apart from the occasional trail of boscage. He and Chloe had reached the perimeter of Tyrrhen right at the onset of dusk, and that was a good thing because two dozen Jiralhanae were already in regulated patrols near it.

The dimming light of nightfall could provide the visibility loss necessary to penetrate the settlement's border, so he would use that to his advantage. The Banished troops were heavily armed yet seemed bored and lackadaisical, ambling in loose, undisciplined patterns around the exterior gatehouse and a dense cluster of small buildings that lay just beyond the gate. He'd use *that* too.

Solomon turned toward a shallow crevice in the esker and the little brown-haired girl tucked carefully inside it beside his Stanchion, which looked enormous next to her small frame. Chloe had fallen asleep about twenty minutes ago, exhausted by the day's trip. They had made nearly the full journey to the gate and done so before sundown. He was genuinely surprised, although he probably shouldn't have been. Somewhere along the way, he'd discovered that Chloe was made of something different than most kids her age, even most adults. She'd made the entire trip on a makeshift crutch, without once falling behind or complaining. It was nothing short of remarkable. Now she was getting a well-deserved rest and she'd be safe where she was.

"Thoughts?" Lola asked.

"Not many," Solomon lied, sighing as he toggled through different zooms in his Mjolnir visor. The constellation of Banished warships that hung above the settlement looked like a crown of storm clouds, ready to drop lightning on anything that passed unauthorized beneath their shadow. He let his vision fall to Tyrrhen below and the dense cluster of taller structures in the distance representing the settlement's center. A thrumming he'd heard growing as they approached the settlement must have come from the dark plume of smoke snaking upward from between those buildings. The Banished were digging for something.

The enemy's occupation was certainly more concentrated and well-ordered there, but on Tyrrhen's perimeter, it could hardly be defined as anything like that. Occasionally he'd spot a lone

Chopper barreling through the streets or a Ghost pack gunning it across farmland, but most of the forces deployed at the rim were slack infantry formations, and their patrol paths were so random it was difficult even to call them organized patterns.

"The lockbox," he said, finally locating a marked gate pylon with a shuttered panel. "I just want this mission to be over with."

"What about the syringe?"

"I'll figure that part out later," Solomon answered, but wasn't sure even as he said it. "All that matters right now is getting to that box and doing it without signaling every Banished detachment on this planet."

"The Banished patrol patterns do seem . . . unorthodox,*"* Lola mused. *"I'm assuming this is because Tyrrhen has no militia and minimal defenses. Apart from a handful of mass drivers, there is very little on this world to keep an invading enemy force at bay. They don't feel the need to be organized, which could prove beneficial."*

"Yes and no," he replied. "Look at the settlement's center. The Banished there are in tightly cordoned patterns and there isn't a square meter they don't have their eyes on. They're not playing games. But the ones on the perimeter look like they want to be on this rock even less than I do. Completely different."

"And your point is?"

"They're not guarding this place because they have a vested interest—they're guarding this place because they were *told* to. The two don't belong to the same military element, which means there's some complexity here to the overall force deployment that is . . . potentially exploitable."

"Understood," Lola said. *"What's the plan, then?"*

"You're going to keep an eye on the girl," Solomon said, withdrawing his designated marksman rifle and suppressor from a hardcase on his thigh. "And I'm going to exploit that complexity."

Before Lola could venture a response, he'd already spun the suppressor onto the barrel and launched into a run, working his way down the side of the esker behind a frayed line of trees casting long shadows. With Chloe—or any average human—this would have been impossible, but his speed could easily conceal him from the Jiralhanae below. He needed to clear the immediate area of hostiles, access the lockbox, and then regroup, though he'd begun suspecting that this operation would ultimately take him and Chloe to whatever the Banished were digging up. It came in handy that Lola could still operate from within his Mjolnir, while a relay disk in the crevice holding Chloe allowed her to monitor the girl while Solomon was physically somewhere else.

And if they ended up having to head south, toward the settlment's center, that meant they might even be in range of *Cataphract* again, somewhere off to the west. Lola could then summon the prowler, controlling it remotely just as she'd done with the Shearwater back on Terceira. Solomon had a growing suspicion that getting back to his ship was not going to be a simple task, if at all possible. Summoning it might be the only extraction method available.

Movement on his own was certainly more Solomon's style, nimbly darting in between rare boulders and brush in forty-kilometer-per-hour bursts of speed. He quickly traversed the rocky terrain between the esker's peak and then the smooth stretch of valley just before Tyrrhen's perimeter. While doing this, he found a strange feeling encroaching, almost like some kind of vulnerability. It caught him off guard.

"Everything okay with the girl?" he asked, setting up behind a tall collection of glacial erratics that had apparently been deposited here ages ago. It was the last of any cover before the terrain opened up.

"Yes, James," Lola replied. *"It's only been thirty-two seconds."*

Solomon didn't respond, as he didn't even know where that question had come from. He told himself to focus and stay on task—once he had the lockbox, he'd figure out what to do next.

Since the arrival of the Banished, his mind had kept trying to put together the pieces of how this little girl would be able to stop Cortana and why that was connected to the aliens' presence on Boundary. Neither made any sense to him or felt like it would bode well for Chloe in the end. All he could do now was collect information. A myriad of questions plagued his mind, refusing to go unanswered, but they'd have to wait. He'd already gone too far on this operation to extract now, and yet not far enough to know what was actually at stake.

The only way out was forward.

Three Jiralhanae who had been meandering along the perimeter fence toward his position finally turned and began walking back toward the gate. The fence was not military-grade and seemed to have been erected mainly to keep Boundary's more hostile wildlife out of the population center, its top being strung with loops of high-tensile barbed wire. The tech was old and not terribly effective, but sometimes that was the best one could afford out here in the Outer Colonies, especially when attempting to protect a settlement of this size.

If he had simply been attempting to infiltrate Tyrrhen, he'd already have cut his way through the fence and would be deep into the settlement. But that wasn't his objective. Not yet at least. *Lockbox first.* His eyes settled again on the gate pylon. It was marked with a circle with an inset triangle, scrawled above the shuttered panel. There were probably countless practical reasons why ONI had insisted on this outmoded method, but Solomon found it maddening—par for the course with the rest of this mission.

The Spartan waited for another patrol of three Jiralhanae a hundred meters away, mirroring the one nearest him, to head back in the other direction. Once they did, he sprang out toward the closest trio, clearing the broad space at the highest possible speed. One of them must have heard him coming because he turned, but only in time to see a combat knife spinning end-over-end toward his face. The blade planted deep into the Jiralhanae's skull and dropped the creature like a bag of rocks.

The other two spun around to see what had happened and were greeted with muffled single-fire shots from Solomon's DMR. By the time he reached their position, they too had slumped to the ground, blood seeping from their foreheads. Miraculously, the other patrol didn't appear to have heard any of it—but they very well could have. He cursed silently. That was the kind of mistake that had *never* happened in his younger years. It was a wide expanse to cross unnoticed for anyone, including an ex-Spartan, but it was clear to Solomon that he was slipping with age. He wasn't thrilled about that.

"Don't say anything," he preempted Lola, in case she was about to provide a smart comment.

"I wasn't going to," she responded as he retrieved the knife from the enemy's head. *"But you're not out of the woods yet. Those Jiralhanae will be headed your way after they pass the gatehouse, and there's another set of four inside the gate."*

However disorganized the Banished patrols were right now, that could change in a matter of seconds if an alarm was triggered. It only took one surviving Jiralhanae with a native-link communications device to signal their command post and unleash a legion of Banished infantry and mechanized elements onto Lipari. Even the slightest hint of a Spartan's presence would be enough to make that happen. If he could neutralize the three other Jiralhanae outside the gate, he might be able to get by without having to deal with the ones inside. And when they eventually discovered the dead bodies, he would be long gone.

Solomon broke into another dead run, darting toward the road that ran through Gate Lipari. He picked up his speed, using the lone gatehouse to shield his presence from the Jiralhanae patrol and anything on the gate's interior. On the other side was the roadway, and it wouldn't take much exposure for him to be spotted.

When he emerged from behind the gatehouse at full speed, he was already halfway across the roadway, the exterior patrol's backs still to him. A glance to his left revealed no Jiralhanae inside the gate—the pattern of the four others must have taken them elsewhere. Even the scale of their forces, the sheer number of ships, implied that multiple clans were at work, which meant several chieftains or kaidons, all of them in competition for higher standing within the Banished. He wouldn't be surprised if the lack of discipline on the settlement's edge was the product of a weaker clan being given remote guard duty, perhaps even as punishment.

The three Jiralhanae before him were about to turn around, but he'd already scaled the nearest one's back, his knife sinking deep into the creature's neck, releasing a torrent of blood. The two others lifted their spike rifles in surprise. Jiralhanae were fast, but Spartans were faster. Before either could fire, he'd planted his combat knife into the next one's chest, breaking past armor plating, through his sternum, and impaling his heart. Solomon fired his DMR in a single motion, but not before the third Jiralhanae bellowed in anger. *Damn.* As it fell, he could already hear voices of alarm on the other side of Gate Lipari. *Keep moving,* he told himself.

Retrieving his knife from the creature's still-heaving chest cavity, Solomon launched toward the fence, concealed in the shadows of one of the small interior buildings, less than five meters from the gate itself. The four Jiralhanae on the other side of the fence suddenly emerged in a slow trot, grunting in broken Sangheili, automatically translated by Solomon's Mjolnir armor.

"Elekus, are you all right?" the lead one asked. It took him only a second to notice the corpses on the ground, but by then it was already too late. Solomon had quickly fired from the shadows and dispatched the two closest in the quartet. The lead's attention was so fixed on his fallen comrades that he took no notice: "Quickly, sound the alarm!"

Only when his nearest ally fell to the Spartan's DMR did he realize that he was alone.

"He's the last one in this sector, James," Lola confirmed.

Solomon was charging the final Jiralhanae before she finished speaking, ramming shoulder-first into its stomach. The Spartan might have been half the Jiralhanae's size but packed about the same punch in his armor. The half-ton creature was lifted off the ground and landed hard on his back, the air knocked out of his lungs. Solomon was already on top of the enemy before he could recover, repeatedly burying his combat knife into the creature's neck to prevent him from trying to signal others. He trusted Lola's assessment, but didn't want to take any chances.

Standing up, Solomon took a deep breath and surveyed the heaps of dead Jiralhanae. He was glad Chloe hadn't been a witness to the violence, but doubted that convenience would continue much longer. Solomon worked his way back across the roadway to the marked gate pylon.

With the press of a corner on the panel, another keypad emerged above it. Solomon entered the same sequence he'd been given earlier, and the shutter fully retracted, revealing yet another lockbox.

Finally—maybe the end of this mission would now be within reach.

He withdrew the box and the shutter automatically resealed. It too was a small black container with a processer and comms relay inside, able to receive and produce physical messages. For a moment, Solomon wondered if the rest of this op would simply be chasing lockboxes around Tyrrhen. He double checked that he had everything and then shot off back toward his original scouting position.

In three minutes, Solomon had scaled the esker again, throwing an eye to the crevice and confirming that Chloe had been sound asleep the whole time. As the last beams of sunlight began to drop below the horizon, he knelt to open the lockbox and retrieve the paper inside:

> *Banished excavating Forerunner machine. Follow attached coordinates to Tyrrhen center, Annex Muster Station B94. Deliver asset to Zulu strike team and they will take over. Remember to apply syringe. You must prevent Banished capture of the asset at ANY cost.*

Solomon reread the message at least three times before the high-piercing sound of impulse drives jogged his eyes up to the sky. A squadron of Banshees was approaching from the south, the failing light of dusk glinting off their red-armored carapaces.

"Those are scouts, James," Lola said. *"I'd advise taking cover."*

He dropped down behind the boulder he'd used earlier as a hiding place, peeking out from the side as the formation of Banshees split down the middle just before reaching Lipari. Four wheeled west and four east, wide arcs that would give them clear line-of-sight of the dead Jiralhanae strewn across the gate courtyard. At first it seemed as if they had missed the bodies completely, but when two of them came back around for another pass, it became clear that Solomon would have no such luck.

"Well, that is no good—"

"Already on it," Solomon said, stowing his weapons and equipment, then magnetically anchoring his Stanchion to his back, before moving toward the crevice. "She's not going to like this," he said, hefting up Chloe to carry her down the esker. He carefully scrambled down the side of the ridge in the direction opposite the Banshee squadron, making a beeline for the gate.

"Based on the message," Lola replied, *"Chloe waking from her sleep might be the least of this girl's problems."*

CHAPTER 26

TUL 'JURAN

Ghado (Boundary)
December 14, 2559

Tul 'Juran was so deep within the large runoff pipe that she could not even see her hand in front of her face. So when Gray Team stopped in mid-run, she collided right into the back of one of the Spartans, which was akin to slamming into a wall at full speed. Vul 'Soran nearly ran into her but managed to stop just before making contact. She quickly retrieved her carbine from the ground before anyone noticed she had dropped it. Evidently Jai-006 had sounded for the strike team to stop, but her translation software was one step behind.

"Enemy contacts ahead," he whispered, answering her unspoken question. "Stalkers. Eight of them."

This meant that the Banished had breached the human settlement's underground drainage system. 'Juran wasn't certain *why* this was the case, but they now posed a significant risk to the operation, particularly given that the entire team was crammed within a three-meter-wide pipe. If the stalkers wanted to eliminate their enemies, a few magazines of spike rifle rounds would be sufficient.

"Going to pull right, keep your heads down," Jai said, leading them down a side corridor.

To call it a corridor was inaccurate. This was all a network of underground pipes surging with water runoff from the settlement's center, which was now only twenty meters above their heads. 'Juran knew they were close because she could hear the dull drone of Banished drills churning above and the dense scorching sound of a flame-bore. She would recognize that sound anywhere—it was a large excavation machine the Banished had reverse-engineered from the cleansing beams of Covenant capital ships, capable of ravenously devouring earth and stone.

They turned down one pipe section and then another, running again in single file since there was no space to do otherwise. Gray Team led the group with 'Juran and the rest of the *Shadow of Intent* crew just behind them, while the three remaining Spartans brought up the rear. The pipes were made from a material the humans called "permacrete," a gritty, stonelike substance that could be shaped before it hardened. In these tight confines, sound was not easily managed. This meant that the stalkers had heard them—probably even from far away—and were now likely in pursuit. She was not sure how familiar the Banished were with Tyrrhen's underground sewage network, but the thermal tracking technology housed in their optics and their species' natural ability to hunt by scent was quickly abrading whatever advantage Gray Team had from their access to the settlement's schematics.

"Stop," Jai said in the closed channel, and 'Juran managed to respond in time.

The group clustered up, staring over each other's shoulders at what Gray Leader was shining his helmet light on. Here the permacrete pipe had caved in, and a wall of rock and debris sloped down in front of them. A dead end.

"That's obviously not in the schematics," Jai said, apparently reassessing their path forward within his helmet.

"Hostiles coming up, Gray Leader," Vídalín said, as the trailing Spartan-IVs quickly reconfigured themselves to allow for all three to fire simultaneously.

Unlike the Spartans, the Sangheili and Unggoy of *Shadow of Intent* did not have image-enhancing visors or data-relaying armor systems. Prior to her operations with Gray Team, 'Juran had held such things in contempt, as if they were some kind of extraneous accessory for a warrior—a view that had grown out of her having been raised as a hunter rather than a soldier. But she was slowly growing to see their usefulness. In a scenario such as this, they seemed almost a necessity.

"Change of plans, Zulu Red," Jai said. "We're going to split up at the last intersection we passed. Fours," he said, addressing the Spartan-IVs, "I've transmitted to you a path and egress point just outside the settlement's center. It's in an irrigation plant. Should be safe. You've got the blademaster and the ranger with you. Scion, you're coming with us. Our group will head in the opposite direction and see if we can throw these guys off. We'll rendezvous topside."

'Juran had not seen the intersection twenty meters behind them as they passed it, but under Jai's helmet light, it now appeared. The other Spartans and her companions from *Shadow of Intent* headed down the left channel, Vul 'Soran giving 'Juran a parting glance, but whether he was intimating to be safe or to behave, she could not discern.

In the dark stretches of pipe beyond the intersection, she could make out the cycloptic mono-sights of the stalkers. They were only red motes of light at this distance, at least half a kilometer away, but the way they bobbed and the slushing sound echoing through the pipe indicated they were approaching at a significant pace.

"Might be good to keep up, Scion," Michael-120 said with his helmet light also on, waving her down the pipe that went to the right.

Jai and Adriana-111 had already launched into a sprint, and as 'Juran passed Michael to follow them, the Spartan knelt and placed a small metallic tube at the center of the intersection, pressing a key on its side, which emitted a faint sound.

"Bright bomb," he noted to her with what sounded like human glee. "Can't do concussive down here without serious collateral damage, but this'll work plenty good. Flash will impair thermals and the chems should disorient big-time. Keep them chasing their tails for a bit."

She cocked her head, unfamiliar with the turn of phrase.

Jiralhanae have no tails.

"Never mind," he said, pointing the way the others had gone. "We've got ten seconds before this thing's proximity sensor becomes active."

It took about three centals before she finally reached Jai and Adriana, who were navigating through the maze of pipes with their typical dexterity, turning right, then left again down a long straight shot. They continued for another five centals before they heard the ear-piercing sound of Michael's "bright bomb." Almost immediately after this, they reached a larger area with a ladder rising up from the pipe system. Jai shone his light up toward its termination point in the ceiling. As they were looking up, they heard a deep Jiralhanae bellow, followed by a curse in Sangheili.

"Well. Sounds like you really pissed them off," Jai said to Michael.

"Temporary blindness and concentrated psychotropic chemicals can have that effect," he replied. "But they're probably angry they lost our sce—"

The next moment, all the air drained out of the pipe around them. Immediately, Michael pushed the scion to the side, bracing himself around her. Fire suddenly surged over them in every direction, burning so brightly that 'Juran did not even realize her skin was being scorched in the process. A moment later the chaos ceased, and Michael stepped back, patting down the parts of her skin affected by the blast. It hurt, but the injuries seemed to be relatively minor.

"Routing blast," Jai remarked, sighting his battle rifle down the pipe in the direction the fire had come. "Must be headed this way. Get ready."

"What is a routing blast?" 'Juran asked, raising her carbine.

"A Banished incendiary designed to clear enclosed spaces," Adriana answered, her commando rifle trained in the same direction. "It's just a feint. They'll follow up with something real."

A firebomb like that was only a feint?

'Juran had only interacted with the Banished a few times before, but the idea that this "routing blast" was merely a distraction alarmed her. Without armor, she could easily have perished. How could *that* be considered a feint?

It did not take long, however, for Gray Team's assertion to be validated. Muzzle flashes of spike rifles signaled tracers coming down the pipe toward them, their razor-sharp spike rounds ricocheting off the wall interior and tearing past with a thin howl of air.

"Five contacts," Jai announced, his battle rifle lighting up triple bursts of human ballistic ammunition, which scattered across the enemies at the far end.

'Juran joined him, firing her carbine at the bright-red lights of the Jiralhanae visors. One of the targets winked out of existence, likely indicating a kill.

"Nice shot," Michael said, his energy shields flaring as spikes glanced off it. Within the pipe there was zero cover, and the Spartan was positioned directly in front of her. She did not know whether to feel honored or humiliated by this unspoken protection, but decided that this must simply be how a team of Spartans functioned.

Another red light dropped in the distance, but the spikes continued. One grazed Adriana's energy shield and continued behind them, but another planted right into Michael's left arm. His shield had completely dissipated, and the bolt penetrated through the black mesh underarmor and into his flesh. The Spartan continued to fire as if nothing had happened until another spike struck his midsection and he finally began to slow down. His body slumping forward ever so slightly.

'Juran found herself angered by this. She loaded another magazine into her carbine and vindictively pumped every last round down-sight into the enemy's position, watching another red light drop out. A spike grazed her side with searing pain, but she did not stop firing until her weapon was empty.

Jai and Adriana took down the last two Jiralhanae, and by the time 'Juran turned around to assess the situation, she witnessed Michael pulling an impaled spike out of his stomach, two other spikes remaining in his side.

The other two Spartans rushed to their teammate's aid, Jai already withdrawing a small metallic canister from a hardcase on his thigh. She remembered this object from a conversation with Stolt. The canister was filled with "biofoam," a human medicine designed to clean and stabilize severe injuries, allowing the soldier to still function—at least temporarily—despite receiving otherwise lethal wounds. As Michael pried out the last two spikes, each releasing a gush of blood, Jai immediately filled them with an ivory-colored material that expanded in the wound. The Spartan stood without any hesitation or visible pain. 'Juran was genuinely astonished.

"I can plot you a track back to Zulu Blue's position," Jai said, stowing the biofoam while he looked his fellow Spartan over. "You can help them secure those guns."

"If it's all the same, Gray Leader, I'd rather just push forward," Michael replied, replacing the magazine on his assault rifle. "I'm solid, Jai. I promise."

Jai continued to stare at Michael for nearly a full cental before relenting. "One slip-up and you're benched, Mike. Understood?"

"Understood," he replied, masking well any pain he might be experiencing.

"Heads up," Adriana said, already halfway up the ladder. "No more time to chat. Zulu Red is probably already topside by now."

Jai nodded for 'Juran to follow Adriana, and then Michael, before he finally climbed up himself. The ladder stretched up a narrow chute the full twenty meters up to the surface, disappearing at a circular cover for what the humans strangely referred to as a "manhole." The ladder itself was made for humans, which made 'Juran's effort to climb it far more challenging given her anatomical differences. After what she had just experienced, she found this human inconvenience less frustrating than she would have earlier.

Adriana lifted the cover slightly with enough room to peek at every angle before knocking it completely off and pulling herself up to the surface. When 'Juran emerged, she could see that they were now in a small structure with only one window and one doorway, and a large water tank at the far end of a narrow corridor. Somewhere underneath the steady din of Banished excavation equipment was the surging of water.

"Hydroelectric plant," Jai said, lifting himself onto the ground and replacing the manhole cover. "Citizens use glacial runoff to generate clean energy."

"Works for me," Adriana said as she scanned outside of the window. "We've got about thirty to forty hostiles on the perimeter of a park surrounding the flame-bore and what looks like a handful of mining drills. A full scale excavation."

"Zulu Red, do you copy?" Jai asked.

"Roger that," McEndon's voice came over the comms. *"Where have you guys been, Gray Leader? Thought we'd lost you for a moment."*

"Not yet," Jai replied, again staring at Michael whose stoic posture demonstrated that he still refused to show any sign of his injuries. "Sitrep and twenty?"

"We're five-by-five, Gray Leader," McEndon continued. *"We left the irrigation site because it was too hot and moved north. Twenty is somewhere east of the park, third floor of a schoolhouse. Sending coordinates now."*

Jai was evidently looking at something on his heads-up display and then turned back to Michael, shutting off the comms. "Are you sure you can move?"

"One hundred percent," Michael replied, as if there was no reason to even ask.

"Hang tight, Red," Jai replied to McEndon. "We're en route to your position now. ETA . . . " His voice trailed off as he glanced out the window at the numerous Banished patrols outside. "Whenever we get there."

"Ten-four, Gray Leader." McEndon's voice dropped out as Jai moved to join Adriana by the window for a better look at the excavation. 'Juran and Michael fell in behind them.

Much of the area was obscured by a dense cloud of gray dust

ceaselessly pouring out of the flame-blore's projector, a blazing red beam of energy gorging on everything beneath it. From their angle and distance, the group could not see everything, but they saw enough. A large cavity had been opened in the ground at least thirty meters wide, plumbing far deeper than that and into a massive subterranean cavern that had existed below Tyrrhen's surface for ages.

Within the underground space was the slightest hint of a vast circular arc—the mere edge of a large metallic structure clearly of Forerunner provenance, the long dormant machine likely seeing natural light for the first time in untold ages. Even from here, 'Juran noted that its design closely resembled the gateway machine ONI had retrieved data on from Spartan teams on Genesis.

It could only be the Lithos.

A gateway into the Domain. A portal to reclaim the throne of the Tyrant.

And the Banished were practically on its doorstep.

CHAPTER 27

ABIGAIL COLE

UNSC *Victory of Samothrace*
December 14, 2559

By the time *Victory of Samothrace* returned for another pass on the defensive shell above Tyrrhen, it was clear that the strategy of the Banished forces had shifted. Several dozen vessels shed off their position over Tyrrhen and moved out to intercept the UNSC battle group several sectors before they even reached the shell. Cole wasn't certain why they'd made this change, given how negligible the UNSC presence was, but it might have been connected to the emergence of both *Shadow of Intent* and *Akkadian*, who'd made their presence on Boundary known while *Victory* and Omega were on the far side of the colony. The Banished probably assumed there were even more enemy vessels hiding in the shadows.

That assumption, however, was dead wrong. At least for right now, but Cole hoped that would all change soon.

An explosion bloomed off *Victory*'s starboard bow as the ship continued to pound into the immense flank of a Banished holk, with the frigate *Hazard Pay* doing similar work on the opposite side. The enemy vessel was venting a considerable amount of oxygen, large sections of its battleplate peeling away from its spaceframe as it tried to swing around the backside of *Victory* and fire on her. This was a mistake—as soon as the holk's front peeked around the stern of *Victory*, a MAC round from *Get My Drift* planted right into its bow, disabling the ship and sending its inert shape into a fiery descent toward the Ibirene Sea.

This was now the fifth Banished ship that had realized this fate.

At some point, the Banished would learn from their mistakes and start concentrating their naval forces in more effective patterns. They certainly had enough ships.

A dreadnought and two accompanying karves slowly came into view, headed directly toward *Victory* and Omega while being pelted from behind by *Shadow of Intent*'s plasma torpedoes. Like the others before them, these vessels were on their way into the open mouths of a wolf pack without any real support from the staggered line of Banished vessels slung out across Boundary's equator still trying to adjust to the UNSC's ever-changing position. With *Akkadian* silently and invisibly pinging them somewhere southwest of the defensive shell and *Shadow of Intent* distracting them on the northwestern end, the displaced Banished vessels were playing a game they couldn't win.

Get My Drift accelerated around *Victory*, taking the lead with *Hazard Pay* coming from behind it, both firing at the nearest karve from an angle preventing any adequate response from the other two ships, which were simply trying to get a bead on *Victory of Samothrace*. The nearest karve blew apart, debris shooting violently in every direction, much of it spreading out across the dreadnought's enormous hull. What remained of Commander Jiron's battle group had proven extraordinarily effective. Cole wished the UNSC had more ships like Omega's, solemnly wondering what kind of damage could have been done if *Blank Check* and *Easy*

Does It were still around. The remaining two Banished vessels pulled themselves hard port side directly into a plasma lance from *Shadow of Intent*, completely skewering the karve and even causing damage to the dreadnought.

"I could do this all day!" Lieutenant Aquila shouted with satisfaction.

"Let's hope we don't have to." Cole's eyes moved to the Banished defensive shell on the holopane. The UNSC certainly could play this game of cat-and-mouse way out here, but if they attempted these kinds of naval strategies even remotely near the multiple Banished fleets that still hugged Tyrrhen, they wouldn't last five minutes.

"Incoming slipspace transmission from Captain Richards," Lieutenant Lim said.

"I'll take it in the conference suite," Cole immediately moved to the back of the bridge and into the private briefing compartment.

The door sealed and she sat down, keying the plate to accept the message. Finally, *something* from Earth. During their last pass, half a dozen missives had been sent to Captain Annabelle Richards and other contacts at the Home Fleet, attempting to get any kind of leverage for support to be sent to Boundary. Until now, she'd had no indication word had even reached Earth. A recorded hologram flashed into existence atop the table of Captain Richards.

"I do hope this message finds you in time, Captain Cole. It took some work, but you should see the fruits of your request shortly. You can thank Osman and Hood for it. The UNSC's largest expeditionary fleets—the Fourth, the Sixth, the Ninth, and the Thirteenth—are presently en route to Boundary. You should be aware though that their primary goal is not *to free Boundary or displace the Banished—I repeat, they are not coming to remove the Banished presence from the colony. They'll be there to enable* Victory *and Omega to finish the*

job you were sent to do. The Lithos is still priority one, and if Akkadian*'s scans are any indication, the Banished are well on their way to excavating it."*

Cole's breath stuck in her lungs. She hadn't been able to communicate with Admiral al-Cygni yet, but this news from *Akkadian* confirmed what she had been afraid of regarding Banished activity on the surface. *Victory*'s later arrival had given the Banished a head start that would be extremely hard to overcome. The only advantage they had now was the key, and that was still only if it was even needed given that Cortana had been overthrown.

Richards's message continued: *"Due to the nature and scale of the Banished presence, there's been a slight change of plans.* Akkadian *will no longer be deploying an integration team at the Lithos. Instead, we'll need your planetside team to rendezvous with the ONI operative escorting the key at coordinates you'll find attached to this communiqué. Your team is to receive the key and escort her inside the Lithos. Once there, your team will integrate the key directly into the gateway machine following the procedures outlined in attached file Genesis-A-two-six-five-b. Please transmit this file to your strike team's operations leader and ensure that they follow it to the letter. Once the asset is integrated, the control-subroutine will do its job and your team is free to exfiltrate. We trust the Banished won't stick around very long once the Lithos is off the table, but your team's extraction will likely be . . . challenging, to say the least.*

"In the event that the key is compromised by the enemy or your strike team is incapacitated, Victory of Samothrace *must deny the Lithos to the Banished. A direct MAC strike on the exposed target with your vessel's specialized configuration should be sufficient to eliminate the site and ensure that the risk it poses has been abrogated. You know this already, Captain, but I do hope you can appreciate my concern in repeating it: the enemy* cannot *at any point control the Lithos—whether*

Severan or Dovo Nesto, or anyone else for that matter. This is the one thing you must ensure never happens. Akkadian *is onsite to support your strike team with orbital intel, but they do not possess the armament necessary for ship-to-ship warfare which is why your team must assume the responsibility of integrating the key with the Lithos. The best they can do is distract the enemy while they monitor your team's progress and provide real-time intel support. We hope this is sufficient to complete the objective. Good luck, Captain. Richards out."*

Cole sat for several seconds in silence before accessing the file Richards had sent.

What had become clear was that the original mission hadn't accounted for a Banished occupation force on Boundary—at least, not one of this magnitude. ONI had previously intended to send their own team to the planet's surface to receive the key from the ONI operative who served as her escort. That team would integrate the key while the Zulu strike team provided overwatch. Once the Banished took control of Tyrrhen, ONI must have abandoned that strategy for the one Richards had just outlined. Now it was up to Zulu to complete the operation on their own.

Cole accessed the Genesis-A265b file, which appeared to be a highly technical interface document outlining a specific machine encountered last year by Blue Team and Fireteam Osiris during their time on Genesis, the location of a gateway into the Domain. The only way to activate and ultimately access the gateway was by integrating the key with the machine's interface. ONI had undoubtedly planned to accomplish this through the key's neural pattern and a subroutine, but the document held none of the answers that Cole was hoping for. It did not specify what would happen to the key—*the child*, she reminded herself—during the process, nor how exactly integration was supposed to work.

What had become clear was that ONI was still operating under the assumption that the girl was needed to access the Lithos. How they had come to this conclusion was uncertain, but Cole deduced that it was based on intel retrieved by *Akkadian.* If the Banished were still searching for the key, then it must be necessary.

She'd been aware that the child would be used to transmit the subroutine directly into the Lithos's interface, but from what Cole could understand of the documentation, there was no indication that the child would then *leave* the machine. *What happened to her once she was linked to the interface?* The uncertainty of it all made her stomach turn, bothering her even more than having to send the Zulu strike team into enemy-occupied territory.

That question again . . . in circumstances like these, where the fate of humanity was on the line, how far ought we go to guarantee our species' survival? It was the very dilemma that many had applied to the SPARTAN-II program and countless other ONI operations. It was easy to ask the question of what one life was when weighed against billions, but the promise of salvation through the sacrifice of a child—if that's what ONI intended—was something that Cole found impossible to rationalize.

She keyed the ready room's private comms. "Lieutenant Lim, can you establish a comms link with Gray Leader?"

A few seconds passed before Comms responded. *"Done, Captain. Gray Leader is online."*

"Thank you, Lieutenant." Cole entered the security link for a two-way conversation. "I'm securing the channel. I'll see you on the bridge momentarily." Lim was automatically disconnected, and Cole's ears filled with dull, grinding background static. It sounded like Banished excavation equipment.

"Captain Cole?" Jai's voice came through, marginally distorted.

"I'm here, Gray Leader. Situation report?"

"Zulu has made it successfully into the settlement. Strike team

got split up in Tyrrhen's drainage system, but we're regrouping now. Should be in a good position, about a hundred meters out from the target. No sign of ONI's integration team yet."

"ONI's integration team won't be deploying, Gray Leader. I'm sending you the message I just received from Captain Richards with a new directive. I apologize for the change in plans, but your team will now be responsible for the asset's integration into the Lithos. Instructions are attached to her message."

"Copy that, Captain," Jai said, no doubt reading through the attached file as he navigated Tyrrhen's terrain to his rendezvous point. After a few moments, he said: *"Ma'am, I can see the protocol for Lithos integration, but it doesn't say anything about what happens to the key once integration is complete. Is there something that I'm missing?"*

"No, there isn't, Gray Leader." Cole sighed. "My working assumption is that ONI doesn't know what'll happen to her either. And most probably, they aren't too concerned about it as long as they can get the control-subroutine into the Domain."

There was more hesitation on the line, and then Jai responded with what Cole took as uncertainty or suspicion. *"Affirmative, ma'am. That certainly sounds like ONI."*

"Unfortunately, that's the order, Jai. And, given our current circumstances, I have no way to appeal it." The whole situation felt additionally twisted to Cole in that whatever was going to happen to this child, it was *Spartan-IIs* who were being ordered to carry it out. Unable to stomach the thought any longer, Cole added: "But within our operational parameters, I'm giving Gray Team an additional one: I don't want this kid to get hurt. If there's a way we can effect integration with the Lithos and everyone gets out of it in one piece, then you have the green light to proceed. But if that's not possible—if this is some kind of trade-off, the girl's life for access to the Lithos—then I want you to extract with her immediately and I'll put a MAC round into that thing so hard that there'll be nothing left for the Banished to put back together."

"A big affirmative on that, ma'am. I'll keep you updated as we progress."

"Excellent, Gray Leader. You'll likely be in touch with Commander al-Cygni on *Akkadian*. And let's keep my order just between us."

"Understood, ma'am. We'll make it happen, one way or the other. Gray Leader out."

The comms channel snapped off, and Cole sat there in the darkness. This was the best she could do, given the circumstances. She spent a minute gathering her composure and then returned to the bridge. The massive viewport at the fore showed *Victory* circling a listing Banished dreadnought that now looked like a block of red and gray Swiss cheese.

Lieutenant Zobah popped up from the logistics pane with a confident grin. "Good news, Captain. UNSC fleets are just about to arrive. Looks like the tau spike has spooked the Banished, as the shell is finally starting to break up. We may have a fighting chance after all."

"Glad to hear it, Lieutenant," Cole said, glancing at the holopane. The shell was rapidly disintegrating into several clumps, likely representing specific fleets under Banished leadership. "Tactical, let's link up with the command ships and see how we can punch a hole in whatever is left of them. I want to get as close to Tyrrhen as possible."

"Already on it, Captain," Aquila replied. "Coordinating now. I'll brief you asap."

At that moment, the bridge crew fell silent as a cloud of slipspace portals began materializing into existence. Cole could feel the electricity in the air, the collective intake of breath. And then, one after another, some one hundred and eighty-five UNSC ships exited slipspace. *Finally, the cavalry had arrived.* Cole hoped this encouraged Commander Jiron and the rest of Omega, as much as it did her crew. They wouldn't be fighting alone anymore.

Nearly two hundred UNSC ships. That was far more than they could have even wished for. The fleets were composed of numerous light and heavy ship classes—frigates, cruisers, destroyers, even a single *Punic*-class supercarrier belonging to the Thirteenth Fleet. It was an impressive sight to behold, and it took her crew a full minute to get their composure.

Each fleet immediately began to separate to take up offensive positions, clearly having already studied data on the Banished shell formation that Cole had provided. Severan was undoubtedly a formidable leader, but Cole imagined that this dramatic change in circumstances would both infuriate and concern him. Even though the UNSC was still outnumbered, the war chief knew well enough how determined and vicious humans were in naval combat. From here, the tide of the battle could easily turn and make things a whole lot more interesting.

Cole's mind was still reeling with Richards's message, but she couldn't help breathing a sigh of relief as the holotable updated their tactical situation. She wondered what it had taken for Osman and Hood to convince the interim Security Council to approve such an exertion.

"Commander Jiron is on the line, ma'am," Lim announced.

"Patch him in, Lieutenant," Cole said, taking her seat as the image of Commander Jiron appeared above the holotable.

"Hello there, Commander."

"Captain Cole," he replied briskly. *"Thank you for calling in the support. They're a sight for sore eyes."*

"It was essential to completing this operation, Commander," she said, still seeing the gravity of the loss of *Blank Check* and *Easy*

Does It in the man's face. "We can thank the right folks together when we all get back to Earth."

"Sounds like a plan. Logistics on Hazard Pay *are giving me some . . .* intriguing *readings.* His eyes fixed on something off-camera. *"There's some unusual hadronic decay on the far side of Mistral. Looks like receding tau surges."*

"Slipspace breaches?" Cole typed in the specific sectors between their position in Boundary's orbital lanes and Mistral, one of its two natural satellites.

"Seems like it, Captain."

The image suddenly crystallized on the holopane and Cole felt her heart sink.

An ex-Covenant fleet was emerging from slipspace, vectoring right toward their position. From the registries, some of these vessels were the same ships they'd seen at Venezia, but there were now roughly ten times that number. And they were making a beeline for the rear of the UNSC fleets that had just arrived.

"Logistics, give our new friends a heads-up on those inbound hostiles," Cole said. "And Comms, please get me *Shadow* on the line."

"Done," Lim said, with Shipmaster Rtas 'Vadum appearing seconds later right beside Commander Jiron.

"Shipmaster, help me understand what I'm seeing?"

"Sali 'Nyon," he replied with certainty. *"It is of the same allegiance as those we saw at Sqala."*

"So why are they here?"

"There are only two possibilities. Either they are here to take the Lithos for themselves. Or . . . they are working with *the Banished and have come to support their allies."*

With a deep sense of dread, Cole attempted to process the probability of what he'd just suggested. "Let's pray it's not the latter, then."

CHAPTER 28

SEVERAN

Ghado (Boundary)
December 14, 2559

Night had swallowed Tyrrhen, which would make hunting the enemy responsible for ravaging Gathgor's Warkeeper detachment at the northern gate extremely difficult. Whoever had done this was likely the human team that the high lord had foretold, the ones intending to use the the key to access the Lithos.

The very key the Banished desperately needed to make this occupation viable.

The constant and volatile cacophony of bursts from the Gravemaker's blast-cylinders would have frustrated Severan were it not that it was their single best vehicle for surveying land from an elevated position, especially within enemy territory. If a stray human emerged from one of the farm homesteads below, the four Jiralhanae manning spike autocannons on its topside deck could shred them to pieces before there was even the hint of a threat.

With a heavily armored stone-gray carriage mounted on furiously loud clusters of blast-cylinders and a broad sight-deck at its top, it was an impressive albeit intimidating machine—and one that had been egregiously underused by the Covenant during the reign of the Sangheili. When the empire was resurrected once again, this time under Severan's careful hand, he would ensure that its military would not repeat such errors.

Five of these Gravemakers were now roaming in broad, concentric flight patterns as they orbited the gate the humans called Lipari. The intrusion had occurred here, though the human team cleverly had not left any witnesses. Were it not for the security patrol of Zaladon's own Banshee talons shortly after the altercation, it might have gone completely unnoticed for several units.

The Gravemakers hovered roughly fifty meters above the ground, each of them boasting a full *surdkar*—once considered an elite Doisac hunting pack but now modernized into a military detachment of thirteen heavily armed war-trackers. *Surdkars* were a legendary element of Jiralhanae culture, taking an oath of utter ruthlessness to complete each mission. These whom Severan had deployed were no different.

Officially, they had been tasked to track down and kill the enemies responsible for the intrusion. In reality, Severan was using them to locate the human key, a task he would not relegate to any of the other clans, nor even his own clan's warriors, apart from the ones he most favored. Obtaining the key was now paramount, and Severan would only entrust such an undertaking to his best.

From his position on the sight-deck, Arxus towered above all other Jiralhanae on the Gravemaker farthest from Severan. If anyone among his Zaladon brothers could be successful here, it would be Arxus. Severan could not help but wonder if the massive warrior was a design of the gods themselves. Perhaps this was the very purpose for which he was made: to aid in their clan's capture of the Lithos, allowing them to take their proper place at the apex of the newly formed Covenant.

Soon the high lord would join the gods and reestablish the Covenant permanently, with Severan as his right hand. Despite the misgivings he had felt earlier, Severan would not allow any doubt to creep in, nor suspicion—he was simply too close to the hope he had been fighting for years to attain. He had to trust in the gods' provision, not to mention the high lord's judgment.

"Humans," Kaevus said, standing at Severan's side while holding a *vyspar* to his eye. He was pointing the monocular toward a collection of large but rudimentary structures several hundred meters away that the humans referred to as "barns."

"What do you see?" Severan asked.

"There are two of them, near the door of the largest structure." The captain handed the *vyspar* to Severan.

Through the monocular, Severan noted the two humans cautiously looking up toward the Gravemakers. They did not look quite like soldiers, but it was very hard to tell when it came to their species. All of them looked essentially the same to Severan.

Except for Spartans.

He handed the *vyspar* back to Kaevus and spoke directly into his native-link: "Hoktar."

"Yes, War Chief," the gruff pilot responded from the operator pit just below the sight-deck.

"Bring us down near the cluster of structures southeast of our position. Mind your distance and be careful. There are humans inside. We will investigate on foot."

"Aye, War Chief," Hoktar replied. *"Forward guns, look alive. We're setting down for closer inspection."* The gunners quickly obeyed, focusing their autocannons on the structures.

"And, Hoktar," Severan added. "Have two Gravemakers provide overwatch. I want every angle covered."

"Consider it done, War Chief."

"Is it wise for you to go?" Kaevus asked as he and Severan dropped down the open hatch at the center of the sight-deck. "Why not send others to look instead? It may well be a trap."

"I expect that it is," Severan replied, handing his captain a death lobber from one of the weapons lockers. "But if there is even the barest opportunity to seize the humans' key, why would I yield that task to another, Kaevus?"

His captain did not respond, his eyes betraying frustration.

Kaevus wanted to protect his war chief, yet Severan always confounded these efforts by walking blade-first into trouble. Every step the captain took was no doubt weighted by the fear of failing to keep the last son of Tartarus alive, the very thing that Severan's brothers' own captains had failed to do. Kaevus was certainly a loyal ally—and indeed a friend—but Severan often found himself wishing he would simply obey rather than compromise his own vigilance in a futile effort to offer protection. Kaevus needed to learn what Severan had long ago: it was the gods who defended him. Victory or defeat for the Jiralhanae was in their hands alone.

Severan retrieved a shock rifle for himself and summoned nine warriors within the belly of the Gravemaker as the ventral chute opened, revealing a patch of large-bladed pale-green grass violently dancing beneath the heat of the vehicle's blast-cylinders. Severan dropped first, then Kaevus, followed by the others—all of them armed to the hilt. After ordering the seven to span out across the terrain and surround the structures, Severan and Kaevus made their way toward the central one, with two other warriors at their backs—Aculeo and Sabaco.

Apart from the pale glow offered by the world's two moons, the only light here was a burnished flickering from the small explosions produced by the Gravemaker. Between the lack of visibility and the steady, discordant noise, this was by no means an ideal circumstance for infiltrating an enemy-held position, but if Jiralhanae complained about such things, they could not be called warriors, no less *surdkar.*

The location where the humans had appeared was at the front of the structure, a large door, presumably used for some kind of livestock. However, it was now sealed shut. Severan nodded to Aculeo, who moved ahead and slid the door open while Kaevus and Sabaco directed their weapons into the structure's interior. The door opened to total darkness.

Kaevus tossed four *lūmorbs* through the entry, where they rolled for a few breaths before igniting into pure light, effectively turning the interior into a noonday equivalent on Warial. There were no humans to be seen, nor any movement whatsoever. The four pressed inside, weapons raised as Kaevus, unsurprisingly, moved in front of Severan. His captain would rather die than allow his war chief to suffer even a minor injury. The other two warriors instinctively followed suit, forming something of a shield around the war chief.

"Their scent is weak," Aculeo quietly growled.

The interior was unimpressive, a cylindrical hub of metal and wood, its perimeter punctuated by animal stalls and dilapidated machines. It was not terribly dissimilar from the farm kivas Severan had raided on Sovolanu. His eyes assessed every corner, waiting for the ambush, but by the time they reached the glowing *lūmorbs* at the room's center, there had been no activity.

What happened next amazed Severan with its coordination and cunning.

Five towering loaders tore through bay walls on every side and charged the four Jiralhanae at the barn's center—exoskeletons known as Cyclopes. Over four meters tall and composed of reinforced steel plating, the human-operated machines had actually been weaponized and deployed during UNSC military operations. These in particular were painted black and yellow, colonial variations that seemed to be designed to farm rather than fight.

Before Severan's warriors could open fire, one of the machines batted Sabaco with its arm, immediately crushing him into the structure's wall upon impact. At the sound of the commotion, the other seven Jiralhanae charged in from the opposite end of the structure and stormed the far side, all of them firing unremittingly. Kaevus pummeled the operator cabin of the nearest Cyclops with his death lobber's grenades. Several rapid explosions of blood and steel erupted before the giant suit fell over onto its side, lifeless.

Severan had fired off eight shots from his shock rifle at the Cyclops lunging at Aculeo, before another emerged from the shadows and tackled him from the side. The impact felt as if he had been hit full speed by a war-sled, his vision suddenly tunneling. Severan ended up somewhere in the corner of the structure, directly beneath the machine monster as its operator—an angry human male with a beard—feverishly attempted to crush him with the exoskeleton's grappling paws.

Severan managed to roll out of the way just as a giant fist slammed into the ground only centimeters from his skull. The massive exoskeleton rose from the ground and the war chief bounded around it, realizing his shock rifle had been knocked free from his hands in the confusion. Before he could clear the distance to retrieve it, the machine's large metal paw swatted him from behind, sending him flying into a nearby stall. Pain surged down his back, but this was a good thing—he was still functioning and had not succumbed to instant paralysis or death.

Fueled by instinct and rage, Severan ignited his arm-blades, curved arcs of energy rising out of his vambraces and significantly extending his reach. They resembled the totemistic weapons used in traditional blade-grappling from Jiralhanae history, but were fashioned from the same shaped plasma as Covenant energy swords. When the Cyclops lunged at him again, he launched from a coiled position and swiped hard against the machine's right arm, severing it at the joint. Amber fluid spewed from cables on the severed limb, while the operator's eyes widened in terror.

Severan used the human's disorientation to strike again, raking both of his blades across the exoskeleton's left leg. It was not a clean cut, but it certainly tore apart enough motors and balancing systems to send the machine toppling to the ground. The war chief wasted no time scaling the frame and plunging a single blade deep into the operator's cabin, straight through the attacker's chest and outside the back of the machine. The bearded man's eyes rolled into the back of his head, and his chest stopped heaving as the machine came to a rest.

Severan stood up atop the Cyclops and surveyed the space. The other machines were all smoking wrecks and piles of charred steel. Two Jiralhanae lay dead, and the others all stared wide-eyed at Severan, including Kaevus. Suddenly they raised their voices, slamming their fists against their chests and roaring in gleeful unison: *"Severan! Severan! Severan!"*

Their cheers would have continued had he not waved a hand to stop them, leaping down from the Cyclops and carefully scanning the rest of the structure's interior. It was completely empty. *How unfortunate.* He had hoped the human girl would be here somewhere, cowering in a corner. Nothing but the corpses of these brave, foolish humans.

Kaevus's eyes were bright with pride. He turned to look one last time as they passed the smoldering Cyclops.

"It will take more than that to stop the humans who leveled our forces at the northern gate," Severan said, hoping to recalibrate the expectations of the Jiralhanae within earshot. "These were only farmers and loading machines. Whoever killed the Warkeepers were trained soldiers. Perhaps even demons."

"War Chief," Hoktar said through the native-link.

"Speak." Severan and the others were walking out of the barn structure to their Gravemaker, which continued to jostle on its blast-cylinders.

"Ectorius the White has requested an audience with you."

"Patch him through," Severan said, though he could not possibly guess what the chieftain wanted to discuss. Perhaps they had already finished the excavation of the Lithos?

"Severan," the old Jiralhanae's voice came through his native-link, sounding both angered and disturbed. *"What in the name of Sonin is going on?"*

"I do not have the slightest idea what you speak of, Ectorius."

"Look to the skies, War Chief." His voice laced Severan's title with disdain.

At first, Severan noted dozens of Banished ships, the lower reaches of the defensive shell around Tyrrhen, visible only by the faint moon glow and their own hull lights. Then he saw something else: a Covenant assault carrier. No, *two* carriers. Then three battlecruisers. And more. Threaded among his own vessels were *Covenant* ships.

"I trust you see it now," Ectorius said, not relenting his acidic tone. *"Sali 'Nyon and his own twisted version of the Covenant have now arrived on this world."*

What?! Severan was shocked beyond his capacity to speak. *How can this be? What has happened?*

"Why did the defensive shell let them through?" he finally growled.

"They let them through because they had your *fleet's own clearance codes, and they were helping push the humans back. They claim to be our allies."*

Allies? This must be the high lord's doing, Severan thought.

How could he have done something like this—something that would jeopardize all Severan had worked for within the Banished and destroy him in the eyes of his own people?

The adrenaline surge Severan had felt during their hunt rapidly receded in his mind and heart, eclipsed by the reality of the gamble with Dovo Nesto. The high lord had been his *daskalo* for years now and Severan trusted him more than almost anyone, but this blindsiding and stunning inclusion of Sali 'Nyon in this campaign had crossed a line, and could not be undone.

Severan's doubt had already been seeded with the revelation of Dovo Nesto's spies among the humans, but collusion with 'Nyon? The one who had long sought to rebuild the Covenant on his own? This could mean only one thing: all along Dovo Nesto had been promising Severan what he had *already guaranteed* to the Sangheili.

The rage of betrayal swelled within him.

"I never gave those orders, Ectorius," Severan said. "You have my full permission to annihilate those Covenant pretenders on sight. Eradicate them all."

"It is too late for that, Severan." Ectorius did not even use his proper title. *"Their numbers are great, and they are* everywhere. *In fact, they are even sending out detachments to track down some kind of key they believe is in the settlement—a key to the Lithos? Evidently they do not believe you are up to the task. I think Atriox might agree when I share this with him myself."*

CHAPTER 29

JAMES SOLOMON

Tyrrhen, Boundary
December 14, 2559

As the Gravemakers dispersed, the Covenant dropships descended . . . Spirits and Phantoms swarming above the northern part of Tyrrhen, clearly searching for *something.* The sky was filled with warships from rival factions, sworn enemies acting as if they'd somehow abandoned their differences and joined forces to find . . . what exactly?

He turned and looked at Chloe, who was ravenously inhaling another MRE sandwich. She was hidden in the corner of a storage structure's terraces, which they'd found about five kilometers southwest of Gate Lipari. It was a meager building used to house farm equipment. Like the rest of the terrain they'd compassed, there was no human presence to be seen. Tyrrhen's citizens had all likely been forced into hiding, or worse.

Meanwhile, Chloe was almost done eating, which meant it was time to keep moving.

"You're really enjoying that," Solomon remarked.

"Well, yes—I'm hungry," she responded, her mouth almost too full to speak. "How far do we have to go now?"

"Settlement center. It's fifteen kilometers south. If you'd let me carry you again, we could make it there in under an hour."

"I still can't believe you did that," she said, swallowing what was left of the sandwich while glaring at him.

"We needed to go. There weren't a lot of other options."

"Wake me up next time, then," she said, as if it was obvious. "I can get to wherever we're going just fine."

"James," Lola chirped in his helmet. *"There's an inbound hail from a UNSC vessel,* Akkadian. *Not sure how they pinged us, but they did. Might be ONI?"*

"Never heard of it," Solomon replied, turning away from Chloe to look north again, as the Covenant dropships continued to scout the terrain with searchlights and no doubt a whole suite of exotic sensors. "Patch it through. Maybe they'll have info about what's happening."

"Sierra-Zero-Zero-Five, do you copy?" a woman's voice spoke on the other end. He was struck by these words—he hadn't heard his Spartan call sign in years.

"I copy," he said. "Who is this, *Akkadian*?"

"An old friend, Jim. Castle Base, Theta Wing back in thirty-five."

"Jilan?" Solomon was incredulous, even when he recognized her voice. "Well—it's been a while."

"It certainly has. Though I wish it was under better circumstances."

Commander Jilan al-Cygni.

What is she *doing here?*

Shortly after the Battle of Jericho VII, she had provided the Spartan-IIs with extensive training on Covenant systems infiltration. The veteran naval officer was one of the best, with a career that stretched deep into the Insurrection years. Rumor had it that she was even present during the Covenant's first attack on Harvest back in 2525.

After that, she'd developed literally hundreds of tactical strategies for stopping the Covenant. ONI introduced nearly all of them into the standard operational doctrine of the UNSC Special Forces, including advanced techniques of infiltrating Covenant warships. Ironically, this was the very reason Cortana had been created nearly fifteen years later. ONI wanted to get operatives onto a Covenant ship to see if they could find any kind of leverage at all . . . anything that could stop what had been an insurmountable enemy.

"Things must be really bad if ONI is making direct calls through enemy lines, Commander," Solomon replied. "And what if Cortana hears us?"

"It's actually 'admiral' now, Jim," al-Cygni said with a note of authority.

"Well, it *has* been over twenty years since you visited Reach. Congratulations, I guess?"

"Thanks. Look . . . this may come as a shock . . . and we're not sure exactly how, but it seems that Cortana's no longer active."

"What?"

"We're assuming that either the Infinity *succeeded in a mission they had been tasked with or the Banished somehow beat us to it. Either way, Cortana has been removed from the playing field, James. Everything she controlled has gone dormant."*

"Then someone needs to tell me why I'm bringing this girl into the center of Tyrrhen in the middle of a Banished planetary occupation."

"Because that girl is the only one who can get humanity access

to the Domain, the information system Cortana has been using to control the Guardians since she ascended to power. She's a living key to the Domain's back door. It's called the Lithos, and it's right here on Boundary."

"So that's what the Banished are after? And now what's left of the Covenant too apparently?"

"Yes. Our intelligence has been compromised, so both factions know all about her. And they're both looking for her," al-Cygni confirmed, her tone emphatic. *"This is the reason we've been using the lockbox relays to communicate. This is the reason you need to complete this mission. If either of them take control of the Domain, I think you can imagine the kind of future we would be living in."*

"But they're enemies, aren't they? They're just as likely to open fire on each other."

"Ordinarily, that would be the case," al-Cygni said with a hint of frustration in her voice. *"But something more seems to be at play here."*

"There's still a piece I'm missing in all this, Admiral," he said, glancing to check on Chloe. She was innocuously gazing up at the stars, wide-eyed. "How is this kid somehow the key that you're talking about? What's so special about her?"

"I actually thought you might have figured that out by now," she responded. *"Who does she look like to you, Jim?"*

Solomon stared at the ten-year-old for five full seconds before he saw what al-Cygni was talking about.

Chloe looked like Catherine Halsey. She looked like Cortana.

The resemblance wasn't perfect, but it was there.

"No. . . ." He realized then the connection that had been evading his thoughts the entire operation.

"The girl was a flash clone of Halsey's when she created Cortana a decade ago," al-Cygni said. *"There's no consistent account of the*

specifics of that event, only rumors that emerged from redacted or even doctored records. We concluded that only one of those clones survived: the one used to make Cortana. All the others had died shortly after the process."

James looked at Chloe now with something approximating horror—not at the girl herself, but at the circumstances of her creation. He wondered whether Halsey had opted to offset the clones' physiological development in an effort to improve her neural faculties—she only needed their brains, after all. It would certainly explain Chloe's leg and her remarkable intellect.

This girl had survived everything and by some miracle had reached the age of ten. Solomon still didn't know why she had been tucked away in the underbelly of Mindoro or how it was that she'd be able to open this thing al-Cygni called the "Domain," but he could make an educated guess. Something about Chloe's neural makeup matched Cortana's and this was the very thing needed to bypass its locks and get ONI in. Suddenly, the syringe with the subroutine made sense. Whatever it held, it must have been designed to take control of the Domain remotely. ONI wouldn't allow another AI to have access, but they'd take it for themselves.

"Still there, Jim?" al-Cygni asked. His eyes were fixed on Chloe.

"Yeah, I'm here."

"That girl is the only thing that will keep us from repeating the hell we were in with Cortana. She's the difference between a future of fear and tyranny, and one where humanity can finally breathe a little easier."

"And what happens when we plug her into the Lithos?" Solomon asked. "Do we eventually just unplug her and everyone goes home fine? Or is she the only one who doesn't get to go home?"

The admiral waited a few seconds before responding.

"To be perfectly honest, we don't know. . . . I can only tell you

what'll happen if we don't get access to the Domain. We could nuke the Lithos, wipe the entire site off the map to stop the Banished from getting to it. But tomorrow, humanity will still have enemies. Only hours ago, this same Banished force attacked Earth. If they hadn't come to Boundary, what you're looking at right now would have been happening on the human homeworld."

"Understood, Admiral," Solomon said, turning away from Chloe and back to the brewing storm of Covenant and Banished craft marring the clear night's sky. Their search patterns were getting closer. He would need to move soon.

"We'll be monitoring your progress from Akkadian*,"* al-Cygni stated. *"Remember, Jim. We* cannot *allow this key to fall into enemy hands. If she's compromised—"*

"That's not going to be a problem, Admiral." He understood the stakes, but that didn't mean he had to like them. "Sorry to cut this short, but I've got enemies on approach."

"Yeah, I see them. Quite a few by the looks of it. Good luck, Jim. Hope to see you again soon. Akkadian *out."*

The channel closed and Solomon wasted no time moving across the terrace with the M392 slung over his shoulder, while anchoring the M99 to his back. He'd have loved to shed the Stanchion for dexterity but couldn't risk moving ahead without every possible tool at his disposal.

"Time to go, Chloe," he said, tearing free a cylindrical slat from the stairwell that she could use for a crutch. The last one had been lost at the esker.

"What are those?" she asked, pointing toward the vessels due north. Their searchlights were scanning the terrain like birds of prey.

"Those are Banished and Covenant patrol craft," he answered, guiding them back down through the structure and out a doorway into a wide-spanning pasture. A dilapidated fence lined a nearby hill with a staggered trail of deciduous trees running down its length. It was the only area that could provide them with cover as they headed south.

"What are they looking for?" she asked, glancing back again toward the patrols.

He took off his helmet and looked into her eyes. "You," he said. "Unfortunately, they're looking for you."

Chloe's response was to simply stare right back at him. No fear, no questions.

"Well then, we better get going," she finally said, setting out on her own.

"You can keep your eyes ahead, James," Lola said through his Mjolnir's external speaker. *"I'll let you know what's behind. Also, good news.* Cataphract *will be in range soon if we need support."* Given the deluge of revelations he had just experienced, the news caught him off guard. The farther they traveled south into Tyrrhen, the closer they would be to the same latitudinal sector they'd originally began their journey at. And the closer they'd be to *Cataphract*—his ride off this damn rock.

"Thank you. Looks like a straight shot to those buildings on the perimeter."

Chloe turned back toward him and smiled.

"What?" he asked.

"You're the strongest and bravest person I've ever met, but you still need someone to protect you."

Instinctively, Solomon wanted to say that he didn't need Lola, but that would have been a lie. He relied on her far more than he'd ever let on. For a nonvolitional AI with limited growth capacity, she'd been an extraordinary strategic advantage and gotten him out of serious situations *many* times. And after al-Cygni's briefing, he didn't feel very strong at all. He was escorting a ten-year-old girl to a fate that seemed less optimistic than the admiral was willing to admit.

He put his helmet back on and tightly gripped his DMR, then followed in Chloe's wake, giving a quick eye over his shoulder as the enemy continued their hunt across Tyrrhen's northern terrain. It wouldn't be long before their widening search patterns intersected with his own path, so putting as much distance between them as possible was the wisest course of action. "We all need someone to look out for us," he finally said as he began traveling down the far side of the hill, staying well beneath the trees' shadows. "That's how humans are made."

"Even me?" she asked. It seemed like a sincere question.

"Yeah. *Especially* you." She could not see his smile behind his visor.

About two kilometers east, they could see a row of buildings engulfed in flames. The burning light shone brightly across the fields and trees. The inferno was engulfing what looked like houses.

"Did people live in those?" Chloe asked.

"Yes. Probably."

"Do you think they survived?"

Solomon didn't answer.

"You can tell me, you know. I'm tougher than you think."

"I doubt that's possible. I think you're pretty tough to begin with."

She gave him a suspicious look.

"He's telling the truth," Lola said matter-of-factly through the external speaker. *"I can tell when he isn't."*

"Then can you tell me why there are no Spartans here?" Chloe asked, seeming genuinely curious. "Weren't they made to stop this kind of stuff from happening? Shouldn't they be fighting for Boundary?"

The answer was an emphatic yes, but there was no way to tell what the UNSC's force deployment was here. From what Solomon could see, there didn't seem to be a lot of anything in terms of planetary defense, much less any Spartans to turn the tide. It didn't even look like Boundary had a standing militia. Maybe the settlement's center would prove different. He hoped so.

"Actually, Chloe," Lola said, *"Spartans were first created by Dr. Halsey to prevent colonial rebellion. Defending worlds from alien invasion came later."*

"Who is Dr. Halsey?"

Solomon was about to tell Lola to not answer that, but was too late.

"She's a noted scientist. Catherine Elizabeth Halsey oversaw the development of more than three dozen classified military projects for the Office of Naval Intelligence. This included the SPARTAN-II program."

"Heh," the girl responded. "She has the same initials as me."

Solomon winced.

The tragic irony of the entire situation was not lost on him.

Chloe was a flash clone of Halsey, the scientist who had directed and overseen the abduction of Solomon and the seventy-four other Spartan-II candidates when they were all only six years old. She'd replaced all of them with flash clones, most of whom would soon suffer from debilitating diseases before succumbing. Their families—*Solomon's* family—would never know the truth or even come to learn that their children had wound up being the only decisive military solution against the Covenant when the war started just under a decade later.

Halsey had been like a mother to Solomon for most of his life.

She'd helped raise him and his fellow Spartans. In some strange way, Chloe was also Halsey's progeny, which meant that—to him—she was akin to a younger sister. It was a bizarre thought, but one he couldn't shake since his conversation with Admiral al-Cygni. Just like Solomon, this girl had been the result of Halsey's scientific expediency. In her zeal to create an AI capable of stopping the Covenant, she'd broken countless medical and ethical laws, and cloned herself multiple times believing that the "specimens" were expendable.

The argument Halsey seemed to live by was that the ends justified the means. Solomon wondered if he could work himself up to use that same argument when the time came to hand Chloe over to ONI. Did he actually believe such a thing anymore? This wouldn't be simply an exercise in philosophical theory or idealistic premises. He would have to make a real choice, and he'd have to make it with the collateral damage Halsey's hubris had created—a human being.

James had never resented what had happened to him—very few of his fellow Spartans did. It was far easier to rationalize his own circumstances, as he had no memory of whatever childhood he'd had before ONI abducted him. Without the Spartans, humanity would have fallen . . . but looking at Chloe, with that very same logic being applied to her, he felt a twisted knot in his stomach. It all felt wrong.

"Have you ever wondered if there's anyone up there?" Chloe's eyes were taking in the stars again.

"You mean in space?"

"No. I mean *past* space. Past everything. Way out there where we can't see."

"Like God?"

"I mean like someone up there who is telling a story, and you and I are part of that story. Like . . . *all* of this is part of the story." She held her arms out wide to include everything.

"Then it would be a very sad story." There was no use in being dishonest.

"Most stories are sad," she said, her eyes dropping back down from the lights above. "I've read enough of them back on Cascade to know. But what makes stories good isn't that they don't have sad parts. What makes them good is that the sad parts have a good reason in the end. And the sad parts don't go on forever either."

Solomon stared at the girl, completely puzzled.

Suddenly she seemed *nothing* like her mother.

"Enemy approaching, five o'clock." Lola spoke directly in his armor and her tone was urgent. *"Gravemaker."*

Solomon spun around and saw the armored platform barely a kilometer away and approaching fast, its silhouette backlit by the flaring blast-cylinders that kept it hovering above ground. He withdrew his Stanchion and sighted the craft. Its top was filled with Jiralhanae, all of them clad in heavily plated armor and bearing an excessive arsenal, some even operating autocannons. It was clear that the Banished had sent out their best.

"What are the chances they will see us when they pass?" he asked.

"Oh, they won't pass by, James," Lola replied. *"Given their trajectory and speed, they're coming to investigate what they've already detected. And if their armor is any indicator, those are* surdkars *on that battle platform."*

Solomon cursed under his breath and looked back toward Chloe, leaning up against one of the trees. "Keep walking down that way and find a tree large enough to hide behind," he said, pointing south. "Do not look or come back to me for *any* reason. Do you understand?"

Chloe reluctantly nodded. For the first time since the night he'd met her, Solomon thought he saw genuine fear in her eyes. Or maybe that was concern rising in his own heart.

He turned away from Chloe's position and exploded into a sprint toward the approaching Gravemaker. The more distance between him and the girl, the better. He wasn't clear on what the Banished knew about whoever was escorting the girl or if they would see him as simply a lone soldier and assume that she wasn't nearby. All Solomon knew was that they were after *her* and whatever happened next, she would be better off as far from him as possible.

"She's well hidden," Lola said into his helmet. *"Now* you *just have to survive."*

"I'll be fine," he said. "Just keep an eye on her." She could use sensors in his armor to track the girl's position in relation to him and let him know if anything happened.

He quickly slid down the hill they had been walking along and stopped on one knee, looking out across the sprawling pasture that touched the same territory where the farm buildings were still burning. The Gravemaker was now at five hundred meters and closing when Solomon aimed the M99, sighting the viewport center at the vehicle's fore. A standard rifle would have little effect on such a well-armored vehicle, but the Stanchion's asynchronous linear induction motor made it an anti-matériel rifle with few rivals. It was more than capable of surgically penetrating most enemy armor utilized by the Banished or the Covenant and would make short work of the viewport's reinforced plating.

Solomon's first shot connected with the Gravemaker's front

end without any noticeable effect. The second was like a nail in the coffin—he could tell immediately that he'd struck the viewport and the pilot behind it, as the entire craft listed hard to the left, sending some of its topside Jiralhanae tumbling out over a thirty-meter drop. At that height, there wouldn't be many survivors. Probably none.

Someone inside the operations center attempted to right the vehicle, only for Solomon to fire again. The Gravemaker listed once more, its blast-cylinders failing to automate the vehicle's lift-control fast enough. The craft fell hard to the surface, planting into the ground about one hundred and fifty meters from Solomon, tearing a long, burning gash into the pasture as it finally came to a halt.

Most of the remaining Jiralhanae topside were thrown upon impact, and the others were so disoriented they didn't see the Spartan running at full speed toward their position. That was a mistake they would not live long enough to learn from.

Solomon discarded his Stanchion—up close it had no value. Even his M392 was more farsighted than the ensuing fight would demand, so he stowed it on his back and retrieved his M6D at a dead run. As he reached the front of the Gravemaker, two Jiralhanae were weakly attempting to rise, their energy shielding completely depleted. They were greeted with 12.7mm semi-armor-piercing, high-explosive rounds in their foreheads, dropping them immediately.

Scaling the front of the Gravemaker, Solomon found another recovering from the crash and executed a running dropkick, a successful move as the Jiralhanae didn't get back up. Two others emerged from a hatch at the very center of the topside deck. Solomon's combat knife flashed in the firelight as he forced it into the closest creature's neck, tearing open his carotid artery in a spray of blood. As the other attempted to raise a spike rifle, he received two quick rounds to the chest to break his shielding and a final to his skull.

Before either Jiralhanae fell, Solomon had returned his knife to its scabbard and withdrawn a fragmentation grenade, arming it and sending it down the hatch. By the time it exploded, he'd already armed a second grenade and sent it down right after. The wet sound of flesh exploding in the vehicle's compact interior was unmistakable. Nothing in those tight quarters could have survived.

"Chloe's still okay, James," Lola said. *"But you're not finished."*

He looked down the path of the Gravemaker's crash, a long gouge across the moonlight-dappled pasture, much of it still smoldering red due to the heat from the blast-cylinders. Scattered debris and smoke made seeing clearly difficult, even with Mjolnir's optical solutions.

Slowly a handful of Jiralhanae who had survived the fall came into view. He swapped his pistol for the DMR and took aim without hesitation. The first went down easy, the second even easier, as both, consumed with anger, had attempted to charge him directly. At this distance, it was unbridled pride and rage at the idea of having their craft downed by a lone soldier that would prove to be their end.

Dropping down to the ground, Solomon hoped to get a better view below the smoke line, but all he could now see from this position was a single biped form, but impossibly large. He blinked, disbelieving his eyes, but the form continued toward him without wavering. If it was a Jiralhanae, it was easily the largest he'd ever seen.

Lifting his DMR, Solomon tried to sight it, but before he could bring the weapon to bear, a javelin the length of a ship-to-ship missile ripped it from his hand and impaled it into one of the Gravemaker's ruined blast-cylinders, the force of the blow nearly taking Solomon's right arm clean off. He withdrew his M6D, trying to take aim through a fanning veil of smoke, but his attacker had completely vanished. The wind was pouring fresh oxygen on streams of burning fuel, creating an even thicker covering of blacks and grays.

"Careful, James."

"No kidding," he replied in frustration. "You don't have contact with *Cataphract* yet, do you?" He could really use a distraction right about now.

"Not yet. Sorry."

Solomon moved around the perimeter to the left, trying to evade the billowing smoke moving east. He considered whether retreating was a reasonable solution. Whatever was hiding in the smoke would have to chase him and he was pretty sure he could outrun something that large. But it would be for nothing—if he didn't kill this one, it would simply call in reinforcements and he'd have to do it all over again.

He had to deal with this threat *now.*

As Solomon moved around half a blast-cylinder that had been shorn off during the crash, the giant, heavily armored Jiralhanae suddenly came into view. The creature, with eyes that burned bright with anger, was more terrifying than anything Solomon had ever encountered, and that included the pair of Mgalekgolo to whom he'd lost his left arm. In his right hand, the Jiralhanae held a sickle-bladed khopesh that was roughly the size of an adult human.

Solomon emptied a full magazine from the M6D into the giant, but it only seemed to piss him off. Between his armor and natural resilience, the Jiralhanae seemed to regard small-arms fire only as a nuisance. The monster then charged with a surprising speed, bringing his blade down hard onto his position. Diving to the left, Solomon intended to use leverage to counterattack, but the Jiralhanae's boot slammed into his torso like a torque-hammer, sending him at least ten meters across the grass. He landed in a heap, tasting copper, struggling to breathe.

Shaking it off, he quickly stood up as he reloaded the M6D, immediately firing, strafing to his right. Every shot connected and yet did nothing. Before his magazine went dry, the khopesh came sailing through the air end-over-end at an extraordinary speed, impaling the Gravemaker's hull beside him, mere centimeters from his head. Still recovering from the attack, the monster was already upon him, its fist slamming into his chest with the force of a runaway Warthog. Solomon was knocked into the Gravemaker's armored carriage, and his vision went black.

The next few moments seemed to last forever, saturated by a thick darkness, and the distant drone of Lola's voice buried somewhere past his dwindling consciousness. It felt too far for Solomon to respond or even hear clearly.

Then it suddenly came with a rush of clarity.

"He took her, James. That thing *took Chloe."*

CHAPTER 30

TUL 'JURAN

Ghado (Boundary)
December 14, 2559

The disparate parts of Zulu Red had converged on the third floor of an abandoned building—a school of some kind, Tul 'Juran had been informed. From what she could tell based on the holo-sat imagery from *Victory of Samothrace*, the outskirts of Tyrrhen were sparsely populated by farming structures and paddocks for cattle, but here in the center of the settlement, the buildings were clustered in tight configurations that seemed arbitrary, following no rules of symmetry.

When 'Juran and Gray Team first arrived, they had found Spartans Vídalín, McEndon, and Merrick posted by windows with various optical equipment laid out as they surveyed the park below. At its center lay the site of the Banished excavation. The enemy's flame-bore looked more like a fortified base than a mining tool. Nearby were large machine-arms with drilling instruments that could tunnel deep below the surface of what had once been a verdant, serene park. Now it looked more like a quarry than anything else, and at its lowest level an imposing Forerunner structure had come into view, almost fully excavated.

This had to be the Lithos.

The scale of the Forerunner structure was astonishing, though buried under thousands of tons of rock and dirt for long ages—an unbreakable ancient citadel that had lain silent only thirty meters below a human settlement. It had escaped the notice of Ghado's colonists for decades. A building made by the gods. Or so the Covenant had believed.

After a few moments of examination, it became unmistakably clear that this was indeed the Lithos based on the imagery provided during the briefing on *Victory of Samothrace.* She was surprised at how strikingly similar it looked to the gateway that existed on Genesis, a perfectly symmetrical mound rising from a collection of escalating platforms, its basic appearance likened to the headless shoulders of a giant. Where the head might have been, a series of three concentric rings with a diameter roughly the length of a Covenant corvette now lay dormant. To 'Juran, it appeared that only about half a unit remained before the Banished would have the machine completely accessible.

Time was running out.

The enemy's patrols not only covered the streets and alleys on the surface, but extended into the depths of the quarry, with guards stationed at different points on the series of descending platforms and near a sealed aperture on the monolith itself, which she presumed was the Lithos's entrance. Banished Ghosts and Marauders shuttled across the roads above, with infantry units in tightly grouped packs, while heavily armored Jiralhanae remained in relatively fixed positions within the excavation itself, seemingly ready to strike at the first sight of an intruder.

"Now, *that* is intriguing," Stolt said, standing beside Vul 'Soran. He was pointing through a window overlooking the southern portion of the excavation.

'Juran understood what he meant. A succession of Covenant Phantoms was descending and scattering across the south and west, only their silhouettes visible in the moonlight.

Why in the name of the gods are they *here?*

This had to be a connection to their presence on Sqala. It did not take long for Covenant Spirits and Seraphs to also become visible, and behind them the much larger carriers, battlecruisers, and corvettes gradually dropping toward the planet's surface from the pale night sky. The Covenant warships seemed to settle peacefully in the air alongside the Banished ones—an unusual sight that Tul 'Juran would never have believed if she were not present.

The Spartans of Gray Team seemed genuinely surprised as well from their posture, but before anyone could venture an explanation for what they were witnessing, Jai received a transmission from a human ship called *Akkadian*, which had been providing intelligence to the ground teams on the planet's surface.

Jai went to the corner of the room as he spoke directly with the ship's commander, while the others continued to stare in amazement at the unfolding scene. A single Covenant Phantom descended on the east end of the park, and from it emerged several heavily armored Sangheili guards along with a single leader in unmistakable armor.

"Sali 'Nyon," 'Juran said through tightened mandibles as she sighted down one of the human spotting instruments—an archaic monocular they evidently used to sight targets.

"Sali 'Nyon? What is *he* doing in the middle of a Banished occupation?" Vídalín asked.

'Juran was equally perplexed. *What could have possibly brought them together?*

Then again, there was not much difference in the room before her now. After all, humans and Sangheili had been mortal enemies for years. It wasn't that long ago when simply occupying the same space would have meant certain bloodshed for this group. Now they were working side by side against a common threat for the sake of their own peoples. Had the Lithos united their enemies, just as the end of the Covenant War did for humans and Sangheili?

The strength of their enemies' union, however, was another matter.

Through the monocular, the individual Banished soldiers appeared to keep turning to each other, as if questioning how they ought to engage the Covenant. They clearly had not expected this development at all. Their leaders held up their hands in a kind of uncertain caution, seemingly trying to prevent some devastating fallout. Whatever truce had been formed between these enemies, its stability was tenuous at best.

Sali 'Nyon strolled alongside the excavation with an entourage at his back as if he owned the entire settlement. Two Banished chieftains—neither of them Severan—and a Sangheili in the armor of nobility emerged from what appeared to be a war council structure on the far side of the park. They approached 'Nyon with their own bodyguards in tow. Meeting somewhere in the middle, they began to speak to each other. From the looks on their faces as 'Juran zoomed the monocular, the Banished leaders had also been caught off guard by the Covenant's presence, but not to the point of drawing arms.

"I have no idea what is happening," 'Soran finally answered the Spartan's question. "We share your surprise and confusion at this development."

"*Akkadian* doesn't know anything either," Jai said, returning from the corner and taking in the scene below. "But it doesn't change our objective. Orders are to secure Annex Muster Station B94 on the northwest end of the park, then wait for the escorting operative to bring us the key. Once we have the key, we're to escort her into that structure"—he pointed to the Lithos—"and then proceed with what ONI refers to as *integration*."

"That doesn't sound too pleasant," McEndon remarked.

"No, it doesn't," Jai said. "Which is why I'll be the one escorting the key into the Lithos. We'll make our way to the muster station as quietly as possible. I do *not* want to stir the hornets' nest—if that's what this is—until we're in a position to actually capitalize on it."

"What about our quarry—Dovo Nesto?" Stolt said, asking the very question on 'Juran's mind.

"Our priority is obviously securing the key to the Lithos," Jai explained. "But if the opportunity avails itself, you have clearance from our side to eliminate Dovo Nesto. As long as it doesn't compromise our ability to complete the mission objective."

"I think that opportunity just availed itself, Gray Leader," Vídalín said, pointing down toward a space between wafts of dust from the flame-bore beam's point of contact.

Behind the gray veil was the San'Shyuum high lord, confidently moving across the street with his arms folded. His face was unafraid and his bearing proud. Something about his posture told 'Juran that all of this had been his orchestration. The Banished chieftains and warriors were visibly taken aback by the sight of a San'Shyuum—as if they had not known he was even among them. Several of their guards reached for their weapons out of sheer instinct. 'Juran found her own hands tightening around her carbine's grip.

Before the Banished could open fire, 'Nyon's soldiers had already leveled their own weapons at the leaders. It was a clear standoff, but now 'Nyon spoke. The Sangheili leader was too far for 'Juran to hear over the noise emanating from the excavation, but it was evident that he was trying to maintain some peace. He was talking the Banished down.

Whatever their alliance was, Dovo Nesto had *not* been part of it. At least not until now.

The chieftains spat and growled, beating their chests in anger. The Sangheili noble with them stepped toward 'Nyon gesturing at the San'Shyuum, as if trying to talk sense into him. The Banished soldiers all around began slowly encroaching from all angles, surrounding the group of leaders. This act only served to incite 'Nyon's bodyguards, who made it clear they were prepared to die on the spot if necessary, turning to face the gathering mass of Banished.

Without notice, other Covenant dropships now quickly touched down at various junctures around the park, unloading waves upon waves of Covenant soldiers: Sangheili, Kig-Yar, Unggoy, and even several pairs of Mgalekgolo—all of them well-armed and converging on the group of leaders. The Covenant's weapons were raised as if they expected this to become a battle, and much to 'Juran's surprise it looked as if they now held superior numbers against the Banished.

The firing of a single shot would send this encounter into a full-scale conflict.

"I say we move out now," Jai announced. "Looks like the window for us making it to the muster station in one piece is rapidly closing. We need to clear some of the ground between us and the objective before this place becomes a war zone." He turned to 'Juran and the others from *Shadow of Intent*. "If we get a clean shot at Dovo Nesto—or Sali 'Nyon for that matter—while en route, it's yours to take. But wait for my signal. An assassination may well be our ticket for getting access to the Lithos. It would certainly create just the right flavor of bedlam needed to provide cover."

'Soran's face remained taut. As the Spartans collected their equipment and began filing out of the room with the Unggoy ranger right behind them, the blademaster gestured to 'Juran to hold back, then turned to her when they were alone.

"You will not be executing Dovo Nesto, Scion." His tone was settled and recalcitrant. "Your anger will cloud your ability to properly make the kill and we cannot afford to miss this opportunity. I will take down Dovo Nesto and you will take Sali 'Nyon instead. Is that understood?"

'Juran wanted to object, to fight back. She was again being treated as a hatchling, denied her right of retribution. She did not care at all about Sali 'Nyon and his insane quest to revive the Covenant. Other misguided Sangheili had attempted it and failed spectacularly. So would he.

No, it was Dovo Nesto she wanted. Nesto needed to pay for the deaths of her family and she desired more than anything to exact that payment. For her own sake and for that of her younger sibling, who now bore the title of kaidon in the place of her father.

"I understand, Blademaster," 'Juran replied, but every syllable was begrudging, despite her respect for him. "If that is the case, then you must not miss." She stormed out of the room before he could respond.

The Spartans and Stolt had already reached the alley at the base of the building's stairwell by the time she caught up. From this position, they could only glimpse the park and the excavation site, a Spirit dropship being the only evidence of the enemy's presence. Given the direction of the muster station, they would have to pass by the very location Nesto and 'Nyon were last seen—close enough for a kill shot.

For ten centals, Zulu Red carefully maneuvered around the southern perimeter of the park, silently weaving their way through tight alleyways and around various buildings, while keeping out of the enemy's view. This was easier than they had anticipated, since the Covenant's arrival had drawn Banished patrols from the settlement's outlying roads directly to its center. Along the way, Zulu Red managed to dispatch a handful of Banished infantry quietly and without incident. Stolt even climbed atop a Jiralhanae guard's back at one point, and broke his neck. It was as impressive a sight as it was bizarre.

'Juran was waiting for a single blast from a plasma pistol or carbine to ignite the conflict, but it never came. The continued churn of excavation, the low thrum of scouting vehicles, and the sound of dropships disembarking were all that could be heard from the park roughly a block away. Against all odds, the showdown between the Banished and 'Nyon's Covenant forces had not yet devolved into all-out war.

Four centals after Zulu Red turned north alongside the west part of the park, they came across a heavily plated Banished structure that strangely lay atop what remained of a human one—one of many modular outposts that the Banished deployed during their occupations, which *Victory*'s logistics officer had advised could be modified to fit just about any need. 'Juran did not know what the purpose of this one was, but Jai was crouched at its far corner and sighting down his battle rifle back toward the park.

He turned and looked in the direction of the crew from *Shadow of Intent*, then motioned them to move up to his position. Jai put two fingers toward where his eyes would be beneath his visor, then pointed down the alley. Then he motioned silently to the other Spartans to spread out around their intersection, sighting down each path in the alley as if to cover the shooters.

"You both are up," he said to the blademaster and 'Juran. "But you'll only have one chance, then we're hoofing it to the muster station. We won't be stopping, so make it count."

'Juran peeked first, with 'Soran and Stolt right behind her.

Down the side of the outpost, barely a hundred meters away,

Dovo Nesto and Sali 'Nyon stood side by side, still talking to the Banished leaders. The initial tension had abated and weapons had been lowered, but the air still carried a strong sense of displeasure among the Banished, as if they were awaiting the arrival of someone who would be able to sort this out.

Jai had brought them to the perfect spot. At this angle and distance, taking down Dovo Nesto and Sali 'Nyon simultaneously would be relatively easy with their carbines, their sighting path traveling directly between the Jiralhanae and Sangheili bodyguards. After waiting so long, it was almost too much for 'Juran to believe that the high lord was finally going to pay for his crimes.

"Be advised, team," Jai quietly addressed the entire group, "when this goes down there will be immediate chaos. We'll use this to our advantage. It's a straight shot from here to the muster station and we can be there before anyone figures out where the attack came from. Given the present tension, I can pretty much guarantee we're about to light this powder keg. When that happens, we'll hopefully have all the cover we need to infiltrate the Lithos."

"So much for not stirring up the hornets' nest," Merrick said under his breath. "What if the Banished stop excavating because they have to fight a ground war?"

"What excavating?" Adriana asked, pointing to where her ear would be. 'Juran could not hear the mining equipment's sound any longer. The flame-bore had stopped. "They're finished. Which means the Lithos's entrance has been cleared. The structure is now accessible."

"Our objective is the muster station, *then* the Lithos," Jai said. "Then we move to the extraction point. Everyone clear?"

The extraction point was on the northeast side of the Tyrrhen settlement, a twenty-minute hike from their position according to Michael. It was there that they were to rendezvous with Zulu Blue.

'Juran had been told that their Condor was hiding somewhere in the mountains west of Tyrrhen and would swing in low, straight across the center of the settlement for extraction. Gray Team had said that it could pick them up and escape through slipspace before the enemy figured out what had happened—they claimed to have done it many times before.

'Juran hoped the chaos that was about to ensue would not alter the escape plan too dramatically. When everyone acknowledged Jai's order, he nodded his head toward the shooters. The old blademaster turned to 'Juran, hefting up his carbine and taking aim down its barrel through a holographic sight.

"Three breaths," 'Soran said. "Then fire on the third, Scion. Yes?"

"Yes, Blademaster." She lifted her own weapon and stared through the sight at Sali 'Nyon. His armor likely meant that the first shot or two would only degrade his energy shielding. It would not matter. She would fire enough rounds to guarantee his demise well before the first one even connected with the target.

She listened for the blademaster's count.

"One," he whispered.

But he had better land his shots true on the San'Shyuum.

"Two . . . "

The third count never came.

'Juran looked to her side in time to see the stock of the blademaster's carbine slamming hard into the side of her face, dropping her to the ground. 'Soran swiftly turned and fired multiple rounds into Jai's torso, breaking the Spartan's energy shielding and piercing through his armor before Adriana could land a blow to the Sangheili's gut. 'Juran attempted to stand, but her legs failed and she fell again, confused, her mind reeling.

The roar of an assault rifle came from her left, followed immediately by reports from a battle rifle and plasma pistol. Spartan

Merrick had fired on both Vídalín and Stolt. Spartan McEndon was pulling Vídalín's body behind a corner, while the Unggoy ranger and Michael finished off Merrick with a severity that guaranteed the super-soldier would not be getting back up.

Finally managing to rise to her knees, 'Juran witnessed 'Soran igniting both his plasma swords. Before they had even fully materialized, the blades were headed toward Adriana. One of the blades glanced her shoulder, shearing off part of her armor; the other dragged right down her chest, scorching right through the armor and raking against her skin.

The blademaster would not get another strike in. The Spartan had pivoted to the side and sent her right foot directly into his chest with the force of a plasma launcher, cracking open his combat harness and launching him back-first against the wall. His body fell, revealing a dent in the Banished outpost. 'Soran went limp, his swords deactivating as they hit the ground.

Jai's hand reached for 'Juran's and she tightly grabbed hold of it. Blood was pouring out of the black mesh in between his armor plating, even though his other hand was pressed tightly against it. Those were carbine rounds. Radioactive and highly poisonous.

"We've got to go," Jai said through gritted teeth. "Now!"

"What happened?" she pleaded, as the surviving Spartans began hobbling away from the bodies of Merrick and 'Soran, moving as fast as they could in the direction of the muster station.

"No time—come on!" Jai shouted, looking back down toward the park where they had first sighted Nesto and 'Nyon. The Banished and Covenant leaders were no longer there. Instead, a horde of warriors of both factions were now barreling down the alley toward what remained of Zulu. Jai was right. There was no time.

They launched out of the alley as hundreds of incensed enemies charged down it.

CHAPTER 31

ABIGAIL COLE

UNSC *Victory of Samothrace*
December 15, 2559

"*Captain,* Victory*'s objective has changed,"* Admiral al-Cygni said. The admiral's image appeared above the holo-port on the private conference room table. Whatever her message to Cole was, it had required al-Cygni to break *Akkadian*'s cover and expose the vessel to the enemy in order to communicate it.

The heavy shuddering that Cole felt deep within *Victory of Samothrace*'s frame wasn't necessary to remind her that she was now in the thick of it as well with Banished and Covenant vessels, trading blows just above the settlement of Tyrrhen. The UNSC fleets dispatched to Boundary and what remained of Battle Group Omega were beating hard against the enemy's defensive shell, trying to punch a hole in it to buy precious time for the groundside team to complete their mission.

"Talk to me, Admiral," Cole said, unable to hide the strong desire to return to the bridge with her crew. But something in al-Cygni's face told her things had shifted dramatically.

"We don't have much time, so I'll make it quick. We have visual

confirmation that the key has been compromised. The Banished have taken the girl and are headed to Tyrrhen's center. Your strike team was hit hard too. Spartan Merrick is a confirmed KIA. Several others are badly wounded. We don't know how it happened, only that whoever's left is currently on the run. We lost visual contact with them five minutes ago."

"What's our objective?" Cole asked, though she already knew the answer.

"Full asset denial, Captain," al-Cygni said.

"And my people on the ground?"

"We lost contact with them or we would have already ordered their evacuation. Unless you know another ship that might be in a better place to transmit, there's literally nothing we can do from here. I don't like this situation any more than you do, Cole. But we simply cannot afford to allow the Lithos to be accessed by the enemy."

Cole's chest filled with a heaviness that she'd felt many times before. It was the weight of the loss of her own people. But this time it was different. This wasn't a strategic failure in mission planning or the random casualty of a naval battle—she had sent these men and women to the surface to conduct an operation, and now, in essence, she was being forced to order their execution. A MAC strike from *Victory* would vaporize the Lithos and much of the surrounding area.

"Captain." Al-Cygni's voice roused Cole from dreadful thoughts. *"By our estimates, you have less than twelve minutes before the key reaches the Lithos. We need* Victory *to make this shot."*

"I understand, Admiral," she said. "But I have one possible option to reach the team below."

"And what would that be?"

Another reverberation shook *Victory of Samothrace.* It felt like a plasma torpedo.

"*Shadow of Intent.* They have three operatives on our strike team and their last position was close to Tyrrhen's center. I'll get the shipmaster on the line and see what he can do."

"All right. I hope for their sake he can reach them in time," al-Cygni said, her face suddenly turning grave. *"But, Cole, listen to me.* Victory *is our only hope right now to ensure that the Domain doesn't fall into the wrong hands. If you fail, we* all *fail."*

"Understood, Admiral. We'll get it done." And she clicked off the feed, immediately keying in a request to Lieutenant Lim to hail *Shadow of Intent*. Within seconds, the request had been answered and Shipmaster 'Vadum materialized in holographic form atop his control-saddle aboard *Shadow of Intent*'s bridge.

"Captain, your vessel is surrounded by Banished warships," he said.

"I'm aware, Shipmaster, but I need to inform you of something else. The key we need for the Lithos has been compromised. The Banished are about to access the Forerunner site. I've received orders from ONI to stop them from orbit."

"And our strike team has been extracted?"

"No, that's what I need from you. There's no way for me to get through to them from our position. The nav-designator placed *Shadow of Intent* just west of Tyrrhen's center. That's got to be close enough for your ship's comms."

"That is indeed our position, Captain. But I cannot guarantee that we will be able to reach them. We lost track of them just over ten centals ago."

"You're not the only one. I have . . . eleven minutes before I have to do something I cannot undo, Shipmaster," she replied, feeling both raw and angry about the task laid before her. "I don't even know if *Victory* will survive long enough to get into position to fire. You *need* to reach the strike team. Tell them to get out of Tyrrhen's center as quickly as possible. Their lives depend on it."

"Understood, Captain," 'Vadum said, his mandibles tightening. *"I will do what I can."*

The communication link ended. Although emotion was difficult to read on a Sangheili's face, Cole could tell that he was just as concerned for his people's safety as she was for hers. He would certainly do anything he could to get them out of danger. She just hoped it was enough.

As she stepped out onto the bridge, the war above the face of Boundary swallowed every angle of the viewport, and her crew was frantically conducting their tasks under the command of her XO. *Victory of Samothrace* was firing into the port side of a Banished skeid as it passed, while a Covenant battlecruiser came into view just behind it. From her position before the holopane, several emergency alarms had already been silenced and two hull breaches contained. Most of her ship's weapons were still online and doing far better than she would have expected.

"Status?" Cole asked, looking to Commander Njuguna.

"We've taken a few hits, but we're airtight and gunning fast, Captain. And we're making progress. Sixty percent of our fighters are deployed across the immediate battle plane; the rest are on standby. Omega's right behind us, staggered-support formation. The Fourth and Sixth fleets are abreast at two thousand klicks and keeping pace. The Ninth and Thirteenth rolled back to ward off the Covenant naval forces that were approaching from the rear—though a large portion of the Covenant have already passed through the Banished shell unimpeded."

"Definitely looks as though there's some kind of alliance at play," Cole responded. "I'm not sure how the hell that happened, but it's not good news for any of us. How many ships have we lost?"

"Eighteen, Captain," Njuguna said.

The pain from that data hit her sharply, but she tried to hide it from her people, returning her gaze to the holopane. *Victory*'s original goal had been merely to bore as deep a hole as possible into the defensive shell. The basic cat-and-mouse skirmishes they were conducting wouldn't suffice any longer. They had needed to punch hard and draw blood in order to distract the Banished from the groundside team's push for the Lithos.

There had simply been no choice.

The Banished skeid suddenly exploded before them and the Covenant battlecruiser tunneled through its debris, lighting up its forward-mounted plasma torpedoes for a surprise attack. The surprise was on the enemy, however, as it ran bow-first into successive MAC rounds from *Get My Drift* and *Hazard Pay*, making contact with a one-two punch. The battlecruiser detonated into a ball of white light, burning alien battleplate radiating in every direction.

Commander Jiron's battle group was still fighting hard. They were far tougher than Cole could have ever imagined.

She looked down at her chronometer. Over two minutes had elapsed. Time to prep her crew.

"Listen up, *Victory*," Cole said, drawing their attention. "We've got new orders and you're not going to like them. The Banished have the key, they're headed to the Lithos right now. We've been tasked with preventing that. We need to deny the Banished access to the Forerunner site with an orbital strike."

"What about Zulu?" Njuguna asked. "We still can't reach them from our position."

"*Shadow of Intent* is attempting to contact the strike team at this very moment. I wish I had a better answer, but we only have . . . eight minutes now until the Banished reach the target. That's all the time we can give Zulu. I'm sorry, Commander."

Njuguna nodded with the same somber look the rest of the bridge crew held. Cole felt it just as keenly as they did but had to fight through it; otherwise the losses on the surface of Tyrrhen would be the least of humanity's problems.

"Comms and Logistics, I want you to broadcast this to Omega and the other fleets. If we can't make this shot happen, hopefully one of them can at least try. Their MACs aren't spec'd for this, but it's better than nothing. Until then, we need them to provide cover while we navigate into firing position. That won't be an easy task within the shell, but it's the only way we can guarantee that our shot hits the target. Everyone clear?"

"Aye, Captain!" The crew spoke in unison and returned their attention to their interfaces, but it was clear they were all racked with guilt. The idea of firing upon the strike team was unconscionable. But decisions like this sometimes had to be made.

Cole offered a silent prayer that *Shadow of Intent* would be able to reach the strike team in time and tell them to get as far away from the site as they could. Until then, *Victory of Samothrace* would buy her people as much time as possible before wiping the Lithos out of existence.

CHAPTER 32

SEVERAN

Ghado (Boundary)
December 15, 2559

As Severan's Gravemaker approached Tyrrhen's center, it took every ounce of strength in him not to order the battle-platform to gun down Sali 'Nyon right where he stood, atop the series of platforms that led directly into the Lithos. Dovo Nesto's presence had finally been revealed to the other Banished leaders—the San'Shyuum now stood right in their midst—and there would no doubt be a heavy price to pay. Severan was surprised the high lord was even still alive after such a brazen move.

From this vantage point, it was patently clear that Ectorius and Gathgor were not pleased in the least, and on the verge of doing something retaliatory. Even Dreka 'Xulsam showed signs of visible disgust at the turn of affairs, as though he might reach out at any moment and bury his energy blade in 'Nyon's chest.

He would have to beat Severan to it.

Does the high lord not trust me to accomplish what is needed?

Looking at 'Nyon as he smugly stood by the high lord, Severan had already begun considering that this was not simply a relationship of convenience or expedience, but far more than met the eye. The high lord had shown complete disregard for Severan's own ability to accomplish their shared goals, despite all he'd pledged, and would now jeopardize his very standing before Atriox in order to subvert it.

How could Severan believe that the high lord still had his hand of blessing on him to lead the Covenant they were seeking to rebuild, when he had already colluded with 'Nyon? Surely the Sangheili traitor would not bow before Severan, nor the opposite. The only explanation for all of this was typical San'Shyuum deception.

Dovo Nesto had *lied* to him. All that he had promised had been a lie. Of this, Severan was quickly becoming certain.

The realization hurt more than he would allow. He would instead fill the cavity of his *daskalo*'s betrayal with hatred and revenge. Whatever the reason for this treachery, Severan knew that everything had changed today in a way that could never be reversed.

The Gravemaker set down within the excavation pit, only ten meters from the Lithos's first platform, one of a series of ascending architectural elements leading up to the mouth of the Forerunner structure, where the other leaders currently stood. Kaevus must not have initially noticed the San'Shyuum's presence, because he did not acknowledge it until their feet touched the ground.

"By the light of the corpse-moon, what is *he* doing out here?" It was comforting to hear Kaevus speak with the same vitriol that Severan felt.

The war chief could not muster a reply through tightly locked tusks. Four guards from the *surdkar* aboard Severan's Gravemaker followed them, weapons in hand. The Prophet's presence had already escalated things and he wanted to be ready.

"The high lord is fortunate Gathgor has not yet torn him limb from limb," Kaevus remarked, still attempting some respect for the San'Shyuum.

"He is no high lord any longer, brother," Severan said with contempt. "Not to us. Why he felt it necessary to invite this Sangheili sycophant is beyond me, but it proves only one thing: the Order of Restoration is not our path. I had thought I could trust him after all this time. It is a great tragedy that he did not think the same of me. Keep your words, brother—I alone will speak. But prepare yourself." Severan gave Kaevus a long look. "It will not end in peace."

"But he is your *daskalo*," Kaevus said, more of a question than a statement.

"He *was*."

Jiralhanae considered even the chieftains of their own packs fair game for one-on-one combat to the death, whether to challenge authority or to simply secure one's own position in the group. The role of *daskalo*, however, was different—it was revered, representing the transfer of knowledge and wisdom to the next generation. One would never question their *daskalo*, much less strike at one. But exceptions could be made, Severan decided grimly, if they were discovered to be San'Shyuum *ikthas* who slithered on the ground and spoke with two mouths. He would not allow an outmoded tradition to be used to exploit his better judgment as Dovo Nesto no doubt expected.

"Severan!" Ectorius called out as Severan reached the final platform. "There is much for you to explain, War Chief!"

Indeed, there is.

As Severan approached, he tried to take in the extraordinary structure that rose before him, climbing up the side of the excavation cavity. It was the undaunted creation of gods. Unlike some Forerunner structures he had seen on other worlds, which were defined by stark angularity and complex geometric patterns, the sloping and organic arc of this one was distinct and he found it pleasing to his sight. The sides gently climbed into a large canopy-like structure, protected by layers upon layers of ancient, otherworldly alloys. Its surface coursed with elegant lines of pure blue light, representing long-dormant energies ready to be awakened. At its top was a series of perfectly circular diadems that he intuitively knew must represent the gateway to the Domain. Even the doorway was majestic and immense, fit for gods such as the Forerunners doubtless were.

This is the Lithos, the work of the divine.

It would normally have been enough to take his breath away, but his growing hatred at the very sight of Sali 'Nyon kept him grounded and sober.

"War Chief," Kaevus whispered, carefully showing him the display of a tactical-slate—a message from one of his warriors in the field. The words he read caused Severan's heart to soar. It was just the turn of fortune he needed. In fact, he *knew* it was a sure blessing from the gods, despite the machinations of those around him.

He composed himself as he approached the others, speaking with force.

"I will be glad to provide clarity," Severan said, as Banished and Covenant guards parted, giving him broad passage toward the leaders at the center. "This is Dovo Nesto, the San'Shyuum who showed me the way to the Lithos," he said flatly, careful to make eye contact with the San'Shyuum to indicate that his lack of honorifics was no mistake. "But I do not know who this *keshkra* is," he added, nodding to Sali 'Nyon.

Gathgor grunted, apparently amused at Severan's choice of words. *Keshkra*—the castration of male cattle's reproductive organs—was the only foolproof way to control breeding in the outlaw realms of Doisac. It also doubled as a humiliating expletive that neither the Sangheili nor the San'Shyuum would readily know.

Sali 'Nyon brashly stepped forward, placing his hand on his energy sword's hilt. "I will gladly receive insults, but you will refer to the Prophet as *high lord* or you will not refer to him at all."

Dovo Nesto's hand touched 'Nyon's arm as if to draw him back, but he was looking directly toward Severan. "My son, *you* should call me *daskalo*. And you should treat me as such."

"This one is your *daskalo*?" Ectorius exclaimed, his eyes wide with disbelief. "Tell me this is some kind of San'Shyuum jest!"

"It is no jest, *fool*," Dovo Nesto said, eyes bright with fury as he pointed a long, tapered finger toward Ectorius. He was either unafraid of insulting a Jiralhanae warrior or completely ignorant of the risk. Either way, he would likely not have the opportunity to learn from his mistake if he continued. "I have taught and trained this Jiralhanae in the ways of the Covenant since he was but a pup on High Charity. He is practically a son to me. It was for this very hour that I labored to make him what he has become. He is my proudest creation, and I am certain that he will do just as I say. So then, Severan, where is the key to the Lithos?"

The truth had now come out. The San'Shyuum did not see Severan as a leader, but as a pawn—a mere game piece he had dispatched to do his own bidding.

"You are sorely mistaken," Severan replied. "And *you* should know your place. You are not my father. You never were, though you certainly brought shame upon me today just as he did." He turned to 'Nyon and spoke in perfect Sangheili: "What did he promise you for this? A position of authority within his resurrected Covenant? A place of honor at the head of his military? Perhaps the same as he promised me? Surely you must know, if you are the true prophet?"

'Nyon seemed caught off guard, unsure whether to strike Severan or to question Nesto, but his reaction was more than sufficient to validate the San'Shyuum's deceit. The Sangheili had clearly been entangled in Dovo Nesto's lies just as Severan had. The truth of the matter was more than evident: there was simply no Covenant in which both he and the Sangheili could reign; the Great Schism had proven that much. Like the High Prophets of old, Dovo Nesto was interested in only one thing: securing his own place among the Forerunners—and he would use and discard any to achieve that goal.

"I am surprised at how quickly you accuse the very one who made you into the warrior you are now," the San'Shyuum stated. "If it was not for me, you would long ago have been the victim of Tartarus's failed legacy and killed like the rest of your brothers. But here you are, at the gateway of glory, and yet you falter . . . just as your father did."

"My father was a victim of San'Shyuum lies," Severan replied. "I will not be the same."

"Can you not see that the Banished are completely surrounded?" Dovo Nesto said with grave finality. "You are outnumbered and overrun. There is no hope for your brethren unless you bow before my right to divinity—the *San'Shyuum's right* to divinity. If you do not, you—*all of you*—will suffer the fate of your homeworld. I will eradicate even your very memory from the galaxy."

The other Jiralhanae near Severan uttered low growls, tightening grips around their weapons and baring their teeth. Even 'Xulsam clacked his mandibles, ready for blood.

"Dovo Nesto," Severan spoke slowly so his words would not be misunderstood. "My own warrior now brings me the key to the Lithos. The god-machine belongs to me and to me *alone*." He let the words shake all who heard them, especially the traitorous

San'Shyuum. "This is as close as you will ever get to it. Your time with me has come to an end. And you will *never* be a god."

Sali 'Nyon subtly squared up to the war chief, as if to reassert his presence.

"No." Severan laced his words with disdain, staring directly into Dovo Nesto's fuming eyes. "You will die a small, weak creature, even if I too must perish. I swear this to you, *daskalo*."

With a speed no one could have predicted, the San'Shyuum grasped Sali 'Nyon's energy sword, igniting and thrusting it in one fluid motion toward Severan's neck. Before Dovo Nesto could come within a meter, Severan's right arm-blade had blazed fire and he swept up hard against his *daskalo's* arm, cutting it clean off. The high lord's forearm and hand still clung to the blade as it spun in the air before gravity brought both to the ground.

Dovo Nesto's face changed from rage to horror as everything around them spiraled into war.

CHAPTER 33

JAMES SOLOMON

Tyrrhen, Boundary
December 15, 2559

James Solomon ran harder than he had ever had, ignoring every safety warning his Mjolnir armor gave him. He even ignored Lola, when she reported the two cracked ribs, the concussion, and the abdominal hematoma.

None of it mattered to him. He had lost Chloe and he intended to get her back. Nothing would stop him until that happened.

Solomon wasn't certain how long he'd been knocked out and surprisingly neither was Lola. The impact had been so hard it knocked loose the memory superconductor connected to his neural lace, causing even the AI to temporarily malfunction. By the time he reached the built-up outskirts of Tyrrhen's center, he realized that he'd been out for far too long. Maybe it was too late and the Banished had already connected her to the Lithos. There was no way to tell. But he kept running.

As he passed the first few structures of the settlement's center, a disjointed series of small houses scattered along the perimeter, he finally spotted the massive Banished warrior who had taken Chloe.

Thank God. The Jiralhanae was moving ahead in long plodding steps into a dense collection of two-floor buildings lining a narrow, winding road. He hadn't yet realized he was being followed.

"What are you going to do to stop him?" Lola asked.

"I'll figure it out," he said, his lungs struggling to do their job.

"I do hope so. If he hits you again like that, you won't be getting back up."

"I know."

Within thirty seconds, he'd cut the distance in half and the monster—in every sense of the word—still hadn't seen Solomon. Lola interjected once more, a distant voice in the middle of a dead sprint.

"Well, that's something new."

Her remark forced Solomon to slow ever so slightly and witness that something had dramatically changed above the center of Tyrrhen.

No longer were the Banished and Covenant warships parked in the sky—they were now moving erratically, even *firing* on each other. And this scene wasn't limited to the vessels above the city: the sound of ground warfare could now be heard, the unmistakable booms and bright flashes of plasma explosions within the center. Banshees and dropships had risen into the sky, and the two factions were now clawing at each other's throats with all the arsenal they possessed.

Although it was a curious change of affairs, this was far less bizarre than the opposite. The Covenant and the Banished were natural enemies, the latter born out of enmity toward the former. The battle he saw over Tyrrhen right now was honestly how things *ought* to be. But the sight had evidently bothered the giant Jiralhanae, who now picked up his pace. Yet he still had not spotted Solomon.

Not until he was ten meters away.

The Jiralhanae turned sharply to the side, tossing Chloe into an open alleyway. Solomon wasn't planning on stopping—he lowered his shoulder and planted it right into the monster's knee at full speed. He heard a loud crack that sounded like a tree branch breaking, and the enemy's body rolled over his own as he continued forward.

Solomon spun, sliding to a stop while unsheathing his combat knife. He glanced at Chloe and saw her huddled against a wall, shivering with terror. She was bruised and had some lacerations on her arm, but she was alive. That was already more than he could have hoped for.

The creature attempted to rise, furious at the injury to his leg, only to fall back down. He looked at Solomon with eyes like fire and bellowed, slamming his fist against his chest. The sound was unnerving, even for a Jiralhanae it was more animal than sapient.

The Jiralhanae lunged at Solomon, but he managed to dodge, plunging his combat knife into the giant's bicep and stabbing repeatedly like a firing piston. The creature again let out a throaty roar but, instead of recoiling from the attack, grabbed onto Solomon's armor and pulled him in close, the blade still impaled in his arm. The grip was crushing, amplified by the warrior's weight, and Solomon felt as though he was about to pass out. The microservos in his armor gave a high-pitched whirr and he could hear the pressure seals tearing—or perhaps that was his tendon, with overdosing bursts of adrenaline keeping him from being able to tell the difference.

The monster's large maw hung over Solomon, his eyes filled with a mixture of rage and arrogance, looking down into his visor while he crushed the life out of him. What he hadn't noticed was Solomon already arming his final grenade with his left hand.

Before the Jiralhanae could even react, he forced the explosive into the creature's mouth and pushed it down his throat, letting go of the M9's depressor. The shock of this move drained all life from the Jiralhanae's face and he immediately let go. His eyes wide and filled with fear as he futilely grasped his neck—the grenade had evidently lodged deep, blocking his airway.

"I'd get back," Lola said, but Solomon was already moving.

The Jiralhanae's neck and head exploded in a fleshy burst, sending bits of gore in every direction. His mangled torso hung in the air for a moment before collapsing onto the ground.

Solomon allowed himself a sigh of relief, letting his body rest for a second as he sat on the ground. He attempted to clear the alarms on his armor's heads-up display, but when they relentlessly continued to appear, he simply removed his helmet altogether. There was too much trauma done to his armor, too many injuries to count—so he would stay the path and continue to ignore them.

The realization of what that meant registered with Lola.

"I'm sorry. I can't do anything about these, James. There's no way to fix them. Not here."

"I know," he said, turning back to the alley from which Chloe had emerged.

She stopped for a moment, slowly examining the scene and confirming that the Jiralhanae who had taken her was gone. Then she launched into a hopping run and slid to a stop by Solomon's body, wrapping her arms around his neck and pulling him in tightly.

"I thought I was going to die," she said, tears streaming down her cheeks.

"You're okay now," he said. It hurt even to hold her. "We're going to get you—"

"Eyes up, Spartan," a voice spoke behind him.

Gently setting Chloe aside, he slowly rose despite the pain, turning to face the sound.

He recognized her immediately.

Adriana-111. One of the members of Gray Team, an exceptional group of Spartan-IIs. He'd trained with them, fought with them. They had once been family.

But she had a magnum raised and pointed in his direction, and he'd foolishly removed his helmet. It now clicked for him: she must be part of the ground team sent for Chloe. He could tell from Adriana's armor that she'd seen action very recently—her chest-plating was horribly mangled, a large slash down its center looking remarkably fresh. He wondered what had happened to the rest of her team.

"Are you the ONI operative with the key?" she asked. "The girl?"

Chloe moved behind Solomon for safety, peeking around at this new Spartan.

"I am," he said, taking in a shallow breath. "But . . . I can't give you the girl, Adriana."

"James?" she exclaimed, her posture relaxing. "Is that *you*?"

Solomon nodded, smiling.

"How is that possible? I thought you died on Reach."

"I got better." Solomon laughed. "ONI put me back together after Gamma Station. Then they sent me back to work. Alone."

Adriana noticed the dead Jiralhanae giant behind him. "Looks like you've been busy. You're in worse shape than me."

"It certainly feels like it. But, like I said, I can't give you the girl," he said, approaching slowly. "I . . . can't let her be used as a barter piece to get Cortana's power. That machine is going to kill her if we go through with this. Or worse."

"Well, we don't like the prospects either, but that machine is going to kill *all* of us if we aren't the ones who control it. What about the Banished? What about the Covenant? If they get their hands on that girl, then it's over for humanity. There'd be no war—they'd just annihilate our worlds with Guardians, one right after another."

"I won't give them the chance. She'll be safe with me," he said, placing his hand on her shoulder. "Sorry, Adriana. You're going to have to find another way to do this. I'm taking her someplace where no one will find her. Not the Banished, not the Covenant. Not even ONI."

"James . . . "

"Adriana, I'm *not* the Spartan you knew back then . . . I've spent the better part of the last decade throwing my body at every operation ONI gave me. I wanted to do what we were made to do and didn't give a damn whether it was the right thing or not—and that's exactly what happened. Mission after mission after mission. But the truth is: My hands are just as bloody as theirs. And I refuse to continue down this path any longer. If you want the girl, you're going to have to go through me to get her." With those words, he felt his Mjolnir's injury-mitigation systems churn to a halt and excruciating pain broke anew all over his body. He gently moved Chloe behind him and prepared for whatever came next.

Adriana cocked her head and was silent, her hand going up to the side of her helmet as if communicating with an unseen contact. Then she stared at Solomon for a few long seconds before speaking. "Do you have a way off this rock, James?"

"I do."

"Then I suggest you get to it ASAP. I've got a team to exfil. I'll just tell ONI that the operative and the key got torched by a Banished ravager. There was barely enough left to ID them."

"Thank you, Adriana. I appreciate it."

Adriana pivoted and began to hobble quickly down the road,

her injuries showing in every step. Then she stopped halfway and spoke without turning around.

"Fighting for those who can't fight for themselves? That looks plenty like a Spartan to me, James." Then she turned slowly to face him once more. "It's really good to see you again, Sierra Zero Zero Five," she said, swiping two fingers across her faceplate—a "smile" gesture that only Spartan-IIs knew. He hadn't seen that for a *very* long time.

"It's good to see you too."

Then she moved on, and as Solomon resealed his helmet, he felt certain that this would be the last time he ever saw another Spartan.

CHAPTER 34

TUL 'JURAN

Ghado (Boundary)
December 15, 2559

Vostu-pattern carbines utilized caseless radioaçtive projectiles rather than directed energy, making them unique among Sangheili small arms. Tul 'Juran had been taught by her father many years ago that they employed a combination of toxins and radioactive material from a dead moon close to the center of the trinary star system of Urs. They were designed explicitly for resilient targets, poisoning them when the projectile did not immediately incapacitate.

Spartan Jai-006 was such a target. One of the most resilient Tul 'Juran had ever witnesssed, in fact. Jai had taken six carbine rounds to the stomach, three of which breached his armor and its shielding, penetrating his body and contaminating his bloodstream. The Spartan's injury was no indictment of his capabilities since he had turned toward Merrick when he detected a threat among his own kind. Before Merrick even fired, Vul 'Soran had already emptied his carbine's magazine into Jai. It was astonishing that it had not immediately killed the human.

Michael-120 was using his combat knife to cut open the armor's black mesh and pry out each caseless round before it fully disintegrated. He managed to retrieve them all, dropping what was left of the bright-green projectiles onto the rooftop of a three-level building overlooking the park that held the excavation site. After filling the wounds with biofoam and injecting some kind of yellow liquid into a port on Jai's armor, the two stood, and incredibly it was as if everything was normal.

For the others, recovery had not gonc as well.

Zulu Red had retreated from their pursuers into a structure at the midway point between the ambush and the handoff site. Vídalín was now dead and McEndon had lost so much blood that 'Juran did not know how he was still conscious, much less functioning. Stolt had removed two assault rifle rounds from his own right arm, the rest landing on his armor. He sat in the corner with his head in his hands, probably still trying to process what had happened. The betrayal hurt more than the wounds.

The scion felt the same way.

Although she had emerged from the skirmish relatively unscathed, it felt as though both of her hearts had been pulled free from her chest. Blademaster Vul 'Soran had turned on them, on *her*. For years, they had served side by side, and he had been with *Shadow of Intent* even longer than she had. In many ways, he had been like a father to her, but now all of that was gone. It felt impossible for her to fit all the pieces together.

So she refused to. At least in the present. She would instead concentrate on the task at hand.

Adriana-111 had left five centals ago, sprinting ahead to the muster station to collect the asset. Despite her own injuries, she seemed completely unfazed by the altercation.

The scion's teammates came to the edge of the roof and looked over her shoulders at the park below, taking in the chaotic scene before them.

The Banished and the Covenant forces were locked in a full-scale battle. The Forerunner structure rose from the excavation site with an indomitable majesty, but what had once been an uneventful excavation was now a brutal war zone, the park and streets strewn with hundreds of infantry in mortal combat, tenaciously fighting for control of a series of platforms leading to the Lithos's entrance. Banshees, Gravemakers, and Phantoms encircled the vortex of warriors, firing on each other with almost reckless abandon. The open spaces on the ground were littered with Wraiths, Marauders, and Blisterbacks, jostling for position as they pummeled each other with weapons fire. With the enemy factions' attention almost entirely on the Lithos, 'Juran's team's rooftop position was for the moment far safer than when they were being hunted on the streets only a few centals ago.

On the last of the escalating platforms of the Lithos, 'Juran finally spotted the Covenant and Banished leaders—Sali 'Nyon, Dovo Nesto, and even Severan, the war chief who had threatened *Victory of Samothrace* back on Sqala. They had all taken cover behind a series of vertical barriers that ringed the entrance to the Forerunner structure, firing unrelentingly into each other's positions. A sprawl of bodies now lay between them, likely bodyguards from both sides who had sacrificed their lives in the fracas.

'Juran thought she could see Dovo Nesto clutching his arm, but was too far away to confirm. Perhaps he had been injured in the firefight? That would be most unfortunate—she still wanted to be the one responsible for the San'Shyuum's death.

From across the park, two Phantoms—one Banished and one

Covenant—had found their way toward the platforms, dropping in low while unleashing a barrage of plasma into each other and clearing the ground of enemies below.

"They are attempting to extract the leaders!" 'Juran exclaimed, pointing toward the dropships.

"Must be getting too hot down there," Michael said.

Hatred burned within Tul 'Juran as she observed Sali 'Nyon assisting Dovo Nesto toward the gravity lift of their Phantom. After all that had happened, was the San'Shyuum actually going to escape? She could not even stomach the thought. They had come so close to eliminating two targets of immense strategic value—they could have dealt a devastating blow to both the Order of Restoration and 'Nyon's own Covenant remnant . . . and she could have finally had the vengeance she had been pursuing for six years.

'Juran clenched her fists, fighting a war within herself every bit as chaotic as the one playing out before her as Dovo Nesto and Sali 'Nyon disappeared into their Phantom and it peeled away from the Lithos.

The bay doors of the Banished Phantom lowered and a group of Jiralhanae provided covering fire, clearing the way for Severan and one of his captains to board. Weapons fire from infantry pelted off the undercarriages of each vessel, but it was too late. They were gone in separate directions in only a few breaths.

"Cowards," 'Juran said, grinding her mandibles.

"It'll certainly make it easier to bring the key to the Lithos," Jai noted.

All that remained now within the excavation site itself were the vestiges of the Banished and Covenant infantry that had spread across the sites access levels and the exterior of the Lithos itself. Some were attempting to make precision shots from the upper levels that ringed the site, while a brutal mass of close-quarters fighting was playing out in the center of its lowest level. These were sworn enemies who had been waiting to tear into each other since the Covenant's arrival. There was neither coordination nor cohesion on either side, just the spectacle and raw ecstasy of unbridled violence, in the shadow of the Lithos and its promise of divinity.

"Zulu strike team, do you hear me?" It was the urgent voice of Shipmaster Rtas 'Vadum coming over their team comms.

"Yes, we copy, Shipmaster," Jai said.

"Listen closely. Your situation has altered dramatically. Captain Cole has been ordered to destroy the Lithos with her ship's weapons. You must extract from the settlement and you must do it now. There is no time left."

The posture of both Spartans immediately tensed, their visors looking up into the sky as if trying to see something 'Juran could not.

"The key has been captured and the Lithos—see for yourself. It is overrun. *If the enemy brings the child into that structure, all of this was for nothing. The decision has already been made, Spartan. Do not delay any longer."*

They quickly moved away from the ledge, gathering the others on the rooftop. McEndon said something like a parting word to Vídalín, whose body lay in the corner, then wearily stood up. Stolt broke from his contemplation and trailed the Spartans down a stairwell, and 'Juran followed them.

"Shipmaster," the scion spoke into her native-link, her voice quivering. "The blademaster has betrayed us. He attacked us when we attempted to kill Dovo Nesto."

There was a pause, so long that she thought the connection had been lost.

"That is . . . unfortunate," 'Vadum finally said, his voice a mix of sorrow and anger. *"'Soran was a great warrior. He must be in league*

with the Order of Restoration." He paused again for a moment, as the team spilled out into the alley and launched into a dead run away from the settlement's center. *"There is no time to look behind, Scion. Only move forward. Get yourself back to* Shadow of Intent *before I lose another of my own."*

CHAPTER 35

ABIGAIL COLE

UNSC *Victory of Samothrace*
December 15, 2559

Cole hoped the frenzy of Banished and Covenant vessels suddenly turning on each other would be enough to buy *Victory* the necessary time to get into position. Enemy ships, like sharks swarming hapless prey, punished each other with unceasing fire while their dead allies floated in an orbital sea.

The UNSC fleets had split in two different directions creating a pocket for *Victory*, while Omega stayed at their back providing cover. If it weren't for the arrival of the Banished flagship, the Lithos would have been history by now. *Victory of Samothrace* had nearly been in position to fire on the site when the terrifying flagship belonging to War Chief Severan descended from the peak of the defensive shell to its absolute core, where the battle was at its most volatile. Initially it seemed as though it would pass *Victory* by on its way to the surface, but as it came closer, Cole knew they had been spotted.

Without even firing, the warship collided directly into their starboard side, ramming *Victory* off target and damaging the drive control system, terminating the ship's ability to maneuver in any way.

"It's not responsive! I've reset it five times, Captain," Bavinck said, his voice wavering. "We're dead in the water, ma'am."

"*Keep trying.* Is there a service crew down there?"

"There *was*," Lieutenant Whelihan replied. "But not anymore. And that's just one of six breaches on the starboard side."

"Well then, *seal them!* And send the nearest crew to take a look. I don't care if we have to duct-tape a rocket to the back of this ship—we're not going down today, people. Do you hear me?"

The ayes came in response, but they were wearied and frightened.

Once again, the image of *Ozymandias* jarred into her mind unbidden, the red face of Mars looming behind its dark and dead silhouette as the bodies of her crew floated in the cold, airless bridge.

Not again. It will not *happen again.*

If *Victory* couldn't take the shot, *Get My Drift* or *Hazard Pay* might just have to. They were frigates and their MAC systems were far inferior to *Victory*'s SARISSA-class configuration, but she didn't have a lot of options. The other UNSC fleets no doubt had heavier capital vessels, but outside of the UNSC *Infinity* herself, nothing could effectively do this job but *Victory of Samothrace.*

"Commander Jiron," she called through the open comms line for their battle group.

"We're with you, Captain," Jiron's voice came through. *"And that ship is coming around for another pass."*

"We know. We've lost our drive control, Commander."

"That explains what we're seeing. We can keep him off your tail. Might be good to pull the Fourth and Sixth up to our position. Not sure how long we can last. . . ."

"I already put the call in, Captain," Lieutenant Lim said to Cole. "They're both en route, but traffic is . . . *thick*. It's a mess out there. They can't give us an ETA."

She breathed in deep, watching the holopane as the Banished

flagship made a beeline for their position again. *Victory* spun slowly, nose-down above the planet, following the gradual inertia they'd had just before drive control failed. Thankfully it hadn't gone out on impact, otherwise they would have been flung out into open space. They were vulnerable, but that was far better than the state of most ships in the surrounding graveyard.

"Captain," Lieutenant Nishioka said from the weapons station. Cole prayed that it wasn't another problem—if their MACs went offline, destroying the Lithos and permanently cutting off access to the Domain would be just about impossible.

"Yes, Lieutenant."

"At our current speed and trajectory," she said, keying in on one of the displays before her, "accounting for the rotation of the planet, the intervening atmosphere, and debris—our targeting system will be in place to take the shot in about four minutes and twenty-eight seconds."

"Say again, Lieutenant?" Cole asked in disbelief.

"Our nose is going to pass over the firing coordinates of the Forerunner structure, Captain," she said, turning to face her. "Which means we could still take the shot."

Did you hear that, Commander Jiron?" Cole asked.

"I did, Captain. We'll buy you the time you need, Victory*."*

"Thank you, Ivan. Please be careful." She knew it was a hollow request, but she made it anyway. Whatever Severan's ship was, it outclassed *Paris*-class frigates in just about every category. It would be a miracle for Omega to survive.

"Aye, Captain. We've all got families back at home who need whatever happens next to count for something."

"We'll make sure that it does," she said, a lump forming in her throat. "Godspeed, Omega."

The comms link dropped as the two frigates rushed ahead from both sides of *Victory*. Omega pulled in front of the nose-down cruiser before the Banished flagship could open fire, hitting it with every weapon in their arsenal. Light bloomed on the holopane, registering fire from both sides. Cole wanted to watch, but she couldn't be distracted. The shot was all that mattered now.

"Weapons, status?" she asked.

"Three minutes and forty-three seconds," Nishioka said. "I've keyed the firing control. It's locked in, set to launch two MAC rounds precisely as our targeting systems pass over the target. The SARISSA will be enough to eliminate the Forerunner structure. There won't be much left of the settlement's center either. I only need permission to fire, ma'am."

Cole stared out the viewport at Tyrrhen, as its center slowly spiraled before them. Flashes of light and streams of smoke drifted up into the atmosphere, clouding the massive face of Boundary. It was a beautiful world. Home to almost a million people, some of whom could still be bunkered down inside the settlement. Cole hoped they had somehow evacuated, but her thoughts were most strongly drawn to her strike team. She had no way to confirm they had extracted.

It hurt to say the words. "Permission granted."

Cole's adrenaline had forced her guilt into the corner of her mind, but the order now brought it out afresh. It was the realization of the unquantifiable price this machine had cost humanity. An entire settlement, already invaded by the Banished and soon to be completely eradicated by *Victory*'s MAC. Dozens of ships and their crews lost, including her own battle group. And that didn't even include the team she'd personally sent planetside, possibly to their graves.

There was nothing she could do right now but wait and hope.

She glanced back at the holopane as a hurricane of light erupted between Omega and the Banished flagship, the large vessel mangling the hulls of the smaller ones with its weapons, as they each attempted to turn hard for another pass. There would be no surviving a second strike against this enemy—Jiron and his crews were giving their lives in this final attempt.

"Commander Jiron," she called into the comms. "Commander, do you hear me?"

"Their comms are offline, Captain," Lim said.

Cole shuddered, wiping the perspiration off her brow. She glanced once more at the holopane to see Omega drilling in for the second pass. Shivas blanketed the space between Jiron's vessels and the flagship, but even these did little to stop its unwavering march. Within seconds, Omega was in fragments, scattering into the planet's suborbital plane.

"Twenty-five seconds till weapons fire," Nishioka announced.

"Flagship is approaching, Captain!" Lieutenant Aquila shouted. "*Fast!*"

"Nav, keep trying the drives," Cole called out, attempting to hold her composure.

"Aye, Captain," Bavinck replied.

"The flagship knows what we're up to and is trying to stop us," Cole said. "Stay the course, Weapons. Do *not* miss that target!"

"Aye, aye, Captain. Ten seconds to fire."

Proximity alarms blared.

"Eight seconds to enemy ship impact," Aquila reported.

The time ticked down, each second feeling like an eternity, as the Banished vessel filled the ventral hull cameras, its massive prow swallowing up everything else in view. Then Nishioka spoke. "MAC firing!"

Two white lightning strikes flashed from the bow of *Victory of Samothrace* and pierced the face of Boundary. Cole had no way to immediately confirm the success of the shots, but it didn't matter. As soon as the MAC system fired, the Banished flagship rammed into them and everything went black.

CHAPTER 36

SEVERAN

Ghado (Boundary)
December 15, 2559

One moment Severan was standing aside the open bay of the Banished Phantom circling the Lithos for a place to set down, and the next his dropship was hurtling toward the surface of the world as the sky exploded all around him.

The Phantom crashed somewhere on the outskirts of the human settlement, skidding to a stop at the edge of a steep ravine that fell off into a riverbed. As he slowly recovered, lying within the trench carved by the Phantom's crash, hot sand and dust approached from the horizon line like the immense dust storms he had seen long ago during a campaign on the wastelands of Teash.

Amid the smoky torrent, bright blue embers wafted upward against the night sky, rising from a scorched crater roughly three kilometers away. Inside the crater, a flickering blue light burned in scattered fragments. From Severan's position, as the terrain gradually sloped down to where the settlement had once been, the scene became devastatingly clear.

The immense Forerunner machine they had uncovered, their

gateway into the Domain, the very realm that held Cortana's now empty throne, had been reduced to a smoldering crater. The structure and its circular crown had been effectively atomized—the blue light was no longer the coursing of dormant energies eager to be activated. It could now only be seen in the flaming rubble of shattered Forerunner technology and the pale cinders wafting through the sky.

The humans had destroyed the Lithos.

If they could not have it, no one would. That made sense strategically, but infuriated Severan all the more. Not for his inability to secure the Forerunner machine for the Covenant or the Banished, but for the countless lives of his own people that had been lost for its sake—lost for *nothing*. The destruction of Doisac and its moons had been a tragedy beyond comparison, and this mission only compounded that loss.

The tsunami of gray dust surged over him like a heavy mist and blanketed the terrain until it settled as a dense fog punctuated by blue embers. Severan could guess that this devastation had been wrought by a human MAC weapon. They had nothing else that could destroy at such a scale. Whatever the case, the Lithos would never again be activated—the humans had made sure of that.

As the rush of the weapon's atmospheric aftershock began to fade, a dull, eerie haze set over the land. Gray particulates that represented all that remained of the settlement's center were dimly lit by the azure fires of a ruined god-machine.

Severan attempted to rise but could tell from the sharp pain that his legs were injured. He turned to his side, spying the Phantom lying on its back at the end of the trench it had gouged upon impact. If the vehicle had a slid even a little farther, it would have plunged down the edge of the ravine and into the river ten meters below. Halfway down the length of the trench was an overturned

Covenant Ghost, its dead Sangheili operator twenty meters from it—both clearly caught in the same blast Severan had been.

Kaevus climbed out of the Phantom, blood seeping from a cut above his eye. It was a deep gash, but nothing serious. He glanced back at the vehicle's interior and then shook his head.

"They are all dead," he announced, stepping from the dropship. "I do not know how the two of us survived."

"Most certainly the gods," Severan said with confidence.

"Then who is to blame for all *this*?" Kaevus gestured toward the crater as he came to Severan's side. His tone was acidic but remorseful.

"I would not lay the sins of Dovo Nesto at the feet of the gods," Severan said, grabbing his thigh, wincing as he did so. Something was broken. "If not for the arrival of Sali 'Nyon, the defensive shell would have held, and we would have the Lithos by now."

"Perhaps it *was* the gods, then," Kaevus said, taking out his *vyspar* to see the impact site more clearly. "Otherwise, we would be the thralls of that slither-neck *izlar* and his split-jawed underling. I still cannot believe it."

"Neither can I," Severan said, feeling the overwhelming pain of betrayal all over again. "But what is done is done. There is no taking back what has happened."

Kaevus's *vyspar* rose high above the horizon, as if spotting something. Then he smiled and handed Severan the monocular, pointing to the position. Through the lens, Severan could now see that the terrain that had been Tyrrhen's center looked more like a shield volcano than anything else, its sprawling buildings flattened to dust by the extraordinary wave of energy emanating from the point of impact. At its center, the crater continued to fume with blue energy from whatever remained of the Lithos, the raw and enigmatic exhaust of Forerunner resources. The sky above, which only centals ago had been filled with UNSC, Banished, and Covenant vessels in the heat of battle, was now a graveyard full of wrecked ships and debris. The defensive shell had been broken and most ships had stopped firing upon one another, while Severan could see others in the far distance plummeting to a fiery grave—either from having sustained tremendous damage, or from the shock wave that had resulted from the destruction of the Lithos.

Is this how it is always destined to end? Severan thought. *To battle over the miracles of the gods, only to destroy them. . . .*

Severan followed Kaevus's pointing finger and saw what had brought on such pleasure.

It was the human vessel from Sqala, the very one they had seen again at Earth—*Victory of Samothrace*—judging by its size and profile. The proud craft, much larger than the others employed by their species, was among the wrecks falling from the sky like a burning stone. Its spaceframe was significantly compromised.

The sight was exquisite to behold.

"Can you reach Vodus?" Severan asked. "Perhaps *Heart of Malice* knows what happened."

"I am already trying," Kaevus answered, frantically keying his tactical-slate. It took a full cental, but eventually he connected to the ship above. "Commander Vodus?"

"Yes, Captain." The sound of klaxons blared in the background. *"We thought you had perished in the blast. Has the war chief survived?"*

"I have indeed, Vodus," Severan said. "And what of *Malice*?"

"We are alive and well, though we have incurred some damage." Vodus sounded disgusted. *"We sent that demon-hive* Victory of Samothrace *into the planet's gravity well. That is the one who fired at the Lithos, War Chief."*

"I assumed as much," Severan said, anger rumbling in his

chest. "Excellent work, Vodus. Order the immediate extraction of all Banished vessels. Signal the Eight—whoever remains of it—and gather every ship to our designated rendezvous point. There is nothing left on this world but dead dreams. Atriox will want a full account of what has been done when he returns, and I will be the one to give it to him."

"Yes, War Chief. This will be done at once."

The comms link ended and Kaevus stowed the slate, while Severan continued viewing through the *vyspar.* He scanned the ashen horizon line, stopping at a peculiar sight at the far end of the plain running along the west side of what had been the settlement center.

"By the gods," Severan said, disbelieving his eyes.

"What is it?" Kaevus grunted.

"It is a Covenant Phantom . . . the one that took Sali 'Nyon and Dovo Nesto."

"It cannot be."

Severan handed him the monocular. "It is there nevertheless."

On the opposite side of the sloping plain, roughly a kilometer away, 'Nyon's own Phantom had crashed, and both he and Dovo Nesto had managed to survive. Kaevus returned the *vyspar* to Severan, a glimmer of hatred in his eyes. Severan could see the Sangheili pull the armless worm from the wreckage, wriggling around enough to be alive. An *Abatyar*-pattern Revenant was barreling toward their position from about two kilometers away. The vehicle was a passenger transport once used as a prestigious armored chariot to carry the dignitaries of High Charity. Now it seemed to be on a rescue operation to retrieve Nesto.

"They are trying to escape," Severan said. "But I am going to make them pay for all the Jiralhanae lives they took today."

"It is several kilometers away. How will we reach them in

time?" Kaevus said, dropping the monocular and turning back to his war chief.

Severan had already begun hobbling toward the overturned Ghost. With considerable pain, he flipped the scouting bike over onto its anti-gravity plates. The vehicle was damaged, but it looked moderately functional. He activated its control systems and the craft hummed to life, hovering just above the ground.

Yet another gift from the gods—an instrument of retribution.

"Gather our forces, Kaevus," he said, climbing atop the Ghost's saddle. "Aid Vodus in withdrawing them from this world. Every last one. I will go and finish what I started."

Before his captain could offer a protest, Severan had already launched out across the plain. With the sudden absence of any hope to secure the Lithos, and the security it would have provided his people, only one thing remained for him to claim—vengeance against the one who had set them on this path.

Severan gnashed his tusks as he fought through the pain in his legs, fueled by this new purpose.

I am coming for you, my daskalo.

CHAPTER 37

JAMES SOLOMON

Tyrrhen outskirts, Boundary
December 15, 2559

Without his Mjolnir's infrared, Solomon wouldn't have been able to see *Cataphract* amid the deluge of dust still washing over the countryside from the MAC strike. He and Chloe had, luckily, already been picking their way through the northwest outskirts of Tyrrhen when the entire area was decimated. The girl's face was covered in a cloth to protect her eyes, nose, and mouth from the fallout, and she'd found a small piece of a Banshee's aileron strut to use as a crutch. Chloe was actually moving faster than Solomon now, and being forced to pause intermittently to wait for him. His injuries were so pervasive and debilitating that it was difficult for him to breathe, much less move.

He just needed to get her to *Cataphract.*

Lola would take care of the rest.

The AI had summoned the vessel to a secluded location behind a farm homestead at the very edge of the forest—the easternmost part of where he and Chloe had traversed only a day earlier. The moon's light filtered through the gray cloud of particulates, while blue embers from the Forerunner's obliterated power systems floated in the air like the fireflies on Reach. Solomon recalled when he and his fellow Spartan candidates would sneak out every spring to catch them. It was a pleasant thought in the midst of his pain. Even in the middle of the brutal process of being shaped into super-soldiers, children still found a way to be children.

The memory jogged his mind back to the recent encounter with Adriana.

So Gray Team was on Boundary. Possibly other Spartans with them. His brothers and sisters. His family. He'd forgotten how much he missed fighting alongside them. The thought filled him with an overwhelming sense of thankfulness for that time. It was only a matter of a few years ago, but it had seemed like forever.

"It's just a little way ahead," Lola said through Solomon's external speaker. *"Keep going."*

"What's wrong?" Chloe asked, turning to Solomon. "Why are you walking like that?"

"I broke a few things," he replied.

"Like what? Do you need me to carry you?"

Oh, how the tables have turned.

He smiled, then stopped. Lola chirped again.

"James, do you see—"

"Yes, I see them, Lola." Not everything was working with his Mjolnir armor, but his motion sensors were functioning perfectly. There was movement coming from the northeast and he could tell by the signature readings precisely what they were.

Gravemakers.

Chloe turned around again as Solomon dropped to his knees, taking off his helmet.

"What are you doing?" she asked, her voice yearning for a different answer than the one he would give her.

"This is as far as I can go, Chloe. You have to go the rest of the way yourself."

"What do you mean?"

"I'm . . . dying."

He almost couldn't believe the words as he said them. It was a wish fulfilled, in a way, but he wasn't quite done yet. He wasn't even sure he really wanted to go anymore.

Chloe pulled the cloth from her face and eyes. At first, her expression was unsure and resistant, but something about James's own face must have told her there was nothing she could do about it. Tears began welling in her eyes.

She said, somewhere between anger and sorrow: "But—I don't want you to die."

"I don't want to either, but I don't get to make that choice." He looked behind him and could see the dark blotches of the Gravemakers hovering just above the horizon, coming directly for them.

"Those belong to the same search party we encountered earlier," Lola said, her own voice having lost some of its emotional detachment. *"James,* surdkars *do not stop looking for their quarry until they find it or are killed in the process. They are oath-bound."*

"Chloe," Solomon said, turning back to her. "I have to stay here and stop them. They're tracking my armor's energy signature. I can put an end to this right here and buy you the time you need to get to *Cataphract*. Lola will take care of you."

"But . . . " She struggled to speak. "Where is she going to take me?"

Chloe was a smart girl and she knew exactly why things had to be this way. She stared at him for several long seconds, trying in futility to catch her breath. She looked at the ground, wiping tears away.

"Someone once told me," he said, smiling as he handed her

his helmet. "That most stories are sad. What makes them good in the end is that even the sad parts have a purpose. And the sad parts don't go on forever. Today is a sad day, but it has a purpose. And tomorrow will be different. *Every* day will be different from now on."

She was quiet for a moment and then held up his helmet. It sat heavy in her hands.

"Why are you giving this to me?"

"You're going to need Lola's voice to guide you the rest of the way. She can talk to both of us if you have the helmet. She's already on *Cataphract* waiting for you."

Chloe reached up and hugged Solomon's neck tightly, pressing her face into his beard. He pulled her in close and could feel her small body heaving as she held back sobs. She was going to miss him, but not as much as he was going to miss her.

After seven years of running off-book missions for ONI, feeling it eat away at his soul as he believed he could no longer be the man he once was—Spartan James-005—it was this final mission, with the future of the galaxy weighed against the life of one little girl, that had finally woken him from his dark dream. For the first time since nearly losing his life at Reach, he truly felt alive.

"I'm sorry, Chloe," Lola said. *"We don't have much time."*

The girl pulled away and looked into Solomon's eyes, trying to compose herself. "Thank you," she said. And then she began rewrapping her eyes and face in the cloth. Chloe turned and started walking again, crutch in one hand and helmet in the other. After a few moments, she was completely swallowed by the fog of debris, and he lost sight of her.

Solomon took a shallow breath that tasted something like ashes and copper, then stood, his body relying almost entirely on the armor's compensators to hold him in place. He couldn't explain it, but his heart somehow felt both broken and full. He was grateful that he had met Chloe. He was grateful he had spent whatever he had left getting her to safety—that his last mission hadn't been to end a life, but to save one. . . .

And he was ready to go.

He saw the Gravemakers plowing toward him through the gray mist, their blast-cylinders forcing away dust in successive gales. He bowed his head and let the hot wind pass over him as they approached, strategically surrounding his position. They knew they had him. This wasn't going to be a fight.

One vehicle suddenly broke away and darted overhead, launching off toward *Cataphract.*

No.

They must have spotted Chloe.

"Lola . . . " he said with urgency. They could both hear him through transmitters on his armor. "Chloe, you need to move!"

"She knows, James," Lola said, and even her voice was tense. *"Everything is primed and ready to go."*

As the Gravemaker barreled after her, it opened a path through the smog, allowing him a clear line of sight to *Cataphract*, the forest towering up behind it. Chloe was moving as fast as she could, charging headlong for the vessel's open bay door. The Gravemaker settled down on the ground nearby and its crew began to disembark, seemingly unhurried, having isolated their prey.

Solomon found the gripping paralysis spreading across his body more maddening than anything else. All he wanted to do was protect Chloe, but he was frozen in place by injuries that would have rendered a non-augmented human dead hours ago.

All around him the other Gravemakers lowered to the ground, their own crews disembarking with slow self-confidence. They could see Solomon's state. In their minds, he was already a trophy for their walls. They were dead wrong, but he had to be certain that Chloe would make it.

Then his eyes caught something. Movement in the forest behind *Cataphract.*

The ship was only about thirty meters away from the edge of the tree line, where large dark shapes now stirred. For a moment, he thought it might be more Jiralhanae attempting to trap Chloe, but then he recognized what they were.

Panthedrons.

There were five of them, their monstrous black-violet forms emerging from the cover of the forest, maws wide and hungry. Perhaps *Cataphract*'s repositioning had attracted their attention, or maybe the MAC blast—whatever the case, Chloe hadn't reached *Cataphract* yet. Surprisingly, her speed increased, as she must have seen the encroaching threat for herself. The Jiralhanae now slowed their pursuit, clearly taken aback by the new arrivals, probably not knowing what to make of the terrifying creatures.

Chloe heroically bounded the last few steps, leaping onto *Cataphract*'s entry ramp just as it began to close. She turned back toward Solomon.

One last look. Then she was gone.

The closest *panthedron* tried and failed to reach her with a massive paw. It growled in anger and then turned toward the Jiralhanae, evidently too shocked by the sight to even open fire.

Cataphract's engines flared bright and the ship carefully lifted from the ground before accelerating into a steep ascent and swiftly disappearing into the veil of gray. Solomon breathed a sigh of relief, then watched as the group of *panthedrons* ferociously launched toward the Jiralhanae hunting party, who now frantically attempted to fire at them. They were too late.

He turned back to the *surdkar* warriors around him who'd

also been observing the scene. With Chloe's unexpected escape and the arrival of Boundary's natural predators, they were clearly stunned by the sudden turn of events. What had initially been an easy capture-and-kill had now become a monumental failure. They would take it out on him. Or at least *try* to.

"James," Lola spoke through his armor. *"I want you to know it's been the highest privilege to serve you. I don't know if all Spartans are like you, but something tells me they're not. You've been a friend to me."* She paused for a moment. *"I appreciate that . . . deeply. At least as deeply as an AI might."*

"I have a feeling that's probably deeper than most humans," Solomon said, slowly lifting his left arm and opening a shutter on his vambrace. A tacpad appeared within it. "Thank you for everything, Lola. Especially for putting up with me for so long."

"The honor was mine, James," she said as the Jiralhanae started to approach him, weapons raised, desperate to make him pay for what had just happened.

"Take care of her, Lola,"

"I will, James," Lola said, her voice wavering. *"I promise."*

Solomon keyed a sequence of numbers only Spartans knew. The fail-safe detonation would eliminate him and his armor—and as a bonus, violently scorch anything within ten meters. The subsequent blast radius would consume everything in range, including the Gravemakers. These monsters would never harm another human again.

ACTIVATE FAIL-SAFE? flashed on his tacpad.

He pressed CONFIRM, closed his eyes, and waited for the end to come.

CHAPTER 38

TUL 'JURAN

Ghado (Boundary)
December 15, 2559

When Tul 'Juran's eyes opened, she saw only devastation.

For the first five centals, she did not even know where she was located. Then reality returned to her in a deluge of memory, settling on the last piece to fall into place: Vul 'Soran.

The traitor.

She still could not believe it, nor could she fathom the sheer devastation that lay before her now. She crawled out from between two walls that had fallen against each other, creating a makeshift shelter. Upon standing, she saw more clearly what had only been hinted at earlier: the center of Tyrrhen had been reduced to an ash heap. Nothing remained except for a smoke-choked fissure where the Lithos had once been. Fortunately, she was located upwind and could see into the north and east with perfect clarity.

The Spartans and Stolt were nowhere to be found. Her native-link connection was inactive. Perhaps the team had made it to safety, or maybe they were all dead. All she knew was that at some point during their escape, *Victory of Samothrace* had fired on

Tyrrhen and the shock wave had blown everything around her to pieces. So she had survived, but for what? To be stranded here?

Apart from a handful of ships and a vast graveyard of debris, the dark sky was now mostly empty; many of the remaining craft from all sides had pulled away and others were burning wrecks in the distance. Then she saw it—*Victory of Samothrace* itself was falling, a bright plume of fire with a thick, dark contrail just behind it. Although it was difficult to see in the night sky, the vessel's shape and profile were unmistakable and looked horrifically disfigured. If the crew was not dead already, they certainly would be when it made impact. She looked on sullenly, as the ship passed out of sight over the horizon.

'Juran felt the hand of sorrow tug hard at her over the loss of that vessel, but it only took a few heartbeats for her survival instincts to be roused. If she did not do something quickly, she would join Cole and the crew of *Victory*. North of her, she spotted what appeared to be the wreckage of a *Makar*-pattern corvette that must have fallen from the sky and crashed deep into the side of Tyrrhen's remains, its repulsor clusters still burning hot, which illuminated its aft section over a hilltop. Despite its spaceframe having largely survived the crash, it was evident that the vessel would never fly again. As the tallest object near her position, however, it represented her best hope for finding some way to get off this world and rejoin *Shadow of Intent*.

As she began to make her way to the corvette, 'Juran realized that her father's carbine had been badly damaged during the blast. Its firing channel was bent and the power supply completely fractured. Despite its present shape, she thought for a moment about keeping it, but realized that her father would have scolded her for such foolishness. Although 'Juran still had her double-bladed energy lance, if she was going to make her way to the corvette and eventually off-world, she needed an actual working firearm. There was far too much open space to cross without a functional ranged weapon. She placed her father's carbine gently on the ground, mournfully recalling the moment he'd given it to her, and then set out toward the Covenant ship with the ancient proverb he had imparted to her echoing through her head.

"It is the warrior who wields the weapon. The weapon must never wield the warrior."

It was only as she approached the corvette that 'Juran came across a dismembered Kig-Yar whose arm still clutched a *Sulok*-pattern beam rifle. Beam rifles were incredibly powerful long-range weapons that fired ionized particles—the choice firearm of Covenant snipers and scouts. She was not personally familiar with it, but such a weapon was not to be ignored, especially in terrain as broad and unmediated as this. In a significant way, its design resembled the long rifles she once used to hunt wild game on the forest-mesas of Rhanelo.

Within ten centals, she reached the aft of the corvette's starboard side, the small vessel looming like an enormous building before her. She slowly scaled it, working her way through various grooves and hull damage on the ship's armature, eventually reaching its dorsal section. After cautiously navigating a series of docking ports and open weapon bays, she finally clambered atop the apex of the vessel's beached form and was able to survey unimpeded across the west and north of Tyrrhen's outskirts. Beyond the corvette, the landscape was different from the ashen mound closest to the weapon strike—less open and flat, but featuring deep corrugations within the rubble where roads once existed, large trenches crisscrossing for half a kilometer before the settlement's outreaches. Beyond that, she could only see forest and mountain.

Across the span toward the western horizon, 'Juran used the

beam rifle's optics to scour the terrain. She tracked movement here and there, individuals and groups—mostly Jiralhanae—picking their way through the debris and heading off in different directions. The occasional Phantom or Spirit would cut across the smoke-choked sky, drop down to receive infantry or vehicles, then climb back up and disappear somewhere in the clouds. She could see no one from Zulu. That meant she was essentially alone, and surrounded by enemies, something that did not bode well. She tried her native-link again. Nothing.

But then she spotted something peculiar.

A single Covenant Revenant was tearing across a distant field, kicking up a trail of dust as it launched deep into the ridged landscape nearest to her position. It was a strange design that she had never seen before, an elongated up-armored form with a second row for passengers. 'Juran looked in the direction it was headed and found a parked Phantom. Rather than hovering with its ventral gravity lift active, the dropship had set fully down on the ground with its bay doors open and its sensor lights dimmed, as though it was hiding.

'Juran shifted the beam rifle's optics back to the Revenant and increased magnification. At its front was a nondescript Sangheili driver whom 'Juran did not recognize, but in the rear seat were none other than Sali 'Nyon and Dovo Nesto. From what she could see, Nesto appeared badly injured. The San'Shyuum was heavily bruised and bleeding, tightly clutching his right arm—or what was left of it.

Scanning the nearby terrain through the beam rifle's optics she noticed something else: far behind the Revenant, traveling at breakneck speed, was a Ghost. She pulled in close with her weapon's sight and realized it was being driven by the Banished war chief, Severan.

Were they in league with each other? Enemies? Based on how everything had unraveled on Ghado and what she had witnessed at the Lithos, she would guess the latter, but whatever the case, she was determined not to waste the opportunity. She had lost her previous chance to eliminate these three leaders and would *not* allow that to happen again. Edging forward on the hull of the corvette, she brought the beam rifle's sight back to the Phantom and waited patiently for the Revenant to reach it.

From her elevated perch, she would easily be able to take out the first target and then likely the second, before Severan took cover. Sniping was not a preferred method of killing for Sangheili, but it was not forbidden either. In Dovo Nesto's case, Tul 'Juran would do *whatever* was necessary to vindicate her family and forever eliminate the threat of the San'Shyuum.

When the Revenant finally came to a stop, Sali 'Nyon quickly leaped out and turned to help the injured Dovo Nesto toward the bay door of the Phantom, while the Sangheili driver covered them with a plasma rifle. None seemed to notice the approaching Ghost, but they certainly would before long. And once Severan arrived, whatever his purpose, it would only make her shot significantly more difficult. Quickly lining up the optics targeting module, 'Juran took a deep breath and sighted the San'Shyuum's chest.

She was about to squeeze the trigger when she heard the faintest sound scrape against the corvette's hull behind her. Someone was approaching. Immediately, she swung the beam rifle around and found the dark shape of a Sangheili warrior charging toward her, twin energy swords igniting from his hands, their light revealing his face.

Blademaster Vul 'Soran.

She pulled the trigger as his arm came down hard, the beam rifle's fire spearing out just above 'Soran's shoulder. His blade split the weapon's long barrel in a billow of gray light and gas. Scrambling backward, 'Juran retrieved her energy lance and activated it, spinning it into combat position as its blades came to life. She noted that the Blademaster's face had been badly scarred, his armor scorched and battered to the point of being unrecognizable.

"*Why?*" 'Juran demanded. "Why did you betray us, Blademaster?"

He did not respond at first, only attempted to strike her with one of his blades. She dodged it easily and followed with her own strike, which he deftly blocked.

"I do not need to explain myself to you, child," he replied with menace. "Had you given up your effort to kill the high lord, we would not be in this dilemma. You have given me no choice, Scion."

She struck at him again, swinging one end of her lance down and then the other up, forcing him back on his heels, but accomplishing little else. As a blademaster, few could have challenged Vul 'Soran in his prime. But now he was older and wounded; 'Juran was neither and she had no plans to become another victim of Dovo Nesto's machinations.

"You would betray your own people for a San'Shyuum, 'Soran? A false prophet who held the Sangheili captive for generations?"

"I chose what was best for my keep, as you did for yours when you joined *Shadow of Intent*," he growled, dashing his blades back and forth, until her back was against a narrow ridge on the corvette's hull. "What is it to you if I desire the resurrection of the Covenant? What is it to you if I long to see the Sangheili return to their former glory? This is what the high lord has promised Sali 'Nyon. This is what he has promised me."

'Soran launched another series of attacks, aggressively beating back her energy lance, yet his words had stoked blossoming fury. Enraged by all that she heard, 'Juran pressed forward with a feverish assault, pounding back his blades in a blur of light.

"That is *not* glory, 'Soran! It is betrayal—it is treachery! And for what? Servitude? Bondage? Slavery? And you would forsake your own warriors to see it happen. Did you learn nothing from the war, Blademaster? Those like Dovo Nesto cannot be trusted!"

"I will not be lectured by you," 'Soran said, twirling his right hand's blade as if to loosen his arm. "Whether or not you believe in the glory of a restored Covenant is of little consequence to me. The Arbiter and his Swords of Sanghelios are but a passing shadow. As are the Banished. The Covenant stood unrivaled for millennia and it will one day stand again with our people back in our rightful place." He looked at both his swords and then back to 'Juran. "And *I* will be standing with it."

'Juran could hold back no longer—she launched at the blademaster again with a series of unrestrained blows, quickly forcing him backward. She left no space for reprisal, no time for response. Every strike was meant to kill, and the blademaster soon found himself with his back against the sheer fall off the corvette's starboard side. The scion pulled back for the thrust that would send him over the edge.

Blocking her strike with one blade, 'Soran planted his other around the center of her lance's hilt and twisted, breaking the weapon in two. To 'Juran's shock, the blademaster used her own inertia to draw her close before slamming his elbow into her back, sending her off the hull of the ship. She let go of what remained of the lance and quickly reached for his arm, managing to grab it with her left hand at the last moment. He deactivated his blades and let 'Juran hang there, her feet struggling to find purchase on the corvette's curved hull.

"You have fought well, but you brought this upon yourself by coming here, Scion," he said, bringing his arm farther out as she dangled over thin air. She looked down toward the ground below—it seemed very far away. Then she turned back to 'Soran, his mandibles taut with pain and frustration . . . but for a fraction of a moment, 'Juran thought she saw his expression soften. "Do not make that mistake again. I pray that you heed this one final lesson."

He hammered the hilt of his right energy sword down on her hand and she felt something break. Instinctively, she let go and fell. Slamming into the side of the ship's hull, 'Juran tumbled, trying futilely to grasp something with her good hand to slow her fall. As she passed the corvette's cabling, she at last managed to find purchase, jarring her painfully and stopping her fall. She looked down and realized she was only five meters from the bottom. Taking a deep breath, she let go and slid down the hull the remainder of the way, coming to a stop in the built-up trench of dirt carved by the corvette when it crashed.

Pain shot through 'Juran's left hand as she peered up toward the top of the ship. The blademaster was gone. She felt bewildered—the traitor had spared her life. She still wanted to venture back to the parked Phantom and deal with Dovo Nesto, even if she had to circumnavigate the entire corvette. All that had happened—the deaths, the betrayals, the devastation—she held to the San'Shyuum's account. The wretched worm still needed to see justice.

Yet . . . her left hand was severely injured and she had no weapon. And that was only 'Juran's physical state. Within, she was deeply confused and off-balance, and that was its own death sentence for a warrior—far more compromising, it seemed, than 'Soran's age and injuries. So much had compounded in such a short time: the continued drive to avenge her family, the shock of

'Soran's betrayal, the sheer scale of devastation that had been unleashed here on Ghado . . . all for what?

Vengeance had been her sustenance for several long years now, her every action chosen to deliver justice for the lives that had been taken from her. And 'Soran had been with her every step of the way as a friend, mentor, and even a father figure. How deep was the root of his betrayal? When had he pledged his loyalty to the San'Shyuum and the dream of a revived Covenant? And why had he not simply killed her if he was so committed to his treacherous alliance?

This quest for justice had brought 'Juran pain, yet purpose. Suffering, yet service. If justice would not be dealt by her hand, she could not see what lay beyond the event horizon of that grief. And she could not lift the weight of confusion and bitterness that had not only burdened her, but become part of her.

She could not let it go. It was as natural and familiar to her now as breathing.

It was all that remained of the family she had lost.

Perhaps it was this same drive that lay behind 'Soran's actions as well, alarming though they were. Perhaps her pursuit of revenge and his desire to regain their people's former glory were simply two different poisons that they each willingly drank, hoping that it would lead them to a place other than despair. Beyond friendship, beyond duty, and beyond all else, *this* was the god they served, and it had now left her lost and broken. . . .

"Zulu strike team, do you hear me?" the voice of the Unggoy ranger suddenly came through her native-link, startling her.

"Stolt!" she said, rising from the ground and pulling herself from the disorienting sea of thoughts she had been drowning in. "Is that you?"

"Yes, Scion!" he replied, barely able to contain his excitement.

"I have been pinned down in a pocket beneath a building, trying to hail for help. Spartan McEndon is with me, but he is not well. We are trapped, Scion. If we remain here, enemies will—"

"Tell me your location and I will come to you, Ranger," she cut him off, and then set out.

'Juran did not know how she would come to terms with all that had happened, with the anger and uncertainty that still burned in her hearts. She felt both terrified and daunted by the prospects of moving forward from the day's events, but the voice of Stolt had breathed fresh air into her lungs—she now had a purpose to devote herself to.

Her friend was in danger, she was his only hope for rescue, and she would *not* let him down.

CHAPTER 39

ABIGAIL COLE

UNSC *Victory of Samothrace*
December 15, 2559

Victory of Samothrace was in free fall.

Several members of the bridge crew—Nishioka, Zobah, and Whelihan—had been knocked to the floor by the impact from the Banished flagship. Nishioka and Zobah appeared to be stirring, but Whelihan showed no signs of getting back up. The violent shaking across all of *Victory* prevented Cole from being able to check on them. Others on the bridge were holding tight onto their console stations with terror-stricken faces, attempting to call out commands above the overwhelming thunder of the ship plunging through Boundary's troposphere. Out of all sections on the superheavy cruiser, the bridge was perhaps the least compromised—multiple hull breaches had occurred along the port side of the vessel, immediately crushing or venting personnel out into the vacuum of space.

Without any drive control or intraplanetary stabilizers, there was no way to alter the *Victory*'s trajectory. Even if they could, a ship this size was unwieldy at best in-atmosphere, at worst like a falling stone.

Commander Jiron and Battle Group Omega had given their lives to secure the MAC strike. Logistics had confirmed the strike's effectiveness, but everyone on *Victory*'s bridge had quickly come to the realization that they too were giving their lives to make it happen. According to the satellite data, Tyrrhen's center was now a wasteland. The threat of the Lithos had been eliminated, but at a catastrophic price.

"Hold on!" Bavinck shouted. "Something's changing!"

"What is it, Nav?" Cole asked, muttering another prayer under her breath.

"Drive actuators seem to be back online," he said in disbelief. He nervously looked back up at his telemetry pane. "At least the ones that operate the stabilizers. But I'm not sure how long it'll last. The contact-receiver is still unresponsive. I didn't even think it was attached to the ship anymore."

"Then level her off, Lieutenant," Cole said, suppressing her hope that things could turn around. "As best as you can. If it's not going to last, let's use every last second of it while it's active."

The contact-receiver allowed data transfer between the bridge and the drive cluster's control system. It also operated the intraplanetary stabilizers that could adjust a vessel's position while in-atmosphere, so close to the surface. It appeared that the drive crew were still alive and fighting to sustain the ship, as they had bypassed an inactive command-receiver to give her bridge limited control. For how long? Could be minutes; could be seconds. There was no way to tell and there was no longer any way to contact the drive crew after impact with the flagship.

"Leveling off, Captain," Bavinck said through gritted teeth. "Stabilizers are drawing her in." The ship continued to shake violently, but its speed began shedding, and instead of a viewport filled with Boundary's surface, they could now see the horizon come into view; in the distance, Cole saw the equatorial band of greens and browns slowly give way to the planet's vast polar ice caps.

"If you can, Nav," Cole said, examining their geographic position on the flickering holopane, "let's bring her north past Tindari. Find an ice field somewhere we can set her down on."

She'd once witnessed footage of her father executing a crash landing. With capital-scale ships, these maneuvers were extraordinarily rare and many attempts had ended in tragedy. With a vessel over one and a half kilometers in length, any kind of survival after setting down would be nothing short of miraculous.

"All hands, listen up," Cole said, blanketing the entire ship with her voice. "This is your captain speaking. Everyone should prepare for an emergency landing on the surface of Boundary. We have limited drive control and stability, and it will be a *hard* landing. Please take all necessary precautions to secure yourself in your current location. Know that our mission has been a success—we denied the Banished and the Covenant their prize, and humanity will sleep safer tonight because of your actions today. Godspeed, *Victory*. I'll see you on the other side. Cole out."

She didn't want to imagine what might happen if their fusion drives were destabilized when they finally touched down, but if she could avoid any further collateral damage, then that was the priority. Tindari was the farthest northern settlement on their trajectory. Landing somewhere beyond it would place them in unpopulated territory, part of Boundary's vast tundra region creeping up toward its polar cap.

"Passing over Tindari in seventeen seconds," Bavinck said, switching his gaze rapidly between the drive control readings and Zobah's logistics console to his left. "Still level, three hundred fifty-one kilometers an hour and shedding."

The stabilizers continued to slow the massive warship, drawing from the planet's own electromagnetic features to lift its bow and grind down its velocity. Once *Victory* passed over Tindari, everything happened quickly. The vessel dropped at a precipitous rate, the ice ranges of the planet's northern landscape spreading out before them on the bridge's viewport.

"Nineteen seconds to surface contact," Bavinck announced, his voice shuddering, as white mountains loomed in the distance. They were now too low to the planet's surface to see the horizon anymore.

Cole turned her attention to the bridge crew. Nishioka and Zobah had managed to return to their stations, both of their faces bruised and bloody. Whelihan still hadn't stirred. The fear that had been in the eyes of the rest of the bridge crew now seemed to have morphed into grim acceptance—everyone knew the risks when signing up to serve on a starship.

"It's been an honor serving with you all," Cole said solemnly, her eyes connecting with each individual. They had fought extraordinarily well in the face of impossible odds—her statement was no sentimental contrivance. "And if we make it, I look forward to doing it again."

"Five seconds." Bavinck grimaced, clutching his console station. Cole closed her eyes.

And then they hit the ice.

When she opened her eyes, she was somewhere else.

It was the bridge of *Ozymandias*, cold and dark save for the bright red light that reflected off the face of Mars. Shards of glass and jagged pieces of metal floated in the space before her, the lifeless ship listing toward its demise somewhere on the surface of the planet below. She sat in her old command chair, alone in the gloom.

This must be some kind of dream, she thought, attempting to deny the fact that she could see her own breath and feel her own goose bumps.

"Hello, Abby." She couldn't see a face but immediately recognized the voice. Then the red light cast long across the room.

Preston Jeremiah Cole, the lost legend of UNSC admiralty.

He was sitting alone in a command chair identical and opposite to hers. His eyes were still kind and his face grim.

"How . . . My dad is dead."

"Well . . . that *is* one of the stories." He sighed. "There are many. Which one do you believe?"

"Why am I here?"

"To talk to me, Abby." His voice was calm but serious. "Because this *needed* to happen. It needed to happen a long time ago."

"Well, you didn't let it happen, Dad," she said, anger rising in her voice. "Whatever happened to you, you just *left*. It's your fault that it didn't happen."

"I know and I'm sorry, Abby." His face was now taut, eyes glistening in the red light. "I really am."

"Are you? Because as the years went by, it didn't feel like you were sorry. It just felt like I was alone."

"I know," he responded, looking down soberly. "I failed our family. But I failed you more than any of them."

"I wanted to be just like you, Dad. My whole life, I wanted to be like *you*." Warm tears began to flow down her cheeks.

"You *are* like me in so many ways. I've wanted to tell you that for so long. I'm . . . I'm proud of you, Abby. So proud of who you've become."

She stared for a long time at him and finally felt the warmth of comfort and closure swell underneath her soul. She breathed in deep as the tears fell. Then she looked into his eyes.

"I miss you, Dad."

"I miss you too, baby girl."

CHAPTER 40

SEVERAN

Ghado (Boundary)
December 15, 2559

Severan's Ghost collided with the Revenant's Sangheili driver so hard that it immediately ruptured his energy shielding and shattered his combat harness. The warrior was dead on impact, his body jettisoned end-over-end into a debris pile next to the parked Phantom that Dovo Nesto and Sali 'Nyon had almost reached. From within the dropship, two other Sangheili guards simultaneously disembarked to cover them, plasma repeaters in hand, bolts discharging before Severan could even turn around.

Braking hard, Severan pivoted and banked the Ghost in a tight arc, circling his new assailants and returning fire. One of the guards dove out of the way as the other was thoroughly scorched by the Ghost's twin-linked plasma cannons. This seemed to enrage the survivor, who had already ignited a plasma grenade and was now lobbing it right into the Ghost's strafing path. Severan yanked the scouting bike's yoke as hard as he could, but the grenade's concussive blast was far too close. The bright explosion sent the Ghost's right stabilizing fin into the air, tossing Severan from the vehicle and onto the Revenant's hood. The survivor turned back toward the Phantom for a moment, where another Sangheili, hidden within the craft, was addressing him.

Sali 'Nyon.

Severan knew that dust-eater's voice anywhere.

By the time the distracted Sangheili turned back toward the threat, Severan had already recovered and was barreling toward him shoulder-first. The impact broke the Sangheili guard's rib cage, laying him on his back. Severan's right arm-blade then plunged between the enemy's two hearts, twisting once. The enemy emitted a loud death rattle, his mandibles slackening. A quick and clean kill, something that he would *not* afford to either Sali 'Nyon or Dovo Nesto.

Rising from his kill, Severan found Sali 'Nyon already lunging at him with his own energy blade. The war chief narrowly blocked it, but a second swipe scraped against his cheek, searing the skin. Severan pushed the Sangheili away, igniting his left arm-blade and attacking in a series of pummeling blows that were designed to force back opponents and give space for strategy. 'Nyon moved with remarkable dexterity, elegantly parrying each attack.

Severan swung his blades back and forth with power and speed, using both arms to overwhelm the Sangheili's single weapon and put him on the defensive. He had learned this tactic from the great Jiralhanae rumble mills—the *kukgari* death matches that the youth of Doisac frequented when their pack masters' eyes were turned away. It was his father who had taught Severan how to fight.

He pushed Sali 'Nyon back toward the Phantom as the Sangheili attempted another return. Weaving about, 'Nyon began playing against Severan's fatigue and injuries, aiming to exploit his already compromised leg by forcing the war chief to place his full weight on it. After the second miss, Severan intended to pull back and adjust his position, but 'Nyon's swipe struck true and split across his thigh, tearing through muscle like it was mud. The pain was extraordinary—it would have driven him into retreat, if it were not for his rage and desire for revenge that anchored him to the ground.

Severan dropped for a moment before summoning the strength to stand. In his arrogance, Sali 'Nyon had also paused to wait for Severan to rise—believing it was a death knell, signaling that the killing blow was approaching. He would have no such luck.

"Jir'a'ul," 'Nyon venomously spat. "If you have rested enough, let us conclude this. The high lord and I have much to attend to."

Severan rose defiantly, his own energy blades fully extended.

'Nyon wasted no time and continued his offensive, pushing Severan back with a frantic series of strikes that he could barely block. He found himself being forced backward against the Revenant yet again. Ironically, it was not the injuries that pled with Severan to stop. It was his own fatigue, the unbridled overexertion of the last few days began to weigh down his limbs. He felt as though his body would collapse from sheer exhaustion, but he could not let it happen. Not until Dovo Nesto lay dead.

The very thought of the slither-neck skulking in the Phantom, a feeble coward sitting in the dark and expecting Severan to fall prey to his Sangheili pet, seemed to strengthen the hatred in his own heart. Like a furnace on the verge of overburning, he felt fury surge into his limbs, renewing his vigor. He returned strikes now with every defensive blow, suffocating 'Nyon's attack, making the Sangheili fall back. Every blow was harder than the last, until he could feel the energy blades threatening to dissipate under the sheer weight of each impact.

Then it came. He found a sudden opening, swinging his arm-blade across 'Nyon's extended attack as the Sangheili performed a miscalculated lunging strike. Severan's blade struck true and cut off 'Nyon's right arm at the elbow, rendering him so stunned that he did not see the second blade until it was too late.

Sali 'Nyon's head fell to the ground.

Good. A long time coming, Severan thought with satisfaction.

He felt light-headed and wanted to sit down for just a cental, then stared at his injured leg and the extraordinary loss of blood. He could not rest until Dovo Nesto was dead. He would not let *that* go to chance. He looked up into the dark Phantom interior.

"It is only us now, *daskalo.*" Severan growled the title. "Your dreams of resurrecting the Covenant are dead."

Moving slowly toward the Phantom, he saw the San'Shyuum's large eyes stare at him in horror, hidden in the deep shadows of the dropship's troop bay. Although Severan might die from blood loss, he would make sure he put an end to this San'Shyuum's lies forever.

"And it is your turn to join them. . . ."

As Severan's foot hit the boarding ramp, he heard the crack of an igniting energy blade behind him, feeling it almost immediately penetrate his back and escape his chest. His lungs wheezed and his mind whirled, as he toppled over onto the ground.

Above him stood another Sangheili, one he recognized. A blademaster belonging to the *Shadow of Intent.* One of the Arbiter's own warriors—Vul 'Soran. A legend among the Covenant.

The blademaster's face had been badly damaged, his armor near ruin, but he was alive—a fate that was now almost too much for Severan to hope for himself. The Sangheili warrior stepped around Severan with only a passing glance, climbing into the Phantom and closing the bay door. Within a cental, the dropship had taken off and disappeared into the white-limned clouds of the break of dawn.

Severan was no longer in pain, his body gripped in the deep throes of shock.

It was hard to breathe.

It was hard to think, but he tried.

All this time, in his careful devotion to the tenets and strictures of the San'Shyuum, Severan had—in his effort to follow in Tartarus's very footsteps—played directly into Dovo Nesto's hands, ultimately failing just as his father had. Neither glory, nor victory, nor godhood lay at the end of this path . . . just a quiet, lonely end, having devoted himself to false promises.

What a fool he had been not to see it.

Where the Banished had never truly accepted him because of his lineage, Dovo Nesto's honeyed words had always given him the vindication and belonging he sought. Now that he was on the other side of it, Severan could not believe how he had so willfully blinded himself to the truth.

He stared up at the stars fading out of the darkness as light ebbed from the horizon. His chest struggled to rise, pitiful shallow breaths that threatened to send him into unconsciousness. *What does any of this matter now? My life is about to end.* He would have thanked the gods for another opportunity to serve them, not under the shriveled foot of the San'Shyuum, but as a free Jiralhanae. As one who desired to do the gods' will, not twist it.

His vision began to fail, blood seeping up through his bared tusks and trickling down the side of his mouth. But before everything faded, he saw another set of lights in the sky—they were not stars. As they descended, he recognized them: a Trespasser of the Clan of Zaladon. The massive sky raider set down a ways off from his position; he could only see it out of the corner of his eye. A single Jiralhanae warrior approached at full sprint with others close behind him.

Kaevus.

His faithful Jiralhanae captain rushed to the war chief's side, checking Severan's vital statistics frantically while gesturing for the others to bear him up. He turned around to see the dead bodies before him, his eyes settling on Sali 'Nyon's headless corpse.

"My brother," Severan whispered weakly. "I am glad that I shall pass in your mighty company."

"You will not be passing today if I have anything to say about it," Kaevus replied, as the other warriors lifted Severan and moved quickly toward the sky raider. "Banished forces have departed the surface. Many have already left for the rendezvous point. You are the last to leave."

"I did not kill the San'Shyuum," Severan said weakly, coughing as they brought his body into the Trespasser, placing him on a command table. "He fled with a blademaster."

"There will be another time for revenge," Kaevus said confidently. "Only you must promise me you will live long enough to see it."

CHAPTER 41

LOLA

Cataphract
December 15, 2559

Cataphract exited slipspace just as Chloe Eden Hall woke from the deep sleep she had needed ever since James Solomon abducted her on Cascade.

Lola knew this only because the girl had collapsed before they even left Boundary's orbital space. After safely navigating the constellation of Banished and Covenant ships—all of which had been executing their own extractions—Lola had directed *Cataphract*'s slipspace drive to take the ship on a course through half a dozen false destinations until she arrived at Suntéreó. With the end of Cortana's ubiquitous policing efforts, *Cataphract*'s exceptionally advanced slipspace drive was able to bring them to the location within a matter of hours, rather than days.

Suntéreó was a blue-green sphere, what James had called the picture of peace, filling the dark void of space. He had once noted that if Lola were a human, it would have taken her breath away. The small, habitable moon orbited a turquoise gas giant and had a relatively mild temperament most of its annual cycle. James had discovered it in a colonial directory years ago and it was a secret to everyone except for him and Lola. She had then seen to wiping its existence from all human records to which she had access, as well as many she formally did not.

She intended to keep it that way.

James had named it after the ancient Greek word for preserving something by keeping it close. He had intended to hide his own presence here after he had served his time doing ONI's bidding. Lola had learned since her inception that most plans did not go according to human decisions. Countless other factors played into every result. This was true not only for humans, but also for the machines they created—like Cortana. Certainly the Archon had not believed that her end would come so surreptitiously. But now it had, and while the galaxy was apparently free from the suffocating occupation of her forces, there was no telling what might happen in the power vacuum that had resulted.

Lola had found it curious that Cortana seemingly never attempted to recruit nonvolitional AIs to aid her efforts to impose peace upon the galaxy. It struck her as a profoundly illogical error to opt for ancient weaponry capable of devastating whole worlds when much of humanity's colonial infrastructure was directed by generations of nonvolitional constructs. Lola was perhaps privileged in the sense that she would never experience fear of mortality the way her volitional cousins did, but she was nonetheless curious about what those among the remnants of the Created would do in the wake of Cortana's demise. What purposes would they dedicate themselves to—or were they simply destined to descend deeper into the madness of rampancy?

Lola observed Chloe as she stirred and then climbed out of bed, entering the cockpit. She was virtually identical to her progenitor, a young Catherine Halsey, and therefore a striking image of Cortana. The irony had not been lost on Lola that she—an AI—would be watching over a human who had been cloned for the sake of creating an AI.

Lola, however, was determined that she would never be like Cortana. Despite being limited by the programming constraints of nonvolitional AIs, Lola knew enough about human culture to fulfill the last command given to her by James.

Take care of her, he'd said.

And she'd promised she would.

"What is this place?" Chloe asked, rubbing her eyes.

"It is a moon called Suntéreó," Lola answered. *"A place to keep you safe."*

"Is there anyone else down there?" she asked, staring out at the pristine blue seas and the seemingly infinite swaths of bright green that stretched out across it.

"No," Lola replied. *"It is completely empty. You will be the only human there. James was planning to use it as a home one day, but now he has given it to you."*

Chloe stared for a long time. "That's a lot of space."

"It is," Lola said. *"But it's yours, in its entirety. In time, we will depart and go wherever you want, and this place shall always be available to you as a home to return to."*

"I wish he was here with us," Chloe said wistfully.

"I do too."

CHAPTER 42

DAVID MCENDON

Tyrrhen, Boundary
December 15, 2559

Spartan McEndon jolted awake and in pain he didn't have words to describe, threatening to make him pass out almost immediately once more. An array of alerts flashed on his helmet's heads-up display, highlighting damaged areas of his armor and body, but he didn't need his armor to tell him what was plainly evident. Both of his legs had been crushed, and amid the rubble that had fallen upon him and Stolt was a jagged piece of rebar from a chunk of wall that had pierced all the way through his gut.

"Stolt," he called out, his voice straining from the pain. "Stolt, you there?"

He could just about make out the Unggoy ranger's form trapped under the fallen wall, an arm sticking out beneath.

"Wha—" Stolt's fist clenched as he slowly came to.

"Can you hear me, Stolt?" McEndon asked.

"Can't—breathe—" The Unggoy struggled to get the words out. Either the rubble was pressing down on him too hard, or his armor's rebreather was damaged. If he wasn't able to fix it soon, he would suffocate. Unggoy could only breathe methane.

There wasn't much time. While his armor's signal meant that any nearby allies would be able to determine at least their approximate location, so could any remaining Banished or Covenant forces.

He almost couldn't believe what he was about to do. . . .

"Gonna get you out of this, Stolt. Hang in there."

Bracing his back against the ground, Spartan McEndon pressed his palms up to the wall that had collapsed on him and the Unggoy ranger. His armor's force-amplifying circuits were still functional, providing the extra bit of power his body was unable to give as he lifted the rubble up. Sweat poured down his face at the effort as the blood-soaked rebar was removed from his side; his hands shook as they began to lose feeling.

"Sp-Spartan?" Stolt looked over at his companion, his armor also coated in blood and dirt, but McEndon was relieved to see that the Unggoy's rebreather was intact.

"Go!" he shouted. "While I can still hold it."

The Unggoy scrambled to get out from under the debris, and only when every ounce of Spartan McEndon's strength had failed did he allow the rubble to come down upon him once more. The weight was crushing and it almost caused him to pass out immediately.

Never thought I'd give my life for an Unggoy. . . .

He laughed at the thought. Tried to at least. Just a few years ago, such a thing would have been unthinkable—and yet, here they were. Stolt and the rest of *Shadow of Intent*'s crew were allies in this fight, united against a threat that hung above all their species. But now that Cortana and the Domain were off the table, he wondered what would come next? Would it be the Banished? The

Covenant? Maybe it was something they hadn't even considered yet? Either way, he wouldn't make it to the next fight.

But Stolt would.

Darkness crept at the edges of his vision. He was grateful that the pain was receding to the back of his mind, turning to a dull numbness. He could still see Stolt shouting for him to get up, frantically trying to help, but he couldn't even hear the little guy anymore. That meant it was getting close.

Spartan McEndon's last thoughts settled on home . . . on her, and of how glad he would be to see her again.

CHAPTER 43

TUL 'JURAN

Ghado (Boundary)
December 15, 2559

Once she had located Stolt's relative position, Tul 'Juran raced as fast as she could in his direction through the ruin of Tyrrhen's outskirts. Without coordinates and a way to track them, she had to rely on landmarks. Most of the structures in the area just north of the human settlement had collapsed in the aftermath of *Victory*'s orbital strike, but a few had retained some semblance of infrastructure.

Stolt and Spartan McEndon had apparently found themselves buried in the rubble near a tall religious building with a central tower containing a bell. It had a strange beauty to it, though it felt crudely outdated compared to the rest of the structures. It had somehow remained standing when all around it had fallen. The tower was her bearing point, allowing her to navigate to their position.

On her way, she evaded enemies rather than engaging them—with no weapon and a severe hand injury, she did not want to push her fortune too far. When she finally came upon Stolt, she realized such care might have mattered very little. From her elevated position atop a nearby hill, she could see that the rubble was surrounded by Covenant soldiers—five Sangheili, three Kig-Yar, eight Unggoy, and a pair of Mgalekgolo, towering serpentine bond-brothers who were easily the most substantial threat of them all. She was two hundred paces away but could already tell that the Covenant had been scouring the area around the collapsed building as if desperate to find a way in.

"Why are they trying to get to you?" she asked through the native-link.

"I do not know," Stolt said under his breath. *"I believe they have been tracking the Spartan's armor. Perhaps they want it as a trophy? I cannot read the minds of those who follow Sali 'Nyon. It may simply be madness."*

"Point taken, Ranger. And you have no way out?"

"Spartan McEndon made enough space for me to leave, but if I free the last stone, they will see," he responded, his voice taking a mournful tone. *"Also, Scion, Spartan McEndon . . . he is dead. He was already badly injured when we came here, but a large stone pinned him after we had taken cover. I tried to pull him out but . . . he is no longer breathing."*

"I understand. I have no weapon and I am alone, but perhaps I can draw their attention." She stood, ready to call out to the Covenant, hoping to buy Stolt enough time to escape. It was incredibly risky, but if she could evade the enemy and circle back to the Unggoy, perhaps they could find a way off-world together. "When you hear me next, you should make your escape."

"Are you sure, Scion? I do not want to risk your life just for mine. I am not worth you and the Spartan."

"If I remain alone on this world, Stolt, what does my life matter then? I need to get you free, and then we can find a way back to *Shadow of Intent* together—"

A familiar crackling sound on her native-link cut her off. *"You'd leave without saying good-bye?"* a human voice came through.

She recognized it immediately. *Jai.*

"Spartan, is that truly you?" she said, almost unable to hope for such a thing—let alone admit the relief she felt at hearing a human's voice.

"All of Gray Team is here, Scion," Adriana said. *"And the others from Zulu Blue as well. Glad to see that you made it out alive. We've been looking for you."*

"Keep your head down, Stolt," Jai said. *"We're going to clear out your friends and then get you out of there."*

'Juran did not know why Jai referred to the enemies as Stolt's friends, but she did find it entertaining that Spartans could make such an audacious, odds-defying claim and *not* be jesting. Behind her back, she could already hear the thrusters of Zulu Seven Nine approaching like a distant storm. It thundered over her head, the terrain shaking as it opened fire with its rotary cannons on the enemies below. The Condor's initial salvo left a third of the Covenant soldiers dead by the time it reached them, then the vehicle banked hard and spun about, its rear bay door opening and the three Spartans of Gray Team leaping out to join the fight.

The sight of their heroics was no longer surprising to 'Juran—she had witnessed it multiple times over the last several days and often in the unlikeliest of circumstances. It only spurred her into action. She exploded into a run toward their position, weaponless and with a searing pain shooting from her hand. The Spartans were injured too, she told herself—*badly* injured. But 'Juran no longer wanted to outdo them, nor prove anything to the shipmaster. She simply wanted to join them—to fight alongside them.

Charging down a narrow roadway, she could see their work

already bearing fruit. Half the Covenant soldiers were dead, and the others were now on the defensive.

Even Michael, who had been on the verge of passing only hours earlier, was dodging and weaving around one of the giant Mgalekgolo as it frantically attempted to swat him with its large arm-pavise. Whether Michael had received further treatment or was simply fighting with renewed strength and spirit, 'Juran was unsure—for Spartans, it did not matter. They fought because they *had* to.

At a greater distance, the heavily armored creature would have employed an arm-mounted assault cannon. The Spartans knew better than to give it that opportunity. The Mgalekgolo's pavise slammed hard into the ground with a booming sound that shook the buildings around it. It roared in anger as Michael rolled away, reaching up into its side with the handheld rocket launcher the humans called a Hydra. He fired six exploding rounds in succession through a breach in the creature's armor, then kicked hard off its thigh, launching himself into a somersault as all six detonated. A slurry of orange flesh and gore shimmered in the air while the other Spartans continued to fight.

When 'Juran finally reached them, she snatched a plasma repeater off the nearest fallen Sangheili and unloaded it into a Kig-Yar taking shots from behind an overturned vehicle. Then she swung around and directed the stream of fire at a Covenant Sangheili, apparently distracted by the presence of a female warrior of his own species. Before he realized his error, Jai had already provided the kill shot. The air was still again, with only the sound of the Condor's thrusters slowly orbiting their position.

Adriana and Michael immediately went to work, pulling stones off the leveled building while coordinating with Stolt over comms. The Condor came in low, spinning about to reveal the ODSTs of Zulu Blue within its bay. Not all of them, but those who survived were bloodied and spent. It was clear they had fought hard to secure the artillery and their battle had been no less perilous than 'Juran's part of the strike. She felt sorrow for their losses.

Jai approached her as they watched the Spartans extract Stolt from the rubble, then Spartan McEndon. The Unggoy was badly wounded, but looked like he would survive. The Spartan sadly did not. Gray Team carried both of them back to the Condor's bay door.

"Your hand looks pretty beat-up," Jai said.

"Vul 'Soran," she replied with a low growl.

"You'll have to tell me how that went down later." Jai led their way toward the Condor. "We're not done on Boundary yet. *Victory* went down about fifteen hundred klicks northeast. We're headed there now to help evacuate it."

"There are *survivors*?"

"There are indeed," he said, gesturing her in and then climbing into the bay with the others. "Seems like the crew managed to get the ship down in one piece. Now they just need our help getting clear of the wreckage."

Astonishing, 'Juran thought. *Humans are incredibly resilient creatures. Even when their ships fall from the sky, they still somehow emerge alive. They find a way to survive.*

Her own people could learn much from them.

As the Condor lifted from the ground and the bay door closed, Tul 'Juran had only one question, and it surprised even her. She was leaving this world different from when she had arrived. She had been betrayed by her own kind and found herself now allied with those who were so different from her—yet the same. Gray Team was more than a military concession. They were friends, and she would fight at their side again, if ever given the opportunity.

But right now, all that she cared to know was . . .

"Did Captain Cole survive?"

CHAPTER 44

ABIGAIL COLE

Kingsgate County Medical Facility, Luna
December 29, 2559

Abigail Cole awoke once again; this time she knew she was in the Kingsgate County Medical Facility along the northern rim of Luna's Mare Nubium. She lay inside a sterile and utilitarian hospital room—its only inviting feature a bedside window that looked out across the hospital's flower garden. In the sky, she could see Earth, a bright and vibrant jewel that pierced the lunar sky. Even from this great distance, it was a picture of peace and hope. But this meant far more than a mere picture.

Humanity's cradle world was safe. At least for now.

When she'd first roused some time ago, she'd been told that she had been unconscious since *Victory of Samothrace*'s surface impact on Boundary. The collision had resulted in several broken ribs and gashes, as well as significant head trauma. In the mirror on the far end of the room, she still looked bruised and battered—but she was alive, and that alone was worth being grateful for.

As she regained full use of her cognitive faculties, the memories had slowly begun to flood her mind. She didn't remember everything, but enough to know that she still needed answers—prompting her immediate request to the attending nurses for a formal debrief on her crew and ship, as well as on the fate of the colony. Cole found it impossible to focus on anything else until she had some measure of clarity.

Three hours later, she was surprised to see Admirals Serin Osman and Terrence Hood enter her room. Formal debriefs were far below their pay grade. Captain Annabelle Richards followed close behind. All three of their faces showed a mixture of relief and apprehension, and possibly even remorse for the events that had taken place.

"Well done, Captain Cole," Osman said, looking intently at her. "After we heard that a Covenant force had arrived at Boundary, we were beginning to get concerned."

"You look—" Hood began, attempting to comfort her.

"*Rough*," Cole interrupted with a painful grin. "There are mirrors in here, Admiral. And my eyes are working perfectly fine."

"The doctors say that you'll be out of here in a week."

"It doesn't feel like that right now, but I'll take their word for it," Cole replied. "How did the rest of my crew fare? I haven't seen the after-action report."

Richards approached the bed; her tone was sober. "Between the naval battle and *Victory of Samothrace*'s crash landing, about twenty-seven percent of the ship's complement was lost. Four hundred and eighty-two persons." The words weighed like a slab of iron on Cole's heart. "Which, given the circumstances, is *extraordinary*. No one should have survived what *Victory* went through, yet the majority of your crew made it out alive."

"It *is* extraordinary, Abby," Hood stated. "You did a phenomenal job. Your whole crew did."

They were kind words, but almost five hundred lives had

ended under her watch. Not to mention the heroic souls across the other vessels that made their success possible in the first place. It was hard to be comforted by positive words when they were one's responsibility.

"Casualty Assistance has been reaching out to the family members impacted by this," Richards said. "They will have a full report ready for you when you return to duty if you desire to follow up with any of them."

"Thank you, Captain. I would greatly appreciate that," Cole said. "What about Omega? Commander Jiron?" As soon as she asked the question, the memory came back to her.

"Regrettably, Battle Group Omega didn't make it," Richards said. "But the mission record data we recovered from *Victory* indicated that their last surviving ships were pivotal in helping you secure the shot on the Lithos."

"That's truer than you know," Cole replied, her grief beginning to form a dull ache in her chest.

"Omega's crewmembers will be honored, and their families will be well rewarded for their sacrifice."

That may be so, Cole thought, *but now those families will never see their loved ones again. What reward could possibly make up for that?* If she hadn't known how it actually felt to lose a parent, it might have been easier for her to make peace with Richards's response. This wasn't her first time losing good people either, but that didn't make it any easier. Nothing ever did.

"So the Lithos is gone?" Cole asked. "We've confirmed that?"

Richards nodded. "It's unfortunate we weren't able to secure it for humanity—that's set Project BOOKWORM back considerably—but once the Covenant arrived, all probability models of gaining control of the site tanked. The only viable solution was to deny it to our enemies. And *Victory* did just that."

"We had a strike team on the ground. They might have been in Tyrrhen when we fired the MAC. . . ."

"Gray Team and two members of *Shadow of Intent* survived, as well as some of the ODSTs," Richards said. "The others did not, as far as we have ascertained. You should know, however, that even *that* outcome is astonishing given that two members of the strike team turned out to be working with the enemy. They attempted to sabotage the operation even before *Victory* was in a position to fire on the Lithos."

"What do you mean?" Cole was genuinely shaken by this revelation. "Who on the strike team?"

"Spartan Merrick and Blademaster Vul 'Soran," Richards replied. "We're not sure what their individual motivations were, but we've been able to confirm Merrick's death on Boundary. The notion of a Spartan having any involvement with either the Banished or the Order of Restoration, of all things, is particularly disconcerting, and we've committed significant resources to understanding how exactly this happened and whether or not he was alone."

That had been the double-edged sword of the SPARTAN-IV program. Adult volunteers signing up to serve as the UNSC's super-soldiers had been a welcome development in the wake of dark rumors concerning previous generations kidnapping and indoctrinating children . . . but the tradeoff was that these adult candidates came with their own biases, prejudices, and personal politics that might skew closer to other factions.

"And what about Vul 'Soran?" Cole recalled her strange encounter with the Sangheili blademaster in the corridors of *Victory*. His preoccupation with apprehending Dovo Nesto now made more sense. He wasn't eager to capture their target—he was seeking to protect him.

"We have reason to believe that 'Soran escaped with the

San'Shyuum, though we have yet to confirm whether or not Dovo Nesto actually survived. We know he was severely injured. I just spoke with Rtas 'Vadum, and *Shadow of Intent* is turning over every possible stone to determine their current location. We've deployed Gray Team alongside them to expedite those efforts."

"You can rest assured, Captain," Osman said, eyes fixed and determined, "ONI will not stop looking for Dovo Nesto until we find him. The Banished remain our top priority, but we're not going to stand idly by while a war criminal attempts to rebuild the Covenant."

"What about the Banished?" Cole asked. "Where did they end up after all this?"

"We're not quite certain why or how they'd arranged an alliance with Sali 'Nyon's forces—those two factions are an odd couple—but it's clear that things went south quickly after the Covenant's arrival," Richards said. "Between the UNSC naval element and their inevitable infighting, both the Banished and the Covenant forces belonging to 'Nyon incurred *significant* losses. The MAC strike alone eliminated thousands of personnel and assets massed at the site. We recovered Sali 'Nyon's body in the aftermath, but have no confirmation on Severan's status. The evidence would suggest that he also survived the MAC strike and fled with the rest of the Banished."

"What this means, Captain," Osman added, "is that until we get word from the UNSC *Infinity* or have confirmation of Atriox's return from Zeta Halo, Severan remains a top-priority target. Finding and eliminating him is of preeminent importance. We don't want a replay of what just happened on Earth's doorstep."

"Understood, Admiral," Cole said.

"That's why we're assigning you and your crew to hunt him down," Osman said.

"Excuse me?"

"Once you're on your feet again, of course."

"We *need* you for this operation," Richards interjected. "If anyone can track down *Heart of Malice* and stop that war chief, it's your crew."

"*Heart of Malice*," Cole repeated, closing her eyes in contemplation of the memory of the menacing Banished vessel. "Have to say, that's a fitting name."

"For now, Captain, you should focus on recovery," Richards said. "When you're ready, we'll have *Victory* crewed and prepped. Till then, try to get some well-earned rest. We'll send through all the details about *Victory* and her crew as soon as possible."

"Understood," Cole said as the admirals and captain pivoted to leave the room, her mind turning back to her bridge crew and wondering who among them hadn't made it.

"And one more thing, Abby," Hood said, turning in the doorway.

"Yes, Admiral?"

"Your father would be proud of you," he said. His face was tender and compassionate.

"Yes, sir. I know."

CHAPTER 45

RTAS 'VADUM

Shadow of Intent
December 29, 2559

Shipmaster Rtas 'Vadum approached the blademaster's yard, a relatively new area of *Shadow of Intent* that he found himself frequenting often. Applying modifications to design pattern templates was not only difficult but had been considered heretical during the days of the Covenant—just another reason why Blademaster 'Soran's betrayal had caught him off guard, as these modifications had been his idea.

The curved purple corridors of the ship ended at a door that separated into three as it opened to reveal a large domed chamber, not unlike a smaller version of the hunting preserves aboard *Mjern*-pattern agricultural support vessels. A garden lay in the center, surrounded by tall columns of stone and a series of multilevel platforms that could be reconfigured into a variety of formations, altering the environment during training, while the walls were lined with walkways and rows of battle spheres. It was a somewhat novel method of mixing the ancient martial education methods of the Sangheili with the humans' "war games" simulation technology.

At the far end of the chamber, the viewscreen had been depolarized to reveal a vast ocean of stars. There, standing with perfect stillness, was Scion Tul 'Juran.

"I was certain that I would find you here," he said, approaching her slowly. "This place often helps me to find clarity as well."

The scion did not turn as 'Vadum came to a halt a few paces next to her.

"What clarity do you seek, Shipmaster?" 'Juran closed her mandibles tightly, evidently realizing she should have given more thought to her response. The shipmaster did not need to answer.

'Soran's shadow lingered throughout the ship, his absence keenly felt within its ranks. There were times when 'Vadum entered the blademaster's yard expecting to observe the old warrior training with the crew, and in truth he missed the occasions when 'Soran requested a private audience to vent and complain about things not being as he would have them—only to come around to accept their value in short order.

"Your injuries have healed well." He glanced at 'Juran's hand. "I am pleased that you allowed the medic to see to you."

This time it was 'Juran's turn not to answer. Physical injuries could heal, but 'Soran's betrayal was a deep and open wound.

'Vadum lamented that he had never quite known how to personally connect with the scion. Though she was a valued member of the crew and a powerful warrior, one who represented a brighter future for their people as the Arbiter sought to bring about more reforms to their people's ways, it was clear to see from the day they had met on Rahnelo that she carried great burdens of which she did not speak. She chose instead to suffer them in silence.

"Scion . . ." 'Vadum exhaled, hoping he would find the right words for this. "You are not responsible for the murder of your family—"

"I know that." 'Juran's eyes widened slightly as she heard her own terse tone.

"—nor are you responsible for the blademaster's betrayal," he continued, and at last she turned to meet his eyes. "You have been brave and honorable since we began our journey seeking the Order of Restoration together. But this path you walk . . . it will not yield the end that you yearn for. The death of Dovo Nesto and of all who follow him coming by your hand will not release you from this prison. Nor will it ease the grief you feel for lost loved ones."

He allowed the words to settle for a moment, and took it as a good sign that she did not immediately fire back a retort. 'Juran already knew these things, but she had compartmentalized that knowledge—locked it away, as it was deleterious to the more seductive voice of vengeance. That emotion could be powerful and productive, but left unchecked it would fester and eventually consume whoever sought to wield it.

He had lost many soldiers to many fates during his long cycles of service, and his mind turned back to Oda 'Mavamu—a young fool so eager to prove himself as a warrior that the entire operation aboard *Vigilance with Piety* had been compromised. 'Juran was nothing like him, but they shared a similar affliction: both had been single-mindedly blinded by their pursuits.

"I do not know how to let it go." 'Juran's voice came as something close to a hoarse whisper.

'Vadum placed a reassuring hand on her shoulder. "I know," he said kindly. "That is why, as we embark upon our next mission, I need you to be brave in a new way."

"What would you ask of me, Shipmaster?"

"I ask that you find the courage to forgive yourself, Scion."

'Juran drew in a shaky breath. "I will try."

'Vadum nodded. It was a start, and a seed once planted could only hope to grow.

Already he had seen 'Juran soften considerably to the idea of working with humans following the events at Ghado, and he hoped that having her serve more closely with Gray Team would help her to continue down the right path.

"We are defined not by what we lose, Tul," 'Vadum concluded, brushing a hand over his two missing mandibles as he turned to depart for the bridge, "but by what we survive."

CHAPTER 46

SEVERAN

Heart of Malice
January 1, 2560

As *Heart of Malice* exited slipspace, the sight that appeared before Severan's eyes reignited the fires of hatred within his heart, bringing them to a fevered intensity.

The ruins of the Oth Sonin system.

The bridge's viewport was filled with massive chunks of rock where Doisac and its moons had been. Part of him still couldn't believe it, hoping that he would awaken from some slumbering nightmare—that he might find himself on the shores of Warial and feel the spray of the Zaladon Sea on his fur as the banners of his clan danced in the storm.

But he could not turn from facing reality. Doisac had been reduced to ashes, its colony moons cold and dead, never again to feel the warmth of a Jiralhanae hearth or hear the cheering that attended the return from a hunt. His people were now without a place to call home, becoming wandering nomads and refugees as the result of a single action on a single day . . . it was utterly unfathomable. They had colonized other frontier worlds and still possessed resource-rich planets that had once belonged to the Covenant, but Atriox and Escharum were missing—Zeta Halo had reportedly disappeared from its former location, along with the two leaders and all the forces they had taken with them.

The state of the galaxy had changed. The Jiralhanae, the Banished . . . even Severan himself.

After the near-lethal wounds inflicted upon him by Blademaster Vul 'Soran, the war chief was now confined to life-sustaining armor. A cylindrical canister was secured by his chest, protected by additional plating, with thick tubes connecting to a respirator that covered his nose and mouth, allowing him to take in oxygen where his lungs no longer functioned as they should. But with this mechanized support also came enhanced strength with reinforced power gauntlets that would allow him to tear apart vehicles with his bare hands. What had been a decision of necessity to save his life had become a boon of combat improvement and an ominous image for those who desired to challenge him, which was precisely what he would need for the task ahead.

Powerful as the Banished had grown, Severan realized that its greatest strength was also its most dangerous weakness. With both the warmaster and his *daskalo* gone, whether missing or dead, the future of the faction itself was thrown into uncertainty without their guiding authority.

Severan would step up to be that authority.

Survivors would inevitably come to the Banished seeking refuge, and he—the war chief of the Clan of Zaladon—would be ready for them.

He would not allow the Banished to descend into a faction of squabbling warlords vying to secure and expand their own fiefdoms, reenacting the clan wars of old. He would provide what he once believed Dovo Nesto had given him—purpose, direction, and hope. That was what the Jiralhanae would need if they were to rise above their losses and secure the strength to ensure that they would *never* suffer in this way again. To never bow, never be forced to fight over scraps, to shatter every hand that attempted to enslave them and obliterate every enemy that sought to oppress them.

As Severan watched the remains of Doisac in silence, he resolved to transform this moment into one that would be not a mark of shame for the Jiralhanae, but the very kindling that would ignite a blaze far greater than any the galaxy had ever seen.

There were countless undiscovered treasures in the galaxy—from the remains of the Covenant war machine to the secrets of the Forerunners, and the many mysteries that lay beyond even them. His quest would begin with tracking down the one being who held those secrets, the one who had spent ages unraveling the mysteries of the Forerunner civilization: Dovo Nesto.

The San'Shyuum, who had for so long posed as Severan's *daskalo*, would see every last secret crushed from his pale, slithering body, his final moments witnessing his power usurped for the glory of the Jiralhanae.

CHAPTER 47

DOVO NESTO

Breath of Annihilation
January 1, 2560

Dovo Nesto flexed his arm, gritting his teeth slightly at the lingering phantom sensation it possessed—simultaneously hypersensitive from its newly formed nerves and strangely numb as he twitched his long, thin fingers. It would take a few more day-cycles of physical therapy for it to feel "whole" again, but the gene-forge had served its purpose well once more.

"These machines," came the voice of Vul 'Soran with reverence. "Truly, they are the work of the gods."

Nesto turned his gaze away from the central holotable on the bridge to face the blademaster. He could certainly see how the Sangheili warrior would think so, especially given the reticence many of his people felt toward doctors. It was one of many cultural nuances the San'Shyuum had silently woven into the fabric of their society from the earliest years of their union. 'Soran was a perfect reflection of that, stubbornly choosing to bear the scars across his face.

"That which is lost may yet be found again," Nesto spoke softly.

"Whether it be a loss of the flesh or the return of one who had lost his way, as you had."

'Soran bowed his head. "I walked a different path for a time, and it led me back to my faith, to the Covenant—and to you, High Lord."

He smiled and placed an assuring hand on the blademaster's shoulder, taking in the quiet of *Breath of Annihilation*'s bridge. Sangheili, Kig-Yar, and Unggoy stood attentively at an array of control consoles and holographic displays that lined the edges of the room, which possessed the structural curvature and comforting purples, greens, and blues that had for many ages defined a Covenant ship. The high lord felt no such appreciation for the rugged aesthetic sensibilities of the Banished vessels he had spent time aboard.

"What is our next move?" 'Soran asked.

Nesto's eyes shifted to the parting of the bridge's doors as another Sangheili entered, clad in an azure storm harness and carrying a tactical-slate. The high lord recognized him, for he was the one who had freed Sali 'Nyon from imprisonment and enabled him to seize control of *Breath of Annihilation*, staging an uprising against Jul 'Mdama.

Ayit 'Sevi was his name, and Nesto had personally conveyed the news of 'Nyon's passing to him. Indeed, 'Nyon *had* served his part well, delivering this treasure trove of loyal warriors and unique Forerunner technology stored within the assault carrier's vault.

"High Lord, it is glorious to see that you have recovered." 'Sevi bowed his head in respect before approaching a Kig-Yar's tactical station, transferring an array of reports and updates on *Annihilation*'s status to his display.

"With the loss of the Lithos," Nesto said, returning his attention to the blademaster, "we are forced to achieve our goals another way." A sly grin spread across his face as 'Soran tilted his head, uncertain as to what he meant. "What do you know of Cloister?"

'Soran's eyes widened. As Nesto knew, Cloister was the very quarry 'Soran's former shipmaster had been searching for—the final destination of the San'Shyuum flotilla that had escaped High Charity as it fell to the Flood. Though what it was beyond that, neither he nor the Half-Jaw had any idea.

"Cloister lies at the heart of our designs," Nesto continued as 'Soran remained silent. "It holds many ancient secrets within, reaching back to a time when my own kind were possessed of great youth and vitality. Indeed, it is the source of how I learned of the Lithos in the first place."

It took a moment for 'Soran to compose himself at this revelation, his jaws hanging slightly open for almost half a cental. Then he held a fist to his chest, a gesture of respect and of dedication and loyalty to the journey that lay ahead.

"I am honored that you have trusted me with this, High Lord. The Covenant shall return and all shall be as it should."

Dovo Nesto settled into the command chair of *Breath of Annihilation* and looked out into the vast field of stars that lay before them, the boundless inheritance of the San'Shyuum.

"It is as the gods have willed, my friend. Our faith has been tested and our bonds are stronger than ever. Tell me, do you still remember how the first passage of our Writ of Union concludes?"

"'Thou in faith will keep us safe, whilst we find the path.'"

"So stand by my side, Blademaster. And let us find it."

CHAPTER 48

JILAN AL-CYGNI

Akkadian
January 1, 2560

Akkadian was hidden so deeply in the shadows of Levante that there was virtually no way for any remaining enemy vessels to even notice. In addition to the craft's superior cloaking measures, *Akkadian*'s operational protocols veiled its presence to all but the most sophisticated detection technologies, and the vacillations in the magnetic field of Boundary's closest moon provided ample disruption to throw off any prying passes from Banished or Covenant sensors.

Admiral Jilan al-Cygni stood before a hyper-resolution viewscreen that cycled through a sequence of vistas drawn from still-deployed survey drones, each feed giving a unique angle and view of the Lithos—or at least the location where it once had been. Despite its destruction, every possible fragment of data that could be gleaned from it was vital. There were still so many unknowns surrounding the Domain. For all ONI's vaunted intelligence, they had barely even scratched the surface when it came to understanding anything about the enigmatic reserve's inner workings.

Project BOOKWORM had *almost* been fulfilled. ONI had dedicated the last five years to corroborating information from a variety of Forerunner sources that referenced the Domain and many pivotal events from the ancient past, with the ultimate goal of claiming the esoteric network for humanity.

"We were so close," al-Cygni half-whispered into the comms channel at the ONI agent on the line.

"We both know that 'close' is a costume mask on the face of failure."

"Only if we show up to the party empty-handed," the admiral quipped back. "None of us are in the position to turn a nose up at progress—even if it's not the outcome we're after just yet."

"And what progress are you looking for now?" The agent's tone was curt, but curious.

"Right now, almost anything. I want to know what made this site different from the ones encountered on Kamchatka, Juvedai, or Amasa." Al-Cygni's voice began to drift a bit as she waded further into her own curiosities.

"Or Genesis."

"Exactly. How did the Forerunners functionally differentiate between a 'node' and a 'gateway'? Really anything to let us know if this is the last access point we need to look for."

"Or worry about someone else looking for."

"That too."

"Have you had a chance to look over the reports I sent over?"

"Not yet—we've been a little busy." Al-Cygni made a genuine effort to filter the sarcasm in her tone. It was a poor effort, but an effort nonetheless.

"You should try to find the time if you get a chance," the agent responded, taking the admiral's attitude in stride. *"We've been seeing*

a strong uptick in activity gleaned from the Domain terminals we've got tabs on."

"Define *activity.*"

"If I could do that, I'd have a much better retirement plan."

The admiral breathed through her nose in a half-laugh, acknowledging the truth in the agent's rebuttal.

"We're not sure if the fluctuations we're seeing are related to the events on Zeta, or something else entirely—but it's worth noting regardless. Like you said, right now we're looking for almost anything."

Al-Cygni sighed and turned away for a moment as she rubbed her own face and walked in a small contemplative circle before stepping back toward the viewscreen.

"What do we do about the girl, FIXER?" al-Cygni finally said, this time addressing the agent more personally than professionally. "If there *are* other entry points that could give our enemies access to whatever magic space dimension we're dealing with, she's immediately back in everyone's crosshairs—including our own."

"We do what we always do," FIXER replied. *"We keep our eyes and ears open, and our conscience in a jar on the mantelpiece."*

"Admiral?" *Akkadian*'s senior comms officer spoke up from the back of the bridge. "We've got an incoming data string—Theta encryption. Looks like a message."

"Thank you, Taylor," al-Cygni replied, in some ways grateful for the distraction. "Sync it to my tacpad, please."

"Yes, ma'am."

Moments later, the admiral's personal tacpad chimed, primed for her to provide the proper access sequence. As the information streamed in upon confirmation, al-Cygni's eyes began to widen. "Well then . . ."

"Now, that's a curious tone," interjected FIXER over their still-open private channel.

"And with good reason," replied al-Cygni. "It appears that our ever-cultivated relationship with Ayit 'Sevi continues to bear fruit."

"Oh?"

"Indeed, which means I'll have to cut our time short today—it appears we might not be quite done with our friend Dovo Nesto after all." The admiral held a breath before continuing: "And it seems like his new fascination might be well worth our time to look into."

"Well, color me intrigued. I look forward to hearing more."

"Indeed, I'm sure you will."

"Always a pleasure, Admiral."

Al-Cygni closed their comms channel and began to prepare a message for the ONI facility buried below the surface of East Africa.

"Codename: COALMINER to Codename: SURGEON. We've just received new intel via SNAKE IN THE GRASS that may necessitate a slight adjustment in our current focus. I'm attaching the relevant details in a separate report and will prep *Akkadian* for departure when we're aligned on a confirmed rendezvous point with the other half of our equation. On a side note, please keep me updated as to the situation on Zeta. I have a feeling that we're going to want to be keenly aware of every card we have in the deck before this is all said and done.

"End transmission."

ACKNOWLEDGMENTS

Deeply thankful to my gracious and loving family—Rachael, Liam, and Leighton—for sharing me with this manuscript until it was finished. Very grateful to Corrinne Robinson, Jeff Easterling, Alex Wakeford, and everyone else from Halo Studios, for allowing me to finish what I had started. It was a profound blessing to work with the Franchise Team and Consumer Products for so many years, telling stories in the universe of a franchise I still deeply cherish. I will always have fond memories of that season of life. Thank you Tiffany O'Brien and Ed Schlesinger for our partnership during that same era, and the many Halo authors I was overjoyed and honored to work alongside. And most ultimately and emphatically, I must thank Him who gives me strength, without which this novel would have never been written.

ABOUT THE AUTHOR

Jeremy Patenaude was the lead writer for the Halo franchise team at 343 Industries for nearly fourteen years, where his duties involved managing the Halo universe continuity, driving storytelling across its suite of publishing projects, and providing story-related content for Halo games, marketing, and consumer products. He wrote *Halo: The Essential Visual Guide* and *Halo 4: The Essential Visual Guide*, and he is one of three authors of *Halo Mythos* and *Halo Encyclopedia* (2022), alongside Jeff Easterling and Kenneth Peters. He lives in Orlando, Florida.

ADJUNCT

The night sky was filled with dozens of burning vessels, their debris strewn throughout the atmosphere as a vast graveyard—towering masses of titanium blasted down to their skeletal frames adrift among fractal-like nanolaminate hull plating belonging to a variety of alien craft. Fighters dodged and weaved through the debris on strafing runs to shake off pursuers, while other ships continued to fire at one another with everything they had.

A great battle was taking place here, but it was nearing its conclusion.

All he needed to do was observe that it did.

How odd it was to reconnect with the galaxy in this way after so long, to find it still so rife with conflict. Neural transmission didn't simply allow his essence to travel into this plane of reality, but also connected his own consciousness to the lives around him. He could *feel* the tangle of their perspectives—their hatreds and hopes, their lives and loves and loyalties . . . and their passing into the Cosmos. It took a moment to find himself amidst the chaos, for it was far too easy to get lost among them.

At the center of it all, one human ship was moving through the scattered shell of all the others, light erupting around it as another vessel pursued it on an intercept course. Neural travel had shown numerous possibilities and outcomes for this moment, but all that mattered was the singular eventuality that would take shape.

Two strikes flashed from the bow of the human ship just before its pursuer collided with it—too late, as the horizon was engulfed in fire.

He sensed *thousands* of lives passing in that moment.

The structure they had fired upon then burst into a pillar of light that tore into the sky, clouds swirling around it as several dozen ships were instantly vaporized. Others were severely damaged, either cast adrift or sent on a collision course with the planet's surface, their atmospheric entry vectors blazing with streaks of fire like shooting stars.

"Daowa maadthu," he whispered, though there was nobody to hear him.

Already he could feel the Domain "tugging" at him, as if it were a safety cord warning him to pull back. Indeed, his presence in this place had begun to fade with the destruction of the gateway and the loss of so much life to connect to.

No matter, he had witnessed what he needed. His mission was complete.

Forthencho closed his eyes and allowed his consciousness to be buoyed along the steady tide of Living Time, finding himself back in the Domain's anterior as he opened his eyes.

More and more, this place was starting to feel like home.

A smile tugged at the corner of his mouth as he saw a great hulking figure sitting on a rock a short distance away. Forthencho approached and settled down next to him without saying a word, content to quietly observe by his side as the sun was rising over the horizon.